The Babysitter

ALSO BY DIANA DIAMOND

The Trophy Wife

The Babysitter

DIANA DIAMOND

ST. MARTIN'S PRESS

NEW YORK

THE BABYSITTER. Copyright © 2001 by Diana Diamond. All rights reserved. Printed in the United States of America. No part of this book may be used or reproduced in any manner whatsoever without written permission except in the case of brief quotations embodied in critical articles or reviews. For information, address St. Martin's Press, 175 Fifth Avenue, New York, N.Y. 10010.

www.stmartins.com

Library of Congress Cataloging-in-Publication Data

Diamond, Diana.
    The babysitter / Diana Diamond.
        p.   cm.
    ISBN 0-312-28047-5
    1. Babysitters—Fiction.   2. Hispanic American women—Fiction.
3. Politicians' spouses—Fiction.   4. Cape Cod (Mass.)—Fiction.
5. Politicians—Fiction.   6. Adultery—Fiction.   I. Title

PS3554.I233 B3   2001
813'.6—dc21   2001019172

First Edition: June 2001

10   9   8   7   6   5   4   3   2   1

April

ONE

"Gordie! Gordie! Gordie!" The shout took on the increasing tempo of a locomotive cheer. "Gordie! Gordie! Gordie!"

Gordon Acton looked at Henry Browning, who was standing at the edge of the stage wing, where he could glance out at the crowd. He gestured with a nod of his head that asked, "Now?" Browning responded with a gesture, shaking his head, "No!" Ellie Acton looked from one man to the other and then out to the stage, where balloons and streamers were landing. "What are you waiting for?" she hissed to her husband. He responded with a nod to Henry. "He says not yet."

There was a roar when the locomotive reached full speed. Then the hand clapping started. "We want Gordon! We want Gordon!"

"Okay, now," Henry said.

Gordon reached for Ellie's hand.

"No! Just you!" Henry snapped.

Gordon looked uneasily at Ellie.

"She comes later," Browning instructed. "When you thank your wife, the crowd will start screaming for Ellie." He took her hand away from Gordon's. "That's when you go on."

Gordon hesitated, then buttoned his suit jacket and strode out under the stage lights. The roar was deafening. He waved into the glare and pointed knowingly at no one in particular. He fielded a balloon and threw it back to the crowd. Then he mounted the podium, examined the cluster of microphones, and raised his hands to still the applause. The screaming kicked up a few decibels, and then the high school cheerleaders started into another locomotive. "Gordie! Gordie! Gordie!" He waved vainly for order, then gestured his defeat and submitted humbly to their worship.

The frenzy lasted for several minutes, loud enough to drown out a local television reporter's interview with the revered senator from Rhode Island. "This is certainly a popular victory," she shouted, and then she and the senator nodded in unison.

Meanwhile, Gordon had stepped down from the podium and was moving along the footlights, reaching down to hands that were reaching up. "Thanks for your help. Couldn't have done it without you. It's your victory, too." He delivered platitudes to faces that were lost in the lights. But when he mounted the podium again, the uproar quieted dramatically. Now there were individual voices. "*Congressman* Gordon Acton!" came from one side of the gymnasium. "*President* Gordon Acton!" came a response from the other side. Then laughter, which Gordon joined.

"My good friends," he tried.

He still couldn't be heard.

"My good friends . . ." Now the screamers in the crowd were demanding quiet. The noise settled to a background murmur.

"I don't deserve to have so many good friends," Gordon shouted. The remark started the whole riot rumbling again. Gordon raised his hands and this time the gesture restored a bit of order.

"And I don't deserve a wife like Ellie!"

"Ellie! Ellie! Ellie!" A new locomotive was starting.

In the wing, Henry told Ellie, "That's your cue."

"Just walk out to him?"

"Yeah!" But instantly, "No, wait!"

Henry plucked a rose from one of the floral displays. "Carry this with you. Give it to him when he takes your hand."

"Oh, Jesus," she moaned in disgust. She walked onto the stage without the flower, heard her name being screamed, and squinted into the lights. Just smile, Ellie reminded herself. Get to Gordon and hang on to him.

Gordon stepped down, took her hand, and helped her up ahead of him.

"Gordon! Ellie!" This new chant brought fresh enthusiasm.

She still couldn't make out a single face. She smiled and waved, pretending she was finding old friends. Then suddenly Gordon flung their joined hands into the air as if announcing a new champion. She felt her bra pull up over the bottom of her breast and tried to ease her hand down. But Gordon sent it even higher in another victory salute. Eventually, he gave up being his own cheerleader and waved the crowd

4

to near quiet. Finally, half an hour after he had arrived at the high school where the district's Republican leaders had gathered an army of supporters, Gordon was able to launch into his prepared speech.

Thank Chris Kirby, he remembered from Henry's outline, so he rendered homage to the Cadillac dealer who had challenged him in the primary for the vacated Republican seat. A clean campaign, and an intelligent debate, were the first positive attributes he had assigned to Chris in the past two months. He invited his defeated opponent and all his followers to join with him in a fight for good government.

Cut taxes, curb government spending, improve education, fight crime, and give the elderly the dignity they deserve were the other points that Henry had wanted him to mention. "No details," Browning had advised. "Just a little something for everyone."

Then the battle cry. The fight wasn't over; it was just beginning. November was only five months away, right at the other end of summer. There was hardly enough time to present the issues to the voters, nor to answer the lies and distortions that were already emanating from the Democratic camp. It would take their greatest efforts to carry this nomination on to victory, and give proper representation to the district in the United States Congress.

"Can I count on you?" Gordon shouted.

Another ten minutes of screaming and confetti showers answered his question. And then it was over. The hired security officers led him and Ellie through the crowd. They slapped greetings to hundreds of offered hands, thanked dozens of well-wishers, but never broke stride in their march to the double fire doors at the end of the room. Then they raced to the waiting limousine like a bride and groom fleeing the church. The car eased out of the glare of the school lights, and headed toward the peace of their Newport home.

As soon as they were in the dark, Ellie began twisting, trying to reach her right hand into the sleeve cut under her left arm. "Did you notice?" she asked.

"Notice what?"

"I hope no one else did."

"No one else did what?"

"Notice."

"What are you talking about?"

"About you lifting my bra halfway over my head."

He looked at where her hand was fishing. "I did?"

5

"When you pulled my hand up over my head, I came right out of my bra cup."

Gordon laughed, a snicker growing into a howl.

"You won't think it's so funny when you see publicity shots of your three-breasted wife. I tried to hide it by folding my arms. Then I looked down and saw that my bra cup was on top of my arm and my breast was underneath. I must have looked like a cow."

"You looked great."

She found the elastic band and was able to pull it down into position. "I'm no good at this. I hate politics," she said, while rearranging her breasts.

"What are you talking about? You're a natural."

"A natural what? What has three breasts?"

"Nobody noticed," Gordon said, drawing her close.

She relaxed into his shoulder. "If Henry Browning says one word . . ."

TWO

The children were awake first, and they charged into their parents' bedroom just as the sun was finding the spaces between the shutter slats. Timothy dove into their bed, as he did whenever they were home, and began wrestling with his father. Gordon feigned terror at the five-year-old's attack, and cowered from the pillow that the boy was wielding. Molly, who was nine, stood patiently waiting her turn. She was too sophisticated to simply jump under her parents' blanket, she was beginning to suspect that their bed was a private place. Still, she wanted the hugs and kisses that went with their homecoming. Gordon surrendered to his children's energy and followed them down to the kitchen where they made a project out of breakfast. A half hour later he sneaked back upstairs to bring Ellie her morning coffee.

The bedroom opened onto a porch that was built over the east wing, vulnerable to the salt spray that blasted off the rocks and soaked the air, and facing into the sunrise. In all the world, this was Ellie's favorite place and she resented every moment of absence. "Politics," she lamented into the steam that was rising from her coffee mug. Gordon's candidacy was dragging her out of her life, far from her children, and away from her work. She had anticipated the intrusions of noblesse oblige when she had married into the Acton family, but she had never imagined just how wrenching those intrusions would be.

"Why?" she had asked Gordon when he told her he was thinking of filling the vacancy in Congress.

"Just something I should do."

"Why *should* you do it? Don't you have a choice?"

"I guess it's something I *want* to do. Other things take care of themselves. This is something that I can affect. It's a place where I can make a statement."

Ellie hadn't discouraged him. She had put aside her academic career so she could be with him at important events. She had surrendered her kitchen to the housekeeper. Most galling, she had turned her children over to babysitters during the days, and rushed home late many nights only to find them already in bed.

"Politics," she whispered again.

But there had also been benefits, most importantly the revived energy of their marriage. It was hard to do anything important for Gordon, who was used to having things done for him. The Actons didn't even have to clip their own coupons. But with her background in special education, she had become a symbol of Gordon's promises for better schools. He had publicly deferred to her views and openly admired her determination to send her own children to the public schools. There was even a hint of her becoming the state's educational czar.

She had also lent a sense of history. Ellie was Ellie Williams, a direct descendant of Roger Williams. Her roots in the state reached back to times when it wasn't even a state, or even a colony. While the Actons had been building ships on the Narragansett since the Civil War, the Williams had been fighting for religious tolerance in the area since 1650. It was who they were more than what Gordon stood for that had crushed the hopes of the state's largest Cadillac dealer.

And, there was her obvious class. Here was a woman of means married to a man of even greater means. She could do whatever touched her fancy. What she had chosen to do was involve herself in solving the problems of failing schools and, more important, failing children. Even if a voter couldn't identify with a rich kid whose family had made a fortune selling lifeboats to the navy in World War II, it was easy to admire his charming wife. Ellie felt important again.

Gordon stepped quietly onto the open porch and slipped into one of the Adirondack chairs, setting his own coffee on the arm. "They're fed, dressed, and hypnotized by television," he announced.

"Something educational?" Ellie asked.

"Wile E. Coyote," Gordon laughed. "It's okay as long as the voters don't find out."

They shared the sunrise and the smell of salt air.

"Gordon, yesterday Henry was talking about seeing me during the summer. You're not going to need me during the summer, are you?"

"I always need you, spring, summer, winter, and fall." He began humming the song from *Camelot*.

"I mean for the campaign."

"Not as much. The primary was the real contest. The last time the district went Democratic was during the Great Depression."

"Then I can plan on having my summer."

He nodded.

"The way we discussed. Out on the Cape where I can finish my damn thesis."

He nodded again.

"With a nanny, so I won't be constantly interrupted?"

"Right," Gordon said. "Away from politics. Away from Henry Browning. Except for an occasional appearance now and then. And I'll be out there every weekend. Maybe even some days during the week."

She leaned back and sighed with pleasure.

"I've even arranged for your nanny," he said.

Ellie sat bolt upright.

"Contingent on your approval, of course," he rushed to add.

"*You're* arranging for *my* mother's helper."

"Not really. That's your call."

"I was thinking of Trish Mapleton. She watched the kids a lot last summer and Molly really liked her."

Gordon nodded. "Then Trish Mapleton it is."

Ellie stared at him for a moment. "What is it, Gordon? What is it that you're not telling me?"

He tried to look innocent of any possible deception. "Nothing. Nothing at all. It's just that there's this girl . . . a nineteen-year-old in junior college . . . the class valedictorian when she graduated from high school. I thought I'd arrange to have you interview her."

"Do I know her?"

"I don't think so. Her name is Theresa. Theresa Santiago. She's from Tiverton. Very blue collar."

"I know Tiverton," Ellie fired back. She looked suspiciously at her husband.

"She's kind of an overachiever. Worked to help out her family while she was winning all sorts of academic honors. Now she's trying to earn money for college," Gordon said to fill in what was becoming a heavy silence.

"This is Henry's idea," Ellie concluded.

"No, it's *my* idea. Henry just pointed out the opportunity. It made enough sense to me that I thought I'd run it by you. And it looks like I have your answer." He pushed himself up from the Adirondack chair. "It just seemed that with your interest in education this might appeal to you." He picked up his coffee mug and started back into their bedroom.

"Santiago," Ellie said slowly. "Is she Portuguese?"

"No," Gordon said, turning back from the door.

"Minority?"

"She's Hispanic. Her family came from Santo Domingo."

"And Henry wants the voters to see you stirring the melting pot. Or tossing the salad, or whatever the politically correct metaphor is."

Gordon bristled, and set his mug back on the arm of the chair. "I told you this was *my* idea. And there's nothing racial about it. It's just simple logic. The state-line area is a Democratic stronghold. The people over there don't care much for the blue bloods on Ocean Drive."

"Because we're all Wasps, and they're all immigrants. And that sounds racial to me."

"Okay, call it racial if you like but that's not my term. I call it smart politics. If we can break the Democrats' hold on the area, we can turn this election into a landslide. It would be great if some of those people reached across to us, and I think one way of getting that to happen would be for us to reach over to them. This girl is a neighborhood icon. She's the poster child for the schools you're hoping to build. It just seemed to me that the two of you together would be a knockout."

Ellie made no attempt to hide her anger. "So, instead of working on my thesis, I'm supposed to entertain the poster child as well as mind my own two children. And show up at every photo opportunity with my Latina companion. God, but this whole thing stinks. It smells just like Henry Browning."

9

"I said it was *my* idea. And I have no intention of you entertaining Miss Santiago. I expect that she's going to watch our kids so that you can get your thesis done."

Ellie turned away in a pout. "I'll bet . . ."

Gordon got aggressive. "That was my thought. Based, in part, on the fact that you weren't all that happy with Trish Mapleton last summer."

"Trish was fine—"

He cut her off. "Didn't you catch her under a blanket with a lifeguard when she was supposed to be watching the kids?"

"That was just one incident."

"And weren't you upset at what Molly might be thinking with all that action happening ten feet from where she was building a sand castle?"

"Well, maybe Trish Mapleton isn't the perfect choice," Ellie conceded. "But I think it should be one of the girls who vacations on the Cape."

"Blond hair, blue eyes, and great teeth," Gordon said sarcastically.

Ellie rejoined the battle. "That's not what I mean. But as long as you bring it up, what kind of an experience do you think a minority kid will have with a summer on the Cape? You think she'll get to spend her free time at the yacht club with the rest of the kids? You think she'll be invited to the clambake?"

"Ellie, I wasn't planning on adopting her. I was thinking about giving her a job, where she could make some money for college, learn from you, and enjoy the beach in the bargain. I was figuring that she would be watching our kids so that *you and I* could go to the clambake."

"And pick up another thousand votes in the process," she added.

"And pick up another thousand votes in the process," Gordon agreed. "Is that so bad? If an idea works for me, and works for you and the kids, why do you think it had to come from Henry Browning?"

That was his parting shot. He stormed off the porch deck and kept moving through the bedroom and down the stairs to join his children and Wile E. Coyote. Ellie stayed out on the porch while her anger cooled to self-pity. "Damn politics," she mumbled to herself over and over again. It took her half an hour to rally her spirits and get into the day's activity.

THREE

Gordon motored away from the slip and turned west toward Jamestown, dead into the chilly wind that was keeping the memory of winter alive.

"Motor or sail?" he offered.

Molly said "sail" simultaneously with Tim's decision of "motor."

"Okay, a little of each," Gordon decided.

They were a nuclear family at its most nuclear moment, all together in the cockpit of *Lifeboat,* their big catboat knockoff, named after the source of his family fortune. Seated at the helm, the wind brushing his salt-and-pepper hair, Gordon was playing the role he liked best. His strong hand on the wheel conveyed a sense of command. He was in charge, capable of taking the ship wherever he thought best. His windbreaker, over an open-collar shirt, portrayed his informal side, a captain whose authority was obvious without special chevrons or symbols of rank. His physique—tall, muscular, trim—announced his strength. Yet his face, with blue eyes wide open and full lips that seemed always to be breaking into a smile, modulated his physical presence with a promise of concern and compassion. This was his self-image, acted out so that it could be shared with his wife and children, and now with his broader political family. Henry Browning had wanted to send a very gifted photographer along when he heard that Gordon was going to spend the day after the nomination sailing with his family. "He'll just be there shooting candids. One little camera. You won't even know he's onboard." But Gordon, anticipating what Ellie's reaction would be, had vetoed the idea instantly. "Not now," he had told Browning. And Henry had accepted the verdict. "You're right. Let's do it later when we can put Theresa Santiago into the family setting."

Ellie was sitting on the opposite side, unable to relax as she eyed her children. They were experienced sailors; Molly had gone on cruises with them when she was only three, and was already captaining her own sailing dinghy in the yacht club youth program. Tim had been brought aboard before he was able to walk. They were both in life jackets and sitting low on the cockpit deck where they were in no danger of being

11

tossed over by waves, or even a broadside hit. But the sea was always uncertain, and Ellie wanted certainty for her children.

She was, in many ways, the opposite of her husband. Where he was physical, she was intellectual. Where he was solid and muscled, she was lean and frail. Not sickly, in any sense of the word, but more straight than curved, more angular than soft. She was over five foot nine and yet weighed less than one thirty, a fact that explained how her bra could ride up over her breast. In the summer, she hardly ever wore one, preferring to put on a fitted shirt so that the shapes beneath could occasionally give provocative hints as she moved. Her face was interesting more than glamorous, with a long nose and hard-etched features that bore a resemblance to the face of her distinguished ancestor, whose portrait hung in the foyer of the state house. Her eyes were brown but took on green overtones whenever she put a light rinse in the brunette hair that she wore short.

"Put up the sail," Molly demanded.

"When we're in the channel," Ellie answered.

It was an exchange that occurred in one fashion or another every time they left the dock.

Ellie still lacked some of Gordon's self-assurance, probably because she had come late into her career, and to the acclaim that her work brought. She had been an indifferent high school student whose best moments came on the tennis court, but even these were never of championship quality. She had picked her college, a small teacher's school in Boston, because it was less competitive, and picked her career in education because it didn't seem as demanding as careers in law or medicine. By the standards of the Williams family, she was a bit of an underachiever, a view that probably accounted for the fact that she had never told students or faculty about her distinguished heritage.

But when she actually began working with public school children, her interests focused, her energy strengthened, and her personality blossomed. Ellie became the tireless advocate of every failing child in the district, and a gadfly to administrators who were terrified at the thought of venturing beyond the status quo. As her new programs were implemented, and lost children were recovered, she was recognized as a tireless overachiever. The Williams name attached quite easily to her new reputation as journalists and toastmasters began to see a parallel between Roger Williams's rebellion against religious conformity, and Ellie

Williams's battle with educational apathy. It was her reclaimed heritage that made her a perfect match for the powerful Actons.

But beneath her daring demeanor, Ellie was still a bit timid, particularly when it came to the safety of her children and the health of her family. Gordon's political ambitions were a threat to the privacy that she wanted for her daughter and son, so she was a less than enthusiastic running mate. In the same way sailing, even with her husband's skill and responsibility, posed a physical danger to the children, so Ellie was a less than enthusiastic shipmate. It had been her preference for a boat that was tame and easy to handle that prompted Gordon to buy a beamy, single-sail catboat design instead of one of the more powerful ocean racers that he would have preferred.

"Molly . . . Tim?" Ellie asked.

Neither gave any indication that they had heard her voice.

"I have . . . actually, your father and I have a question that we want to ask you."

Molly looked up with attention while Tim kept knotting one of the mooring lines.

"We're thinking of hiring a full-time mother's helper for the summer. A girl who would be living with us, and with you all the time."

Gordon focused on her. Very fair, he thought. She could have used words like *babysitter,* or *different kind of girl,* or *new girl,* which would have instantly prejudiced them against the idea. Instead, she was putting the idea in a positive light. Someone who would be with the family for the summer, and with them whenever they needed supervision.

"What about Trish?" Molly asked, seeing through the inoffensive wording of the question. "Is she going to take Trish's place?"

"No," Ellie lied. "Trish will still be there to take you out. But she has things of her own to do. She can't be with you all the time. This girl would be around all the time with nothing to do except be with you."

Gordon found himself smiling, not so much to sell the idea, but rather in admiration of Ellie's skill. She was the politician, able to make any decision sound pleasing to all the diverse constituencies. He knew she didn't like the plan, but she was giving it every chance to win favor.

"I like Trish," Molly decided. "But, if the other girl is around just when Trish can't be, that's okay."

"What if they both were around sometimes?" Ellie asked, unwilling

13

to let her daughter think that the new girl would function only as a pinch hitter.

Molly shrugged her indifference.

"Then should I invite her over so that you can meet her?"

"Sure!"

"And what about you, Timmy?"

He looked up blankly from the rat's nest he was tying into the mooring line.

"Would you like to meet her?"

He rubbed his nose on his sleeve. "Meet who?"

"The new girl who might be with us on the Cape."

"What new girl?"

Ellie looked up at Gordon, smiled, and shook her head. "I don't think he cares one way or the other. Probably doesn't even remember Trish from last summer."

Gordon leaned across the wheel so that he could whisper to her. "Thanks, for the way you handled it."

She accepted the compliment.

"Okay," he called out to his crew. "Let's get the sail up."

Ellie slipped aft and took her station at the wheel, keeping *Lifeboat*'s bow into the wind and the telltales blowing astern. Molly unlocked the mainsheet so that the wishbone could move freely. Gordon began cranking in the main halyard, lifting the sail up the mast where it began to unfurl and snap with the wind. Ellie turned a few points to starboard so that it would billow into the shape of the wishbone.

"Ready about," said Ellie on Gordon's signal. Molly and Tim scampered into the cabin, safe from the lines that would be moving across the deck. "Hard alee," Ellie called as she turned the lumbering boat across the wind and aimed it down the channel. She slowed the throttle while Gordon trimmed the sail. Then she switched the engine off. The instant quiet was overwhelming, her first chance to get in touch with herself since Gordon had announced his candidacy.

Ellie hadn't wanted him to run for Congress, nor had she been enthused over any of his earlier grabs for power. She had married the well-to-do heir to a profitable and honored business, expecting that his position would allow him more time with her and their family. And, for the first year, that was how it had been. But then inflatable boats had become too small a kingdom for her prince. He had sought and won the presidency of local business organizations, headed state commerce commissions, and chaired redevelopment programs and trade commissions. Gordon was perpetually involved and he seemed to thrive on the exposure. Gradually, Ellie had realized that she occupied only one small compartment in her husband's express train to the top.

It was a pleasant compartment. When he was with her, his love seemed genuine. He was solicitous of her pregnancies and proud of his children. On days like this, the quiet moments between his public activities, he was a perfect husband and devoted father. But as his career broadened, the days between commitments had become fewer. Other interests demanded more and more of his time.

She hated politics and the blind ambition that it seemed to nurture. But the campaign had at least reestablished her place by Gordon's side. Congressmen had to be sold to the public, and the family image was considered an essential part of the sale. She and the children had been brought forward, and despite the frantic campaign schedule she was seeing more of her husband.

For the first time in her marriage, she knew that she was needed. She had rationalized Gordon's dalliances with other women, but now his faithful devotion was mandatory. She was his only love interest. He had shown little awareness of Ellie's career in education, but now her role as an advocate for children was invaluable. His arm was around her at nearly every public event, and she suddenly was being treated like the queen of his expanding empire. She would prefer his admiration in the privacy of their family, but there was no longer any privacy in her family. So she would accept it in public even though its sincerity was always tinged with comments about how important she was to his image.

"Ellie?" It was Gordon's voice from the front of the cockpit.

She smiled in embarrassment, realizing that her mind was back somewhere in their wake.

"It's so lovely," she answered.

He looked over the side at the silver water reflecting the golden clouds, and then to the rocky shoreline colored with spring. "It really is," he said as if he had suddenly found time to look outside of himself. "Fantastic."

"You were going to ask me something," she reminded him when he turned his attention back to her.

15

"Just the girl. You will at least consider her, won't you?"

She nodded without any great enthusiasm. "It seems to be okay with the kids."

"Because it's important. Henry thinks it will help erase the blue blood stigma. He thinks it will give me a much broader following."

Henry, she thought, taking care not to show her exasperation. His strategy was intruding into every corner of their relationship, even to the choice of her children's companion. God, but how she hated politics.

FOUR

Ellie was as nervous as if she were the one being interviewed. She paced the hallway, glanced down at her watch—which didn't seem to move at all—and peeked out through the panel windows at the empty drive-way. Theresa Santiago wasn't scheduled to arrive for another five minutes, but Ellie had been fussing and pacing for the past twenty.

For Gordon's sake, she wanted the meeting to go well. Ideally, Theresa would charm her, the kids would be thrilled, and she could go to Gordon and agree that her nanny and his olive branch to the mi-nority community were one and the same person. But her instincts argued that the meeting was going to be a disaster. Molly had already decided that she wanted Trish Mapleton to be their summer babysitter. She was a year older now, and Ellie suspected that she wanted another chance to find out what was going on under that blanket. Timmy had gone one step further, announcing that he wanted his mother to spend the summer minding him, and he wasn't going to be nice to either Trish or Theresa. And, of course, the minority poster child was Henry Browning's idea. As a result, Ellie was predisposed to dislike Theresa. She had planned a productive, yet relaxing, summer interrupted by only a few obligations to Gordon's campaign. Now she was awaiting the arrival of the young woman who might foul up everything? She saw the car as soon as it turned into the long driveway. Instinctively, she went to the window and pressed her nose against the glass, hoping that the girl's manner and appearance would be a ray of sunshine. But her spirits sunk as the car moved closer and came into focus.

It was an old car, two design eras behind the industry's current aero-dynamic styling, and painted in a color that could have been anything between a dirty gray and a faded black. Japanese, she thought immediately. One of those cookie-cutter, faceless coupes that tried to pass itself off as a European roadster. As it pulled to a stop in front of the porte cochere, she could see the worn edges of the tires and the faded rims that were missing wheel covers. On the Cape, the car would have been towed into the harbor and sunk as a permanent mooring.

Then Theresa stepped out and glanced up at the front door, catching Ellie in the act of peering down at her arriving guest. Ellie winced; the hair was deranged, and the dress was a nightmare. The young girl, who stepped around the front of the car clutching a purse that she had probably borrowed, was floating in space between two generations. She had traded the jeans of her contemporaries for the formal business dress of her elders, and her discomfort was apparent.

Ellie fixed her warmest smile and threw open the door. "Theresa?" she said, using the name as a question. The young girl stopped dead, as if she had been caught carrying a television out of a broken store-front. "Yes. I'm supposed to see Mrs. Acton."

"I'm Mrs. Acton. Please come in." Ellie stepped aside, clearing the doorway, but still Theresa managed to keep as much space between them as the dimensions of the entranceway allowed. Then, as she moved inside, her face stretched out ahead of her body so that her saucer eyes could take in the size and appointments of the living room.

"Go right in," Ellie said pleasantly. "I'll get us some refreshments. Would you like a soft drink? Or a lemonade?"

Theresa kept staring into the living room as if she were looking through the bars of the heavenly gates. "Sure. Thanks," she answered off into space.

Oh God, Ellie thought. Disaster. Worse than I could have imagined. She filled two tumblers with ice, and poured a can of Diet Coke over cubes. "Have you eaten? Can I fix you a sandwich, or get you a snack?" she offered as she entered the living room.

"No thank you," Theresa said from the center of the sofa on the other side of the huge coffee table. She was still clutching the purse under her folded arms as if she were carrying her paycheck through a dark alley.

Theresa's physical assets were instantly visible. She had smooth tan skin of mulatto coloring, a perfectly proportioned face, and incredibly

17

light blue eyes. Caucasian, with perhaps a black slave anchoring her genealogy, and clear evidence of an Irish overseer who had gone through the cabins. She was a world child, the ideal recipient of adulation by a politician who needed to be a man of the people. But her liabilities were equally visible, and far more numerous.

First, was her hair. It stood out from her head forming an oversized frame for her face. It needed pruning.

Then there was the dress. The gray and blue pattern was tastefully conservative, certainly appropriate for a secretary in a law office. But the neckline was edged in white lace that was heavily embroidered and well over the top. It seemed almost like a trellis as it rose into her hair. The same lace outlined the patch pockets and finished off the hem. The stockings were gray, and the black shoes were right out of a shoe box.

She seemed a bit overweight, not for an adult who would have been comfortable in the dress, but rather for the young woman that went with the face. Her figure was obvious and attractive, but more mature than typical *Cosmo* covers. The girls on the Cape, who had personal trainers and flaunted their anorexia, wouldn't recognize her as a contemporary.

"Well, tell me something about yourself," Ellie tried as a starter.

Theresa cleared her throat, and kept her eyes fixed on her hands, which were now folded across the captive pocketbook. "I'm a high school graduate," she began, "in the top ten percent of my class and on the honor roll."

"I heard you were your class valedictorian," Ellie prompted her.

Theresa nodded. Then she suddenly opened the purse and took out a sealed business envelope. "I have a letter of reference from my principal." She stretched across the table to hand the letter to Ellie, who took it, opened it, and made a great show of reading it carefully.

"You were first in your class," Ellie blurted out, as she read the school official's comments.

Theresa nodded.

"And you held down a job after school and on weekends?"

Another nod.

"What kind of job?"

"With Digital Electronics in Fall River. I'm there full-time now. I'm a quality inspector on the circuit board production line."

Ellie couldn't hide her surprise. "That's a very responsible job. Do you like it?"

"It's kind of boring. And you never finish. The boards are coming down the line when you get there, and they're still coming down the line when you leave." She smiled at the irony, which gave Ellie a reason to laugh.

"Then why did you choose it?"

Now Theresa seemed surprised at the density of the question. "The money. It pays much better than retail jobs. It's a union shop . . ." She trailed off just after she said "union," remembering that the word was very offensive to the people who lived on Ocean Drive.

"What about school activities?" Ellie wondered.

"I'm in junior college now. And there aren't any activities. But in high school I was in the orchestra. I play the flute." She went back to staring at her hands until she remembered that there was salvation in her purse. "I have a recommendation from my music teacher." She pulled out another official envelope and delivered it across the table.

Ellie read quickly, then stopped, and read again. "This says that you were first chair. And that you were soloist in the annual concert."

Again, Theresa nodded.

"What did you play?"

"The allegro from a Mozart flute concerto."

"How long have you been playing?"

"Since I was five. But then it wasn't really a flute. More like a tin whistle."

Ellie stared over the letter, trying to find the person who was across from her, hiding in someone else's dress. This was a very talented young lady, obviously on another academic planet from Trish Mapleton and her friends, who would be pressed to draft a note for the milkman.

Theresa was back into her purse, retrieving still another envelope. "I also have a letter from my foreman at Digital Electronics," she said. Ellie opened the letter eagerly, half expecting to learn that Theresa had invented a new computer chip.

Miss Santiago is our best quality control inspector, allowing production flaws in only .06 percent of units on her line, less than half the errors of our entire inspection staff, and less than a quarter of the industry average.

Ellie read several similar paragraphs from a company that clearly had a measure on its quality, and had documented that Theresa exceeded all standards. But it was the last paragraph that overwhelmed her.

Miss Santiago achieves these results despite time she spends assisting her coworkers. When she finds a mistake, she doesn't simply reject the board. On her own, she takes the error back to the appropriate workstation and helps the technician to develop corrective procedures.

Ellie was very impressed with the credentials, and honestly admired the girl's nearly self-effacing modesty. But, it just wouldn't work; the people on the Cape didn't give a damn about production lines. They were into cars, boats, fashion, and parties. Quality became significant only when their stereos gave out. And while many of them were patrons of theaters and orchestras, she couldn't think of one who even knew what a flute allegro was, much less identify the composer. Theresa Santiago simply wouldn't fit in, and that would be painful for her, as well as a problem for the children.

Theresa's soft voice interrupted her thoughts. "The job description said that you were a teacher, working on a thesis?" She turned up the last words of the question as if she could scarcely believe what she was saying.

"That's right," Ellie answered. "Unfortunately, the thesis has been dragging on for several months without much progress. I really have to get it finished!" Maybe that would be her excuse. That her back was to the wall and she simply couldn't take a chance with a new and inexperienced mother's helper.

"Maybe I could be helpful," Theresa suggested, as if the thought were preposterous. "I'm very interested in education. I'd like to be a teacher. And I'm really good at finding my way through a library. When your children are taken care of, I might . . . maybe I could help as . . . kind of a research assistant." She paused at the temerity of her own suggestion. "Well, not really an assistant, but maybe just . . . kind of . . . a gofer."

"That's a very interesting idea," Ellie said, surprised that it actually was a good idea. But then she realized that she didn't want to let herself sound enthusiastic. The girl simply wouldn't work, and there was no point in getting up her hopes.

"Tell me about your experience with children. Have you ever worked as a full-time babysitter? Or as a mother's helper?"

Theresa shook her head slowly. "No. Between the job and school . . ."

"Of course," Ellie said to bail her out. "When would you have time? But, you know that really has to be my first concern. Children can find so many ways to get into mischief. You can't take your eyes off them."

"I know," Theresa said. "I take care of my little brothers and sister on Saturday nights and most of Sunday. It's hard just keeping them together where I can watch them all at once. Sometimes just getting them all into shoes for church is all I can handle."

Keeping them all together? Ellie had images of shepherds trying to keep the flock going in one direction. "How many brothers and sisters do you have?" she asked.

"Five. I have four brothers and a sister. That's just the younger ones. I have two older sisters."

"You take care of *five* children on Saturday nights and Sundays?"

"Most weekends. My parents have to go down to Bridgeport to take care of their parents. And my older sisters are married. So I take over."

Ellie stared dumbly, knowing that she needed help just to keep up with her two children. The young woman was already measuring up to more family responsibility than she or any of her friends could manage. Yet she was calm and composed, while many of Ellie's contemporaries were tuned out on Xanax or Valium.

"Who'll take care of your brothers and sisters if you're working with me?"

"My parents will alternate weekends. And my sisters will help out if they run into a problem. They're all sort of pitching in. My mother says this is a great opportunity for me."

Ellie sat back into her chair and drew a deep breath. "Would you like to meet my children?" she suggested.

FIVE

Gordon was surprised by Ellie's enthusiasm.

"Five brothers and sisters," she kept repeating while shaking her head in genuine awe. "And she didn't even bring it up. I brought it up."

"It wasn't on her résumé?" he asked.

"She didn't have a résumé. Just a few letters of recommendation, and she didn't even play up her strong points. She told me she played flute in the orchestra. The letter said she was first chair and soloist. She said she worked in electronics assembly. Her boss says she's the best quality control inspector they have, and that she works with some of the slower people to help them upgrade their skills."

"No wonder you were sold."

"I was run over. This kid is more competent than I am. But I was still looking for a way out. I mean, you should see her. She's never going to be happy on the Cape. So I raised the issue of kids so I could let her down lightly. I wanted to be able to say very positive things to her, but tell her I really needed someone with more experience."

"Like Trish Mapleton?"

"No, not *that* kind of experience. But that was when she mentioned the five kids she takes care of. And the most amazing part of it all was that she didn't make it sound like it was any big deal. Like everyone spends their weekends trying to keep five kids from killing themselves. And do you know what she thought the hardest part of it was? *Getting them all dressed for church!* God, I've found reasons not to go to church since I learned that I was pregnant with Molly. I've been dreading going back when she starts preparing for confirmation."

"So, you hired her."

"No, first I wanted to hear from Molly and Tim. So I introduced them, and then left them alone together."

"And they loved her?"

"Tim did. Or at least he said she was nice."

"Molly didn't."

"No! And that's exactly what made up my mind. Gordon, do you know that our daughter is a nasty little racist?"

22

He looked appalled. "Molly?"

"I could have throttled her! She didn't want Theresa living with us because she's darker than we are."

"She said that?"

"I quote. 'None of the girls will want to be with me if I have to bring one of those people.' "

" 'Those people'?"

"That's what she said, and it only got worse when I pressed her. She doesn't like blacks, or Hispanics, or even Portuguese. 'They have funny hair, and they dress stupid,' according to our oldest child. I felt like wringing her neck. I mean, where did she get such ideas?"

"Maybe she learned them in school, or from her play group. You said yourself that there is no more segregated society than the kids in a school lunchroom."

"Well she's going to unlearn them this summer. Theresa has accomplished more, against greater odds, than any person Molly has ever met. I'm going to make damn sure that our angelic daughter appreciates that."

Gordon was suddenly having second thoughts about the benefits of associating his family with the poster child. He had assumed that Theresa would fit into one happy family, with hundreds of delightful photo opportunities. He had never considered that the relationship might not work out. Molly was perfectly capable of making life miserable for a mother's helper. In conspiracy with the other Wasp kids out on the Cape she could easily create an incident. The last thing he needed was the champion of Hispanic opportunity standing in front of a television camera and explaining how the candidate for congress had racist children and racist friends.

"Well, maybe we're rushing things," he tried on his wife. "After all, Molly is just a baby."

"What do you mean, 'rushing things'? Molly is a long way from being a baby. I'm beginning to think she's already a rotten adult."

"What I'm saying is that you were right. This wasn't a very good idea. If Molly doesn't take to Theresa, that's just going to mean more work for you. Particularly if you're refereeing racial tension. The first task of the summer is to help you finish your thesis."

"Which just happens to be about creating remedial opportunities for disadvantaged children. Hell, I'd be doing exactly the opposite of what all my work champions."

23

"But if Molly . . ."

"Molly has to learn. What do you think I'd be telling her if I knuckled under to her Ku Klux Klan ideas?"

"You're exaggerating," Gordon said.

"Exaggerating? Our little girl's first social utterance is that 'those people dress funny and have bad hair.' And you think I'm overreacting?"

"No, no, not in the least. I'm as shocked as you are. And I think we should set her straight in no uncertain terms. But you were worried that this could be a terrible experience for someone from Theresa Santiago's background. And now I'm worried about the same thing."

Ellie paused thoughtfully. "Then we'll just have to make sure she has the time of her life."

He shook his head. "Nice sentiment, but it won't work. The fact is that Molly is right. Most of our friends, and her friends, would be very comfortable wearing hoods and bedsheets . . ."

"What?" Ellie was visibly angered by the thought.

"Well, that may be too strong," Gordon said, backing down a bit. "But we're all first-class passengers, and we really don't involve ourselves with the problems down in steerage."

"That's exactly what I involve myself in, to use your metaphor. And I've never heard any of our friends who didn't think what I was doing was important."

He laughed. "Sure. So tell me how many Hispanics own houses on the Cape. Or tell me what you think would happen if one of the realtors rented to Hispanics. The only blacks we associate with are the ones who park our cars."

"Well that's going to change," Ellie insisted. "Our friends are going to have to live with Theresa, and she's going to have to live with our friends. And Molly is going to learn not to judge people by the way they look and the way they dress."

"How do figure you're going to do all that?" Gordon said sarcastically.

"By paying Theresa to start watching our children right now, so that by the time the summer rolls around, we'll all be used to one another."

SIX

So it's not completely honest, Ellie rationalized as she swung her Land Rover into the parking space. But it's for a good cause; Theresa will thank me.

She guided her children onto the sidewalk while Theresa took out the backpacks that contained the afternoon's snacks. Ellie helped Molly into her backpack while Theresa maneuvered Timmy's uncooperative arms into his shoulder straps.

"Can't I stay with you?" Molly asked for the tenth time since her mother had explained the day. For the tenth time Ellie told her "no," promising that she and Timmy would have a better time at the mall amusement park than at her hairdresser. Molly's eyes rolled toward Theresa, but she didn't wail that her friends might see them as she had before Theresa had arrived. Reluctantly, she marched off with her new mother's helper, and Ellie turned into the hair stylist shop that called itself I'm Worth It.

She had decided that Theresa's introduction to society had to start with her hair, but she couldn't think of a tactful way to raise the issue. Maybe it was a cultural thing and the girl would be offended by any suggestion of change. Or maybe she simply didn't know any better; with her many adult responsibilities, grooming might not make the first page of her list. But she had to find some way of telling her that her hair had all the style of a burrowing animal. The young ladies in the Cape community wouldn't be nearly that tactful. And it had to be more than just a hint. Once she got the message, Theresa might not know how to act on it. She might go back to the same barber that had put her in her present predicament.

The plan she had decided upon solved both problems. If she could pull it off, Theresa might never realize that she had been insulted. And she would be delivered into the hands of a professional stylist who would know what the in-crowd was wearing. Ellie had booked two appointments, one for herself and another for Theresa, with the second appointment beginning fifteen minutes after the first one ended. When Theresa came back with the children, Ellie planned to announce that

I'm Worth It had received a rare cancellation, and coax the young girl into the chair. As she had reminded herself a dozen times, it wasn't really an honest approach. But it was certainly kinder than simply telling her that she needed to shape up.

Other improvements, Ellie figured, could be made without Theresa's direct involvement. She could give Theresa gifts of clothing with innocent comments like "I thought of you the instant I saw it," or, "It was on a great sale and I thought you could wear it at school." The niceties of etiquette and surefire leads into polite small talk would be picked up through association. Everything would work together to give her the self-confidence she clearly lacked. But the hairstyle had to come first, and there was no completely safe way to handle it. Theresa might see right through her plan. But even if she did, she would be able to see the necessity of the deception every time she looked in the mirror.

Ellie was hardly paying attention to her own styling, much less to the flattery that Harold used as conversation. As he tipped her head with his fingertips he would sigh over the artistry of her bone structure. When he tilted her forward, he would gasp as if he had turned a corner in a gallery and come face to face with a great piece of sculpture. "You *must* wear things that show your shoulders. Such an extraordinary neckline!" In his earlier days, Harold used to join in the local gossip, but a trade magazine had advised that if he shifted to flattery, he could raise his prices.

"Mrs. Acton?" Ellie suddenly realized that he had asked a question. She looked blankly at the mirror. He was asking her something about the cut, and she had missed it completely.

"What do you think?" she said as a cover.

"Oh, I'd try it. You certainly can handle it," Harold answered.

It turned out to be a lock of hair that fell down onto her forehead. Thank God it wasn't a variation of the Mohawk, she thought.

She became more and more nervous as her hour wound down. With fifteen minutes left, her scheme seemed demeaning. How would she like it if a well-meaning friend delivered her to a pair of strange scissors? The insult would be unmistakable. Theresa would have every right to simply refuse, and tell her that she had a stylist of her own.

With ten minutes to go, Ellie began to feel indicted. If she preached tolerance and acceptance, then why was she trying to change Theresa? Shouldn't she just accept her for what she was? At five minutes, she was a transparent hypocrite, trying to make the young girl look and act like her friends, as if her associates were better than Theresa's. Damn it, she was trying to turn the kid into a Wasp, and she was convincing herself that the transformation was some sort of favor. Why would Theresa be grateful for being turned into something that she wasn't? She had never given even a hint that she was unhappy with who she was.

Ellie wanted to leap from her chair, get back to the Land Rover and drive to the amusement area before Theresa and the children started back. But Harold was doing his interminable fussing, another gem that the trade publication had recommended. He was peering over her head, examining her image in the mirror, his lips pursed as if something simply wasn't right. Then his eyes exploded in recognition. He snatched up a brush and began rearranging the piece that fell over her forehead, moving it lower over one eye. He had no sooner satisfied himself than Timmy's face appeared at the window. It was too late for evasion. Harold was expecting the second appointment, and she was already at the door.

"Guess what?" Ellie said with great enthusiasm as she stepped outside the shop. "They've had a cancellation." She took Theresa by the hand and began leading her inside. "As soon as I heard, I booked it for you. You'll want something quick and casual for the summer."

Theresa was holding back, her eyes showing fear as she glanced in through the window. "I haven't . . . I can't . . ."

"Of course you can. It's on my bill." She gave Theresa a conspiratorial hug, and whispered, "We'll let Mr. Acton pay for both of us."

Harold did his best to hide his disdain for the unkempt head she was leading to his chair.

"Where are we going now?" Timmy wailed when he realized that he was being dragged back into the mall.

"I thought we could have some ice cream while we were waiting for Theresa."

"They'll run out of ice cream before *she* looks nice," Molly said, looking back at the beauty parlor. "What are they going to do for *her?*"

Ellie wanted to throttle her daughter, but she realized that all Molly was doing was putting words to her own feelings that Theresa would be an embarrassment.

They had ice cream that Tim dribbled down the front of his shirt. Then they killed half an hour in a clothing store where she soothed her guilt by buying Molly a new sweater. Ellie kept checking her watch,

27

dreading the end of the hour when Theresa's embarrassment might be unbearable, but at the same time anxious to get it over with. She had decided that Theresa would know immediately that the cancelled appointment was simply a sham and that her appearance had failed to make muster. But she was hoping that the results would win forgiveness for her meddling. She tried to steal a glance through the window as they approached I'm Worth It, but she couldn't see Theresa in any of the chairs. She was expecting the worst when she pushed the door open.

Harold spun the chair, unveiling the new Theresa, lifting his arm as if to accept the applause that was due. Theresa's light blue eyes showed nothing but anxiety. Ellie looked back and forth from the beautician to patient.

"Wow!" Timmy said, leaving his mother and walking toward the person in the chair. "You look nice."

Theresa's face broke out in an enormous smile.

"Great!" Ellie said. She could feel the burden lifting from her spirits. And she noticed that Theresa had still another asset: her smile was dazzling.

Harold had thinned and trimmed. Then he had shaped her hair to fall loosely on her forehead, and turn in over the tops of her ears. Finally, he had rinsed in a full black, covering over the original mousy brown. The look was casually professional, like the standard cut for television anchorwomen. Theresa looked more mature, and several IQ points brighter, but it was still Theresa. Harold hadn't turned her into someone else, but rather had focused attention on the woman who was already there. The light blue eyes were inescapable and they sparkled when her generous mouth illuminated in a smile.

"Beautiful," Ellie complimented Harold.

He waved away the praise. "She knew what she wanted," he said as he swirled the cloth from Theresa's shoulders. "And what she wanted was perfect."

Theresa stood up and then stooped to hug Timmy. She raised her eyes to Ellie. "Thank you, Mrs. Acton."

Ellie was nearly beside herself. It was as if she had worked a miracle.

SEVEN

Gordon was getting bored. He had been sitting for almost three hours at the hotel conference table, listening to Henry Browning's managers report on the planning for his campaign. At first the reports had been interesting, even exciting.

The advertising looked great. The print ads were bold quotes from his speeches, some of which he couldn't remember giving. The quotes, all innocuous endorsements of American values, served as both headlines and body text. Dynamic shots of Gordon appeared inside the oversized quotation marks. His name floated in clear space, well above the slogan "Government that works."

The television campaign, organized around fifteen-second spots, ran action footage of Gordon greeting the voters. The quotes, which were no more familiar even in his own voice, ran as a voice-over.

He particularly liked the design for the posters. They were dramatic, mezzotint reproductions of candid photos taken as he spoke. The quotations were printed across the fragments of torso and hands, leaving the face clear.

"We're playing down the glamour," Henry had repeated several times, "and we're not pouring on the charisma. After Clinton, people have gotten suspicious of just a pretty face. We're trying to project substance."

"I thought content put the electorate to sleep," Gordon had questioned.

"It does. When we did our testing, no one remembered a damn word you said," Henry chuckled. "But they all remembered that you were a man of ideas."

The rally schedule was pretty reasonable during the summer months, just as Gordon had promised Ellie. But it began growing in September, and by early October, there was either a planned or spontaneous rally scheduled for every day.

Browning had arranged for over a hundred radio talk-show interviews, and thirty appearances on daytime talk shows. Reluctantly, he had agreed to one debate on late-night television, and two on daytime

29

radio. He didn't want exposure for the debates because all they would amount to was free airtime for the financially strapped Democratic opponent.

Now the reports were getting down to the nitty-gritty. A bookish type was explaining the forms that were needed to account for all campaign financing. Waiting in the wings was a budget report. Gordon had to stand and pace around the table to keep his eyes from closing. He feigned interest, assuring himself that Henry would handle everything. All Henry wanted in return was total control of the Acton administration's patronage.

Finally, there was just he and Henry, slumped at opposite ends of a table littered with used coffee cups and mustard-stained sandwich wrappers.

"I didn't see much that was aimed at the blue-collar set," Gordon said, just for the sake of having some input to Henry's campaign.

"We have some quotes about keeping jobs at home," Henry answered. "We'll run them heavily in working areas."

"Blue collar, yeah," Gordon agreed, "but I was thinking more specifically about the minorities. Shouldn't I be identifying with some of their interests?"

"Not in our ads. It would sound like pandering. We'll handle them with events and with a PR effort."

"What kind of events?"

Henry Browning leaned back wearily and pushed his glasses up to his forehead. It was the first time Gordon had seen him fatigued and looking his age, which had to be somewhere in the sixties. Henry had been a fixture in state politics for over thirty years, always vitalized by the battle. Now, despite his trim physique and full head of hair, he seemed an old man who might even be vulnerable.

"I was hoping that we might get Ellie to visit a couple of schools in minority and immigrant areas. She has the credentials to be there, so it might not seem entirely political. She could make a point that these are the same public schools you trust for your own kids. Might make you look a bit concerned, maybe even a little human."

"That drastic?" Gordon teased. "Next you'll want me to referee one of their cockfights."

"And we'll try to get our Hispanic overachiever into the family photos. Maybe have her with Ellie, helping her mind the kids. We can't say you're not a bigot. But maybe we can show it."

Gordon nodded. "I think we can count on Ellie for a couple of appearances. And she might not mind having Theresa Santiago along. She's very impressed with the young lady."

"That's fine!" Browning was honestly pleased. "I thought she might empathize with someone from Theresa's background."

"Empathize? She's awestruck. She thinks Theresa is the most competent kid she's ever met. And modest besides. All she does is compliment our poster girl and trash our friends."

"Great! I'm glad it's working out. You never know with troubled youngsters."

"Troubled?" Gordon laughed. "Hardly troubled. Number one quality control inspector at Digital. Soloist in the school orchestra . . ."

Henry nodded. "Yeah, I tried to arrange for her to play at the Governor's inauguration."

"All while she was taking care of her family. Ellie says Theresa did a better job with five than she does with our two. Even took them all to church on Sundays."

Henry registered surprise. "What family? Who says she took care of five kids?"

Gordon was taken back. "Well, she wasn't bragging about it or anything. In fact Ellie said she had to drag it out of her. But she has five younger siblings that she was responsible for over weekends."

"She said that? The Santiago kid said she took care of five brothers and sisters?"

Gordon nodded.

Browning shook his head. "News to me. If she has brothers and sisters they must be scattered around town because there is no family home. Her father took off when she was a kid, and her mother was renting out her ass to keep her suppliers happy. Theresa grew up in a foster home. An older couple who takes in a couple of kids to help with the rent. She lived with them until she turned eighteen. And then she took a room on the same street."

"But she said . . ." Gordon tried, but stopped because he had already reported what Theresa Santiago had said. And Henry had just told him that it was a bold-faced lie.

EIGHT

Gordon followed the traffic from downtown to the interstate, and drove one exit to the north into the old mill district. The red brick buildings with their endless rows of tiny windows had spent a generation as warehouses after manufacturing had taken its leave of New England. Now they were being renovated into fashionable loft space for artists, and into eclectic offices for the advertising and marketing industries.

He pulled into a ground-level parking lot, and rode the old, steel-cage elevator to the penthouse offices of Simpson and Weyer Public Relations. When he stepped out, he was in a black-walled reception area illuminated by an overhead rack of stage lighting. The receptionist, seated behind a glass desk furnished with a computer screen and keyboard, smiled as soon as she saw him.

"Congratulations, Mr. Acton. You already have my vote."

He nodded his appreciation. "Is she in?"

"Sure. She's in a meeting, but I know she'll cut it short for you."

"No hurry," Gordon said as he settled into one of the designer director chairs with a copy of *Graphic Arts*.

He knew he wouldn't have to wait long. The *she* was Pam Lambert, a vice president of the firm, responsible for promoting Action Inflatable Dinghies, the only boating properties left in the Acton family. The fortune made in World War II lifeboats had moved almost entirely into securities, properties, and shopping malls. Action Dinghies, named to sound like the family name but keep it separate from other interests, had become more a hobby than a business.

But when Gordon had first met Pam she had been a young account executive on the make, and the dinghies had been billing enough to make them a very desirable account. They both knew that their love affair was built on a firm foundation of mutual greed. And they both had good reason to keep it secret, she to shelter it from associates who would whisper that she was sleeping her way to success, and he to keep it from Ellie who was totally involved in her then-new baby daughter.

They had been on and off ever since, mostly off in the role of old friends and occasional business associates, but sometimes on with a

32

passion that surprised both of them. They had gotten together for a long, hot summer six years ago, when Pam had been dumped by a man whom she thought would be her husband. And then again, four years ago, when Timothy had been born and Ellie had taken him to the solitude of the Cape. There was little doubt in her mind that she and Gordon would be a time-to-time couple for the rest of her business career. And there was no doubt in his mind that if it weren't damaging to his public image, he and Pam would be keeping house together.

He had enhanced the prestige of the Acton name when he linked it to the Roger Williams lineage. He had kept himself in the social register by occasionally displaying Ellie, much as he might win points in the art community by occasionally displaying a priceless Picasso. An affair that blemished his marriage to a Williams would be like splattering the Picasso with house paint, or hanging it with motel-room art. Pam had always been well-disguised as a simple business associate.

His other indiscretions had also been handled discreetly. There had been a young model who had appeared as a bow bunny in numerous yacht ads, a dancer with the Providence ballet, and, for one stretch of time, the wife of one of his sales representatives. Gordon always had the good sense to choose women who had their own reasons for keeping secrets, or who could be set aside with a modest gift or a career favor. Did Ellie know? He assumed that she had probably suspected. But he knew she had the good sense not to search for evidence, and the good breeding never to voice her suspicions. She had his name, his children, his houses, and the wealth needed to pursue any of her interests. He assumed that she would always give him a relatively free rein outside his home.

Did his marital sophistication extend to any affairs that Ellie might have? Gordon had never even considered the possibility. But if the question had been put to him, he probably would have decided that such behavior was demeaning to her status as his wife, and an act of ingratitude that would be difficult to forgive.

Pam stepped into the foyer with a smile, and with an affectionate kiss on the cheek that held no deeper meaning than business as usual. Then they walked back, through the maze of secretarial cubicles and small private offices, to her large executive office that held a massive desk with its side chairs, an arrangement of sofas around a coffee table, and a bar with two padded stools. Pam went behind the bar, and Gordon slipped onto a stool as comfortably as if it were his private club.

She set up two flat glasses of ice cubes, and poured generously from an outrageously expensive single-malt Scotch.

Gordon examined the bottle. "Business must be very good."

Pam nodded as she raised her glass in a toast. "Better than we deserve. But that doesn't mean we couldn't handle another five-million-dollar account if you happen to have one."

"Not a one," Gordon said, returning the toast. "That's why I'm here. To apologize."

"Apologize for what?"

"My campaign publicity is going to another agency. I just found out today, and I thought I should be the one to tell you."

"Thank God I hadn't already written you into my business plan," Pam said with no hint of disappointment.

Gordon explained, "It's the damn campaign funding laws. If I'm doing business with you, or my company is doing business with you, then it's hard for you to be working on the campaign. The accountants claim there's no way they could prove that I'm not paying you through Action Dinghies for work you're doing for my election campaign. They want everything kept separate."

"It makes sense," Pam said.

"So I'm increasing the Action Dinghies budget," Gordon filled in immediately. "I want to dominate the industry."

Pam nodded. "That wins you another drink." She topped off his Scotch. Then she asked, "Will I be seeing a bit of you this summer?"

"Only a bit. Henry Browning has me on a short leash."

"I assume you'll be in town and the family will be out on the Cape."

Gordon nodded. "Not only that, but Ellie will be full-time on her thesis. I'll be pretty nearly full-time preaching the virtues of good government. But . . . I'd love to see you whenever we can steal a minute."

She leaned across the bar and kissed him on the cheek. "I wasn't sure whether I was going to take a trip this summer. I just decided that I would rather stay home."

"Can we do an early dinner?" he asked.

"Give me five minutes," she said. Pam walked around the bar, carrying her drink, and stood behind her desk while she made a few quick phone calls.

They had dinner in a very public restaurant where they could never be accused of trying to hide anything. Gordon went over the campaign plans that he had reviewed that afternoon, and Pam filled in with intelligent suggestions. She listened carefully as he explained the reasons for hiring the poster girl as Ellie's mother's helper. "Be careful with that one," she advised. "Any hint that you're sucking up to the Hispanic community, and you'll get crucified by all sides. She better be a legitimate employee doing legitimate work. And for God's sake, don't forget the payroll taxes."

Gordon told her about Theresa Santiago's background, and why Henry Browning had introduced her into the Acton family. He mentioned the five children, and Henry's comment that the five kids must live in Theresa's imagination. "Ellie is ready to vote her into sainthood," he concluded, "but I'm having second thoughts. If she's lying, then she's using us. And if she's using us, then the whole shy, innocent demeanor is a lie. I mean, I might be hiring a complete nut to live with my wife and take care of my children."

"You can't stand people who use people," Pam teased.

Gordon allowed a conspiratorial laugh. "Of course I'm using the girl. But I know I'm not dangerous. I guess I'm not really sure about her."

They sifted through the possible reasons for Theresa's lying, and then Pam decided, "I'll bet it's just wishful thinking. Her family is a mess. She sees Ellie's *perfect* family, and she wants to have what Ellie has."

"Sounds weird," Gordon answered. "Like some sort of split personality."

"Don't be melodramatic. This is just a young woman taking her first steps into a very sophisticated corner of the adult world. She's just putting on a new dress to help her get past the interviews."

"But lying! That worries me."

"Have you always been so honest?" Pam was smiling as she waited for his answer.

Gordon nodded. "Okay. We all bend the truth. I guess I'll have to give her a little room to maneuver."

"Good for you!" she said sarcastically. "And speaking of room to maneuver, do you have to get back tonight?"

"Yeah," he said wearily, "but I don't have to be very early."

"Then we'll say goodnight in front of the restaurant. And I'll leave the key in the flower pot."

He examined her carefully. "Do you think that's a very good idea?"

Pam bunched her napkin and pushed her chair back. "You think about it," she said. "The key isn't going anywhere."

NINE

Ellie was stunned when Gordon told her that there were no little brothers and sisters in Theresa Santiago's home. "There is no family," he said, "and there really isn't a home." He explained that she had been placed in foster care by the court, which was how she first came to Henry Browning's attention. The couple who had taken her in were probably her aunt and uncle, but they certainly wouldn't admit to that for fear of losing the monthly payments that the state provided.

"I wonder what else isn't true?" Ellie thought aloud.

Gordon assured her that the rest of the girl's references seemed to check out. Her class standing, her musical skills, and the job in quality assurance were all as represented. She was, indeed, a most extraordinary young woman. He eased into the explanation that Pam Lambert had offered, without attributing it to the other woman. "You know, she's still a kid. It probably hurts her that she has no family, and she probably doesn't want to admit it. She wants to say, 'Look, people love me too!' So she invents a home filled with love and concern."

"You don't think she was lying just to get the job," Ellie countered. "I think she might have figured that I was going to reject her because she had no experience with children. She said what she had to say."

He nodded. "I suppose that's possible, but what if it is? You're dangling everything she wants in front of her face. A family. Nice children. A vacation at a summerhouse. Even the chance to work with you on a graduate level academic project. Would it be so awful if she exaggerated her credentials to get the job?"

"No, I suppose not. We all blow our own horns when we have to. But this was more than just an exaggeration. Exaggerating is if she tells me that she minds her brothers and sisters every weekend, and it turns out that it's only twice a month. Inventing brothers and sisters who don't exist is an outright lie."

"Then you want to get someone else? Trish Mapleton, maybe?"

She didn't decide right away, but took a few days to ponder the problem. She could put up with a momentary lapse in honesty, espe-

36

cially when she put herself in Theresa's place and considered what was at stake for the girl. But she could accept no risk with Molly and Timothy, and the truth seemed to be that Theresa had no experience in dealing with children. It was also possible that she might be lying about other things as well. "Can we find out if she's ever been arrested?" she asked Gordon. "If she's ever harmed anyone? For all we know she might be a hatchet murderer."

"Officially, I can't check up on her," Gordon answered. "Any police or court records she generated before she turned eighteen would be sealed."

But he promised to inquire, and he put the question to Browning. Henry called in a few favors, and was able to assure them that the kid had an exemplary record. "Never even late for school," he had laughed. Gordon brought this information home and vouched for its truth.

In the meantime, Ellie was receiving assurance from another source. Theresa was coming to the house in the afternoons, and watching the children under Ellie's supervision. She saw great patience when Theresa easily managed one of Timothy's tantrums. She saw understanding as the girl glossed over Molly's superior attitude and even outright insults. And she saw imagination as Theresa invented games and stories that captivated Timmy and that Molly reluctantly joined.

"I've decided I'm going to keep her," she told Gordon one evening when he phoned to tell her that he would be very late. "But I'm going to tell her that I know she lied to me, and explain that there is never a reason for lying."

"I think that's a good decision," Gordon told her, even though he was in the midst of a lie as they were speaking. He was calling from his car, on his way to Pam Lambert's apartment where the key was waiting in the planter.

TEN

Theresa was playing with the children while Ellie was organizing their clothes for the move to the Cape. She could hear a game in progress with both Molly and Timmy laughing, and realized how well her household had been running since the new mother's helper had joined the family. She had developed complete confidence in Theresa, and was less and less inclined to confront her about the status of her family and the experience she had claimed in minding her brothers and sisters. But avoiding the issue, Ellie realized, was the easy way out. She had to make it clear that there could be no deceptions between them. She waited until the children were settled into the projects that Theresa had created for them. Then she called the young woman into her bedroom, nearly choking on her words. Theresa came instantly with her white smile flashing beneath her light blue eyes.

"They're wonderful children," she said to Ellie.

"You seem to bring out the best in them. They're not always this cooperative. But then you must have had bad days along with the good days with your own brothers and sisters."

Theresa nodded curtly, but made no answer. She was plainly uncomfortable with the subject.

"That wasn't really true, was it?" Ellie continued.

"What?" Theresa's discomfort was rising to alarm.

"About your brothers and sisters. You told me there were five of them, and that you took care of them on weekends."

"Well . . . no. Not brothers and sisters . . . not exactly." She was fumbling the question badly.

"Theresa, I think it would be best if you told me about your brothers and sisters."

The girl stood stone still, her eyes blank and her lips squeezed together. She didn't seem to be searching for an answer. Rather, she was crushed to have been caught in a deception.

"Please, Theresa. I'm going to be trusting you with my children. There's no room for doubt. You and I have to have complete confidence in one another."

38

The girl's eyes came back into focus and the color returned to her face. "For a while my foster parents took in some other kids. Sometimes I had to take care of them. But I couldn't handle it. I was only twelve. Mostly I was too busy."

"That was a terrible responsibility," Ellie sympathized.

"I couldn't do everything," Theresa went on. "They were crying a lot. Sometimes they would just go out into the street, and neighbors would have to bring them back. So the social workers moved them in with other families."

"Your foster parents were . . ."

"It wasn't their fault," Theresa was quick to say. "They both did what they could."

"Why didn't you tell me the truth?" Ellie asked. "You hadn't done anything to be ashamed of. There was no reason for you to lie."

"It's not something that's easy to talk about."

"I can understand that," Ellie said sympathetically.

Theresa allowed a small smile. "No you can't," she told Ellie. "I don't think you have any idea at all."

They stood for an instant, facing one another as adversaries. Then Theresa turned and walked slowly from the bedroom, into the family area where the children were playing. Ellie decided not to follow her, to give her a moment to herself. But suddenly, Theresa was standing in the bedroom doorway, this time with her sweater over her arm. "I'll be going now," she told Ellie. "I just wanted to say thank you for everything. I've enjoyed meeting you and your children." She moved quickly toward the front door.

Ellie followed right on her heels. "Theresa, I'm not firing you. I just want to be sure that there will always be honesty between us."

"I know," the girl answered. "But I think I should leave. We don't know the first thing about each other. This isn't going to work."

"We can make it work," Ellie tried. But her mother's helper had already slipped through the door and closed it behind her. Ellie thought for a moment. Was this the right way to end their relationship? Or were they both making a terrible mistake? She knew that Theresa wanted the job. And she knew that she wanted the girl as part of her summer household.

She bolted to the door when she heard the tubercular auto engine gasp for air and then catch. But the car was already pulling away, and Theresa didn't look back in her direction. She seemed to be crying.

Ellie spent the rest of the afternoon arguing both sides of the issue.

At one moment, it seemed that she had every right to confront the girl, and Theresa's response had demonstrated her immaturity and lack of responsibility. Her leaving was probably for the best. But seconds later, she hated herself for having dredged up an insignificant lie. She had put Theresa through agony for no good reason. No wonder she had walked out on the job. When Gordon pulled into the driveway, she was still undecided whether she should be blaming herself or blaming the girl. But by the time she began telling him what had happened, she knew that she wanted Theresa back.

Gordon was surprised at Ellie's report, and apprehensive over the effect it might have on his campaign. Not hiring the girl would have been a nonevent, but forcing her out of the job could easily be used against him. Technically, as Ellie explained several times, Theresa had quit. But it would be easy for his opponents to put a very different spin on the parting. It could logically be made to sound as if a girl from a broken immigrant family wasn't good enough to associate with Gordon Acton's kids. Not the kind of reputation a candidate wants, even in a safe district.

But he sympathized with Ellie, telling her she had every right to ask for a clarification of Theresa's claims. "If the kid wants to hide her upbringing, that's her business. And if she'd rather quit than tell the truth, that's her business too."

"Well, I certainly feel like the heavy," Ellie countered. "It's just like she told me; I don't have a clue about the kind of life she's had to lead."

"She said that?"

"Not in so many words. But when I told her I understood why she might not want to talk about it, she told me that I didn't understand at all. That we didn't know anything about one another. And she's right. I was way out of bounds."

He nodded in agreement that Ellie might have been too hasty. But he made his words sound reassuring. "All you did was check up on a reference."

Ellie shook her head. "It was a lot more than that. I judged her. I measured her against our damned superior morality. 'Thou shalt not tell a lie!' She's not supposed to lie to get a job. But it's okay for us to lie just to pad our pockets."

Gordon looked defensive. "I'm not sure it's the same thing."

"Damn right it's not. People like us lie to save on our taxes. She lies for a shot at a better life. So, which one of us is worse? Our friends pretend they're not dealing on inside information. She pretends she's had experience. Which one of us is the criminal?"

"I don't think we're criminals," Gordon decided.

"But I'm right, aren't I? She and her people cheat in their way, and we and our dear friends cheat in our way. What right do I have to judge her unless I know what she's been through? And when it comes to that, she's absolutely right. I don't have a clue."

"So what do you want to do?" He was pleased with the way she was leaning.

"I want to apologize to her and ask her to reconsider the job."

May

ELEVEN

The house on the Cape was in Chatham, on the elbow of the landmass that resembles an arm flexing its muscles. Built just before the Civil War, by a sea captain who had enormous respect for the power of the waves and wind, it stood like a fortress on a stone outcropping overlooking Pleasant Bay and the distant barrier sandbar. Its foundations were a full twenty feet above the high-tide markings and another ten feet above the sandy beach. Even the storm of the century had fallen short of the porch steps. The peaked roof was low in the front, reducing the resistance to onshore breezes. The hurricane of '44 had ripped away some of the shingles, but the rain had never been able to break through into the attic.

Still, the weather had exacted a price. The wooden shakes were stained dark green by sea air that had triumphed over paint and varnish. The deck boards on the ground-floor porches were turning up along the edges. And the windowpanes were shrunk inside mullions that had thickened with repeat coats of putty and paint. It was, in the jargon of the year-round inhabitants, well-weathered. But to the realtors who catered to the new fortunes of Boston financiers, it was too small and a bit too quaint for the neighborhood.

Architecturally, it was a classic, with all the limitations of the bygone era. The upper floor had four equally sized bedrooms with inadequate closets. The two white-tiled bathrooms, each with a giant freestanding tub, were at the ends of the halls, making bathrobes essential attire. On the lower floor, the outside porch with its full roof, posts, and railings actually served as a family room. Screening played the dual roles of air-conditioning and bug protection. Just inside the massive front door, a wide flight of stairs separated a big, generally unused living room from a smaller, always busy dining room. The kitchen, pantries, and still another tiled bathroom were across the back of the house.

The kitchen, remodeled a few summers back, was the only contemporary room, with an island cooking area, two wall ovens, a built-in refrigerator, and a snack bar countertop. The dining room was wainscoting, chair rails, Victorian paper, plate rails, and a center chandelier. The furnishings were dark, carved, and heavy. The living room was overstuffed, with dust covers that stayed on throughout the season. Its only vital area was a massive desk and high-backed chair that served as Gordon's summer office. Ellie was in the process of taking it over.

She had driven over in the fully loaded van with Theresa and the children, and met the caretaker at the front door. Herman had greeted her, as usual, with a litany of all the disasters that had been averted only because of his constant vigilance. Though he regarded himself as the protector of all the waterfront properties from Pleasant Bay to Nantucket Sound, most of the new residents with the big shorefront homes had replaced him with security services and motion detectors. Gordon kept him on because he had always been there, and because he was always on call whenever a handyman was needed.

Theresa had carried in the children's bags, unpacked their beach clothes, and led them down the steps to the small waves that lapped against the sand. Ellie had stationed herself at the front door and directed Herman toward the destination of each of the packages he carried around from the garage. She had noticed the cardboard carton that was headed up to Theresa's room, holding everything she would need for the summer. It was embarrassing for Ellie when she compared the box to the steady parade of suitcases and hampers that were intended to hold her over only until Gordon could make it down with the rest of their things.

"Over there, on the desk," she told Herman when he carried in the first installment of her computer gear. The processor tower would stand next to the desk with the terminal on the desktop. The paper file box that held her research notes could stay under the desk where it would be out of sight, and the printer went into the hall closet, to be brought out and connected only as needed. The telephone line could be disconnected from the desk telephone and plugged into the back of the tower whenever she wanted to go on-line. It was a perfect arrangement, giving her all the office space she would need in a location that overlooked the porch where the kids would be playing. She would be only a few seconds from the steps that led down to the beach.

Ellie busied herself with setting up her office until Herman announced that the van was empty. She tipped him extravagantly, and then ran up to her room to get into her bathing suit and beach robe. Her dormered window looked straight over the bay, and as she undressed she went close to the glass so that she could see down to the beach below. Theresa had rolled her jeans up above her knees, and she was at the water's edge supervising the construction of a sand castle. Molly seemed to be the master builder, and Timmy served as the contractor, supplying the wet sand and needed stones. It was a scene of domestic joy, and Ellie was once again thankful that Theresa had reconsidered her decision. She had been a big help not only in packing the children's things but also in organizing and packing the computer gear and research files. Ellie was already thinking of her as indispensable.

Theresa hadn't been easy to win over. She hadn't been home when Gordon and Ellie had driven to her house, and she never seemed to be available when Ellie called. Ellie had met her on the steps of the junior college, apologized for making too much of the discrepancy, and asked her to return. Theresa had thanked her politely, but told her that she was going back to her manufacturing job. She had a lot of friends there, she explained. They were people she knew and who knew her. Ellie got the message; the young woman would be more comfortable with people who knew all about her, and who accepted her as she was. Theresa promised to give it some more thought, but it seemed to be more a courtesy to Ellie than a real chance that she would change her mind.

Ellie had apologized again in two telephone conversations, and pitched the benefits of the mother's helper job. She had talked about the vacation setting, the free-time opportunities, and even the advantages of stretching her relationships and meeting new people. "It sounds like *you're* the one applying for a position," Gordon had commented. "Let's keep it clear that you're the one doing the hiring." She had finally gone back to the school and offered the job to Theresa one last time before she hired someone else. "I think you'll be good for us and we'll be good for you," she had argued, "and you'll meet people who are on the same success track that you're on." The last argument seemed to be the winner, and Theresa had smiled, said she would come back, and then joined Ellie in a laughing embrace. She had returned the next day, and Ellie had been careful about her requests and comments ever since.

She climbed down the wooden steps to the beach, holding her straw sun hat on against the wind. The kids rushed to greet her, and Theresa stood back by the water's edge enjoying the family reunion.

"Go up and get your bathing suit," Ellie said. "We'll wait for you before we take our swim."

Theresa smiled nervously. "I don't have a bathing suit. I'm not much of a swimmer." She noticed Ellie's disappointment, so she quickly added, "But I don't mind getting my jeans wet. I can wade in as far as Timmy will want to go."

When Gordon called, Ellie told him more about her mother's helper than about the children. "I think she likes the place."

"She should. It's not exactly shabby."

"What I mean is that she seems comfortable with it. You should have seen her expression when she saw her room. She just stood in her front window looking out at the bay, and then the ocean. I don't think she suspected that places like this really existed."

"Maybe we should tell her what a room with a view goes for during the season," Gordon laughed.

Ellie's hand was cupped around the phone. "Gordon, I don't think she knows how to swim. She doesn't even own a bathing suit."

"Great!" Gordon said sarcastically. "Maybe if the dinghy tips Molly will be able to rescue her. How does a kid grow up in a fishing town and not learn how to swim?"

"Dinghy racing may not have been part of her social scene," Ellie said with equal sarcasm.

"Well get her a bathing suit and whatever else she needs. I suppose when you hire an amateur carpenter, you have to buy him a hammer."

"Let's remember who suggested hiring the amateur carpenter," Ellie reminded him.

Gordon was silent for an instant. Then he answered, "Mea culpa! You're right of course. I started all this. And I'm sorry if it's causing you problems."

The next morning Ellie announced a shopping trip to Hyannis, which would certainly have drawn protests from the children had she not added that they would pick up new beach toys. These, as she carefully planned, were best found in a surf shop that also featured long aisles of swimsuits and beachwear.

"Get yourself what you'll need," Ellie said to Theresa, trying to

48

sound casual. "I'll steer the kids to the safer toys." Theresa hesitated, not moving in any of the appropriate directions. "For this job," Ellie prompted, "a bathing suit and sun hat are career clothes. And you better get some shirts and a good pair of sandals." Still, Theresa wasn't moving into the aisles. "They come with the job," Ellie told her. "I expect to pay for the things you need to take care of my children."

"Mommy! Look!" Timmy was already running toward her with an inflated shark that was twice his size.

"Get some clothes," Ellie ordered, taking Timmy's hand and heading to the other end of the store.

She tipped the clerk to carry sand toys, life rings, and the oversized shark out to the van, and then led her children back to the clothing section. Theresa had a pile of shirts and suits draped over her arm, and wore a large straw hat on the back of her head. She was standing in front of a shelf that displayed sandals.

"Let's see," Ellie said, already showing excitement over Theresa's selections.

The T-shirts with sailing scenes and leaping fish were what she expected. None carried the more popular four-letter words or sexual double entendres. The hat was practical, if a bit too matronly. "You'll need something that fits tight for sailing," Ellie said, and she selected a baseball cap that displayed the logo of Narragansett Ale. "These are adjustable to any size." And she picked a pair of shower clogs that were the rage with the younger set. "Get these for the beach. Around here the sandals are more for dress up."

The bathing suit was the problem. It was a one piece in a florid pattern, with fake nautical rope outlining the shoulder straps and neckline. Not terrible, but certainly not what a young woman with a good figure would wear to a coed beach. Ellie was tongue-tied, wondering how to suggest that she get something a bit more revealing.

"You're not going to wear that!" Molly whined.

Ellie could have kissed her.

"You don't like it?" Theresa asked. Ellie could tell that Theresa wasn't thrilled with it either. She had picked it because it was on a special sale.

"It's gross," Molly answered, turning her face away as if she had detected an unpleasant odor.

Ellie moved quickly, picking up a one-piece racing suit in dark blue with light green piping. Then she grabbed a simple white bikini with high cut thighs and strings serving as bra straps. "Try these on," she said to Theresa. And then added, "Maybe you'll like them better." She didn't want to appear to be giving orders.

Theresa took the two suits and leaned down to Molly. "What do you think of these?"

Molly glanced. "They're better than the one you picked."

Theresa disappeared into the dressing room and stepped out in the one-piece. Ellie was startled. She was well-curved, a speck too busty and hippy for a fashion model, but certainly a very well proportioned young woman. Her skin was glorious, a deep tan that showed an almost polished sheen. The white smile and the light blue eyes were even more evident. There was no doubt that Theresa was competitive with anyone that the neighboring families could field for the clambake.

"Much, much better," Ellie said.

But Theresa was modeling the suit for Molly. "Do you like this one?"

Molly was fascinated by all the curves and by the softness that pressed against the skintight fabric. "Yeah! It's okay!"

"Should I try the other one?" Theresa asked Ellie.

"Sure, if you'd like." But Ellie didn't think that anything would improve on the present look.

Theresa returned a few minutes later, and the pink flush of embarrassment made her dark complexion even more glowing. The white suit seemed minimal, fully revealing of a perfect cleavage. Nipples bulged against the curve of the bra. And the waistline seemed even smaller than it had in the one-piece.

"Wow!" Ellie said with a smile.

Molly's eyes were popping, filled with the hope that someday she might look like that. "That's much better," she allowed.

"I feel naked," Theresa whispered to Ellie.

"Well, as long as you don't wear it in a heavy surf."

"Would you wear one?"

"No, but I wouldn't fill it out the way you do."

"Then I won't get it," Theresa decided.

"Get it!" Molly ordered. She was thinking of the crowd that Theresa would attract, and how envious the other kids would be.

"Yes," Ellie agreed. "You certainly can wear it, so there's no reason why you shouldn't."

"I will, if you will," Theresa answered.

"Oh, God. I have a figure like a flagpole."

"But I'll be embarrassed if I look bare and you look fully dressed."

"Go ahead, Mom," Molly joined in. "Haley's mom wears a bikini."

"Haley's mom isn't really Haley's mom," Ellie whispered. "A second wife."

"Then you shouldn't back off," Theresa encouraged. "At least try one on."

Ellie flushed with embarrassment, even though she was pleased that her daughter regarded her as a contemporary of Haley's second mom. "Oh, I don't think so . . ." But she was already pushing through the rack to find her size.

In the dressing room, she turned slowly in front of the mirror. The suit she had picked was a horizontal stripe that at least added the appearance of width. She had to admit that it didn't look bad. Her legs were good, long, and slim. And the widest part of her midriff was the bottom of her ribs. Her bust was small, but at least the suit didn't add pre-shaped padding. It was natural and even provocative.

She couldn't! If she wore this to the yacht club her friends would wonder whom she was kidding. She really didn't need to be competing with a teenager. But as she pirouetted, she remembered that she was a few years younger than most of the women in their circle. Why should she be in a hurry to catch up with them?

Hell, she decided, she could wear it on their small private beach. Let Gordon decide whether he wanted her to show her midriff and, when she leaned forward, all that there was of her breasts. If he liked it, and wearing it on her own beach gave her courage, she might just wear it at the club.

TWELVE

That night, Ellie began the long-postponed work on her thesis. While Theresa marched the children through their baths, she sat on the porch and reread her outline. She paused when they came downstairs to say goodnight, and took another break when she heard Molly defying Theresa. After she had restored order, she reviewed her statistics and tabulations, isolating the data that she still needed, and listing the authorities whose views would be essential. She was organizing papers on her desk when Theresa finally came down to announce that the children were both asleep.

"How's it going?" Theresa asked, nodding in the general direction of the papers.

Ellie sighed. "Discouraging, I guess. It seems I'm not as far along as I thought."

Theresa sat cross-legged on the floor, next to the desk. "What's it about?" she asked.

Ellie was going to give her a casual answer, but she detected real interest and so she began to explain the work. She was attempting to show that in deprived communities, scarce teaching resources were better directed toward the parents than the children. In head-start programs, the professional educators should work with the parents, and then let the parents work with the children. Both approaches had been tried and there were some valid reports. Her task was to gather this data from the professional journals published by the states, and then relate the data to the viewpoints expressed by university and government experts.

"Well," Theresa said, "I know I can help you with the tabulations. I'm real good at math."

"I'd appreciate that," Ellie said.

"And I know how to use a library catalog. I might even be able to get some of the information over the Internet."

Ellie sat back, her expression showing her delight. "I've used computers at the libraries," she said, "and I've gone on-line just to see what was out there. But actually doing the research . . ."

"It's part of a course that I just took," Theresa said. "If you want, I could at least try to see if I can get anything."

"Okay," Ellie said, relinquishing her chair. Then she looked over Theresa's shoulder as her babysitter launched into the Internet, picked a search engine, and began loading in subjects. Ellie watched with fascination as they traveled from state to state, constantly narrowing the description of the target articles.

"Maxwell," Ellie suddenly yelled as the name appeared in a list of authors. "He's one of my sources."

Theresa brought up titles and summaries of three articles by the man, and then downloaded all the text onto a disk. Ellie pulled one of the soft chairs over to the desk, and began offering words and phrases that might speed the search. Theresa ran them through the search engines, generally running into dead ends, but occasionally coming up with a hit. They had identified three of the databases, and downloaded two more articles before Theresa wiped her eyes in exhaustion.

"My God, it's nearly midnight," Ellie announced.

Theresa laughed. "I stopped thinking half an hour ago. I guess we didn't get very much."

"You got a great deal. You made more than a dent in the work. I don't know how to thank you."

"I like doing it. And I like what you're trying to show. Would it be okay if I read your files? I might get some ideas."

"Okay? I'd be thrilled. Gordon's eyes frost over whenever I tell him about my work."

"I think I'd like to get into education," Theresa said. "It's so important."

Ellie could have hugged her.

She sat at her desk for several minutes marveling at the performance she had just witnessed. She had never had a brighter student. Student? It was unfair to think of Theresa in that way. She had been the teacher, showing Ellie how to maneuver through cyberspace, a place where Theresa was perfectly at home and she was just a visitor. It seemed that with just a few hours a night, Theresa could help her download hundreds of articles.

Ellie looked at her watch, wondering why Gordon hadn't called as he did nearly every evening when he was away. And then she remembered; the phone line had been tied to the computer. Gordon probably couldn't get through. As soon as she reconnected the line to the phone, it began to ring.

"Who in hell have you been talking to?" he demanded. There was an angry edge in his voice.

"I'm sorry, but wait until I tell you. Theresa had me on the Internet, doing my research on-line. I got so much done!"

"You? On-line?"

"Well, really Theresa. I was just giving her words and watching over her shoulder. But it was amazing!"

"Computers are the future . . ."

"Not the computer. Theresa! She has to be the brightest kid I've ever worked with. She was great with the kids, and then after watching them all day, she pitched in and helped me."

"She's not a graduate student, Ellie. She's just a babysitter."

"She could be a graduate student. For the first time I'm feeling confident that I'll have this thing finished by the end of the summer."

"Just watch her work."

Ellie detected alarm. "Why? What do you think she'll do?"

"Nothing! But she won't understand what she's reading. She could make a mistake that would embarrass you."

She sighed. "Good God, all she's doing is fetching some data. I'm writing the thesis."

"Good," he said, and then he began to tell her that he was missing her. She leaned back, cradled the phone against her shoulder, and wondered if he couldn't make it out to the Cape a day early. "I've got a surprise for you," she said, thinking of her daring bikini.

Gordon didn't tell her his surprise news. Henry Browning had called to warn him that the police were interested in Miss Santiago. Stolen semiconductors that had come from the Digital Electronics plant where Theresa had worked were showing up in the area black market. Someone had figured out how to alter a computer-based inventory program so they wouldn't be missed from the warehouse shelves.

The next morning, Ellie showed Theresa how to use the camcorder, and sent her out to the National Seashore with the children. The season was opening with a sand-sculpturing contest that Molly wanted to enter, and even though she had no special talent, each of the under-twelve contestants would receive a ribbon. "Get pictures of Molly and Tim working," Ellie asked, "and then shots of their entries. Their father will enjoy them. And take some of the adult entries. Some of them are terrific."

When they had left, she sat at her computer, and began shaping her discussion around the information that Theresa had pulled off the Internet. As she worked, she realized the importance of the young girl's contribution, and pondered the contrasts that lived within one personality. She was so skilled in her schoolwork, in her factory job, and so amazingly comfortable with the computer. And yet she was at a loss when it came to grooming, attire, and other things that were typically important to women her age. It was as if she had gone from childhood straight to adult responsibilities without ever pausing at adolescence.

She heard the roar of a downshifted engine, and then the skid of tires. When she went out to the porch, an open-top Jeep was parked halfway into a dune. Trish Mapleton was dashing up the steps.

"Trish!" Ellie was honestly happy to see her. In her athletic shorts, tank top, and baseball cap, she was in a familiar uniform. The sunglasses were expected, and the hiking boots with the rolled-down socks were in step with the latest trend. Ellie was very comfortable with Trish.

"Mrs. Acton! I just heard you moved back. How was the winter?" She was already settling into one of the stuffed wicker chairs.

"Wonderful! Busy! I guess you heard about the nomination."

"Sure. My folks think it's great. So, how are the kids? I'll bet Molly is all grown up."

Ellie's joy faded. Trish was expecting to take up her babysitting chores. Ellie wasn't looking forward to delivering the bad news.

"They're out at the seashore. The sand castle contest."

"Oh!" Suspicion appeared in Trish's eyes. "Who are they with?"

"My assistant," she answered with as much nonchalance as she could muster. "I had to get someone back in Providence to help during the campaign." *Assistant* seemed to suggest someone taking care of her rather than the children. It didn't sound so threatening.

"Oh, great!" But Trish's enthusiasm was feigned, and suspicion still lingered in her eyes.

"She'll be here on and off during the summer," Ellie struggled ahead, "helping me with my schoolwork and . . . with the kids." She hadn't been able to make *the kids* sound nonchalant. And she could see it had registered quickly with her guest.

"Well then, you probably won't be needing me."

Ellie still couldn't deliver the news. "Of course I'll be needing you. And Molly is dying to see you. I might not need you as much, but you're welcome to come over whenever you want."

"Oh, thanks." The girl was polite, but it was clear that she had gotten the message. "I'll be pretty busy myself, but I'll try to get over to see the kids." She was up and moving toward the steps.

"How about a Coke or some iced tea?" Ellie offered with little enthusiasm.

"No thanks. Just wanted to say a quick hello."

She bounded down the steps and sprang into the Jeep. The car whirled in a tight U-turn, kicking up a sandy rooster tail. Then it flashed by the side of the house and disappeared around the garage.

Ellie looked after it sadly. "Well, you sure handled that beautifully," she berated herself. She could picture the cold reception that awaited her when she ran into the Mapletons at the yacht club.

She returned to her thesis, but her mind kept wandering to her meeting with Trish. She wished she had telephoned her the minute that Theresa had been hired and told her the truth up front. Then she reconsidered. It would have been just as difficult telling her then as now, and her parents would have had that much longer to poison the atmosphere at the club. She found herself toying with the idea of burying Theresa in her research work so that she *would* need Trish for the kids. That might make everyone happy, particularly her preadolescent daughter. But she had hired Theresa to watch the kids, with the added promise of a summer on the beach. It wouldn't be fair to lock her indoors like a librarian. Finally, she put her papers aside. Theresa, she reminded herself, was far more competent than any of their friends' daughters and she needed the job more, and probably took it far more seriously. There was no way she could compromise the girl just to avoid a few awkward moments.

She went upstairs, noticed that the door to Theresa's room was ajar, and went to close it. Then, when she reached the doorway, she couldn't help peeking inside. Ellie was immediately taken by the near military sparseness of the environment. There were no personal items, no posters, no women's magazines, and no beauty guides or clothes reviews. The requisite CD player was missing along with the familiar tower filled with disks. There were no pictures of parents nor any snapshots of friends. In fact, Ellie could find no sign that there was any life at all.

She looked across the shelves of the bookcase that stood opposite the bed. There were groupings of schoolbooks, in math, English, computer science, biology, and history. No novels, or picture books, or anything that hinted of a hobby or suggested fun. She found herself feeling sorry for the girl. Her possessions reflected a dreary existence.

Ellie tiptoed noiselessly into the room even though she knew she was alone in the house. She was spying shamelessly and trying to hide her actions even from herself. She eased open the closet door. The things she had bought the day before were hung neatly on one side of the closet. The things she had brought with her—two ordinary dresses, a few pairs of jeans, and a few shirts and blouses—were relegated to the other side as if one group of clothes might contaminate the other. On the floor, next to her new sandals and old sneakers, was a flute case with worn corners.

She closed the door and turned toward the dresser. "You shouldn't be doing this," Ellie reminded herself. She leaned toward the bedroom door, knowing that was the path she should take, but then stepped toward the closed dresser drawers. She found a basic assortment of socks and underwear, all the cotton athletic type. There was nothing that could qualify as lingerie. There wasn't even a nightie, just a pair of striped pajamas. To Theresa, clothing seemed to be nothing more than modesty and warmth.

She looked at the desktop, with a single pencil resting next to the blotter. Then she slid open the desk drawer. Inside were the pens, stationery, and paper clips that Ellie had provided. There was also a single white envelope, with photo prints visible under the flap. She lifted it carefully, and began slipping the pictures out.

She recognized Theresa. She was standing next a boy her own age in front of the weather-worn car that she had driven to Ellie's house. There was a plastic cooler at their feet. Then there was another couple next to the car, a slightly overweight girl with a tall, thin boy. They appeared to be neighborhood friends, all from a neighborhood on the other side of the world. The car, the attire, the grooming, and even the mannerisms would cause concern on the Cape Cod beach, and raise the suspicions of the local police.

The next few photos showed combinations of the same people, now at a sandy beach. They were on a blanket, with the open cooler resting in the sand next to them. Each of them held a bottle of beer and mugged for the camera. Ellie found herself smiling, delighted that Theresa seemed to have at least a few friends and some sort of social life.

She slipped out the next photo. It showed Theresa and her boyfriend plunging from a rock into deep water. Ellie was stunned at the evidence that Theresa must know how to swim. She was even more surprised at the very minimal bikini she was wearing. There was obviously no reason why she should have been shy about trying on a bathing suit in the store.

"Why you little phony," Ellie said out loud. Then she took a deep breath when she remembered that Theresa had her children out on the barrier beach.

THIRTEEN

When Gordon stepped into Henry's office there was already a man sitting in one of the side chairs.

"Gordon, this is Sergeant Edward Wass . . ."

"Was-*chay*-vitz," said the sergeant, who had obviously been through this routine many times before. "Fall River department."

Wasciewicz was of medium height and round-shouldered, with the sunken chest of a chain-smoker. He was somewhere between thirty and fifty with thinning white hair and a pale complexion. He would have been absolutely nondescript except for penetrating blue eyes that warned he was not to be trifled with. Gordon shook his hand and then sat beside him, across the desk from Henry Browning.

Henry set the stage. "The sergeant has generously agreed to brief us on the state of his investigation into the Digital Electronics matter. His captain knows of my interests in Theresa Santiago, and he was kind enough to call me when her name came up."

Gordon understood the truth of the matter. Henry's political clout washed across the state line into Fall River. Someone in the department was watching out for his interests and had ordered Wasciewicz to keep him informed.

The sergeant hunched his shoulders in response to the introduction. No big deal, he seemed to be indicating. Clearly, he didn't know what all the fuss was about. "There's not much to brief you on," he began. "Microprocessors from a plant in our area have been showing up in repair outlets in half a dozen cities. The company doesn't sell to repair centers, so it checked everything from its own warehouse right down to its customers' receiving docks to try to find the source. Turns out the stuff was coming right off its own shelves."

Gordon glanced at his watch. The policeman picked up his cadence. "It looks like some local hood had gotten to someone in the plant who was putting the components out with the garbage. Routine stuff that we can easily stop. But someone had changed the computer inventory programs so that the missing components wouldn't show up. We got a list of people with access to the company's computers and Theresa Santiago was on the list. Way down the list so that she isn't really a suspect, but someone saw her name and thought that Mr. Browning should know about it."

Henry closed the loop by saying, "And since you've hired her, Gordon, I thought you should find out immediately."

Gordon nodded, then turned to Wasciewicz. "You say she's not suspected of anything."

"Not yet," the sergeant answered. "Probably never. But if we get that far down the list we may want to interview her."

Gordon looked back to Henry. "I don't see any problem. She works at a place where there's been a theft, but she's not suspected of anything." He glanced back to the policeman. "Is that about it?"

"That's about it. But we're just getting started. Maybe when we know more . . ."

"You'll let me know," Henry said, finishing the thought.

"Sure." Wasciewicz was already standing. He wasn't comfortable promising to deliver someone's political favor.

He shook hands across the desk, and then reached out to Gordon. "Nice to meet you, Mr. Acton. And if anything develops on your end I hope you'll return the favor and give me a call."

"What could develop on my end?"

"Oh, you know. Strange characters calling on Miss Santiago. Or maybe she takes off without telling anyone where she's going. Or even that she seems frightened."

"Does she have anything to be frightened about?"

"Probably not. But the guy who was putting the components out with the garbage has disappeared. We don't know what happened to him."

FOURTEEN

Gordon drove out to Chatham late Friday night from a fund-raising dinner and arrived at the house long after his children had gone to bed. Even though there was a light in the living room window, he closed his car door quietly and moved carefully up the steps. He was surprised, when he stepped inside, to find Ellie and Theresa working furiously at the desk.

Ellie jumped up and greeted him with a kiss. Theresa scarcely raised her eyes, remaining absorbed in the computer.

"We're making so much progress," Ellie announced, and rushed back to the desk to gather up the printed pages.

"Great!" He joined her behind the desk, but focused on the work that Theresa was doing rather than on the papers that Ellie had handed him. "What's that?" he asked, nodding toward the display.

"We're in the Yale library," Ellie told him, "picking up sections of Wortheimer's study of teachers' children."

"Columbia," Theresa corrected. "Robinson's stuff was at Yale."

"Of course, Columbia," Ellie agreed.

Gordon watched the girl manipulate the information, highlighting sections for downloading. It was obvious that she knew enough of the content of the work to know which of the tabulations were relevant.

"You're really good at this," he complimented.

"I like computers," Theresa said, still completely absorbed in her work.

"Not just *like*. You understand computers. I'll bet you could write programs of your own."

Theresa nodded. But then she suddenly pulled back from the keyboard. "Oh, not real programs. More like changing a few instructions. Just things we learn at school." Gordon was staring down at her, and Theresa began to fidget. "We just learn the simple stuff . . . the mechanics . . ."

"It doesn't look so simple to me," he persisted. "You really understand file organization. And you certainly know the points that Ellie is trying to make."

Theresa slid out of the chair. "I'm just copying whatever Mrs. Acton needs. I don't know what it's all about."

"Oh, you're much more helpful than that, Theresa," Ellie responded. Then she told Gordon, "I don't know what I'd do without her."

"I better be going up," Theresa said. "It's kind of late."

"Yes, of course," Ellie called after her. "Busy day tomorrow."

She and Gordon took a bottle of Pinot Grigio out onto the screened porch and settled together in an oversized chaise lounge. To their left, there were the anchor lights of the boats moored off the yacht club, with an occasional flash of light from inside the cabins.

Straight ahead, the road lights out on the barrier beach were reflected in Pleasant Bay.

He listened attentively while she explained exactly where she was in the developments of her arguments, and all the work that Theresa had done to get her there. The kid was an amazing researcher and certainly learned quickly. She had even drafted the connectors between some of the quotations and had demonstrated unusual writing skills. "It's no wonder Yale wants her," she said in summary.

"Yale?" Gordon was amazed.

Ellie nodded. "She has a scholarship along with full credit for her junior college work. All she has to do is cover her expenses."

"Maybe you should let Theresa write the thesis for you," he said with an ironic laugh.

Ellie sat bolt upright. "I'm doing no such thing!"

"Hey, I was just kidding." Gordon's hands went up in mock surrender. "It's just that she wasn't playing video games in there. That's pretty sophisticated stuff she's doing. If our average high school graduate is that talented, I'm not sure we'd *need* new teaching methods."

"She is *not* your average high school graduate. She's already a terrific research assistant. But these are my ideas being presented in my way. Just as she said, she's doing the mechanical stuff."

"I know, I know," Gordon agreed. "And I'm thrilled that she's such a big help to you."

Ellie sipped, taking a moment to organize her words. "You know, she really is far more valuable helping me with my thesis than just watching the kids. I was thinking . . ."

"Just watching the kids?" he interrupted. "You're always saying that's the most important work that you do."

"It is. I didn't mean to put it that way. But I thought I might talk to Trish Mapleton tomorrow about giving me some help with the kids so that Theresa can spend more time on my paper. She could go into Brown and up to Harvard for some of the research we can't get off the Internet. Overall, it might give me even more time with the children."

Gordon eyed her suspiciously. "Sure, if that's what *you* want. But it sounds to me as if maybe you're really thinking about what Molly wants. Has she decided that she wants to be with Trish? Is she giving Theresa a hard time?"

"There's some of that. Molly seems moody, and I don't want her to have an awful summer. But the truth is that I don't have a hundred

61

percent confidence in Theresa. I'm just not that sure that she's the person she makes herself out to be. That's okay with the research. I know I can take care of myself. But I don't want any doubts when it comes to the children."

He asked if she were still worried because Theresa had lied about her family responsibilities.

"Well, that. But there are other things. Like the pictures I found in her drawer."

"You were looking through her things?" He was completely surprised. Ellie had the highest respect for other people's privacy.

She admitted her crime, but then told Gordon about Theresa's shy act at the store, and the contradicting photo of her in a string bikini. She reminded him that Theresa wasn't supposed to be much of a swimmer, and then described her dive into deep water. "I mean, there's nothing wrong with jumping off rocks if you know what you're doing. But why act as if you don't? There's nothing wrong with a revealing bathing suit, especially if you have her figure. But why act as if you've never been in a locker room?"

He nodded slowly and mumbled words of agreement. But he didn't share his uneasiness about the semiconductor swindle at Digital Electronics. That was too unlikely a connection to bring up even though the possibility had been reinforced by her demonstration of computer expertise.

"Tell you what!" he proposed. "Let's sleep on it until after the weekend. The guys from Newport are bringing the boat around and should be docking at the club first thing in the morning. Then Henry is sending out a photographer, who will want to get us all together on the dock, climbing aboard, and all that sort of stuff. So we'll really be watching the kids ourselves."

Ellie nodded thoughtfully. "Okay. I wasn't going to do any work on the thesis over the weekend. And Trish should be around the club, so Molly might not be as much of a pest."

"Then we agree."

"Except the part about 'sleeping on it.' I was hoping you might not want to go right to sleep."

He smiled, tossed down the rest of his drink, and helped her out of the lounger. "I got enough sleep at the dinner," Gordon promised.

FIFTEEN

The next day began badly. Molly whined that she didn't want to go to the club. She didn't give a reason, but Ellie knew that she was afraid to being left out of activities because she would be in the care of someone who didn't fit in. Molly dragged and delayed until Gordon got angry because there was a photographer and a boat crew waiting at the dock, and then Ellie found herself arbitrating between her husband and her daughter.

When they finally got to the boat they found the photographer arguing with the boat crew. He was an effeminate young man with cameras, meters, and film cases hanging around his neck. He was standing toe-to-toe with the waterfront types, demanding that the boat be moved to another slip to provide a more scenic background. The captain of the three-man crew was insisting he had no authority to move into anyone else's slip, and was physically restraining one of his sailors who wanted to drop the photographer over the side. Gordon signed off the crew and added a very generous tip. Then he motored the boat to the slip that the photographer had selected.

Henry Browning had promised an inconspicuous photographer who would get a few quick candids, and then be out of their way. But the young man had much loftier ambitions. He posed Ellie at the wheel with Gordon peering over her shoulder, apparently out to sea, but actually into the gawkers on the next yacht. Then it was Gordon instructing Timmy in reading the compass. Then the kids on the foredeck with Ellie and Theresa, and then the family and mother's helper in the cockpit with Gordon at the wheel.

While he posed his subjects, he ordered his assistant—a pierced and tattooed young woman—to position reflectors, straighten attire, and even towel a few beads of sweat that formed on Gordon's forehead. The activities on the boat, together with the array of equipment cases on the pier, drew a crowd of onlookers. And the commotion eventually brought the commodore with complaints about the interference to normal club decorum. By the time the few simple candids were completed, Gordon was furious and Ellie was embarrassed.

They sent Theresa to the beach with the two children and the club card that would enable them all to have lunch at the snack shop. Then they went to the porch lounge, and ordered gin and tonics even though the sun had yet to pass over the yardarm. Jack O'Connell, who had the loudest laugh in the club, and who thought everything he said was hilarious, joined them without being invited, and waved his wife Mary to the table as soon as she arrived. He teased Gordon unmercifully about the faked sailing photos, and offered to throw a bucket of seawater on him so that he would seem to be battling through a storm.

While Jack was wiping away his tears of laughter, the Mapletons came in for lunch, Cecil pausing to comment on the "piece of Caribbean ass" that Gordon was keeping under the pretense of minding his children. Pricilla never approached the table but managed to exchange a knowing glance with Mary O'Connell. By the time the Actons were left to themselves, Gordon was halfway through his second drink.

"When I get elected," he told Ellie, "the first thing I'm going to do is have the EPA shut this place down for a wetlands violation."

Ellie could only shake her head. "It can't get any worse than this," she announced.

It did, and at the very moment that lunch was brought to their table. Molly came out onto the deck in her bathing suit, begging to be taken home. Trish and her crowd had paddled a chain of air mattresses out beyond the breakers, and the other young children—watched by the older girls—had gone out to join them. Molly hadn't been invited, and Theresa didn't want her swimming out alone to join the fun. Her pouting was just loud enough to be heard at the other tables, and to stretch a thin smile of satisfaction across Pricilla Mapleton's lips. Then Theresa came looking for Molly and, because she was in a bathing suit, was ordered off the deck for violating club rules of attire. Timmy ran to his parents, leaving Theresa to suffer her disgrace alone. "Well, what can you expect," a woman's voice commented with overtones of Puritan righteousness. Ellie and Gordon decided not to stay for dessert.

Theresa took Timmy upstairs for his bath, and Molly went down to the private beach to brood. Ellie sat on the porch until Gordon finished unpacking the van and sat beside her with a half pitcher of martinis. "Christ, what an awful day." He poured the potent mix over a glass of ice cubes.

"Maybe the worst yet," Ellie agreed.

"Well," he continued after a lapse into silence, "I'll promise you this. There will be no more photos at the yacht club. Anything else Henry needs, he can take right here at the house. And he'll have to come up with another photographer."

"Was that a penis that the assistant had tattooed on her arm?" Ellie wondered.

"I think so. It had an erection every time she lifted something heavy. And how did she manage to speak with that chain hanging from her tongue?" He drained the glass and poured another.

"Be careful with those things. You're barbecuing tonight. I don't want you to set yourself on fire."

Gordon nodded toward the upstairs rooms. "As far as she's concerned, it isn't going to work out. I think you should hire Trish and lose Theresa in the stacks of a library. Christ, lose her in the root cellar for all I care."

"No," Ellie said instantly. "I'll find someone, but it won't be Trish. There's no way I would give the Mapletons the satisfaction of pleading with their daughter. Cecil practically accused you of perversion, and right in front of me as if I weren't even there. And damn Pricilla! Her face is as tight as her ass!"

"Well, you better do something." He looked down to the beach where his daughter was lying face down, her chin propped up on her elbows. "At the rate we're going, Molly will be the only kid on the Cape without a friend. She might even break out with a mental disorder."

"I'll find someone," Ellie promised.

Timmy came downstairs, dressed in shorts and a sweater, his face scrubbed and his hair neatly parted. Molly came up from the beach and passed through without any acknowledgment, either gestured or spoken.

"I better talk to her," Gordon said, pushing himself out of the chair. He wobbled a bit as he tested himself against the alcohol. "Hell, I won't set myself on fire. I'll be killed falling down the stairs."

"You don't have to go up. She just wants to be bratty."

"Yeah, but I'm responsible for all of her problems," Gordon said. "I ought to tell her I'm sorry."

As he started up the stairs, he realized just how tipsy he was. His grip tightened on the banister, and he paused halfway up to get control of his legs. "You never could drink," he told himself, remembering that it had been a very long time since he had tried a half dozen drinks before dinner.

He heard the bathroom door at Molly's end of the hall slam just he reached the top of the stairs, and the water was already running by the time he reached the door. He knocked abruptly and called, "Just a minute, young lady. I need to talk to you." The sound of the water stopped instantly. Then the doorknob twisted and the door eased open. Gordon was already speaking when Theresa's face looked out at him.

"Oh, God, I'm sorry."

Theresa didn't seem in the least embarrassed. "Can you give me a second, Mr. Acton? I'll just get back into my swimsuit."

"No, that's not necessary . . . I mean, you're the wrong person. It wasn't you I was looking for . . ." His babbling was nearly incoherent, and his embarrassment so obvious that Theresa was beginning to smile. Gordon stopped explaining and stood perfectly still, his eyes fixed on the mirror that was slightly ajar over the sink. Theresa thought that she was hiding behind the door, but in the mirror she was standing completely naked, showing the full profile of a wondrously adult body. Gordon was drinking her in as if she were a porno flick.

"I'll just be a second," Theresa repeated. But as she turned away, she could see herself in the mirror, now in complete frontal nudity. And she could see Gordon standing in the narrow space of the open door. Their eyes met in the glass.

"Oh, hell, I'm sorry," Gordon said, suddenly snapping his gaze away. "I was looking for Molly. I thought she was in there."

When he looked back, Theresa was once again peering out around the door, smiling coyly at Gordon. Her full profile was still available in the mirror. "I don't think she's here," Theresa said, "but if you want to, you can come in and look." She was still smiling when she eased the door closed.

He retreated to the sanctity of his own shower and pushed his face into the ice cold stream, trying to wash away the alcohol induced stupor. But while his body came around quickly, there was still a leaden feeling in the center of his brain. And there was the image of Theresa, her perfect dark skin contrasting to the pale blue of her eyes and the white flash of her smile. It was a knowing smile, amused by the thoughts that Theresa must have known he was thinking. And seductive, like the smile a hooker might flash across a bar to her mark. "You seem to like what you see," she was telling him. "The next move is up to you."

Gordon shook his head, trying to dislodge the cobwebs. His mistake had been innocent so it wasn't really his fault. But he had lingered, drinking her in lustfully. And she had caught him. *Why, Mr. Acton, what would your wife think?* But she had been more brazen than that. Her smile made it clear that this was going to be just their secret. He remembered Ellie's description of how embarrassed Theresa had been just to try on a bathing suit. "Embarrassed, my ass," Gordon whispered into the roar of the shower. "That little bitch has been around." He found himself wondering if maybe that was how she had gotten such marvelous endorsements from her employer and her teachers. Maybe she had given *them* the same kind of previews of coming attractions.

He toweled himself vigorously, relieved that the clouds were lifting from his mind. Henry Browning's poster girl was a very dangerous young lady. She had to go, and based on the kind of day that had been inflicted on Ellie, he doubted that his wife would put up any argument. He'd just tell Henry . . . *tell Henry what?* That he had the hots for the girl so he had to get away from her? That she was such a big help to Ellie that he didn't want her around anymore? Get control of yourself!

What had Theresa done wrong? Kept Molly from swimming out to the kids on the rafts and maybe drowning herself in the process? That was a very responsible decision. Come to the clubhouse to retrieve Molly so that he and Ellie could finish their lunch? That was what they were paying her for. Help Ellie with her thesis? Where was the crime in that? Or smile alluringly when he had barged into her bath? She had concealed herself behind the door. And there was no way she could have known he was coming and adjusted the mirror to a revealing angle.

The problem, when he got right down to it, was that he had drunk too much and had made a damn fool out of himself. And he couldn't fire the girl as if it had been her fault. She hadn't tried to climb into his shower. Just keep your mouth shut and let Ellie handle it her own way, he decided. He'd be going back to Providence tomorrow, and by next weekend all of today's problems would be forgotten.

He stepped out into the hall wrapped in a full size towel. At the same instant, the bathroom door at the other end of the hall opened and Theresa walked out, wearing a robe with a towel wrapped around her head. Gordon started back into his bathroom, realized that it was

67

inappropriate, and rushed toward his bedroom door. He heard Theresa laugh, and when he looked up she was thoroughly enjoying his embarrassment.

"Oh, hi!" Gordon mumbled, with a quick nod that acknowledged her presence. He ducked into his bedroom and then mumbled, "Smart ass bitch!"

Gordon cooked burgers and franks on the charcoal grill while Ellie boiled corn and heated canned beans in the kitchen. Theresa pushed Timmy on a tire that was hung from a tree. Molly sat by herself on the front porch, brooding and sucking on a can of cola. When Ellie announced that dinner was ready, they all came together at the picnic table, each isolated in a personal cloud of silence. Timmy was entirely absorbed in putting mustard on a frankfurter, Molly was snubbing everyone to punish them for the indignities she had suffered, and Gordon and Theresa were both doing their best to avoid eye contact. Ellie was busy serving, and it wasn't until she was fixing her own plate that she noticed the embarrassing silence. She decided to plunge right in with her plan to move Theresa out of babysitting and into academic research.

"Theresa, the material we can't get from the Internet; do you think you might be able to find it in the libraries? Maybe at Harvard or Brown?"

Theresa welcomed the opportunity to talk to the other end of the table where she wouldn't be eye-to-eye with Gordon. "I guess so. Most of the libraries have only the last few years on their servers. For the rest of the stuff, you still have to search the catalog and the shelves. Harvard and Brown probably have copies of everything ever published, so if we can't find it with the computer, we can probably get it out of the stacks."

"Is this something you might be able to help me with?"

"Sure," Theresa answered enthusiastically. But then her interest faded. "But I don't think I could bring . . ." She glanced from Molly to Timmy. "I don't think they could come with me."

"Who wants to?" Molly snarled, showing that she followed all the bends in the conversation.

"That wouldn't be a problem," Ellie said thoughtfully, as if she were still grasping for the pieces of the puzzle. "I think I could get one of the other girls to fill in for you."

"Trish?" Molly asked, with a hint of the enthusiasm that she had not shown for the past few weeks.

"I don't know, but someone must be available to help out in a pinch."

Molly was ecstatic.

Theresa's clear eyes darkened. She understood precisely where Ellie was going and knew it was pointless to object. "However you want to handle it, Mrs. Acton," she said. She used a paper napkin to blot the remnants of a hamburger from her lips. Then she eased out of the bench. "I wonder if I may be excused," she said toward Ellie, and then she looked directly at Gordon. "That was delicious, Mr. Acton. I hope you're going to do a lot more."

Gordon tried to answer, but he was suddenly choking on his food. A nod was all that he could manage.

When Theresa was gone, Ellie looked at Gordon. "What do you think?"

"A bit obvious," he answered. "I think she knew exactly what you were up to."

"I want Trish to stay with us," Molly said. "Can you call Trish?"

Ellie hated to give in to her daughter. "I'll have to think about it," she said. "And besides, Trish may not be available. She may be working for someone else."

"I bet she'd rather work for us," Molly persisted, "if you'd just give her the chance." She jumped up and started down to the beach. Gordon came out of his end of the bench, prepared to catch up with her and bring her back.

Ellie held up her hand. "Let her go. She has to work it out for herself. We can't just promise her everything she decides she needs."

Gordon settled back onto the bench and reached into the cooler for a bottle of beer. Timmy leaned against his mother, his eyes beginning to close.

They looked up at the first sound from the flute. It was just a few notes and then a very quick scale as Theresa oriented her fingers and tried out her lip. There was a silent pause, and then the strains of a flute sonata began, hushed, ethereal, as if they came from another place and another time. The sounds stretched soulfully, and then notes began to cascade rapidly. Ellie found herself smiling, and when she looked across at Gordon, his eyes were wide in astonishment. Tim sat up straight. "Is Theresa doing that?" he asked. Ellie nodded. "I think she is," Gordon said.

The hollow sound danced joyfully, as if imitating laughter. Timmy giggled, and the playful sound turned all their heads up toward the lighted window of Theresa's room. And then Molly appeared back from the beach, following the music as if she were powerless to resist its charm. "Wow," she said.

"Wow, indeed," Ellie answered.

The music took a steady tempo, almost like the call to a reel. But then the light dance motif turned on itself, and slowed into a heart-tugging plea.

"That's Theresa," Timmy told his older sister.

Molly nodded, stepped past the picnic table and moved silently toward the front steps. "That's beautiful," she allowed, suddenly without the overtones of self-pity that had recently become part of her personality.

They were all perfectly still, Gordon holding a beer bottle that was hovering above the table, and Ellie with a plastic fork poised in midair. Even Timmy, who was always fidgeting, was motionless in his wide-eyed pleasure.

The music soared majestically, repeating its theme over and over in ever-higher tones. And then it dropped pathetically to almost the airy gasp of a dying breath. Always there was the unique sound of the flute, echoing the breath that it was turning into life. The melody launched into a finale, and then the last note joined with the soft wind that was blowing in from the barrier islands. The music turned into silence, which seemed just as dramatic as sound itself.

"Isn't that beautiful," Ellie said, still lost in the trance that Theresa's music had induced.

"Some talent," Gordon agreed.

"Will she do it again?" Timmy asked, looking first to his father, and then his mother.

Molly said nothing, but simply stared through the door at the steps to the second floor. Then she opened the screen door and dashed up the stairs.

"I think Molly liked that," Ellie said.

"Why wouldn't she? She's impossible, but she's not deaf," her father said. He stood and began gathering the paper plates for the trash, and collecting the silverware for the kitchen.

Molly came running down the stairs, flung open the front door and charged down to the picnic table. "Theresa is going to teach me how to play the flute," she announced. "She says it's easy and that I'll pick it up in no time." She turned abruptly and flew back into the house and up the stairs.

Ellie and Gordon looked at one another.

"I think she's decided that she likes Theresa," Gordon said.

"I guess I won't have to go crawling to the Mapletons," Ellie added.

SIXTEEN

Timmy broke through the silent treatment on the next day. Theresa had taken the two children to the club beach, set up their blanket, and walked down to the water's edge to supervise their swim. Within minutes, the other girls and the children they were minding, led by Trish Mapleton, had arrived behind them. Trish looked left and right, and then directly at the spot where Theresa was standing. She had made eye contact with Molly who was knee-deep in the water, and then gestured her company to end of the beach, nearest to the club-house. They positioned their blankets and chairs in a tight pattern that served to emphasize the isolation of Theresa and her charges. Then they picked sides for a tag race, and began setting up their boundaries at the water's edge.

Molly stormed angrily out of the water and threw herself face down on her blanket where she could at least pretend to be totally oblivious to the snub, and unconcerned with the rest of the world. But Timmy broke away from Theresa, and ran to the group, where he positioned himself directly in the middle of the playing field and began running back and forth in imitation of the older children, unaware that he was disrupting the game. Twice, older girls took his hand and lead him to the sideline, and twice he ran back into the center of the races.

Theresa thought of sending Molly to retrieve her brother but knew that the young girl would rather be tied up and tortured than face the people who had snubbed her. So, she steeled herself and started down the beach toward the club. At the same time, Don McNeary, the yacht club lifeguard, came down from the deck, lifted a delighted Timmy to his shoulders, and came toward Theresa. His ploy was to appear helpful to Trish and the others while taking the opportunity to introduce himself to the great-looking new girl in the form-fitting bathing suit. Theresa thanked him with a shy smile that flashed against her dark skin, and McNeary lingered long enough to walk her back to her blanket. Within seconds, two other young men came down to the beach to meet the new squeeze that McNeary was hitting on, and then two of the college-age girls broke from the original gathering, and wandered up the beach to keep an eye on the boys. Now there were two groups on the water's edge and in one, thanks to the lifeguard, Theresa was being made to feel welcome. As the younger kids whined to resume their game, the two girls invited Theresa to join their group, and Molly accepted the invitation before Theresa had a chance to refuse.

Her novelty made her a celebrity. She spoke differently, her words accented by her family's native tongue, while the others sounded the flat vowels of New England. She looked different; her color much deeper and more exotic than the sunburned pink of the European heritages that surrounded her. She was different, her attitude more serious and adult than the confident indifference of the privileged club members. At least for this day, she was the center of attention, and Molly basked in the attention being lavished on her new friend. "She's teaching me to play the flute," she told the other grade schoolers, and they responded with the proper reverence.

When Ellie and Gordon came to claim their family, prepared for a repeat of the previous day's horrors, they were stunned by the normality of the scene. During the ride home Molly chattered continuously, enthused by her own achievements but more excited about Theresa's new celebrity. "The boys were all showing off for her," Molly said, and when Theresa denied the attention, Molly challenged, "Didn't Don McNeary ask you out?"

"No," Theresa answered, "he asked what nights I had off. And I told him I was busy at night with schoolwork."

"You can have all the time you want," Ellie said.

"I know," Theresa laughed, "but I'd rather work with you on the thesis."

They had a noisy dinner at the picnic table. "A lot different than last night," Ellie whispered to Gordon.

"Looks like she's finally going to fit in," he answered, as if the previous night had been her fault, with his martinis playing no part at all.

It was dark by the time the children were tucked into bed, and Gordon headed back to Rhode Island for the week's campaigning. Ellie settled at her desk, and Theresa laid out the new research results she had gathered from the Internet. They were hard at work when they heard a car pull past the garage, and they were waiting expectantly when Don McNeary tapped lightly on the outside screen door.

He fumbled for conversation until Ellie suggested that he might like to come in and then he hovered around Theresa like a hound who senses a bitch in heat. Finally, he stationed himself behind the desk where he could look over Theresa's shoulder at the display screen while stealing glances down the front of her tank top.

"So, what's this all about?" he asked when his confusion became embarrassing.

"Theresa can explain it," Ellie said, and she gathered up her papers and headed for the isolation of the porch. Don sat next to Theresa, leaning against her as he nodded at her description of the thesis. "Cool!" was the best he could manage.

"So, do you want to take a walk on the beach?" he asked, getting down to the business at hand.

"Be back in a minute," Theresa promised Ellie, and then she and Don went down to the small strip of sand directly in front of the house. Ellie stayed near the window where her presence would discourage the young man's longer-term ambitions, and where she would be sure to hear Theresa's cry for help. After all, she was responsible for the girl's safety.

The next day, Theresa brought the children back to the club, and used the video camera so that Ellie could share in the fun. At night, Ellie laughed through a well-photographed production of Molly and Timmy's day at the beach, including a private swimming lesson that Don McNeary gave to Timmy. It was obvious that he had personally assumed responsibility for Theresa's happiness. The mood of the video, with its background of the other girls and their charges, was joyous. Only Trish Mapleton stood off from the activities, glancing an occasional dagger toward Don and Theresa.

The surprise, in footage shot by simply placing the running camera on the club railing, was the public unveiling of the bikini that Theresa had been too embarrassed to try on. She didn't seem at all shy about displaying the best figure in the crowd, and she looked absolutely provocative when she emerged from the water in her wet bathing suit.

Ellie was thrilled with the way things were working out. Her kids were happy and safe, and her academic treatise was moving ahead rapidly. Most important, Gordon had been freed up from parental responsibilities and household chores, and seemed to be pleased with the way his campaign was progressing. He was particularly impressed with the warm reception he had received in the state-line communities. Henry's subtle release of family photos that included Theresa had been well received. "A decent guy," was the neighborhood opinion of Gordon, even though he was a Republican. "Not like the other rich guys," was another way that the compliment was worded.

She had no misgivings when Henry suggested another photo shoot, this time a taped television interview with a local network affiliate. Gordon sat in an Adirondack chair as he knocked the cover off questions that were served up like slow-pitch softballs. He proclaimed his concern for the environment as he walked barefooted at the water's edge, and helped Theresa and his kids build a sand castle. He cooked on the open grill while Ellie served Theresa and the kids at the picnic table.

Theresa, covered in a sweatshirt, was interviewed as she watched Molly and Timmy swim. She offered her candid view that the Acton children were treated "just like any other kids," and bubbled over with joy at being part of the Acton family. Ellie was caught at her computer, where she reaffirmed her dedication to public education, and exaggerated the importance of her research work. Then she was photographed walking hand-in-hand with her husband along the shoreline.

It was a full day's work for the thirty-second spot that the station would run in its soft news time, but Henry Browning had arranged rights to the tape and intended to use the footage for final-week commercials. He refused an invitation to stay overnight, and went back with the photographers to get a head start on the editing. "I hope that little girl is working out for you," he said to Gordon and Ellie as they walked him to his car, "because she certainly is doing the job with the voters." Their polls, he reported, had Gordon only five points behind in a traditionally democratic, blue-collar section of the district. "We're beginning to think in terms of a landslide. Something that might be the election night lead story all over New England." Gordon was so pleased with the day that he decided not to return to Providence, but to get an early jump on the weekend.

Late at night, when the children were asleep, Gordon and Ellie left Theresa in charge and went for a walk on the beach. They slipped into the sand dunes and made love like guilty teenagers, then laughed at their daring all the way back to the house. The next day they repeated their amorous adventure in the cabin of their sailboat as it drifted off-shore, its sails luffed in light air. Their mood was joyous when they returned to the club for cocktails and found a cabaret table overlooking the bay. But then Jack O'Connell wandered out from the bar with his fifth gin-and-tonic in hand, and pulled a chair over to join them.

"Well, you two certainly put on a show out there," he said with a knowing wink and an obscene laugh.

"Out where?" Gordon challenged.

"You know where." He patted Ellie on the knee. "One minute she's sailing along, and the next she's dead in the water with you two gone from the cockpit and down below." He turned his head in the direction of the bar. "We were giving odds on how long you'd stay down there."

Ellie reddened with embarrassment at the thought of the club regulars looking in on her private life. She excused herself and headed for the ladies' room, never once glancing in the direction of the men at the bar.

Gordon's color was more a product of anger. "We were having lunch," he said.

Jack O'Connell leaned in confidentially. "Yeah, well I'd like to have lunch with that babysitter of yours. Have you seen her coming out of the water in that white bikini?"

"No, I haven't," Gordon answered, his tone icy cold.

O'Connell winked. "Yeah, you probably get to see her *without* the white bikini."

Gordon flared. "Jesus, Jack, she's just out of high school."

"Prime time," Jack joked. "There ought to be a law protecting them." He feigned a punch into Gordon's chest. "But hell, you're the one who makes the laws, so I guess you know what you can get away with."

Gordon jumped angrily to his feet. O'Connell pulled back suddenly, tipping his chair precariously. He struggled for balance, and then fell over backward, sprawling out on the deck.

"You're drunk!" Gordon shouted down at him. "Stupid and drunk!" He stormed off in the direction of the rest rooms to find Ellie and leave.

Cecil Mapleton came out of the bar area, alarmed by the clatter of the falling chair. He saw O'Connell stretched out across the deck, and turned on Gordon who was flashing past. "What the hell happened?" Gordon kept walking away, never bothering to answer. Mapleton rushed over to help Jack to his feet. "You okay? What happened?"

"Our candidate doesn't like people talking about his young Caribbean friend."

"He hit you?"

"He came at me. I lost my balance."

"What did you say to him?"

"Just what we've all been saying. A girl like that doesn't belong at this club."

Mapleton nodded in agreement. "I'm not sure that Gordon Acton does either."

Gordon decided not to tell Ellie the things Jack O'Connell had been saying. He realized he probably should have cut O'Connell a bit of slack because of his mindless condition. His reaction had been too abrupt, probably because he was still feeling a bit guilty about stumbling in on Theresa's shower, and about the image in the mirror that he couldn't put out of his mind.

June

SEVENTEEN

The next week started badly for Gordon. It began with the loss of a significant piece of business when a yacht manufacturer cancelled an ongoing order for inflatable boats. What made it bitter was that he could blame no one but himself. All the yacht builder had ever asked was a little bit of personal attention to show that he was a friend and a social equal rather than just a customer. Gordon had neglected him in his quest for the nomination, and now for an overwhelming victory.

He called Pam, hoping that she could come up with the right promotional strategy to win back the contract, but she was away on a short vacation. He was handed over to a new account representative who advised an immediate press release indicating that the business was insignificant. "We'll want to let the Street know right away that this won't result in disappointing earnings," the young man counseled solemnly.

"Screw the Street!" Gordon fired back. "How the hell am I going to win him back if I make a public statement telling him that his business isn't important to me?" He decided to do nothing until Pam returned at the end of the week.

Then Ellie called. Her doctoral mentor was going to be available in Providence on Friday. Could Gordon possibly cut his week short and come out to the Cape on Thursday night? That would give her a full day to review the work she had done and remind the professor just who she was and what she looked like. "I haven't seen him in over a year, and if I miss him now, I won't be able to meet with him until the end of the summer."

Gordon called Browning to cancel his Friday dates, and had to listen to Henry's pouting about how difficult it was to arrange publicity events and how much would be lost by disappointing the people involved. When he called back to promise Ellie he would be there, she suggested that he might want to make appearances at the yacht club over the weekend. Don McNeary had told Theresa that some of the members were stirring up trouble for him and trying to drag him in front of the disciplinary board.

"That's just bullshit," he yelled at his wife.

"I know. But it's easy for O'Connell and Mapleton to bad mouth you when you're not there. I don't think either of them will have the guts to say anything to your face." So that became the plan. Get out to the Cape on Thursday night, and spend Friday with the kids at the club. And in the process, he could field calls from Henry Browning asking sarcastically when he intended to get back on the campaign trail.

Pam called him at his Providence apartment on Wednesday night. She had heard about the lost business and had dug enough to find out that the contract hadn't yet been moved to another supplier. "I think if we move quickly, we can probably get it back."

He was in her office first thing Thursday, and with Pam listening across her desk, Gordon phoned the customer to eat crow, reading from a script she had prepared.

"You have every right to dump us, Lennie. I let a lot of friends down over the past few months, and you're the one I regret the most. You've been good to me personally as well as financially."

Lennie recounted his grievances; it wasn't the boats. "You still have the best quality in the business," he complimented. "But there have been service problems, and when I called about them I was routed down to some junior clerk who said he'd have to consult our contract. I just couldn't get ahold of you."

Gordon listened while Lennie gave case histories of the many instances on which he had been abused.

"You're right. I've put you through hell. And no matter what you do with the business, I'd like the opportunity to apologize in person."

Lennie played hard to get. He had a very busy calendar and didn't know when he could squeeze in Action Boats. "I have to tell you that if it's just an apology, then you already apologized. We don't need a meeting for that. And I don't think I can afford to open myself up to any possibility of more neglect."

He had his hand over the speaker when he told Pam, "Schmoozing isn't going to do it. I think he wants sucking . . ."

She moved her thumb over her finger to simulate the feel of money. "Start sucking," she said with a pleased smile.

"Lennie, it would be a favor to me. I need your views on everything we're doing here at Action Boats. Maybe I can impose on your lunchtime. Or even your dinner hour. We could find a dark corner at my club and just talk."

Pam sucked in silently and nodded her approval.

Lennie rustled some papers while he delayed his verdict. "Gordon, tonight is the only time I have free until well into next month."

"Then let's do it tonight," he answered with feigned enthusiasm.

He tried to reach Ellie to tell her that he wouldn't be in until very late, but he had to settle for leaving a message on the answering machine. Then he went back to his apartment to shave and put on a fresh shirt for his meeting with his disgruntled customer.

The dinner dragged on and on, with Lennie offering sage advice while he went through three bottles of an overpriced Bordeaux. Gordon listened, nodded, asked clarifications, and threw remedies out for consideration. By eleven o'clock, he was longing to bring things to a close, and prayed silently that his guest would stop jerking his chain and reinstate their agreement. But that was the one caution that Pam had offered. "Don't ask for the business. That cheapens the whole evening. And if he offers it early, tell him that it's not necessary." So he waited patiently, stealing glances at his watch, and realizing that the combination of the hour and the wine would make it impossible for him to head out to the Cape.

"I'd like to continue doing business with you," Lennie allowed as Gordon was signing the check, "but I do understand how busy you'll have to be with your campaign. And then, if you're elected, well, the business will only be a sideline to you."

Gordon assured him that Action Boats would never be a sideline, and hinted at the potential benefits to their respective businesses of having a friend in Congress. When they parted at the doorway, Lennie volunteered that he would "talk to his people" about reinstating the order, and would call with the decision.

He went straight to Pam's apartment and found her up and waiting for him, anxious to learn about the meeting.

"Just as you predicted. He spent the whole evening being a big shot, and then left me hanging."

"He'll probably ruin your weekend, and on Monday let you know that he's giving you one more chance."

Gordon shrugged. "That's the impression I got." He loosened his necktie.

"There's something else that might ruin your weekend," Pam went on. "I guess I'd be disappointed if you tell me that it won't."

He refocused through the fog of fatigue and wine. "Oh God, you're dropping my business."

"I hope not. But I'm afraid there's going to have to be a change in our relationship."

"You're getting married!"

She laughed. "I'm not that far along, but I have to tell you that I've met somebody."

The air squeezed out of his lungs. "Oh . . ."

"It's not all that serious, but I guess I'd like it to be."

"Sure, sure. You deserve it," he said without conviction. "I mean, I'm happy for you . . . and for him . . ."

"You're a terrible liar. And I'm happy that you can't generate any genuine joy. It would really hurt if you didn't care."

Gordon pushed the knot of his tie back up to his collar button. "I do care. But I'm not in play so all I can do is waste your time."

Pam took his hand. "You've never wasted my time."

He nodded, stood up, and tossed his jacket over his shoulder. "I'll let you know if Lennie sends back the business."

"He will. You can count on it."

He drove carefully to his apartment, realizing that if he were stopped he probably couldn't pass a breath test. There wasn't much that he could count on.

EIGHTEEN

When he woke up the next morning the sun was already streaming in through the window. He blinked into the glare, found enough evidence that he was in his apartment, and then traced back to the previous night. He winced at his disgusting fawning over a man he didn't really like and dragged himself into the shower to wash away embarrassment. As he was waiting for the water to warm he thought of Pam's admission that she had found someone else. "Class," he said shaking his head. The lady had made the bad news as painless as possible.

Gordon was slumping in the shower when he remembered that he was supposed to be heading out to the Cape. He left wet footprints across the bedroom carpet as he hurried to the phone.

"You just missed her," Theresa answered.

"Damn it," Gordon cursed. "Was she mad?"

"I don't think so. She didn't say much."

"She was mad."

"She told me to keep the kids around the house. Waiting for you, I guess."

"Yeah, well I'll be on my way in just a few minutes. Tell Molly and Tim that I'll bring them to the club this afternoon."

"I can bring them over," Theresa offered. "Don told me he would pick us all up."

"No! Stay at the house. I'm on my way." He knew Theresa would be an incendiary for the tempers of his detractors. Best if he took the kids and smoothed things over. And then maybe Ellie could suggest that Theresa save the bikini for their private beach.

He pulled into the driveway just before noon and found the children waiting impatiently, already in their bathing suits and carrying their beach things. He changed quickly, told Theresa that she had the rest of the day off, and then left for the club.

Molly and Tim ran out onto the beach, and Gordon climbed the steps and walked out on the deck. He couldn't be sure, but he thought he noticed a few heads turn, and several pairs of eyes look up over book tops and underneath raised sunglasses. He took a deep breath, and walked confidently into the bar.

"Mr. Acton." The bartender was cordial.

He leaned across the bar. "Jack O'Connell been in yet?"

The bartender brought his head close. "Mr. O'Connell is resting at home. He suffered whiplash when he fell the other day."

"Oh, Jesus." Gordon could already imagine the ambulance chasers lining up. Then he asked, "What about Mapleton?"

"Mr. Mapleton hasn't been in yet."

Gordon walked back out onto the deck. He looked for signs of life aboard Mapleton's boat that was docked at the main pier. Nothing; the covers were still on the sails. Then he noticed Tom Cameron aboard his sloop, his head bobbing up and down from behind an open engine cover. Cameron was the club commodore, chairman of the governing body, and the person who would sit in judgment if O'Connell's charges ever came up for a hearing. Gordon tried to look casual as he sauntered out onto the floating ramp and climbed aboard next to Cameron. He skipped the usual sailors' small talk, and didn't even ask about the apparent problem with the engine. "Tom, is there any truth to all this talk about me being brought up on charges?"

Cameron talked with his face down in the hold, allowed that O'Connell had demanded a hearing and that Mapleton had supported his story. "But I don't know if it will actually come before the board." He popped up to smile at Gordon. "People tell me he was pretty drunk and that his language was a bit salty." His face went below again and he grunted as he pulled on a wrench. "Of course, if you did actually hit him . . . or push him . . ."

"That's bullshit. I got up to leave and I guess he thought I was coming at him. He tipped his chair over backwards."

"Were you?"

"Was I what?"

"Were you coming at him?"

"Of course not. I was trying to get away from him. Ellie had already left to avoid saying something to him, and I went after her."

"Trouble is, no one saw it. So it comes down to 'you said, he said.' No way the board can know what really happened."

"Ellie was there. She heard what he was saying."

"But she wasn't there when he had his accident."

Gordon stood and leaned back on the gunwale. "Oh Christ . . ."

Cameron sat back on his haunches and wiped his hands on a grease rag. "To be honest with you, Gordon, I don't think the *alleged* altercation is the real issue. I think what's bothering some of the members is that girl you have minding your kids. I've heard some complaints that her manner and her dress aren't in keeping with the standards of the club."

"Is that what O'Connell says? That he doesn't like her *'manner?'* Because what he was saying to me—after he accused Ellie of balling me in public view—was how much he'd love to get into the girl's bathing suit. He even accused *me* of banging her."

Cameron nodded. "That sounds like O'Connell. But it wasn't just him. Some of the women seem to be offended."

"Sure," Gordon agreed eagerly. "Because their daughters are bitching about the competition. A couple of the young studs have dumped a couple of our young ladies so they can hang around Theresa. The daughters want her out of here."

"You're probably right," the Commodore allowed. "And I'm suggesting that some of your troubles might go away once the girl tones down her presence. At a minimum, Jack O'Connell would have to find something else to talk about."

"That's sick. We're supposed to punish the girl because O'Connell has a dirty mind."

"No, we're supposed to consider the idea because O'Connell is a dues-paying member in good standing."

Gordon seethed, but nodded his surrender. "Tell me, Tom, if the girl were fair-skinned and golden blond, do you think our members would still consider her such a bad influence? Like that Danish au pair Ed and Tracy Lawrence had a couple of seasons ago? She was topless behind the boathouse and no one thought she was unsuitable."

Cameron considered the point. "You may well be right, but the point is moot. Our members pay big money to come out here so they can protect their children from *undesirables*. If we really wanted fairness and equality, I don't suppose there would be any reason to have a club like this."

Gordon climbed over the gunwale and onto the dock. "I'll say this for you, Cameron. You tell it like it is."

"Only in private. In my official position, I lie like everyone else."

Gordon laughed and turned away.

"There's one more thing you might consider," Cameron called after him. "Why don't you stop by at O'Connell's house and see if you two can't work this out with a handshake. I think we should avoid a disciplinary hearing at all costs. It would be divisive."

He left the kids at the club day-care program under Donald McNeary's supervision. The lifeguard was anxious for the opportunity to bring them home because it would provide an excuse to see Theresa, and perhaps get invited to dinner. Gordon drove to O'Connell's house, told Mary how sorry he was for Jack's difficulties, and visited Jack on the screen porch where he was lying on a chaise, exaggerating the difficulty he had in moving. He apologized for "anything I might have done to cause your fall," and O'Connell allowed that he regretted, "anything he might have said that embarrassed Ellie." He offered Gordon a drink as a sign of friendship, and Gordon sipped through a rum collins to seal their pact of silence. Mary cut to the issue as she was showing him out by expressing the hope that one of the local girls might still be available to help Ellie with the children.

As he started home, Gordon was in a mild rage over having subjected himself to still another humiliation within twenty-four hours. But by the time he reached his house, he was drowning in self-pity, induced by the depressant effects of a rum collins poured into an empty stomach. He cursed when he found the front door locked, and mumbled threats against the yacht club while he tried several of the keys on his ring. His first act in Congress, he fancied, would be to turn the place into a navy base. Once inside, he changed to his shorts and sweatshirt, and found the makings of a gin and tonic. Then he sat out on the porch planning how to tell Theresa that she wasn't wanted at the club. He had to persuade her that devoting all her time to Ellie's thesis was a promotion.

He didn't see her coming up the steps from the beach, so he was startled when she was suddenly standing on the porch steps. "Oh, hi! I was . . . just . . ." She was wearing the white bikini and the little bit that there was of it was wet from her swim and clinging to her curves like a shrink wrapper. He realized he was staring, but couldn't tear his eyes away. "I was . . . over at the club . . . with the kids . . ." It was a stupid thing to say. She knew he had the children, and she knew where he was taking them. "They're at the day camp . . . with Don . . ."

His eyes finally found her face and the slightest hint of a smile. She knew exactly what he was looking at and, if her skeptical expression was any indication, had a pretty good idea of what he was thinking.

He stood up abruptly. "Can I get you a drink?" Theresa glanced down at the telltale lime floating in his glass, and then back to him. Her smile was a bit wider and her eyes a bit more knowing. "A beer? A soft drink? What do you drink?" Jesus, he was babbling like an idiot.

"I heard about the people at your club," she said. "I'm so sorry for all the trouble I seem to be causing you."

"What trouble?" Gordon tried to look as if he had no idea what she might be talking about. "What people?"

"Don called and told me they were giving you a hard time. Because of . . ." Theresa looked down at her bathing suit. "Because of me."

"No, no, nothing like that. It's about some drunk who fell down and thought I had pushed him. It's all straightened out."

"Don hears everything at the club. He told me that some of the girls were mad at me because they wanted the job of watching your kids."

"Oh, I suppose there might be a little of that . . ." He shrugged as if a little jealousy on the part of the debutante daughters was of no consequence. "You know how girls are . . ." He winced at his own words. Of course she knew, she was one herself. He seemed to have lost the ability to speak intelligently.

"Don thinks you're being blamed because I don't fit in. And, you know, it's true. I really don't fit in. I'm not really one of . . . them."

He reached out carefully and touched her chin to keep her from hiding her face.

"Thank God you're not one of them."

Their lips were only inches apart, and Gordon wasn't even trying to hide his desire for her. "None of them can touch you," he whispered.

Her eyes closed slowly and she leaned toward him. Her movement was the tiniest fraction, but it said clearly that she wanted to be kissed. His arms swept around her and he pulled her wet figure close to him. God, she was gorgeous, and the taste of salt spray on her lips was exciting. Her mouth opened hungrily, and Gordon plunged in. He knew there were thousands of reasons why he shouldn't be sliding his hand under the bikini top of his wife's mother's helper, but none were as compelling as the touch of her skin. And now her arms were locked around him, pulling him even closer. His hand was now pushing down on the elastic waist of her briefs, and he was tilting her toward the couch.

Theresa pulled her head back. "No . . . please . . ."

Gordon didn't know whether he could let her go.

"Not here . . ." She took the hand that was already halfway into her pants. "Upstairs. My room."

He followed her through the door and almost raced her to the top of the stairs.

"Just a second," Theresa asked when they reached her bedroom door. Gordon let her slide away and watched the door close in his face.

"What in hell are you doing?" he demanded of himself. His hand went to his forehead. Good God! She was half his age. He was throwing away everything. Tell her now! Be sorry now, before it was too late.

No! Don't tell her. Don't wait around. Just get out of here. Down the stairs, out the front door, and down to the beach. Go for a walk.

A run! Put as much distance between them as he could in the next ten seconds. His weight was back on his heels and he was about to turn away when the door opened slowly revealing the room inside. The top of the bathing suit was in the middle the floor. The bottom was in a small wet spot directly beneath the bookcase. He could hear her sliding into the bed.

Gordon looked back down the hallway. Then he eased into the room, and shut the door quietly behind him.

NINETEEN

He was lying beside her, enjoying her embrace, but just beginning to feel the first pangs of guilt, when he heard tires crunching onto the gravel driveway. He sprang out of the bed and danced in a small circle while he jumped into his underpants and pulled up the Bermuda shorts.

"You're wonderful," Theresa said, her arms outstretched to welcome him into another embrace.

His sweatshirt was inside out and he was tying it in a knot in his efforts to reverse it.

"It was *so* good!" She looked as if she were still at the heights of orgasm. "I can't let you go."

"Someone's coming," he said, and as if to make his point car doors slammed shut behind the house. The sweatshirt was over his face, and he was shuffling his feet trying to slip them into his docksiders.

"I don't care," Theresa answered.

His eyes were wide when his face popped out above the neckline. She didn't care? Was she crazy? Of course she cared. "We have to talk," he told her as he turned for the door.

"I know. I've wanted to since I first met you."

"No. I mean *talk*. And don't come down until you . . ." He gestured his confusion as he tried to think of a way to tell her that a nun could see that she had just had sex. "Until you get dressed," he decided. He opened the door and darted out into the hall just in time to hear Molly yelling at Timmy. He prayed silently in gratitude that it wasn't Ellie. He needed a few minutes to get his act together.

He was sitting on the porch next to the now watery and warm gin and tonic when McNeary and the two children reached the steps. The kids scampered by without interrupting their argument, both threatening that they would "tell Mommy."

"Hey, no hello? No kiss?" Gordon called after them, trying to sound as if they had been his only concern.

"He's a brat," Molly answered.

"I'm telling Mommy," Timmy repeated.

He shifted his attention to McNeary. "Everything sounds normal," he said.

"Yeah, we had a pretty good day," the lifeguard said. He rocked awkwardly from one foot to the other.

"Can I get something for you?" Gordon asked.

"No . . . I just wanted to tell you that I'm sorry . . . about the club."

Gordon nodded his appreciation and Don went on. "I mean, everyone over there knows that Mr. O'Connell is all . . ." He sorted through all the things that he could call O'Connell, and decided on caution in the presence of another club member. "A bit difficult."

"He's a prick," Gordon said.

McNeary smiled. "Yeah. That too."

"Can I get you a drink? A beer?" He didn't know the young man's age, but judging by the empties in the trash barrel outside the guard shack, he knew this wouldn't be Don's first.

McNeary popped the top, and then asked if Theresa was around.

Gordon shrugged. "Don't know. Just got in myself. Sit down while I check upstairs."

But when he reached the steps, Theresa was already coming down in jeans, T-shirt, and sneakers, which combined to give her a bit of the tomboy. "Hi, Mr. Acton, I didn't know you were home." Gordon marveled that she didn't display even a hint of familiarity as she passed him. "Hi Don," she said to McNeary. "How were the kids?"

She took a soft drink for herself while listening to his review of the day. Then she walked him to the door without paying the slightest attention to her employer. She wasn't acting innocent; she was acting as if there were nothing to be innocent of.

Theresa hurried back into the house when Molly and Timmy launched into a shouting match, and raced up the stairs to make peace. It was all so normal that Gordon wondered if maybe they hadn't just been making love. Was it all in his sick imagination? Could she have forgotten about it already?

He had the chicken breasts on the grill when Ellie came home. He had thought of several different ways to play the moment, fearful that an overwhelming show of affection might raise her suspicions. He decided on a smile, a quick kiss, and the encouraging report that he and Theresa had dinner well under control. But Ellie was still smarting over his broken promise to arrive home in time to take the children to the club. Her kiss was perfunctory. "Glad you finally made it," she said, and turned all her attention to the children and Theresa.

As he turned the chicken, he heard each of his children list a day's worth of grievances, and Ellie respond with sympathetic sounds. He kept his eyes on Theresa, watching her walk through the normal activities of preparing for dinner. She fussed with the children, responded to Ellie, and played the part of a cheerful and grateful mother's helper. He couldn't believe that she was the same woman who only an hour earlier had been sitting astride him, smiling at the pleasure she was reading in his face.

Who in hell was she? The poster child with the bad hair and mournful eyes? The pathetically shy young woman too embarrassed to try on a bathing suit? Or the calculating liar who made up brothers and sisters? And the sensual woman who had led him into her bed? The contrasts were impossible to reconcile. He remembered their sweaty, physical lovemaking. And then he watched her run up the stairs with Molly, two children dashing off to play.

He took the draft of a speech out onto the front porch, but couldn't bring his mind to the words on the page. All he could think of was how he was going to tell Theresa that their romp had been a terrible mistake that would best be forgotten. He also had to figure out just how he was going to move her out of his house and off the Cape. He had to find exactly the right words because in those few intimate minutes he had given her the power to destroy him. Her knowledge was like a virus that once let loose would spread rapidly and broadly, proving deadly to his marriage, his family, and his political career. He had to get her away from people who would be infected by the virus. Don McNeary, to whom she might want to boast about her experience. Trish Mapleton, to whom her seduction of Gordon Acton would be a tasty bit of one-upmanship. His problem was that he no longer had the employer's power to determine the fate of a hireling. Theresa now had the power to determine his fate. Anything he did to protect himself

90

would probably make Theresa angry. And he could no longer risk making her angry.

He heard the lilt of the flute coming from upstairs, pure and almost angelic, and dropped the speech to one side as he gave the music his full attention. The beauty was overwhelming, making his activities of the afternoon seem unspeakably corrupt.

Ellie got up from behind her desk and walked out to the porch. She stood behind Gordon's chair, listening, her hands falling gently on her husband's shoulders. "She certainly is an artist," Ellie said.

"No doubt about it," he answered, trying not to sound cynical. "An artist . . ."

TWENTY

Ellie solved part of the problem. She had returned from the meeting with her mentor carrying a dozen pages of comments, criticisms, and suggestions, the sum of which was that she still had a good deal of work ahead of her. Theresa, she decided, would be much more valuable helping her with the research and organization. The children, for the few weeks involved, would be entrusted to Trish and her friends, and to the day-care center at the club. Theresa agreed to the new arrangement with generous enthusiasm even though it promised to keep her in the library rather than out on the beach. Molly protested that just when she had gotten to like Theresa, her life was being uprooted. Timmy cried because he didn't want to go to day care. Gordon was ecstatic; it was Ellie who was keeping her away from the club rather than he.

He knew he wasn't entirely out of the woods. He remembered Theresa trying to lure him back into the bed even as the car came down the driveway. It was obvious that she thought they would be seeing more of each other, and possible that she might be reckless in arranging their meeting. He still needed an opportunity to get her alone, apologize for his moment of weakness, praise her discretion, and assure her of his fatherly concern for her well-being. He needed to put her behind him, but with assurance that she would never do anything to hurt him.

Theresa plunged into her new assignment with incredible energy, organizing the research suggested by the mentor, and spending ten consecutive hours connected to promising sources all over the country. By midweek she was able to present Ellie with a plan that involved computer time which she could handle, two days at Cambridge in the Harvard social sciences library, and two days at the Brown University library in Providence. While one of them was drafting the material from the Internet sources, the other could travel to the libraries. Theresa suggested that she could take care of the children while Ellie journeyed to the universities. "They can be at the club during the day, just like you planned," she explained, "and then I'll be here for them when they come home at night."

Ellie fretted over leaving her children. She had every confidence in Theresa, but there was always the possibility of an emergency. Libraries frowned on patrons who left their cell phones on, so she would be hard to reach for hours at a time. And even then, it might take her half a day to get back from Cambridge.

Theresa suggested that she could always reach Mr. Acton, and Ellie thought that might be a solution. But then she realized that Gordon's schedule had him on the road most days, lunching with even the most insignificant organizations of voters and committees for every type of civic cause. He might be harder to reach than she would be.

As a solution, Theresa suggested that she could do the library research, leaving Ellie close to Molly and Timmy. It was a generous offer, and Ellie thanked her profusely. But she felt a bit uneasy about having Theresa Santiago's footprints all over her thesis. The Internet offered a screen of anonymity, but a library card identified a specific researcher. As Gordon had warned her, this had to be entirely her work.

Almost as if sensing her problem, Theresa blurted out a solution. "I don't have library cards at Harvard and Brown, but I'll bet I could use your university card in both places. So, I'll have no trouble getting the stuff you need." Theresa thought she was solving a problem of access, but Ellie realized that what she was proposing would also solve questions of authorship. Ellie's university credentials were honored at all academic libraries on a reciprocal basis.

"Okay," she said after churning the idea for several minutes, "if you're sure that it won't be putting too much of a burden on you."

Theresa was sure. "I'll start right away," she offered. "The faster I get this done, the sooner I'll be back with the kids."

Ellie couldn't wait to tell Gordon how well everything was working out, and when he called during the week she forgot to even ask how his campaign was doing. "She is the most remarkable young woman," she said. "I think you ought to tell Henry Browning that we're forever in his debt."

"Remarkable . . ." Gordon mumbled.

"She was at Harvard all day yesterday. Left here at six-thirty in the morning, and didn't get back until nearly nine. But she covered two days of work in one. You should see the information she brought back. I mean, this is my field, and I don't think I could have done any better in figuring out what was relevant, and what parts of it were most significant."

"Remarkable . . ." he repeated.

"She's up at Brown today, and then she's going to spend the night with friends in Tiverton, so that she can get back to Brown first thing in the morning."

"She's here? In Providence?"

"At Brown. Maybe you could stop over and take her to lunch."

"Probably not. I'm scheduled for more chicken and peas. I wish someone would do something politically dangerous and serve peanut butter sandwiches." He was thinking that she was only a few minutes away, and that this might be the perfect opportunity to put their momentary liaison in its proper light.

"Oh, and guess what she did this morning."

"Turned lead into gold?"

Ellie laughed. "No, something cute. So darling I could have cried."

"Oh, she did the windows!"

"You know all those videos she shot of the kids on the beach?"

The only one he could remember was the shot taken by the camera resting on the porch showing Theresa coming out of the water. His memory was even more intense now that he had seen what the bathing suit was hiding.

"Well, she bought a new tape while she was in Cambridge, and spent most of the night holed up in her room with the VCR. This morning I asked her what was so important and she told me she had made a copy of all the footage of the kids. She wants to take it to college with her so that she can remember them."

"Tell her she can take the kids," Gordon teased, but his thoughts were elsewhere. Even if he couldn't meet her for lunch he could probably get over to the Brown campus early in the afternoon. It would be safer to be seen with her on the campus than in a restaurant. Hell, it might even look as if he were involved in her education.

The luncheon was a waste of time. There were three tables of the Daughters of Liberty, all women concerned with the intrusions of government on the personal freedoms that had motivated the founding of Rhode Island. More specifically, they were afraid that environmental groups might interfere with the expansion of their waterfront homes, lessening their property values.

"Why are we talking with these people?" he had asked Henry on the way to the restaurant.

"Publicity opportunity. We'll get photos of them standing around you, and then they'll make sure the pictures get printed on the society pages. Nice thing about it is that the only people reading the society pages are their friends. Environmentalists generally go straight to the funnies."

He was still thinking about a conversation with Theresa while he struggled through small talk with the two chairwomen who flanked him. He listened humbly to a fifteen-minute introduction that chronicled his family's contributions to the Narragansett region. Then he spent ten minutes telling the women exactly what they wanted to hear. He favored Christian values and private property. He was a family man who had opened his household to the less fortunate. He treasured his sea-faring heritage and would always support the interests of those who loved the sea. Two of the women dozed during the question-and-answer period.

Gordon had Henry drop him at the Brown social sciences library where his name and political credentials got him through the turnstile. Then he wandered from floor to floor, glancing into all the student kiosks, and searching through the stacks. When he didn't find her, he went back to the desk and asked for books on Ellie's subject. Then he went back to that section and waited around for half an hour hoping that Theresa would return. He didn't want to attract attention, but he hated to miss the opportunity to straighten out their misunderstanding. So he waited still longer in a quiet, empty corner.

"Theresa, before anything else, I want to apologize for what I did the other day," he rehearsed, practicing his crestfallen expression as he mouthed the words. "What *we* did the other day," Gordon corrected, and then decided to soften the apology even more. "What *we allowed to happen* the other day."

She would probably nod. He doubted that she would put the affair into its proper context by saying, "You mean when you fucked a young female employee?" But he didn't want to give her a chance to interfere with his speech. So, he decided, he would hardly pause. "As you know, I had a terrible day, completely abandoned by my friends. I was exhausted from the week's campaigning. I had a drink and in the hot sun, it must have gone straight to my head. I want you to understand that I wasn't at all myself when I reacted to . . ." No, that was too clinical; he had to at least acknowledge his obvious passion. ". . . when I *clung* to your expression of sympathy."

"But . . ." He knew he couldn't allow her to interrupt. "But, nevertheless, what I . . . what *we* did was terribly wrong. Fundamentally, I'm a moral man, and my sense of right would never allow me to compromise a girl . . . *young woman* . . . half my age, much less dishonor my marriage."

He liked the way he sounded. He was admitting his guilt without giving up his aura of personal integrity. She would have to admire that. But he didn't want her admiration; he wanted her silence.

"So, I hope you will be able to forgive me and put Friday afternoon completely out of your mind . . ." That sounded a bit too much like begging. He didn't want her to think that it was *entirely* his fault. She had undressed herself. He remembered that she had taken a private moment behind her closed door, probably to tend to her contraceptive needs. And it wasn't as if he had been the first. The young lady was very familiar with the basics of lovemaking.

"So, I hope *we'll* be able to forgive *one another,* and put last Friday afternoon behind us. I hope you can still care for me, and I know I will always hold you in the highest regard."

Gordon took a last look around the library, hoping that he could find her alone so that he could rush right into the words. But there was no sign of her. He would have to find her alone sometime over the weekend when he was scheduled to be back out on the Cape.

He went across town to a chamber of commerce meeting, where Henry had arranged for him to receive an award as a champion of downtown revival. He sleepwalked through all the usual platitudes, and posed with the director as they held a wooden plaque between them.

The evening was a waste until Pam came in, nibbled at the wine and cheese, and then joined the line to offer her congratulations.

"You still involved?" he asked her while he was feigning small talk.

She rocked her hand like a boat floating over ground swells.

"I'd love to see you," he told her, "if . . ."

She smiled. "I don't think it's that iffy. Just not moving as quickly as I hoped."

Gordon nodded. "You'll keep me posted one way or the other."

"And you'll let me know how things are going with your wife."

They both laughed, and then Pam drifted off to the wine and cheese, leaving him to greet perfect strangers as if they were the oldest and dearest of friends.

It was late when the business group adjourned. Henry signaled Gordon into a private suite where there was a full bar setup waiting on the kitchen counter. Henry fixed the drinks and then joined Gordon in the sitting room, the two men on opposite sides of an enormous coffee table.

"So, how are we doing?" Gordon asked, pretty sure that he would be pleased with the answer.

Henry nodded. "Not bad. Not bad at all. Actually, we're a little ahead of where I expected to be at this time. You're still ahead by twenty points, and when I get the polls in the morning, I'm guessing more like twenty-three points."

"And that means . . ."

"A landslide," Browning allowed, raising his hand to ward off Gordon's congratulations, "assuming that all your supporters get out and vote. That's where I'm particularly pleased. We seem to be generating some real enthusiasm for your candidacy. People who haven't voted in the past four years tell us they're planning to get out and vote for you."

What about the border-area folks?

"I'll know for sure first thing in the morning. But I get the feeling that you're making very serious inroads. Having you photographed with Theresa has certainly given you the common touch."

"Oh, Ellie says to tell you that she's wonderful. We don't know what we would be doing without her."

"I don't either," Henry admitted. "We've gotten great play on the stills that we took. They have appeared in all the ethnic papers — Spanish, Portuguese, Russian, and even in English."

"So then we're in big," Gordon concluded.

"Probably. You're the only one who can hurt us now."

"Hurt us how?"

Henry hunched his shoulders and took a thoughtful sip from his glass. "I saw Pam Lambert tonight."

Gordon thought of feigning surprise, but knew that few things surprised his friend. "Yes. We chatted briefly."

"Are you two still a thing?"

"Pam and I!" Now he had to pretend to be surprised. "She's in business. She does some work for my company."

Browning nodded. "You know of course what would happen if it became known that there was something more between you than a business relationship."

"Henry, it's just business. What are you driving at?" Gordon already knew the answer. What he wasn't sure of was exactly how much Henry already knew. And if Henry knew, how many of his political sidekicks also knew.

"Your wife, Gordon, is a distinct asset. Through her work, she's become a beloved figure. Cheating on her will cost you the family vote. And Miss Lambert is a working woman in your employ. If it seems you're extracting sexual favors for your business, you'll lose the women's vote as well."

"Henry, you don't think that—"

He was silenced by the older man's upraised hand. "I don't want to prolong the discussion. You know that you've been sleeping with her, and I know that you've been sleeping with her. As far as I can ascertain, she's the only other person who knows all the details. So, there are two things we can't allow to happen. We can't let anyone else find out, and we can't do anything that might aggravate her. That means you can't be seen with her. It also means that you can't simply dump her because hell hath no fury. She is smart enough to know that blowing the whistle on you would be a very effective way of getting back at you. So, there is a bit of a dilemma."

Gordon sat silently, looking like a chastened child. "I don't think we have anything to worry about," he said softly.

Browning continued in his no-nonsense manner. "I know we have nothing to worry about. I've arranged for her to dump you, so that she will be feeling sympathy for you rather than anger." Gordon's head rose slowly, his eyes narrowing as he began to understand. "What we don't need is for you to complicate things by making it attractive for her to

97

return to your bed. You need to break if off completely while the young lady thinks that she's still ahead."

"You got someone for her. You hired someone to put a move on her—"

"The details are unimportant. What's essential is that you let her new romance run its course until after November."

Gordon was on his feet. "You heartless bastard. You're playing games with an innocent woman. Don't you give a fuck about her feelings? Or his?"

"*His* are paid for. And I don't think I've treated *her* any more shabbily than you did. Haven't we both dangled the suggestion of romantic bliss in front of her?"

"But I never lied—"

"That's bullshit, and you know it," Henry fired back, raising his voice for the first time in Gordon's memory. "What did you tell her when you were in bed? That it was just for kicks? You lied to her and I'm lying to her. The only difference is that your lie can destroy you and everything you hope for. My lie might just save you."

Gordon slumped back into the chair. The two men sat quietly for several minutes. It was Henry who broke the silence. "I'm sorry if I appear unnecessarily brutal. But I can't stomach all the stupidity that comes with protestations of love. You got what you wanted, and you got away with it. I hope you'll be as fortunate throughout your life in politics."

Gordon was sputtering. "But you can't . . . just . . . use people."

"I do it all the time when it achieves something of value. The way you were using her, it could only have ended up in destruction. That's what I hope to avoid. The destruction of a very promising political career. Since it's your career, I hope I can count on your support."

He paused and watched Gordon sink into his own foolishness. Then he asked, "I can count on your support, can't I?"

Gordon made eye contact. Then he nodded and looked away.

TWENTY-ONE

He raced through the streets on his way to his apartment building, and screeched around the hairpin turns in the underground garage. He was in a rage, but he couldn't focus his anger on anyone, which made it all the harder to control. It wasn't Henry Browning's fault. All Henry had done was remind him of the realities of his situation. Maybe Henry shouldn't have stuck his nose into his private affairs, but Gordon had chosen to become a public figure and had opened up his life for scrutiny. He counted on Henry to promote his public persona. He certainly couldn't be angry with Pam; she had never demanded nor refused anything. Yet, she was being violated for the sake of his public image. The only one he could rage at was himself.

He slammed the car door and stomped to the elevator, his head down and his lips forming silent curses. He sputtered as the elevator groaned its way to the fifth floor, and sulked down the corridor to his apartment. When he opened the door, he was startled to see that there was a light on in the living room. He was stunned when Theresa Santiago's face rose above the back of the sofa.

Gordon stepped in slowly, easing the door closed behind him. "How did you—"

She held up his car keys. "Your spare apartment key is on the ring. And the address is on all the magazines that you bring home." Theresa smiled at her own inventiveness.

Gordon was still in shock, but slowly he began to understand the situation. Theresa thought their tumble at the Cape Cod house had been the beginning of an affair, and she was thrilled that she had found a way for them to be together. Obviously, he had to get her out of his apartment. But how? He certainly didn't want to be seen walking her out the front door. Or did he? Maybe that was exactly what he wanted if someone had seen her coming into the building. His mind began swirling, hunting for a way to make it seem that she wasn't there at all.

"I used the fire stairs," Theresa said as if reading his thoughts. "I didn't want to run into anyone in the elevator. And I made sure no one was in the hallway while I let myself in."

She was still sitting on the sofa, looking over the back toward the entrance foyer. He was still standing in the entrance foyer, afraid to take even a step in her direction.

"Aren't you glad to see me?" Theresa asked.

Gordon came back to life. "Of course. I'm delighted." He strode into the living room with all the enthusiasm he could muster. "As a matter of fact I was over at the library looking for you this afternoon. I thought we might have lunch, because there are things we need to talk about."

"That would have been nice," Theresa said.

"In fact," Gordon went on, "why don't we go out for dinner?"

Theresa stood up slowly and stole a glance at her watch. "It's ten thirty!"

"Well, maybe just a snack. Or a drink." Jesus, why was he offering her a drink? That was the last thing they needed. "A Coke . . . or something."

She walked slowly around the sofa. "I had a Coke and a snack. I hope you don't mind."

"Mind? No, of course not."

She was coming slowly toward him. "I've been thinking of you all week."

"And I've been thinking of you . . ."

She smiled. Her arms reached up to encircle his neck. The white smile and the light blue eyes seemed unreal against the deep tan of her skin.

"No," he gasped, spinning away from her. He crossed around to the other sofa so that the coffee table was between them. "What I meant was that I was thinking about what I was going to say to you. What I had to say to you."

She seemed amused at his obvious panic.

"Theresa, you shouldn't be here. It could give the wrong impression. People might think . . ."

"That's why I took the stairs. I know you have to keep us a secret."

"It's more than that. I'm a married man. I love my wife. I can't give you . . ." He wasn't sure exactly what to say he couldn't give her.

"I don't want you to give me anything." She was moving slowly around the coffee table in Gordon's direction. "I certainly don't want to come between you and Mrs. Acton."

"But then you must understand . . ." She was close enough so that he could feel her breath.

"All I want is right now. What we can bring to each other now, before I have to go away. You're wonderful, and I want to feel close to you."

He backed away. "This could destroy . . . both of us."

"Only if someone finds out, and I'll make sure that never happens. I'll never tell anyone. Never! And I'll only see you when I know we'll be alone."

"But it's not right for me to . . ."

"I want you so much." She had reached him, and her hands were pushing back the lapels of his jacket. "Don't you want me?"

Her arms were around him, inside his suit coat. He could feel her breasts against his chest and her thighs against his legs. "No one will ever know," she whispered. "Except us. It will always be our secret." Theresa pushed the coat off his shoulders and began loosening the knot in his tie. Gordon noticed that his bedroom door was open and that the bed had already been pulled down.

TWENTY-TWO

He awoke with a start and found himself staring into the folds of his pillow. There was a fraction of confusion, and then total recall of the night's events. His crotch was sticky and sore, and his lips felt swollen. Tiny scratches stung across his back. They had been wildly physical in their lovemaking, and every toss and turn was fixed like a graven image at the front of his brain. Oh my God, he thought, what have I done?

Gordon lay still, keeping up the same breathing pattern so that she wouldn't know he was awake. He listened carefully for the sound of her breathing, hoping that she was still asleep, but she was deathly silent. Slowly, he moved a hand under the covers, reaching carefully behind him toward the other side of the bed, feeling for her and hoping that she wouldn't feel him. He inched the hand further and further until it was stretched out behind him. She wasn't there.

He bolted upright and looked to his left, the side where Theresa had been when he fell away in physical exhaustion. There was no sign of her. She had straightened her side of the blanket and even fluffed up her pillow. Gordon blinked in disbelief, and spent a second fantasizing that she had never been there. He looked around. The clothes that he had peeled onto the floor were folded neatly on his silent butler. The underwear that had been balled next to the bed was gone. There was no sign of her clothes in the bedroom doorway where she had left everything but her panties. Maybe it had been a dream.

But he knew better. His side of the bed exuded the aroma of sex, and his body ached in all the telltale places. He swung out of the sheets and found clean underwear in his dresser. Then he hunted for his seldom-worn bathrobe and tried to make a casually gracious entrance into the rest of the house, assuming that she was lurking about some-place. He glanced through the living room and dining room and then eased open the swinging door to the kitchen. There was no sign of her. Absolutely nothing seemed to have been disturbed. Apparently she had gotten up, dressed, and left the apartment without so much as leaving a footprint in the carpet. The FBI forensics lab, he decided, couldn't have placed her at the scene.

Who was she? *What* was she? His mind was spinning as he searched in vain for any clue of her existence. This was a disadvantaged minority woman who wouldn't look up during a job interview. Yet, she seemed to be a computer expert, skilled in graduate level research. She was certainly a very accomplished lover. And now she was displaying an uncanny abil-ity to carry on an adult affair without leaving any hint of incriminating evidence. She had even buried his underwear in the laundry hamper. She wasn't just good for her age. She was unbelievable for any age, so skilled in such divergent personalities that she was positively frightening.

He showered quickly, dressed, and charged out of the apartment. There was a man in the elevator whom he greeted perfunctorily and then searched for any sign that he might know Gordon's guilty secret. There was no hint of recognition. In the lobby, he went to the door-man's desk, and asked if there were any messages for him. The man glanced in the empty mail slot and shook his head. Gordon bored into his eyes. Had he seen anything? Did he know anything? Was he enjoy-ing a secret laugh at Gordon's expense?

"Is there something else?" the doorman asked, unnerved by his ten-ant's scrutiny.

"Oh, no. Nothing. I was just expecting a . . . an express delivery. It must have gone to my office."

He got back on the elevator and rode down to the parking garage. Then he drove to the Brown University social sciences library.

He saw Theresa as soon as he reached the second floor. She was wearing the jeans and tank top that she had worn the night before, and was sitting in a carrel, surrounded by a mountain of books. She jumped up as soon as she saw him coming toward her.

"Mr. Acton!" The marvel in her voice made it seem as if he were a total surprise. "What are you doing here?"

He glanced around uneasily. "Can we go outside for a minute?"

"Sure!" Theresa spent a few seconds folding the books into one another to mark her pages. Then she walked with him down the steps and past the front desk. "I didn't know you were in town," she said just loud enough to raise disapproving glances from the librarians. As they were passing through the detectors she added, "I didn't think I'd see you until you got home on Saturday."

She was absolutely convincing. Even Gordon couldn't have guessed that it was anything more than an unexpected meeting. And she was fresh and scrubbed, looking like a Miss America candidate and nothing like the seductress from last night.

He led her to a bench, waited while she sat, and then settled uneasily at the opposite end. "I was . . . concerned . . . when I didn't find you in the apartment this morning."

"I thought it was best," she said from behind her smiling mask. "I got out before anyone was up. Before daylight, actually."

He nodded. "Sure. I appreciate that."

"I caught a few winks in the car before the library opened."

"Theresa, this was a terrible mistake. We can't let it happen again." Her eyes dropped sadly. "We could ruin your whole life. You're very young, with a wonderful future ahead of you. I'm much too old for you."

She looked up with a tiny smile. "I thought you were wonderful."

"You know what I mean."

She nodded. "You mean that you could lose everything. Your wife and children. Your career . . ."

"I'm thinking of you."

Theresa ignored the obvious lie. "I'd never do anything to hurt you, or Mrs. Acton. All I was doing was stealing a minute of what she has all the time. I know it's wrong. But lots of things are wrong."

"But if anyone found out . . ."

"No one will. Look how careful I was. No one ever has to know."

Gordon hesitated for an instant, regrouping his thoughts. "It's not just that people might find out. For me, it's very wrong. I'm the older man. I'm the one who is supposed to keep things straight. I shouldn't be taking advantage of you."

"You're not! I know what I'm doing. I'm not some silly kid."

"I know that. You're a . . . beautiful . . . talented . . . young adult. But it's wrong for me to take advantage of your feelings. You understand that, don't you?"

Theresa seemed about to cry, but she steeled herself and nodded vigorously. "I know."

"So we're agreed. This will never happen again."

Another nod. "If that's what you want."

Gordon exhaled slowly. "That's what I *have* to want. I have no choice. Neither of us does."

She forced a smile. "Okay, Mr. Acton."

"Thank you, Theresa."

She stood abruptly. "I've got to get back to the research." Then she wheeled and dashed up the library steps. Gordon watched her until she disappeared through the enormous double doors.

TWENTY-THREE

Ellie was thrilled with the material that Theresa brought back from Providence. "This is terrific," she told Theresa as she glanced through the work. "Just perfect." She held up a page. "How did you know that these tables could be integrated?"

Theresa was sitting next to her on the floor. She laughed with delight. "Because you told me that if it was the same study and the same sample—"

Ellie cut her off with a hug. "You're marvelous. Absolutely marvelous. I can't tell you how many hours—days, really—that you've saved me."

"So, should we start drafting it into the paper?" She was already moving toward the computer.

"Not you! You've done enough of my work. You take the day off. You can take the children down to the club and leave them in the day camp. Go swimming. Lie out on the boat. Whatever you want."

"I'd like to help you with—"

"Absolutely not. No more work on the thesis. I've taken advantage of you too much already."

Theresa brought Molly and Timmy to the club and stayed to watch as they joined in the waterfront games. She chatted easily with Don McNeary and the other boys who seemed to lean on McNeary for support. They, in turn, attracted some of the girls, most of them on vacation from college. Trish, with a small contingent of followers, stood at a distance, throwing dartlike glances in Theresa's direction.

Molly called to Trish, who had been watching her for the past few days, and asked her to join in a game. Trish used the excuse to get back closer to the other boys without seeming to be giving ground, and when her friends followed the two hostile camps fell into an uneasy truce. When the decision was made to leave the counselors in charge of the children and move up to the pool for a soft drink, Theresa was included. She spent the afternoon at the center of the young people's group, in full view of the disapproving elders. The Mapletons, Stuckys, and O'Connells lay in a row of chaises, taking the sun along with their afternoon cocktails.

"Acton's hired girl seems to have wormed her way in," Mrs. O'Connell observed.

"Great tits sure attract a crowd," Cecil Mapleton noticed.

"What big eyes you have," his wife chided.

"It's not his eyes that are big," Phil Stucky said in support of his friend.

"That's what attracts the boys," Emily Stucky answered. "It's the only thing they're interested in."

"And it's the boys that attract the girls," Jack O'Connell slurred, waving his glass toward the circle of young women in revealing bathing suits.

Trish's mother took umbrage. "It's a very sad commentary when a girl like that can become the center of attention. Isn't there a rule about the help using the members' facilities?"

"That's just the club's hired help," Phil Stucky answered. "Au pairs have always been treated like members' families."

"Well, maybe that's a rule we should look into," Mrs. Mapleton suggested.

"I know what I'd like to look into," Jack O'Connell said in a throaty laugh.

"Have another drink, Jack," his wife suggested.

"Don't mind if I do."

The comments continued on the weekend when Gordon brought Theresa and the children to the club and took them out sailing. He stayed in the bay, always in sight of the members on the porch, always at the helm while Theresa had the children herded at the front of the cockpit.

"Bet he'd like to get rid of the kids for an hour," Jack O'Connell cackled.

"I feel sorry for Ellie," Pricilla Mapleton said, shaking her head sadly. "It's so obvious that she's more to him than just a babysitter."

"Gordon isn't the kind to cheat on his wife," Emily Stucky said forcefully.

"What do you mean, 'isn't the kind'? He's a man isn't he? They're all the kind."

"But not here! Not right in front of her," Emily protested.

"Don McNeary was telling Trish that little Miss Hot Pants was over in Providence during the week," Pricilla revealed. "That's where Gordon is while he's campaigning."

Emily Stucky gasped at the irrefutable evidence.

"I'll bet he's campaigning," Jack O'Connell laughed.

Gordon had brought the boat about at the southern end of the bay and had lined up a straight run to his anchorage. Molly had grown bored with the repetitious runs and was letting a hand drag over the side. Timmy was asleep, his life jacket serving as a mattress while Theresa's lap was his pillow.

"Great sailing day," Gordon allowed for at least the fifth time. He was staring alertly out to sea and then up at the set of the rigging in order not to have to make eye contact with Theresa. But conversation became inevitable when he had no sailing commands to fill the silence. "So," he said to announce that he was going to break open a new topic, "what's the latest news from Yale? I guess you must be getting pretty excited."

"Why do you want to go to Yale?" Molly asked without lifting her gaze from the bow wake. "It's too far away. We'll never get to see you."

"I'll see plenty of you," Theresa answered, "because I won't be going away at all."

Gordon was startled. "I thought you were into Yale. With a scholarship."

Theresa nodded. "The scholarship is just the tuition, and that's only a fraction of the cost. I'm way short."

"Your summer job doesn't help?'

"It helps . . . a little. But you should see the fee schedule they sent me. Room and board. Lab fees. Books. And then there are clothes. It's about fifteen-thousand dollars that the scholarship doesn't cover." She looked over at Molly. "So I'll probably be right back in Tiverton, which means you'll be seeing a lot of me." Molly's smile indicated that she couldn't be happier.

"That's too bad," Gordon said. "I hate to see you give up on such a terrific opportunity."

"I guess I'm used to coming up short," Theresa sighed. Then she looked straight at Gordon and added, "But at least I'll be seeing a lot of you and Ellie."

He felt his guard go up, as if the words were a threat. "That's nice," he mumbled for Molly's ears, but he was thinking that it wasn't nice at all. The girl was a ticking time bomb who could blow him out of the water with a simple slip of the tongue. The anxiety she brought was bearable only because he had thought that she would be going away before the end of August to a new life in a different place. A revealing remark would probably go unnoticed in New Haven, but it could be fatal in his headquarters or his living room. He had also been counting on the healing properties of time. An accusation now would have instant credibility. But should she decide to mention their indiscretion six months from now, after she had been far enough away, anything she might say could be instantly denied. Gordon had even rehearsed the words. "It's just her imagination. Maybe something *she* wanted to happen. She's very young. She probably has no idea how embarrassing her fantasies are for me and my family."

But if she weren't leaving then there wouldn't be enough separation. All she would have to do was show up at his campaign headquarters once a week and anything she said about their relationship would be taken very seriously.

She was looking directly at him, her eyes narrowed as if searching his thoughts. Oh my God, does she know she owns me? Has she known all along? It was suddenly very clear. She had maneuvered him into bed. Put him in a position where he could deny her nothing without great risk to himself. She had him by the short hairs and she knew it. Now she was naming the price.

Her eyes left him, and softened as she looked away from the sun and toward the eastern barrier beach. "This is so beautiful, Mr. Acton. Thanks so much for taking me along."

Jesus, get hold of yourself, he thought. She's not threatening you. She hasn't even hinted that she might tell someone. She hasn't asked for anything. All she did was say that Yale was too expensive, which was certainly true. Of course it made more sense for her to go someplace cheaper and closer to home. He was making the worst possible mistake in taking such an innocent remark as a threat.

He turned the buoy at the entrance to the yacht club harbor.

"I should have brought the camcorder," Theresa said suddenly.

He didn't understand.

"It's so beautiful, coming into the harbor like this with all the boats riding at anchor, and the sun going down."

Gordon looked over the bow. "Beautiful, indeed. I guess I get so used to sights like this that I stop seeing them."

"It's still new to me," Theresa answered. "That's why I try to take pictures of everything. So I'll always have them with me."

He remembered that she had copied the footage of the children. She really is a nice girl, he thought, glancing back into the cockpit where Timmy was sleeping peacefully in her lap. Maybe we should give her the money she needs to go to Yale. Of course, he would have to be ready to come up with that amount, maybe even more, in each of her four years. So it would be more than a gesture. He was thinking about serious money. And there was no point in kidding himself. The only reason he was even thinking about it was to get her as far away as quickly as possible. Even if she weren't trying to hold him up, he realized that he was frightened of what she might do with a single, careless word. What did it amount to? Something between sixty and seventy-five thousand. That was a lot of money to assure her silence. But, hell, his entire future was at stake.

"Should we start taking the sails down?"

He was suddenly aware of Theresa, and more important that he was sailing right into the narrow channel between slips.

"No, I'll just free the sheets and go in on the engine." He let the sail blow freely while he skillfully swung the boat into the slip. Then he sent Theresa on home with the children while he tied everything down and walked up to the bar. He made a point to move in next to Jack O'Connell.

"Haven't seen a lot of Ellie," O'Connell said in greeting.

"She's swamped with her doctoral dissertation. She's been living in front of the computer, buried in books."

"I thought your little Latin lady was helping her with that."

Jesus, was every part of his life conversation on the pool deck? "No," he said patiently while his gin and tonic was set before him. "Ellie is doing the whole thing. Theresa just helps with some of the legwork."

Jack snickered. "I'll bet she's an expert on legwork!"

The McNeary boy was right, Gordon thought. Jack O'Connell really was difficult. But he contained his anger; he wasn't going to give O'Connell another excuse for falling down. "She's a very attractive girl," he said in pleasant agreement. Then he raised his glass in toast. "To all attractive girls."

"I'll drink to that!" O'Connell agreed.

You'd drink to anything, Gordon thought.

Cecil Mapleton was suddenly at his elbow. "Good to see you, Acton." He raised a finger to the bartender, who automatically started pouring a single-malt over ice. "Pricilla and I were just saying that we don't seem to see much of the Actons."

"It's a busy summer for us. Ellie has her doctoral work, and the campaign keeps me away most of the time."

"Hell, you're not worried about the election. Seems to me that you're a shoo-in."

"I still have to go through the motions. In politics, you take nothing for granted."

Mapleton sipped and exhaled. "Heard you had the whole family over in Providence. They're not all going door-to-door, are they?"

Gordon was puzzled. "Not really. I've tried to keep them out of it. Ellie and the kids have been here all summer."

"Oh, well didn't I hear that your mother's helper was in Providence? I just assumed . . ."

They're both pricks, Gordon thought. "She may have been. Ellie's been using her to look up data that she needs. She's been traveling up to Harvard. Could be that she was over at Brown."

"Gordon calls it 'legwork,'" Jack interjected. He and Mapleton broke out in laughter, and Gordon felt obliged to join with an embarrassed smile.

He hurried the drink. "Have to run," he told the two men. "I've got kitchen duty."

"I hope you're not going to miss the clambake," Cecil called after him.

Gordon shook his head. "Not a chance. See you at the clambake."

He checked his anger so that he could smile at members in the parking lot, looking thrilled to see people whom he barely knew. Once in the car he screamed a curse. Were they following him? How in hell did Cecil Mapleton know that Theresa had been to Providence? Jesus, had they hired an investigator to hound him out of the club? What had he done to them except hire an outsider for a job that generally went to the members' daughters?

Poor Theresa, he thought as he turned into his driveway. She thinks that she can keep their secret, that no one will ever know. "Well, welcome to the upper crust, kiddo," he said out loud. "They make it a point to know everything! At least, everything they can use against you."

He tried to look at ease as he came up the steps, but one look at Ellie told him that something was terribly wrong. She had been waiting for him just inside the screen door, and came charging out to meet him the second he reached the porch.

"Oh, Gordon . . ."

She looked pale, except for her red-streaked eyes.

"What's the matter? What's wrong?"

She took a folded letter from her jeans pocket. "This came this morning. Right after you left."

"What is it?" he asked as he opened it.

"It's from the dean. About my thesis . . ."

He read her mentor's terse letter requesting that she meet with him and members of the doctoral board to clear up certain ambiguities with her work. Then he shrugged. "So? It's probably something routine. Some obscure academic procedure that—"

Ellie interrupted him. "No, I called as soon as I got it. They want to be convinced that it's all my work."

"Of course it's your work," he assured, but he felt an instant uneasiness in his stomach.

She shook her head angrily. "No, they suspect I'm using a ghost-writer. Someone must have told them that Theresa was writing my thesis."

He took her into his arms. "That's ridiculous," he assured her. "We'll get all this cleared up in a hurry." His uneasiness was rapidly becoming a point of fear. He and Ellie had both taken advantage of the young mother's helper. Now it was payback time for his wife.

July

TWENTY-FOUR

Ellie and Gordon suffered private agonies during their rare Sunday morning church service. They sat up front, each holding a prayer book and gazing attentively at the preacher in the pulpit who conjured up images of a loving savior. But it was Theresa's image that was fixed in the front of each of their imaginations. And it hurt both of them to think about her.

Gordon saw a naked nymph who had twice drawn him into her bed. He was ashamed of his weakness, but he was terrified of the inevitable revelation of his dirty secret. Sooner or later it would come out. Maybe he would slip, thoughtlessly mentioning something about her that could be known only to an intimate lover. A birthmark, a mole, a private tattoo. He began searching her body for some identifying mark, intending to banish it from his memory.

"There are sins that cry to heaven for vengeance," the minister's dramatic voice intoned. Gordon realized that he was remembering her breasts, and snapped his head to erase the thought.

Most likely it would be something that she blurted out, maybe to the girls at the yacht club during one of their locker-room sessions. A mature man, particularly a public figure had to count for more than one of the cabana boys. His downtown apartment had to carry more points than the shadows under the boardwalk. It was too big a conquest for her to keep to herself.

Or maybe something whispered into the ear of a young lover. *"Oh, Gordon,"* when she meant, *"Oh, John"* or *"Oh, Jose!"*

"To God, our thoughts are as clear as our words," he heard from the pulpit. He was thinking of Theresa in the embrace of some fraternity lover, and again he shuddered to free his mind.

He stole a glance toward Ellie and drank in the innocence of her

115

expression. Once the word was out, people would be trampling one another in the rush to tell her about her unfaithful husband. The news wouldn't be incredible, but once it was public it would be unforgivable. Her pride would be terminally damaged.

Ellie looked back, and smiled at him but she felt no joy. Her image was important to his political career. Her academic disgrace could be a fatal blow to his hopes as well as her plans to reform the state's public education system. And he had warned her. He had seen the danger of her dependence on Theresa and correctly predicted her downfall. What could she say to him when her idealistic career was exposed as a fraud?

"Sooner or later, we all face the truth about ourselves," her pastor's voice reminded her. That was exactly what she had to do: face the truth. It was easy to pretend that all Theresa had done was run errands to the library. That was all that anyone would expect of a junior-college student. But the truth was that Theresa had done some very original work. She had used her computer skills to search far more widely and thoroughly than Ellie would have done herself. She had made judgments on the value of materials that were uncannily accurate. Ellie could certainly claim that the basic thesis was hers and that she had imagined and structured its presentation. But she would have to admit that the development of the evidence was at least a team effort, with the big plays being made by her mother's helper.

How could she explain to Gordon that defending herself before an academic board wouldn't simply be a matter of laying out her notes? The handwritten outlines and notes would show clearly what a major role Theresa had played. Ellie couldn't explain even the techniques by which massive files had been downloaded.

"Our deeds reveal our intentions, and our intentions reveal our souls," the sermon continued toward its predictable ending. Ellie's deeds stood out like channel markers. People must have noticed the young girl in the libraries who had asked for such specialized materials. How long would it take them to prove that she had signed them out under Ellie's name? If she was just an errand girl, why was she lying about her identity? Why was Ellie lending her name to what was obviously someone else's work?

She glanced at her husband and was humbled by the integrity that gleamed in his eyes. What would he say when she told him? What would he do?

They were quiet as they began the drive home, absorbed in their own thoughts. But while Gordon needed silence, Ellie needed to speak.

"It's true, Gordon," she said out of nowhere.

"What's true?"

"The work wasn't entirely mine."

"Ellie, don't be ridiculous. How could they suspect a nineteen-year-old of writing a doctoral thesis?"

"She made substantial contributions. She was much more than just a gofer."

"No one will ever believe it. All she has to do is tell them . . ." He suddenly went silent.

"You see what I mean?" Ellie said. "She has to tell them. My career hangs on what she tells them, and I'm frightened stiff over what she might say."

Gordon fumbled for a response. He knew exactly what his wife was feeling, but he had to be careful not to let on *how* he so clearly understood her feelings. "I think she's crazy about you, Ellie. I can't see her doing anything to hurt you."

"Gordon, who do you think could have told the university about her role?"

He shrugged. He had never thought of the question.

Ellie went on. "Who knew besides her and me? Even you didn't really understand how much she was doing for me."

He nodded.

"It had to be her," Ellie continued.

"Why? Why would she do that?" Gordon asked. But even as he asked he knew the answer. It would be the same for her as it was for him.

"So that she could get anything she wants from me. Don't you see? My life is dependent on her. If she asks me for the moon, I'll have to give it to her."

Gordon let his eyes widen as if he had just realized the implication. But he had already answered the question in his own words. Why did she screw me? So that she could get anything she wants from me, and I would have to give it to her.

"She'd have to have some sort of proof," Gordon finally offered. "You're in a good position. The presumption would be that she couldn't do that kind of work."

A hell of a lot better position than I am in, he was thinking as he

117

spoke. One look at her body and everyone would know she could do that kind of work.

"Like what?" Ellie asked.

"You tell me. What would she need to prove beyond a doubt that she had authored substantial parts of your thesis?"

Ellie thought. "Notes. Extensive notes in her handwriting. Photocopies of documents where she had initialed the original, or copied her driver's license on top of the original. Things like that, I suppose."

He nodded, and then asked, "What about the computer stuff?"

"That would be hard. It was all downloaded to my computer address. But maybe she could have done something during the log-on that left her footprint. I really don't know exactly what she was doing . . ."

"So, she'd have to have a file somewhere. Probably in her room."

Ellie nodded. "For positive proof, she'd need documents."

They sent Theresa off to the beach with the children, suggesting the ocean-front barrier bar because it would take them longer to get there. Then, after waiting to be sure that they wouldn't be returning for something they had forgotten, Ellie and Gordon tiptoed up the stairs. There was no need for quiet; they were alone in their own house. But neither said a word as they walked carefully down the hallway to Theresa's room.

Ellie led the search under the assumption that she had a better idea of exactly what they were looking for. She began in the dresser drawers, lifting the underwear, blouses, and stockings only far enough to peek under them. She was satisfied when she ran her hands around the edges and found nothing out of the expected. But Gordon wasn't satisfied. As Ellie finished with each drawer, he pulled it out so that he could look at the bottom. He remembered that at school he had taped letters that he didn't want his roommates sharing to the bottom of his dresser drawer.

They made the same thorough search through the desk, with Gordon sliding it away from the wall to be certain that nothing had been taped to its back. Then they lifted chair cushions, took up the cushions in the window seat, and turned back the corners of the carpet.

"I really appreciate your help," Ellie said as her husband lifted the bed footboard so that she could lift the rug a bit higher.

He nodded. "If she has it, we'll find it."

"Unless she took it home with her when she was over in Providence."

"I doubt it," he assured her.

Ellie looked up. "Well, it is possible."

"But not likely," Gordon said confidently.

"How do you know?"

His head snapped up and there was a hint of panic in his eyes. How did he know? Because she never went home. She spent her days in the library and her night in his bed. Exactly the kind of slip he had been dreading. "Well, I don't figure that she would leave something like that lying around a house where she probably has less privacy than here. I mean in a small room with her foster parents next door." He stared into Ellie's face until her expression told him that she was satisfied with his explanation.

The fact was that he probably shouldn't be helping Ellie with the search at all. Not in this room, where he might even have left semen stains on the sheets. Everything was so familiar that it seemed inevitable that he would blurt out some suggestion or observation that would announce that he had been in the young girl's room before. But he had to stay close to his wife; he had to be ready to spring on any piece of evidence that might incriminate him.

A diary! He had thought of it as soon as Ellie decided that they were going to search. If Ellie found a diary, it would make sense that she would read it looking for comments about the work she was doing on the thesis, or maybe even an admission of her call to the deans at her university. But it was far more likely that she would find something else. Didn't young women fill their diaries with romantic fantasies, and excruciatingly detailed descriptions of their lovemaking? If there was a diary, he wanted to page through it first.

Or letters! Theresa must be sending brag notes to her friends back home. She was in charge of the children, tanning on the exclusive yacht club beach, helping a doctoral candidate with a thesis. And her friends would comment on all her successes when they wrote back to her. Ellie would want to read those responses for any hints that Theresa was wrapping her around her little finger. Gordon was determined to find them first in case there were words of congratulations for seducing the head of the household. He had to stay right by his wife's side with his eyes wide open and his mouth tightly closed.

Ellie was already in the closet, sliding the hangers across the bar so that she could look between the clothes. She ran her hands down the sides of each shirt, and dipped her fingers into the pockets of each pair of jeans. Gordon crowded in next to her and stood on an overturned wastebasket while he searched the shelf. He took down a folded sweat-shirt and shook it out. All the while, he kept glancing at Ellie, secretly rejoicing that she was finding nothing. They put everything back in order and then swung the door to the closed position in which they had found it.

"That's everything except the bookcase," Ellie announced. She took a step toward it but then stopped abruptly. "Gordon, have I gone com-pletely paranoid? Am I searching for something that doesn't exist?"

He shrugged. "We'll know that when you get done searching." He went to the bookcase and began leafing through the books on the top shelf. Ellie started at the bottom shelf, which enabled Gordon to watch the pages she was turning as well as the ones he was examining. He was completely absorbed when his hand reached for the next book and bumped into the video camera.

"You don't suppose she made a video of the notes. Or maybe set the camera on a library shelf so she could photograph herself doing your work."

"It would be a damn dull video," Ellie said without looking up from her search. "Not the kind of thing she could sell on the Internet."

Gordon felt his heart skip a beat, and the breath rush out of his chest as if he had been punched in the belly. His hands flew off the camcorder as if it had suddenly burst into flames. The camera! The damn camera, sitting on the shelf with its one good eye looking down the length of her bed. He leaned down carefully, turning his head and setting his cheek on top of the box. He closed one eye so that he could sight with the other, down the axis of the camera and out over its lens. He was seeing what the camera was seeing as it sat on the top shelf, and it was Theresa's bed that was the target.

But the light, there was a little red light that came on when the camera was running. If she had the damn thing on, he would have noticed the light. He gave a half sigh of relief and looked for telltale beacon. But he couldn't see it. It was hidden behind the decorative brace that supported the shelf. When it was set at the every end of the shelf, as it was now, the light couldn't be seen.

His throat was knotting, and the first beads of sweat were trickling down from his hairline.

"Nothing here," Ellie said, standing up next to him.

"Nothing here either," Gordon lied.

"Well, let's look around and make sure we don't leave anything out of place."

All he could look at was the camera. The power switch was on the side of the unit, near the front, but the recording trigger was at the back. She couldn't have turned it on. He would have seen her if she had gone to the bookcase.

His head panned automatically in response to Ellie's request, but his mind was trying to reconstruct everything that had happened that first afternoon. They had come up the stairs together and rushed down the hall. She hadn't gone into the bathroom, but instead had taken his hand and led him through the door. Then they had gotten undressed. No, wait, she was already undressed. But how could that be? She wasn't naked when they were running down the hall. She was in her bathing suit. Had he watched her take it off? Had he *helped* her take it off?

"I don't see anything. Do you notice anything out of place?"

He never heard the question. He was trying desperately to remember how she had gotten out of the bathing suit. Because he was sure that she was naked when the two of them began undressing him.

"Gordon?"

"What?" He blinked.

"Everything back in place?"

"Oh, yeah. It looks good to me."

They backed out of the room, he first and then Ellie. She closed the door behind her. As they walked toward the stairs she said, "Okay, so I'm paranoid. I'm imagining enemies where there aren't any."

"Didn't you tell me that she had copied a videotape? Something about wanting to have pictures of the kids."

Ellie went ahead of him down the stairs. "Yes. She wants to take their pictures to school with her."

"Then where is it?" he asked.

Ellie turned to find him still on the top step. "Where's her copy of the tape? If she made one, wouldn't it be in her room?"

"I guess so," Ellie answered, not certain that she understood the significance. Gordon couldn't actually believe that Theresa would have made a videotape of her notes.

"Then why didn't we find it?"

"She must have . . . put it someplace else." As she answered, she understood. If the tape was somewhere else then her notes and letters might be somewhere else. She had obviously found a place to put the tape for safekeeping. She could have done the same with her diary.

"Oh God, Gordon. Then I haven't found out anything. Except that she must have brought some things home when she was in Providence."

"Or hidden them someplace here in this house. Maybe in the garage, or in one of the cars."

"But we can't look everywhere."

Gordon ran down the stairs past her. "Maybe not, but I can start in the garage." He was out the door and down the front steps. It was only a few seconds later when she could hear him banging around the garage shelves.

We went down the hall and right into her room, Gordon kept reviewing mentally. So then why don't I remember her getting out of her bathing suit? He squeezed his eyes closed, trying to rewind the image of the night two weeks earlier. Theresa was in the bikini, still wet from her swim. And she embraced him, feeling sorry for the trouble she was causing him at the club. And then they were kissing, and pawing. He remembered. He had pulled down the top of her suit. No! She had stopped him. She had said something about not doing it on the porch and had led the way up the stairs. So she still had the suit on when they reached the bedroom door.

Of course! She had asked him to give her a second. And he had figured that she needed an intimate moment for contraceptive purposes. He remembered that he wanted to turn on his heels right then and there. She had been gone for several minutes. No, not minutes. Maybe one minute. But more than enough time to turn on a camcorder and get out of her bathing suit. Then, when she opened the door, she was already undressed. And the camcorder was running, capturing all the action taking place on top of her bed.

And then she had probably copied it. Ellie thought she had taken the VCR up to her room in order to make copies of the kids' activities. Maybe she did, but she could also have made a copy of Gordon Acton, candidate for the United States House of Representatives, in the act of adultery. She was past the age of consent, so it wouldn't be a felony. But what difference did it make? If the video ever got out, he would be without a career and probably without a wife. Hell, with the kind of settlement Ellie would get he might also be without a company, an apartment, and a car.

He was soaked through with perspiration from his futile search through the stuffy garage. Where else, he thought? Maybe in her apartment, or at her foster parents' flat. He hadn't found her in the library, and then he had gone off to a political dinner. She could have checked into the library, then walked out, gotten into the car, and driven to Tiverton. But he didn't think she would let her ticket to fame and fortune out of her hands. So, if she had anything incriminating, it was most likely still in the house.

Ellie was waiting as he came in through the front door. "Gordon, let's stop this right now. I feel like an idiot searching for something that probably doesn't even exist."

"You said she'd need hard evidence."

"If it's her, and if she wants to disgrace me. But is that realistic? She's just a girl, and she seems so grateful for everything we've done for her."

"I know, but there's so much at stake. Let's keep looking." He was past her and headed back up the stairs. It wasn't really Ellie's thesis that he was worried about. But he would have to let her go on believing that it was. He tried not to think of what it was that he had done for Theresa.

He went into her bathroom, searched the cabinets and the linen closet, turned over the hamper, and got down on all fours to search under the tub. Then he went into Molly's room and looked hurriedly through her mountain of toys, searched her closets and tossed through her dresser. Gordon was nearly frantic when he began looking in Timmy's toy chest.

"Gordon, I really appreciate your help. But I think we should let it go. They'll be back soon."

He looked at Ellie who was standing in Timmy's doorway, stared uncertainly for a moment, and then nodded. "Okay. I'll find an opportunity to go through the car. And tonight, I'll take a look around the basement."

Ellie hugged him in the doorway. "Thanks for all your help. You warned me to make sure that it was *my* thesis. If I am in trouble, it's my own fault."

He couldn't agree with her. The real problem wasn't hers at all. So he held her close for just a moment and then headed outside to start the grill for dinner.

Don McNeary wandered in while they were eating, and made small talk until he had an opportunity to get Theresa alone. He took her for a walk down the steps and along the shoreline of the private beach, then held her hand as he brought her back to the front door. When Theresa turned to face Ellie and Gordon her face was aglow.

"Don asked me to the clambake dance," she said.

"Oh, Theresa, that's wonderful," Ellie cooed.

"Great!" Gordon said. "It's a hell of a party."

They both sounded completely overjoyed, hiding their suspicions and even the slightest hint that they had spent the day searching her room.

"You'll need a dress," Ellie said. She was gushing with concern.

"Oh, I don't think so. I don't want to be a bother."

"Nonsense! It won't be a bother," Gordon said, putting in his bid for survival.

Theresa looked from one to the other. "Well, I really don't have anything . . ."

"First thing tomorrow," Ellie insisted.

TWENTY-FIVE

They left in the Land Rover shortly after Gordon had returned to his campaign trail in Providence. Timmy was bratty about being forced to miss day camp, and whiney about wearing shoes. Molly, to Ellie's delight, was overjoyed to be part of the buying team for Theresa's dress. She envisioned a gown studded with pearls, somewhat in the Disney image of Cinderella.

They were in and out of three stores in Hyannis before they faced the inevitable of a drive into Providence or Boston. "They'll just have more choices," Ellie said, making light of the long trip. With Boston traffic and the hell of parking, they would be in the car for two hours.

"It's such an imposition," Theresa argued. "I'm supposed to be letting you relax at the beach." But she had to agree that the things they had seen on the Cape were more suited to a mother of the bride. They used ornaments and feathers to hide the inevitable defects of age, whereas Theresa had nothing to hide and everything to show.

"Theresa, I was just wondering if you saw anyone in the library while you were getting my material?" Ellie tried as they approached the canal bridge.

The girl was clearly stunned by the question. "Who?" she responded. "Who do you think I saw?"

"Oh, no one in particular. I was just wondering if someone saw the work that you were doing. Anyone who would know that it was for my dissertation."

She sensed that Theresa was grasping. There *was* someone, and the girl was stumbling for a plausible lie.

"I don't think so. Where? Which library?"

"Oh, either one. I have nothing particular in mind."

Ellie heard Theresa's sigh of relief. Then the girl answered confidently. "The librarian at Brown asked me what I was working on. But I don't think he listened to my answer. He was a graduate student, and I think he was really trying to pick me up."

"What did you tell him?"

"I said I was a teacher, and that I was doing research for a course." Theresa hesitated until she saw Ellie smile. "I hope that was okay."

"Of course it was okay. The reason I'm asking is that my faculty adviser seems to have heard that . . . well that it's really *your* work. So, I . . ."

"That's crazy," Theresa interrupted. "All I was doing was saving you the trip."

"No," Ellie corrected. "You were doing a lot more than that. You've been a tremendous help. But I think you'll agree that you were working under my direction."

"Of course. I don't know anything about writing a thesis."

"You know quite a bit. As I said, you've been a lifesaver. But wouldn't you agree that you were simply gathering information that I directed?"

"Sure. I was like a messenger."

Ellie didn't know what to believe. Theresa's first reaction had practically been a confession that she had met with someone at one of the libraries, but her denial rang true. And she was, if anything, minimizing her contribution to the dissertation, which didn't sound like someone who intended to take credit before a graduate review board.

"I mean, I guess I was pretty much on my own when I was on the computer. But that's only because we just had a computer-networking course in school. It was all stuff you *could* have done."

Ellie felt suddenly sick. *Pretty much on my own* was not what she hoped Theresa would report to her mentor. And the emphasis on the computer! Ellie didn't have her own net ID and password. If they could be traced, Theresa would have electronic proof that it had been her doing the research.

"Theresa, an answer like that could be very embarrassing to me," Ellie said, suspecting that the girl knew *embarrassing* was an understatement. "If you were 'pretty much on your own,' then portions of my dissertation would be your work, not mine."

"Oh no! We were always working together."

More nausea. Theresa was smiling as she claimed coauthorship. Ellie was fumbling in an effort to explain her dilemma, but she suspected that it was Theresa who had thrown her on the horns. Was the kid sitting there and laughing at her?

"Yes, we were working together," Ellie agreed as pleasantly as she could manage. "But we were in different roles. I was deciding what information we needed and what we would write; you were gathering the information that I specified."

"Sure," Theresa said agreeably. "Except sometimes, you remember, we didn't even know the information existed until we found it on the Internet."

She can destroy me, Ellie thought. She can absolutely destroy me.

"What kind of dress do you think you'll get, Theresa?" Molly asked to override the boring conversation.

Theresa blushed and looked at Ellie. "I don't know. We'll find something we all like."

"You'll need shoes to go with the dress," Molly observed.

"Oh, I don't know if the shoes have to match," Theresa answered.

Ellie knew what she had to do. "Of course you'll need shoes. And we'll have to think about them when we're buying the dress. We won't have time to dye them."

Timmy started to whimper. The top had come off his water cup and he had spilled the drink down the front of himself.

"I'll take care of it," Theresa offered as she leaned over the back of the front seat.

You're already taking care of everything, Ellie thought.

In Boston, they went from store to store with Theresa in and out of dressing rooms. Clerks kept dragging out flowered and feathered dresses, assuming that a Latino girl would want something very flashy for her first formal dance. Molly liked everything that was bright and colorful, and Timmy busied himself tying and untying his shoes. Theresa had no opinion, but simply posed for Ellie and awaited a reaction. Ellie had no reason to care about anything except making sure that Theresa was happy. But aesthetically she couldn't abide the fussy decorations that did nothing to showcase the young girl's features. "You don't want people to see the dress," she explained. "You want the dress to help them see you." And Theresa blushed at the thought that she should ever be the center of attention.

Ellie was more confused than ever. In the car, her mother's helper had demonstrated how easily she could sound like a coauthor of the dissertation. It was almost as if she were warning Ellie. She had appeared tough, smart, and determined. Now she was back to her wall-flower persona; shy, embarrassed, and hardly able to look at herself in a mirror. She had gone from being intimidating to being helpless in the time it took to walk through the doors of a store. And yet Ellie was genuinely concerned that Theresa should find exactly the right dress for dancing on the deck of a very self-satisfied yacht club.

"Something like this, maybe," Theresa said lifting a gray-white dress from a rack of size eights. She held the hanger up to her shoulders so that the hook seemed to be hanging from her nose.

"Yes, I think so," Ellie said, her eyes squinting critically. "Try it on."

When she returned from the dressing room, Ellie caught her breath. Against the near-white background, Theresa's dark skin was like silk. The bit of gray in the color made the blue of her eyes even deeper.

"That's it!" Ellie said. "Absolutely gorgeous."

Molly's hands went up to her mouth to contain her delight. "That's beautiful," she said in her most mature voice.

"You like it?" Theresa asked.

"Like it?" a saleswoman said from behind a row of hangers. "It's marvelous."

Within seconds, store clerks and shoppers surrounded Theresa, all stunned by her appearance in the dress. "I know just the thing," a floor manager said, rushing off to select lingerie and stockings. "We have shoes in that color," a clerk remembered. Bras, slips, and panties materialized. Then the crowd moved in procession to the shoe department.

"Is this all right?" Theresa asked, thinking of the expense.

"It's perfect," Ellie answered, thinking of the ensemble.

The next thing she knew, she was standing at the cash register, looking at a seven-hundred-dollar total and handing over her charge card. She was no longer caught up in the beauty of the dress and the thrilled glow in the young girl's face. Instead, she was beginning to count the cost of Theresa's silence.

"You wouldn't believe what she looked like," Ellie told Gordon during their evening telephone conversation. "A perfect ten. Honest to God, you should see her cleavage."

"Should I?" he asked as if it were the farthest thing from his mind. He was pleased that he had adopted just the right tone of feigned interest. He sounded innocent of even a lascivious thought.

"Well, no, you shouldn't. But I'm afraid you will, and when you do you're going to wonder which of my ancestors was run over by a steamroller. Next to Theresa, I'm a two-dimensional object."

"You're kidding," he lied.

"You know what she needs?" Ellie went on. "A single pearl on a platinum chain. Something absolutely simple and elegant."

"Is that what she suggested?"

"Oh no. She didn't ask for a thing," Ellie answered. "And I'm not about to spend another penny. I was just commenting from a fashion point of view."

"It sounds to me as if you've spent more than enough already," Gordon said. And then he asked, "Any thought about who might have written to your mentor?"

"Nothing I'm sure of. While we were driving, I felt pretty sure that it was her. Just the way she put things seemed a little threatening. But at the store, she really seemed embarrassed that I was buying anything for her. She acted as if she would have been grateful for just a simple dress."

"So maybe it's not her," Gordon said, as if supporting Theresa's innocence somehow proved his own. "I really hate being suspicious of her."

"But, still, I'm quite sure that she met someone when she was in Providence."

"Who?" he nearly shouted into the phone.

"I'm not sure who, but when I asked her she really panicked. Then she covered with a story about a graduate student in the library trying to pick her up."

"That could be true. The young studs at the yacht club have all tried to pick her up."

They had decided that they were being a bit too suspicious, and agreed that if she had to give a statement to the faculty board, she would say whatever Ellie wanted. They both sounded at ease with the situation. But as soon as they hung up, Gordon went back to his deliberations on where Theresa might have hidden her tape. Ellie got back to work on her thesis, and instantly turned down Theresa's offer to help her with the typing.

TWENTY-SIX

Gordon awoke to the annoying buzz of his front doorbell, mumbled a "go away," and pushed his face back into the pillow. When he heard the sound again, he cursed, got up, and snatched his bathrobe out of his closet. Before he could tie the belt, the buzzer sounded again.

"Okay!" he screamed across the living room and into the foyer. "You better be a fireman telling me that the whole building is in flames!"

He screwed his eye up to the peephole and saw the distorted image of a man's face. He recognized the sallow complexion and the thin white hair, but he couldn't think of a name that fit it.

"Yes!" he called through the door.

"Sergeant Wasciewicz. Fall River police . . ."

Nothing seemed to fit. "I'm not up yet," he called back. He was turning away when he remembered the policeman who had been investigating a semiconductor theft. Now why in hell would that be important to him?

The buzzer sounded again. Gordon opened the deadbolt and pulled open the door. "The semiconductor affair," he said drowsily, but he woke up quickly when he saw the authority in the man's eyes. "Come in!" He stepped aside as Wasciewicz entered, whispering an insincere apology for having awakened him. "Sit down. I'll put on some coffee.

How's your investigation coming along?" Gordon called from the kitchen. Wasciewicz came up to the dining room side of the counter where he could watch Gordon spooning coffee into a basket.

"Slowly," he said. "But some things are starting to fall into place. Like the guy who was putting the components out with the trash. He turned up in a landfill packed into an old refrigerator."

"Jesus! A mob hit?"

Wasciewicz smiled. "Probably not. We're closing in on a small-time crook who would be an embarrassment to a professional gangster. Though I have to admit that he's done a pretty good job covering his trail. People say it's him, but there isn't any real proof."

Gordon adjusted the coffeemaker controls. "So, how can I help you?"

"Your babysitter, the girl who used to work at the factory. Remember she was one of the names on the list of computer operators?"

"Yeah! She's very good with computers."

"Well, she's also on a list of people who knew this slug we think was behind everything."

"Theresa?" Gordon squinted in disbelief. "She's a little young to be a gangster's lady."

"This particular gangster is only twenty. And there's no doubt that he and the Santiago girl were very close."

"Theresa?" Gordon still couldn't buy it.

"He picked her up after work on several occasions, all while the thefts were going on. His car has flames painted down the sides, and about half a dozen tailpipes, so it was easy for witnesses to remember. It's not much to go on, but she's the only person at Digital Electronics who knows the suspect and has access to the computer."

Gordon whistled softly. "Little Theresa," he said more to himself than to the sergeant.

"Anyway, I was wondering if you'd mind looking at some mug shots." As he was talking he was retrieving the photos from his pocket. He spread them on the counter facing Gordon, three shots of the same man taken from different angles, one with a well-trimmed beard and mustache. He had dark features, more obviously Hispanic than Theresa's. His eyes were wild with anger.

"Not your typical altar boy," Gordon allowed.

"Have you ever seen him? Near your home out on the Cape? Or anywhere close to Miss Santiago?"

Gordon shook his head. "Absolutely not, and that's a face I'd remember." Then he wondered aloud, "Are you sure about this? Because Theresa is a very gentle young lady."

Wearily, the policeman gathered up his photos. "Well, our friend here is a man of the world. The girls seem to think he's *bad,* and he probably has more money than any of them can ever hope to make. She might have seen him as an opportunity."

Gordon took out two coffee cups and filled them, then went to the refrigerator for the cream. Yeah, he thought, she might well see him as an opportunity. That seemed to be the way she looked at the Actons.

He talked about her with great enthusiasm while they had their coffee. She was bright, and not likely to be taken in by a smooth-talking thug. She was great with the children, patient and understanding. There was nothing he could say about her that would justify the policeman's suspicions. He concluded with a challenge. "Why don't you interview her? You can come up to my place and take a walk on the beach. If she knows this guy, she'll tell you. And even if she does, I'd give good odds that she knows nothing about the changes to the inventory program. I'll bet she'll be as bewildered about the theft as I am."

Wasciewicz thanked Gordon for the invitation, but said that he wasn't ready to confront Theresa. He didn't want to give anyone advanced warning that he had made the connection between the girl and his prime suspect. "But I think this guy will try and contact her. He'll want to satisfy himself that she would never turn against him. Otherwise . . ."

Gordon understood. He remembered what happened to the man entombed in the refrigerator.

"I guess it's good that she's with you and your family. That gives her a good measure of safety. But if she decides to take a trip on her own, or if she starts getting unusual phone calls, I'd really like to hear from you."

"Of course," Gordon agreed. "But do you really think she's in any danger?"

Wasciewicz used a paper napkin to blot his lips. "Not as long as we don't make her look like a potential witness."

TWENTY-SEVEN

The clambake, always scheduled for the last weekend in July, was the major event in the yacht club's annual social season. The time was picked to accommodate members who might be renting their homes and traveling abroad during August, and to handicap the odds on fair weather. Only once in the memory of the club's old timers had the clambake been cancelled because of rain.

Festivities began on Friday night when the male officers traveled out to the barrier beach to supervise the digging of a roasting pit in the dunes. The actual digging was done by the young cabana boys, waiters, and other club employees, who were given full access to the keg, and then tipped lavishly by their beer-bloated elders. Several years back, one of the returning officers had driven off the road with three other officers as passengers. The car had gotten caught in soft sand, and the group spent the night watching the tide fill and then cover a Jaguar sedan. Since then a school bus was hired and used to provide round-trip transportation.

Saturday morning, a truckload of driftwood was dumped into the pit and set afire. Then layers of lobster, clams, and whole fish were set on top with intermediate layers of dry wood and fresh seaweed until the whole pit was filled with light smoke and hissing steam. Members began arriving in the early afternoon with blankets, folding tables, and coolers of top-shelf gin, rum, and vodka. Swimming, sunning, and sack races filled the afternoon, and at twilight there was a beach volleyball tournament. By then, most of the members were filled, sunburned, dislocated, and gin-stunned. The wounded wandered home at their leisure while the more adventurous found some sort of amorous liaison on top of a beach blanket in the towering dunes.

Sunday morning featured a dinghy race from the club, around the southern tip of South Beach Island, and back up the Atlantic coast to the site of the prior day's festivities. Club employees and many of the younger members bolted oversized outboards onto undersized dinghies creating blazingly fast and generally unstable racers to compete for a chipped glass trophy. The real purpose of the race was to get a cleanup crew out to the beach before the park opened to the public.

Sunday afternoon was given to a dockside cocktail party. By tradition, every member with a boat at a slip prepared fingerfoods and stocked a bar. Then every boat was open to every member. The visiting back and forth across the docks was boisterous and, after a few hours of cocktails, dangerous. Every year, at least one of the members stepped off the wrong side of a boat or fell into the space between two of the docked yachts.

The finale of the weekend was the Clambake Ball on Sunday night. Dress code dictated elaborate cocktail dresses and white dinner jackets. Reckless behavior was discouraged so as to get the more dedicated revelers back on even keel before they returned to their dignified professions as money managers, physicians, and board directors.

Ellie spent a good part of her week meeting with the ladies of the various committees. She was consulting on the flowers for the dinner dance, was in charge of the place cards, and was coordinating the program with the printer. Conversations varied according to the group. The older women who dominated the flower committee were overly solicitous of her opinion and sympathetic to her difficulties. Ellie assumed that they realized that her thesis and her husband's political needs were stretching her to her limit. "I'm doing fine," she responded to questions of concern, and "I love working with flowers," assured them that she didn't mind her committee assignments. She never suspected that they were aware of the rumor about her husband and her mother's helper. Ellie didn't even know that there was such a rumor.

The place cards were difficult because the seating preferences changed constantly. People who were seated with the Browns suddenly wanted to be seated with the Smiths, which left one table with empty chairs while another was overcrowded. Changing the floor layout was only a partial solution that left some requests impossible to honor and brought gasps of outrage from women who were told that they would have to stay put. The outright anger, she guessed, was as much due to resentments over Theresa as to her inability to solve a seating problem.

The program arrangements demonstrated that every young woman in the club had been an art major. Committee members who were supposed to simply bring in advertising from their husband's companies suddenly decided that they were graphic designers. Changes were being made without Ellie's comment as if she were known to be spatially challenged and color blind. She was annoyed because people were acting as if her opinion didn't matter, unaware that she was considered a public fool for turning her husband over to her babysitter.

"You know, Gordon," she said in a phone conversation, "I'm not sure that I like our *friends* at the club. Maybe next summer we could try a different kind of vacation."

He had agreed with her, but when he returned late Friday, he climbed onto the yellow school bus and joined the other members in supervising the pit digging. For most of the evening, he stayed with the crowd guarding the keg atop the sand dune, trying not to be singled out by Cecil Mapleton or Jack O'Connell. But the insinuations of his relationship with the family au pair had apparently found a much wider audience. Several of the men who came up for refills made remarks that hinted at his supposed affair.

Phil Stucky asked about Ellie in a perfunctory way, but showed all his bridgework when he asked about "that little girl who's been *servicing* you." He instantly corrected himself, "I meant *serving* of course," but then chuckled at the men standing around them. Harvey Smedler, a Boston urologist who spent four-day weekends aboard his forty-foot power cruiser, reminded the group that Don McNeary was escorting Theresa to the dance. "Tough to compete with those young studs," he said to Gordon with professional sincerity, and then laughed so vigorously that he spilled his beer down the front of his shirt. "Maybe you ought to see me for an implant," he howled between his breathless guffaws.

"Maybe you shouldn't drink more than you can handle," Gordon said. He grabbed the cup from Harvey's hand and poured out the little that was left. "Oh, touchy, touchy!" Phil Stucky cackled, encouraging Harvey Smedler to reached out and knock Gordon's beer up into his face. Reflexively, Gordon slapped Harvey's hand aside, which was all the jarring that the doctor needed to lose his footing atop the dune. He flailed wildly for an instant, clutching at air, and then tumbled down the sandy slope.

"For Christ's sake, Gordon, he was just joking around," Stucky protested.

"My arm!" Harvey Smedler screamed once he had stopped rolling. "I broke my arm." He tried to sit up but succeeded only in losing his balance. He yelped with pain as he rolled even farther down the slope.

Stucky led the rescue party down the dune, leaving Gordon in the company of two totally sloshed members at the top. They got Smedler to his feet and then looked back up at Gordon, screaming and shaking fists, like a mob below the walls of a palace.

"You didn't have to hit him!" someone hollered.

"Call the police," another voice demanded.

"You'll pay for this," Smedler threatened. "You'll hear from my lawyer!"

Gordon refilled his paper cup and wandered down the other side of the dune. He took the next shuttle back to the club so he wouldn't have to face Stucky or Smedler again.

At home, he explained his early return and wet shirt to Ellie as the result of some "good-natured kidding." He didn't want to be specific over what the teasing was about, nor did he add he would probably be charged with assault before the weekend was out. But he did refer to his fellow members as "a bunch of assholes," and repeated his support for a different summer vacation next year.

In bed, they lay silently, side by side, staring up at the moving reflections on the ceiling, cast by the moonlight on the bay. Ellie was thinking of the damage that an academic scandal could cause to both their careers. Gordon was rehearsing for the moment when Ellie became aware of the snide talk about him and Theresa. He figured it would happen the next day when the details of his slapping match with Harvey Smedler became general news. He had decided to acknowledge that he had overreacted to Harvey's comments, which certainly were never meant to be taken seriously. But, he would say, he was just being protective of the girl's feelings. Theresa, he would explain, wouldn't understand the kind of ribbing that went on among the members, and might think that she was actually being accused of something.

But the difficult moment never materialized the next day when they arrived at the beach with their picnic gear, children, and mother's helper. Most of the members greeted them with a wave and a shouted "hello," and those who didn't were plainly involved in arranging their own picnic tables and blankets. The children dashed immediately to the beach with Theresa right at their heels. Ellie was dragged away by a woman who simply couldn't sit with the people assigned to her table and demanded one last change to the seating. Gordon was left alone, feeling as if he had been locked into Puritan-era stocks and was being stared at by everyone in the community. As he looked around he caught

Tom Cameron looking back in his direction, which seemed to confirm his suspicions.

Cameron ambled over, accepted the offered beer, and slumped into one of Gordon's beach chairs.

"I suppose you heard about last night," Gordon said, getting right to the inevitable.

Commodore Cameron nodded. "Sure did. Smedler made a perfectly innocent comment intended to be humorous. You flew off the handle, cold-cocked him when he wasn't looking, and sent him tumbling down the hill, severely bruising his right shoulder and elbow."

"I thought his arm was broken."

"No! As a doctor he was able to figure out that it wasn't broken, but he has pointed out that severe sprains and damaged ligaments can take much longer to heal than a simple broken bone."

"Did he mention that he was suing me?"

"He did, and then he added that he was also suing the club, hinting that he would drop that action only if the board agreed to banish you from our midst."

"Consider it done," Gordon said. "I'll resign effective the end of the season. I'd like to stay on for the rest of this year only because it's probably too late for me to get a decent slip."

Cameron was shaking his head while Gordon spoke. "Absolutely not. The first rule of running a stuck-up club is that it's better to lose a urologist than to lose a United States congressman. I told him that if he persisted in suing us I'd have to ask for his resignation. So he decided that suing you would be justice enough."

Gordon mumbled a few words of gratitude. Tom Cameron usually found a way to get to the heart of the matter, which was why he was continuously elected as the club's commodore. "Just tell me what will make it easy for you Tom," he added. "I could always be too busy to show up for any of the club functions."

"No, I wouldn't go that far. Just resist the urge to kill Dr. Smedler. And try to ignore the remarks of some of the members. Your babysitter is creating quite a sensation, and the lads need room to react to her."

"Tom, she shouldn't have to—"

The commodore's hand was in the air demanding silence. "You don't have to tell me that you're not having your way with the young lady. The whole idea is disgusting. But when you overreact to a bit of rib-bing, you just lend credence to the rumor."

"I'm a public figure," Gordon answered. "They can say what they want and there isn't one damn thing I can do about it."

"I'll put a stop to it whenever I can," Cameron assured, pushing on the arms of the chair to raise himself back to his feet. "And you just ignore it."

Gordon nodded. "I'll do my best."

"Give me a day or two," Cameron added, "and I'll tell Smedler that a suit would hurt the club's reputation. I'll urge him to be satisfied with an apology."

"Seems I'm apologizing to everyone."

Tom Cameron paused. "Probably it wasn't the best idea to bring a girl like that into a club like this. If she were hanging out with one of the Puerto Ricans in the kitchen everyone would probably think it was cute. But when she starts winning boyfriends away from their daughters, that isn't cute."

"Jesus, Tom. I didn't ask young McNeary to take her to the dance."

"No, but you did set her in front of him. No one is forgiving you for that."

Ellie and Gordon spent the day with their kids, and even took them as partners for the sack race and the egg-throwing contest. They made repeated trips to the pit to fill their plates with lobsters and clams, and both were enjoying a contented glow by the time the softball game started.

Gordon found himself catching. When Harvey came up to bat he used the occasion to apologize. "Fuck you," came the reply, and while still facing the pitcher, Smedler added, "you can tell it to my lawyer."

"Well, at least I'm happy your arm has healed," Gordon said, bringing a howl of laughter from the umpire.

Most of their other tormentors were completely civil. The women complimented Ellie on the program, praised her children's behavior, and showed open-mouthed awe when they learned that she had finished her dissertation. They even marveled at the praise she bestowed on Theresa. "She was a great research assistant," she said, stressing *assistant*.

"Amazing what they're able to do," a woman complimented, talking about Theresa as if she were a trained seal.

The men seemed to realize that they might have gone a bit too far. "Too bad about your run-in with Smedler," Jack O'Connell said when they were both standing on second base. "But from what I hear, *he* had it coming to him." The emphasis on *he* was a signal that Jack certainly

137

wasn't admitting any responsibility for his own altercation with Gordon. Even Cecil Mapleton seemed to go out of his way to offer a greeting once he was sure that he was out of his wife's earshot.

After the game, Theresa took the children home to get them ready for bed. Ellie and Gordon gathered around the ashy embers with some of the other couples, sipped wine, and watched the sun turn into a fireball as it dropped into the bay behind them. Darkness came quickly, and the last points of light disappeared from the bottom of the pit. Slowly, couples gathered their things together, and began lugging them back to the cars.

In their earlier search for isolation, Ellie and Gordon had pitched their camp far down the beach. Now, as they carried the final cooler to the van, they realized that they were almost alone. Their Range Rover stood in empty space, and the long line of tail lights was already moving off in the distance.

"Are we in a hurry?" Gordon asked suggestively.

Ellie smiled. "I have no place that I have to be."

"It's been a long time since we went skinny-dipping," he said.

She winced. "I'm not sure I liked it even then. Cold water, and then trying to pull underwear over wet sandy skin." She gave an exaggerated shudder.

His hand was falling down onto her butt. "You said you liked it."

"I lied. What I really liked was what came afterwards."

"After you pulled on your sandy undies?"

"No, after the swim, before we got dressed. That was my favorite part."

"Mine too," Gordon said. "So why don't we skip the swim and get right to our favorite parts." He began steering her away from the parking lot and back into the high dunes.

"Suppose we run into somebody?" Ellie asked mischievously.

"We'll just look the other way, and hope that they have the good sense to follow our example."

They began climbing the first hill into the tall grass. Ellie said, "Caught screwing on the beach after a drunken clambake! What would that do to your political career?"

"I'd be symbol of virtue once the word got out that I was with my own wife. The people in Washington would be flabbergasted."

They stopped abruptly as someone moved in the grass directly ahead.

"Who's there?" said a woman's voice that was instantly muffled by a man's "Shhh!"

Ellie giggled.

"We're here!" Gordon answered. "Who's there?"

He heard scurrying. Amid muffled voices there were sounds of legs sliding in pants and blouses being pulled over hair.

"Hey, don't hurry on our account," Gordon said. "We'll find our own place." But two figures jumped up to a half crawl and tried to escape up the next hill. The girl's footing failed in the soft sand and she began to slip backward. The man turned to catch her hand.

"Don," Ellie blurted, catching a glimpse of his face in the pale moonlight. The man stopped scrambling toward the top and turned full face to his accuser. "Eh . . . hi, Mrs. Acton," Don McNeary said.

Trish Mapleton rose up next to him, straightening her blouse in the process. "Hello Mrs. Acton . . . Mr. Acton."

"The Actons aren't here," Gordon said. "In fact, no one is here." He took Ellie's hand and pulled her away toward the parking lot. But her open-mouthed face kept looking back at the two young people. "Goodnight . . . " Ellie managed to say.

Trish waved feebly. "Goodnight . . ."

"Yeah, see ya!" Don added.

Gordon was chuckling on the way back to the car. "Boy, that was close. If we had started ten minutes earlier it would have been them walking in on us."

"That's terrible," Ellie said.

He laughed louder. "Lighten up, will you? You said that was your favorite part."

"It's awful!"

Gordon still didn't register her concern. "Boy, I wish Cecil Mapleton knew that I knew what I know. That would be the end of all his shit about Theresa not being right for the club. 'Not the same standards,' " he said, mocking Cecil's reserved voice. " 'Not the right breeding.' " He could hardly contain his glee. "Well the ones with the right breeding are screwing around by the fire hydrant!"

"Theresa will be devastated," Ellie said, interrupting his reverie.

"She won't find out. Who's going to tell her? Not either of them!"

They were driving around the bay when Ellie suddenly said, "My God, I'll bet they're the ones."

"What ones?"

"The ones who turned me in. Theresa is telling Don how much she's done on my paper, and Don is telling Trish."

"I don't follow."

Ellie turned in her seat and leaned into Gordon's face. "It's so simple! We suspected Theresa because she was the only one who could know how much of my work she had done. But we had a hard time believing it because Theresa had no reason to hurt me. But she might be telling Don just to score points with a college man. And Don is telling Trish under a beach blanket. So little Trish knows everything that's going on, and she hates my guts because I hired a Latina girl to do her job."

He pursed his lips for a moment and then decided, "It's pretty far-fetched. And it doesn't explain the missing videotape."

"Theresa wouldn't have made a tape of my notes. She has no intention of turning me in. And Trish wouldn't need a tape. All she's going to do is write anonymous poison-pen letters."

Gordon pretended to be weighing her problem, but he was really thinking of his own. Theresa had told him how much money she needed not thirty seconds before she had mentioned that she taped everything. Coincidence, perhaps. But she had certainly made a video of the kids and then made a copy of that. So there *was* a tape and it *was* missing.

"Do you think I'm right?" Ellie interrupted.

"It's possible," he conceded. Theresa could have been bragging to Don, perhaps even showing him some of her notes just to prove she was doing college-level work. And when Don was with Trish, he might well have ridiculed Theresa. "Dumb jerk thinks she's smart enough for graduate school." But the whole scenario was a bit of a stretch. Don probably didn't have to pretend to be interested in Theresa's mind in order to win her over. And he certainly didn't need to compromise Theresa just to get Trish out of her underwear. He was a big, good-looking stud. The girls were falling into his arms.

"Or maybe," Ellie considered, "they're working together. Maybe Don just hangs around with Theresa so he can get information for his bed partner."

"Now that's beginning to sound paranoid," he cut her off, leading his wife to turn away abruptly and stare angrily out the window.

Paranoid, my ass, Ellie thought. Trish was furious when I brought

Theresa on the scene, and it's perfectly reasonable that the little bitch would want to get back at me. And what's paranoid about believing that Don McNeary would drag information out of Theresa to score points with his favorite squeeze?

The evidence couldn't be any plainer to Ellie. McNeary had come on big time to Theresa, inviting her to the main event. And now, the night before he's supposed to show his affection for Theresa, he's off in the dunes with Trish. What more proof did Gordon need?

Gordon was still hung up on the tape, and his biggest fear was that Theresa might have given it to Don. You're being more paranoid than Ellie, he berated himself. And yet, he could imagine a scenario where Theresa would brag to McNeary that she had been woman enough for the future congressman, and McNeary would call her bluff. "Oh yeah," Theresa would say, *well I can prove it. I've got it all on tape!*"

Was McNeary really stringing Theresa along? Were he and Trish telling their friends about Mr. Acton and his babysitter? Was that why so many of the club members were intimating that he was sleeping with the young girl?

But it hadn't been McNeary or Trish Mapleton who had hinted they could use a little financial support. That had been Theresa, and she had coupled her comment with a reminder that she had all her summer experiences on tape.

The possibilities were endless, and none of them were good. Or, was it just his own feelings of guilt that were torturing him with images of his disgrace?

They heard Theresa playing the flute as they stepped through the porch door. The tune was simple and mournful, much more emotional than the intricate Mozart pieces that she usually practiced, and Ellie and Gordon paused outside the front door until she had finished. When they entered, they found Theresa seated cross-legged in the center of the living room, her head down, the flute lowered into her lap. There was no sheet music to be seen, the piece had come from memory.

Theresa looked up when she sensed their presence but didn't seem at all startled. "It's something I wrote," she said.

"Beautiful!" Gordon complimented sincerely.

"I'm nearly crying," Ellie added. "It's so sad . . . so emotional."

"I thought I might teach it to Molly. She says she loves it."

"She'll never make it sound like that," Ellie answered.

"I think she will. Not right away, but it's a piece that she'll like to practice because she's able to feel it. Most of the music I was taught was just notes. So, whenever I was getting bored, or discouraged, I'd just kick back and play this. It sort of reminded me what I could accomplish when I made up my mind."

Gordon realized that the last few words had been delivered directly to him. For an instant he imagined that he was hearing a warning.

Theresa unwound herself and stood up with her flute. "I was wondering," she asked, "if you could spare me for a few minutes tomorrow? Real early, like five o'clock?"

"I suppose so," Ellie allowed.

"I should be back before breakfast so I'll be able to feed the kids."

"We still remember how to feed them," Gordon joked.

"I just wanted to wish Don good luck in the dinghy race. It starts at dawn."

Gordon glanced to his wife. If Ellie thought she should tell Theresa whom they had met in the dunes, this was the time to do it. He was relieved when she answered, "It's no problem, Theresa. And stay as long as you want. We'll get the kids started."

Theresa bubbled with gratitude, and ran off as if she had just seen the Easter Bunny.

When Ellie heard her door close she told Gordon, "If Don McNeary is using that girl I swear to God I'll . . ." She shook her head at the thought of punishments too terrible to mention.

"I thought it was Trish you wanted to kill!"

"From what we saw tonight, one bullet would get them both."

TWENTY-EIGHT

The dinghies had been lined up the night before with their bows pulled up on the sand and the engines lowered into the water. They were a ragtag collection of boats, some rowing skiffs used to get out to the moorings, some sailing dinghies with their masts now down and stowed, and several rubber inflatables. All were dwarfed by their oversized engines. They usually moved quite briskly on the two-to-five horsepower outboards that their designs specified. But in this event, engines of up to fifty horsepower were allowed. The idea was to use enough raw power to lift the tiny hull almost completely out of the water. The speeds were spectacular and admittedly dangerous.

The contestants, a man and a woman for each boat, stood at the shoreline with life jackets over their bathing suits. They all looked east, where the sky was pink above the dune line of the barrier beach. The cannon on the yacht club porch would fire the starting signal the second that the sun popped up over the far edge of the ocean.

Spectators were assembled on the porch: parents and friends of the young people racing, fitness freaks who had planned to take in the start as part of a morning jog, and the more socially interested members who were nursing last night's hangovers with this morning's Bloody Marys. Commodore Cameron and the heads of the weekend planning committee were grouped around the ceremonial cannon. Cameron touched the glowing wick to the powder charge as soon as the cherry-red shape appeared, and the report was still echoing across the bay when it was drowned in the roar of outboards.

Like the other crew members, Trish had grabbed the bow of Don's rubber inflatable and spun it off the sand into the water. She was jumping aboard as Don pushed the boat off and leaped in over the motor. The engine growled into life on the first pull of the cord, and screamed to full power within two or three seconds. All along the beach, the contestants kicked up churning wakes that crested into breakers. In an instant, the fleet of twelve racers, carrying twenty-four volunteers for the morning cleanup, was screaming in a line out into the bay.

One boat was lost within seconds. It fell slightly behind the boats to either side, bounced in the churn of their wakes, arced into the air, and landed on its side. Its captain and crew skidded across the water and came up laughing. The chase boat, which pushed off from the yacht club pier, sped to the rescue.

The pack began to spread out. Some of the captains moved closer to the barrier beach hoping to pick up speed in the lee where the sea was smoother. Others tended to the mainland side of the bay, trying to catch a current that generally flowed outward. But the boats that had made the quickest starts clung to a straight-line course toward the turning marker at the end of South Beach Island. McNeary's boat led this group, dueling with an eight-foot fiberglass dinghy. Don figured that with the boats in the air as much as in the water, sea conditions and tide wouldn't make up for a longer route. The throttle on his thirty-horse outboard was turned wide open, and he planned to duke it out on raw speed.

Trish sat on the wooden floorboard, her knees locked under the rubber rowing seat to keep herself from bouncing out. Basically, she was ballast, positioned just forward of center to counteract the weight of Don and the engine at the stern. The greater weight at the back assured that the boat wouldn't bury its nose and flip. But still, some weight was needed up front to keep the inflatable relatively flat so that it would skim across the wave tops.

McNeary kept repositioning her with loud, angry commands. "Forward, damn it! Get your ass under the seat. You let the bow come up and we'll flip over backwards."

"Shut up, Don. I can't get any more forward."

"Then lean over the seat. Get your weight up front!"

He was leaning forward against her back, his arm stretched back to the outboard tiller. "Slide under the seat," he screamed.

"I don't fit. The space is too small."

"Put your head back, damn it!" He tugged her hair down between his knees. "Now slide forward." He pushed her shoulders, sliding her forward along the deck until her life preserver caught under the seat.

"I can't move," Trish screamed.

"Don't!" he yelled at her. "That's good. We're flattening out."

She kept inching herself forward, trying to get her shoulders and head out from under the seat.

"For Christ's sake, stay put!" Don ordered.

"This bouncing is killing me. I've got to sit up!"

"Stay put. We're going great."

They were skipping like a rock, hopping from wave top to wave top, and pulling away from the fiberglass dinghy. McNeary hunched lower until he could barely see over the air-filled rubber bow. By cutting wind resistance, he added even more to his lead.

Trish kept inching herself around in a circle, working to get her head past the seat so that she could sit up on the other side. Then she would be able to stretch her legs rearward, still using the rowing seat to keep herself from flying out.

They were nearing the turning point, a shallow draft marker at the far end of the South Beach Island sandbar. One of the club officers had motored out to the marker before sunrise, and was beached on the bar to make sure that none of the contestants cut the turn short. Don planned to cut back on the power when they reached the marker, and have both Trish and himself lean to the inside. He knew he would lose some of his lead to the dinghy that was trailing him. But if he stayed flat, the inflatable would skid sideways, increasing the risk that she would flip over. The dinghy, which had a rounded bottom with the suggestion of a keel, could easily turn inside of him.

They came to the marker, with the dinghy just ahead of their wake. Don noticed that one of the inflatables that had chosen the lee near the barrier beach was converging toward the turning point. "Lean in!" he screamed into Trish's face, indicating the marker side. He turned the throttle back. His boat buried into the sea and heeled to port, giving him a tight turn around the marker. The dinghy came up inches behind. And, at that moment, the other inflatable came sliding sideways toward the marker, lost control in the double wakes, and slammed into the dinghy. Both boats spun off the track, the dinghy burying its stern and filling with water while the inflatable flipped and dumped its crew.

Don glanced back to see the committee boat power off the bar and head out to the laughing foursome bobbing in the waves. "Yahoo!" he yelled, waving his fist in victory. "We've got this thing won by a mile." He turned up the throttle.

"Yahoo!" Trish echoed, for an instant actually enjoying the race.

At that moment, the air-filled freeboard on the port side burst in an explosion that was followed by the hiss of escaping air. The boat turned sharply into the beach, ripping the speed control and tiller out of Don's hand. The power increased their rate of spin, throwing them both over the side. Then the boat fired like a pinwheel until its engine broke free and sunk to the bottom. The boat listed to its deflated side until only the starboard hull was above water.

Back at the turning marker, the rest of the racing fleet slowed to be sure that the two crews from the collision were safe with the committee boat. Then they throttled up in the final dash for the clambake site and the second-place ribbon. Everyone assumed that McNeary's boat had maintained its considerable lead and had the first place trophy easily won.

It was half an hour later when all the beached crews were working on the cleanup that someone noticed Don and Trish were missing. They wasted another ten minutes speculating what the captain and his crew might be doing *instead* of helping with the cleanup, and ten more minutes searching the dunes. Only then did someone count the beached boats and realized that McNeary's inflatable hadn't finished the race.

"Bet the son of a bitch turned around the north end of the island and went straight back to the club," someone guessed. "Yeah, that's why we didn't see him ahead," another young man added. But even while they were agreeing on the possibility, other voices couldn't believe that Don would ever pass up the winner's trophy. "Not with Trish aboard," they agreed.

The first call from the ranger station came as owners of the docked yachts were setting up their boats for the afternoon's guests. "The kids here are asking whether Don McNeary and Trish Mapleton are back at the club?" the ranger asked. "Their boat didn't make it out here to the beach."

The sense of alarm was mixed with a bit of skepticism. Ellie and Gordon were pretty sure they knew where the two young people probably were. Other members, who didn't know what the Actons had interrupted in the dunes, guessed that they might be playing some sort of prank. "Someone ought to kick their asses," Jack O'Connell advised. "You don't play games when it comes to boating safety."

Commodore Cameron couldn't afford to be cynical. He ordered the committee boat to turn around and run back over the racecourse. Then he commandeered three boats to search the shoreline of the barrier beach and the island. "You're wasting your time," some of the party crews told him. "They're pulling your leg."

"I guess they're not your kids," Cameron answered as he cast off. But only a few moments later, all the naysayers were casting off lines and putting out to sea. The park rangers had found the wreckage of the missing inflatable, with no one near or aboard.

Ellie and Gordon were tight-lipped as they motored across the bay, their makeshift cocktail bar still set up in the cockpit. They turned at the northern tip of South Beach Island, and ran south, as close into the shore as they dared. Within minutes they were joined by the rest of the fleet, assembled as an armada on the eastern shore where the inflatable had been found. Boats turned across and between one another as they conducted a disorganized search, threatening collisions that might put more survivors in the water. Gordon turned away, deciding to search farther out to sea.

"What do you think happened to them?" Ellie finally asked.

He shook his head. "Maybe they were involved in the collision that

146

sank the other two boats. Maybe, in the confusion . . ." He shrugged indicating that he really had no idea.

"I was really hoping to be rid of Trish Mapleton," Ellie confessed. "But not like this."

Gordon agreed, "No, not like this." But if Theresa had been sharing her sexual conquests, then he wouldn't mind being rid of *both* of them, and maybe Theresa as well. He knew he could never feel comfortable with his whole future in the hands of a bunch of malicious frat rats. And *like this* wouldn't be all that bad. A nice public accident at sea where an inquiry would open and adjourn in about ten minutes. *"What are we looking for?"* a coroner would say. "We all know what happened."

"Oh my God. They've found something on the beach." Ellie's knuckles were pressed against her teeth. Gordon looked toward the shore and saw all the boats converging on one point. "Looks that way," he agreed, swinging the bow at the beach and opening the throttle.

I don't really want them dead, Ellie told herself. Please, God, don't let me think about it. She had to want them alive no matter what the consequences to herself. Only a monster would put her own graduate credentials ahead of the lives of two young people. There had to be some other way to keep her secret; something less drastic than having two people drown.

Gordon was peering anxiously over the bow. Several of the powerboats had beached. The deep-draft sailboats were standing off just a short distance. "Doesn't look good," he said. "There's a lot of arm waving going on." Theresa had sworn that she would never tell anyone. So his secret was probably safe with her, particularly if he anted up her college costs. But Don and Trish couldn't be tactfully bought off. If Theresa had told them anything, or shown them the tape, then those two were the end of his marriage, and, even more painful, the end of his political career. He had mixed feelings about the activity taking place on the beach.

"They find them?" he called to another sailboat that was heading away from the shore.

"Yeah, they found them."

"They okay?"

"They wouldn't be if they were my kids."

Ellie shook her head slowly. "Thank God . . ."

Gordon maneuvered up close to another sailboat. "Where were they?" he shouted.

"Over on the bay side. They said their boat broke up. When the race passed and nobody missed them, they went over to the bay side where they figured people would see them. The McNeary kid says they've been standing over there for the past hour."

Both captains shook their heads in disbelief. "They didn't see all the boats heading to this side?" Gordon wondered aloud.

"Sure, that's why they came back across the island. But that don't explain why it took 'em half an hour to walk a few hundred yards."

Gordon thought of the night before. "What could have delayed them?" he asked.

"I been wondering that myself," the other captain said with a leering laugh.

They motored away from the commotion, and Gordon poured two of the Bloody Marys that they had prepared for their guests. Ellie slipped to the back of the cockpit and settled next to him.

"I'm glad they're safe," she said, trying to convince herself as much as her husband.

"Of course you are." Gordon supposed that he was happy too, although *lost at sea* would have gone a long way to ease his anxiety. He was getting desperate to find out exactly who knew what, whether there was a videotape, and when they would play their hand. He might even welcome a blackmail note just to end the suspense. A drowning might even have been more welcome.

They moored stern-to and opened their cockpit to the guests who were beginning to recapture the party spirit. Jack O'Connell settled in and informed everyone in the area that the lost boat incident had been a prank. "Kids hiding in the tall grass while the rest of us are looking for them! I think they ought to have their butts kicked."

The Mapletons were incensed that anyone would think their daughter would be party to a scam. "The kids were right to cross the island to the bay side. Made it possible for them to signal for help," Cyril grunted. "Only sensible decision anyone made all day." Pricilla added that they had done exactly what she would have done.

The Stuckys thought that the kids were lucky to be alive. "Those hopped-up boats are too damn dangerous," Phil said. "We ought to cancel the whole event, or maybe change it to a sailing race."

By early afternoon, the bar business at the Acton boat slowed enough so that Ellie and Gordon could visit some of their neighbors.

They were walking carefully along a floating slip when Tom Cameron caught them from behind. "Mind if I borrow your husband for a few minutes?" Ellie protested that she didn't like to drink alone. "Order a soft drink," Cameron answered. "I'll have him back in just a couple of minutes."

Gordon saw the seriousness in the commodore's manner. "Something wrong?" he asked.

"I hope not. But I'm afraid you're going to tell me that something is very wrong."

"Me?"

"You know anything about those inflatables your company manufactures?"

"Sure. But that wasn't one of my boats."

Cameron nodded and kept walking, leading Gordon around the clubhouse to the workshop where motors were tuned and rigging repaired. Don McNeary's boat, deflated and wrinkled like a prune, was hung across three sawhorses. The fabric had been pulled smooth along the port hull to show a jagged tear.

"Jesus," Gordon gasped. "It's a wonder they weren't killed. This thing must have turned somersaults."

"What do you think about the tear?"

Gordon took the heavy fabric in his hands and folded it away from the gaping hole. He noticed thin slices at each end of the wound and deep cuts above and below. "Yeah, I see what you mean. Something is very wrong. This was no accident."

"You're sure?" Cameron questioned.

"Well, not positive. But these things never fail in the center of the material. If they go, it's always at a seam or a fitting. And you can see cut marks through the canvas and right into the rubber. Looks like someone took a knife to this thing. A very sharp knife."

"It couldn't have been a rock, or maybe clam shells?" The commodore was giving Gordon every chance to modify his opinion.

"I doubt it. The only natural thing that could have done this would be coral, and I don't think we have any coral reefs off Cape Cod."

Tom Cameron took a deep breath. "Well, you're confirming what the Coast Guard told me. It looks as if someone cut it so that it would blister and explode. They could have just punctured it and let it deflate on the beach. But it looks as if they wanted it to fail during the race."

"Sick," Gordon offered as the only possible explanation.

"Or damn foolishness by one of the competitors. Remember a couple of years back when someone drained one of the two-cycle outboards and replaced the fuel with straight gasoline."

Gordon smiled. He remembered the engine seizing and the boat dying so rapidly that it took water over the bow. "Yeah. It was pretty funny until we all realized that the engine could have overheated and exploded." He spent another minute examining the fabric. "Sick, or damn stupid," he concluded. "I assume you want this kept quiet."

Cameron nodded. "For the time being, although I have to ask people questions so I suppose it will get out pretty quickly."

Gordon turned away from the wreck. "Well, I won't tell anyone."

Cameron spoke as he followed out of the shed. "You're one of the people I have to ask a question," he said, pulling Gordon up short. "You know that your girl was down here real early? Our watchman noticed her hanging around the boats."

He recoiled from the implication. "Theresa? Oh, for Christ's sake. She came down to wish the McNeary kid good luck. He's taking her to the dance tonight."

Now Tom showed surprise. "That'll be interesting. He's taking the Mapleton girl, too."

"What? That can't be."

"Well, maybe I'm wrong. But that's beside the point. She got down to the beach early, even before the contestants. She was alone with the boats for half an hour."

"Tom, I don't think she's strong enough to cut through that skin. And she's never seen an inflatable before in her life. She wouldn't have any idea of how to cut one so that it would blister under pressure."

"With a razor, or one of those box cutters, she wouldn't have to be all that strong."

Gordon's temper was beginning to heat up. "She doesn't have a razor or a box cutter. And if she did, she wouldn't know what to do with them. Christ, Tom, this *has* to be one of the guys in the race who wanted McNeary to lose."

"Most likely," Cameron conceded. "But I have to check up on everything. Maybe you could ask her if she saw anyone else around there early this morning. Or, can she remember who were the first people to show up."

"I'll ask her," Gordon promised. "But do me a favor and don't mention anything about Theresa. She has enough problems with some of the members already."

Cameron agreed. "Yeah, I suppose there are some folks who would like to see her blamed."

Gordon was morosely silent when he returned to the dockside party. He barely nodded to acknowledge conversations, and never refilled his near-empty glass. It was still early in the afternoon when he pulled Ellie aside and told her that they should be leaving.

"I knew something was wrong," she said, as soon as they were in their car. "When you came back from your stroll with Tom Cameron you looked like you were getting sick."

"I was. Damn sick!"

"What did Cameron say to you?"

"That our mother's helper tried to kill a couple of people."

Ellie gasped and tried to form words. The best she could manage was an astounded "What?"

He told her about the hole in the inflatable boat, going into detail about the way the canvas and the rubber had been cut. He didn't think it could have been an accident. Ellie understood his analysis, and felt her own sense of rage that anyone could do something so obviously dangerous. She echoed her husband's initial reaction, "Sick son of a bitch!" But then she went on the defensive. "Theresa couldn't have been involved in such a thing. She wouldn't know how. And besides, why would she want to hurt Don McNeary? She's crazy about him. She's going to the dance with him."

Gordon told her that Theresa had been seen around the boats early in the morning. "She told us she was going down to the beach to see Don," he reminded his wife. "Don probably wasn't even out of bed yet."

Ellie got legalistic. "So, she had the opportunity. But she doesn't have the skill to do it, and certainly doesn't have any motive."

"That's what I thought," Gordon agreed. But then he told her what Cameron had said about Don being paired up with Trish.

"Oh, Jesus, he wouldn't. No one could be that much of a bastard."

"Maybe not. But if someone is pushing it as rumor, and Theresa got wind of it, then she'd certainly have a motive. Hell, if I had heard about it I probably would have tried to kill the two of them myself."

She sat quietly until they pulled into the driveway. "I guess I'm beginning to believe it," she announced quietly.

Gordon didn't move to get out after he had stopped the engine. "I thought it was ridiculous myself. But then I saw that it kind of fit a pattern." Ellie, who had reached for the door handle, took her hand back and gave him her full attention.

"Remember, the first thing she did was lie to us. Hungry brothers and sisters to take care of. Fed them, dressed them, and got them to church every Sunday. None of it was true."

Ellie didn't need reminding. True, there had been mitigating factors, and she had pretty much put the initial interview behind her. But on the face of it, the girl had played very loose with the truth.

"She didn't swim," Gordon went on, "but you found a photo of her swimming with a group of her friends. And she didn't know how to dress, but she picked bathing suits that knocked the guys' eyes out."

Ellie was nodding. "All true," she agreed.

"Then she turns out to be a computer whiz. She never told us that she knew anything about computers, but we find out that she can break into half the databases in the country. So at a minimum, we know Theresa is devious, and maybe a downright liar."

Instinctively Ellie jumped to her defense. "I can't go that far. I think she's made a lot of mistakes trying to belong. She played humble and downtrodden, thinking that was what we expected. I think she may have been afraid of coming on too strong."

Gordon knew that Theresa had no trouble coming on strong, but he couldn't argue that point. His evidence was between the sheets.

"But, frankly, this boat thing disturbs me," Ellie continued. "If she learned that Don had been stringing her along, I would expect her to be crushed, disappointed, embarrassed, and damn angry. I wouldn't expect her to do something violent."

"Maybe she found out when she got down to the boats and just went berserk!" Gordon wondered out loud.

"No," Ellie contradicted. "If she did it, then she brought the razor, or the box cutter, or whatever with her. One of the kids from the clambake may have told her that Don and Trish were headed into the dunes. Maybe someone told her that Don was going to stand her up for the dance. By the time we got home she already had plans to be down at the beach first thing in the morning."

Gordon nodded, suspecting his wife was right.

"So, I guess I don't want her around my children," Ellie concluded. "I think we have to tell her that the summer is over."

Gordon felt instant panic. Throw her out, and she'd be talking to the press within hours. If Theresa had tried to hurt Don McNeary, she certainly wouldn't have any problems hurting him. "Let's not be too hasty," he advised. "Remember, she can still make things very difficult for you with the graduate committee."

Ellie sighed. "I know. But whatever problems she can cause me are nothing compared to what she might cause Molly and Timmy. The kids will be safe with a sitter tonight while Theresa is with us at the dance. And tomorrow, I won't let them out of my sight."

"Maybe we should give this just a bit more thought. She may have had nothing to do with that boat."

"I know, but just the fact that we think she might have done it shows that we really don't trust her. And if we don't, then why are we leaving her with our kids?"

"So, when do you want to tell her?"

Ellie thought. "Tomorrow, or Tuesday at the latest. I want to tell her when we're prepared to move her out right away. I don't want her living here for even a day after we've told her she's leaving. That would be the time when she would be most apt to do something that would get back at us."

"What she'll do," Gordon suggested, "is go straight to the phone and call your thesis mentor."

She nodded. "I suppose so. But that's not really the important issue."

Gordon opened the car door and led his wife quietly around to the front of the house and up the porch steps. All the while he was thinking of how he could dissuade Ellie from firing Theresa. He suspected that her first call wouldn't be to Ellie's school but rather to the local papers. Maybe Ellie's doctorate wasn't *the important issue,* but his reputation certainly was. If Ellie dumped Theresa then his political career was over, not to mention his marriage and his lifestyle. Before Ellie did anything, he had to find out if Theresa had made a video in her bedroom. And if she did, he had to find it and destroy it.

TWENTY-NINE

Don's call came late in the afternoon while Theresa was down on the beach with the children. Ellie knew that she should simply take a message and stay clear of whatever painful joke he and Trish were planning. She had already decided that she wanted Theresa out of her family life, and this wasn't the time to start feeling sorry for her. But none of that could overcome the loathing she had for people who could be intentionally cruel. "What time are you picking her up?" she asked the young man.

She heard him gulp down some air. "Ahh . . . that's what I want to talk to her about."

"Just tell me. I'll make sure she's ready." Ellie wasn't going to let him off the hook easily.

"Well, I've got a little problem. I need to see how she feels about it?"

"Feels about what?' Ellie persisted. She knew she was way out of bounds. He was entitled to a private conversation. But if he were going to stand Theresa up, she wanted him to know that it wouldn't be a private giggle among the junior members. She and Gordon would know, and he could assume that all the other parents and members would know as well.

"Ahh . . . well . . . Jack Brewer tore up some knee ligaments during the boat crash today . . . and . . . he was going to take Trish Mapleton."

"How sad for the two of them," Ellie said, her tone dripping in mock sympathy.

"Yeah! Well, Jack can't drive, so I'm going to pick up Trish."

"And then you're coming here?"

"No. My car's a two-seater. So I'm going to Jack's and trade my car for his. Then I'll drive Trish and Jack over to your place and pick up Theresa."

"Oh . . ." Ellie's hostility cooled instantly. "That's very thoughtful of you."

"But I'll be late picking up Theresa, and I wanted to tell her."

Ellie was overjoyed that Don was only going to be late. "I'll tell her as soon as she comes up from the beach."

"Thanks. And could you sort of explain to her why we're all taking her to the dance and not just me?"

"I'll tell her exactly what you told me." She asked after his parents said her good-byes, and then hung up. And suddenly she was bewildered. The accident had happened just this morning, so Theresa couldn't have known about a change in plans last night. And Don was still taking her. So, there was no motive for her to have carved a hole in the boat Don and Trish would be racing. Then exactly why was she sending Theresa packing, especially if she might still need the girl's cooperation for her academic survival?

Gordon was relieved when she relayed the content of her conversation. "You know, I was thinking that we were being too harsh on her," he said. "I'm going to have Tom Cameron deliver that boat to the company lab so that our guys can go over it. Maybe the whole thing *was* an accident." The droning fear that had been with him all afternoon suddenly went silent. He still had time to find a hidden tape.

The deck of the yacht club had been turned into one of the beaches at Bali. Tables were clustered under potted palm trees, and blue lighting rippled across the dance floor like moonlight at the bottom of a lagoon. The white jackets made all the men look like the French planters of the South Seas, and all the women could have been the navy nurses who fell hopelessly in love. The waiters and waitresses were in sailor suits, and the dishes they served were curries and fruits straight from the kitchen of a Trader Vic's. It was hokey, but effective.

Ellie and Gordon were at a table with Emily and Phil Stucky, and Noah and Mary Singleton. Noah, who claimed ancestry from the Mayflower, had the longest European family history on the Cape, and spent most of his time despairing of any changes that had occurred since the turn of the century. Mary ordered his drinks, brought his food, and nodded in agreement to anything he said.

At Phil's insistence, Gordon was discussing the problems of running for political office and in particular the need for substantial advertising dollars. "It's all money these days," Noah lamented. "Used to be that you could just stand up on a soap box and tell folks what you thought."

Not since I was born, Gordon thought, but there was no sense in disagreeing with Noah who would simply remind listeners of his heritage as proof of his position.

"There's no way you can *lose* this election," Phil assured the gathering, "so why do you need to do so much campaigning?" Gordon got into the need to gather widespread support if he hoped to accomplish anything. "Oh, horseshit," Stucky sneered. "All politicians do is take money and screw interns."

"A seat in the Congress used to mean something around here," Noah said.

Ellie was explaining the gist of her doctoral dissertation to Emily and Mary, documenting the superior classroom performance of teachers' children. "But what's the point?" Emily asked, and Ellie explained her idea of using school resources for teaching parents how to teach. "It multiplies the effectiveness of limited funds."

Mary Singleton sneered. "I think we have to go back to corporal punishment."

But while they chatted socially, Ellie and Gordon had their attention fixed on a cluster of tables across the dance floor. The younger set, all children and friends of members, were partying loudly, practicing the tipsy boorishness that was their birthright. Theresa was sitting next to Don, and so was at the very center of the hilarity. But her pretended smile and forced laughter showed that she was really at the periphery. The references to prep schools, coming-out parties, and foreign travel were a strange language to her. She was trying to enjoy jokes that she didn't really understand.

"Do you think she's having a good time?" Gordon whispered to Ellie.

"She's fitting in. It can't be easy for her, but at least she seems to be accepted."

"I just don't believe that she sabotaged Don's boat."

"I don't think so either."

He was hearing what he wanted to hear, but he had to be sure. "So we'll just forget about sending her home. We'll keep her here for the summer."

Ellie was smiling at something that a passing woman was saying. When she had a chance she whispered, "We'll talk about it later."

Gordon waited until he had her attention. "Why later? You still have misgivings?"

She nodded while she pretended to listen to Mary Singleton.

"What misgivings?"

"I'm not completely comfortable leaving her with the kids. Like you said, there's been a pattern. And if we could believe for even a minute that she wanted to hurt someone, then I think we can manage without her." She was immediately commenting on Mary's point of view as if the older woman had her complete attention.

Gordon got up and wandered to the men's room. On the way back, he paused at the bar for a fresh drink, and then ordered another wine spritzer for his wife.

"Great party, Mr. Acton!" It was Don McNeary on his way to the men's room.

"Looks as if you guys are having fun," Gordon said. And as Don was continuing past he called after him, "How's Theresa doing?"

McNeary stopped, puzzled by the question. His expression seemed to ask why wouldn't she be doing fine like all the rest of us. He stepped back to the bar. "She had no problem with my turning it into a double date, if that's what you mean."

"No," Gordon assured. "I didn't mean anything in particular. It's just that she's new here, and I try to make sure that she's happy."

"Oh, no worry there. She loves the place, and she really likes living with you and Mrs. Acton. In fact, she has a video that she keeps promising to show me. All sorts of things that she's been doing during the summer."

The wine spritzer shook in Gordon's hand and splashed out onto the front of his dinner jacket. "Show you?" he gasped.

"Yeah, maybe you can remind her not to forget." Don was smiling broadly as he turned back toward the men's room.

Gordon set both drinks on the bar and dabbed at his coat with a handkerchief. He had to get a look at that tape. Or, at least, he needed a long frank conversation with Theresa. He needed to make her understand that there were a lot of things he could do for her. Tuition help. Summer jobs. Introductions. But he couldn't do any of them if he were run out of Rhode Island on a rail.

"Thanks," Ellie said when he handed her the drink.

"Listen! We need some time before we get rid of Theresa."

Ellie frowned. "Not now, Gordon. Why don't we dance? We haven't danced all evening."

On the dance floor, he held her close and hummed the show tune that the band was playing, but his mind was whirling. She had told Don about the video. Why? Why would she think he would want to see home movies of my kids? Had she told him what she had photographed? Is that why McNeary had on that stupid grin when he mentioned that he was looking forward to seeing the tape? Christ, did Theresa tell him to mention the video? Was this the next step in a shakedown?

"I think we ought to sit on it for a couple of days," he suddenly blurted out.

Ellie pulled away abruptly. "Is that what you're thinking about while you're dancing with me? Theresa, and what she's going to mean to your campaign?"

He could see the anger in her eyes, and he drew her back to him more forcibly than he intended. "That's not it at all. I am thinking about you, and how you ought to get through this hearing before we make an enemy out of the girl."

"I can handle that," she insisted.

"I suppose I can too. But it would be a lot easier to work the press if I weren't being asked about my wife's cheating."

Ellie pulled away. "Everything begins and ends with you, doesn't it. Your only interest in my doctorate is how it affects *your* career."

Nearby eyes focused in their direction. He took Ellie's hand. "Let's walk down to the dock."

"Sure," she answered. "If you promise to talk about something else."

They walked off the floor, nodding politely to friends, and went down the steps to the boat slips. Gordon began talking about fall tides, and the problems they would cause for boats at fixed docks. He commented on the benefits of the floating slip where their boat was moored, but also allowed that they might be a little more vulnerable to a heavy tide. He talked about anything he could think of except Theresa in order to give Ellie's anger time to cool.

"Look," she finally interrupted him in order to get back to the topic she knew he had in mind. "Let's not do anything tomorrow. On Monday, I'll call my mentor and see how things stand. Then we'll know whether we need Theresa to back me up at a hearing."

"Fine with me," Gordon said as if it had been the farthest thing from his mind. "I think that's a sensible approach." He pulled her close so they could share a kiss, which they both enjoyed.

"How would you like to join me under the boardwalk?" he teased. The sandy beach covered by the edge of the club house deck was a dark and private place that had seen many summer romances consummated. Ellie giggled at the suggestion.

"Hey, I'm serious. We could get in a quickie between dance sets."

"Wet sand is just what my dress needs," she told him.

"Oh, is that what you think of when I'm trying to seduce you? Your couture's reputation?"

"Touché," Ellie admitted.

At that moment, two figures emerged from beneath the deck, pausing to wipe sand from their clothes. The girl was having an impossible time because of her basic black, and the man was wiping at his pants legs.

"Let's go," Gordon suggested, "before we become witnesses to this year's scandal."

Ellie turned slowly. "It's them!" she whispered.

"Who?" he asked as he led her back along the deck, away from the new arrivals.

"Trish Mapleton and Don McNeary."

"Oh, shit!" Gordon sighed.

"Our motive is back," Ellie said.

August

THIRTY

They woke up slowly with dry mouths and the taste of last night's liquor still in their throats. Ellie raised her head to the clock and saw that it was nearly ten. She nudged Gordon, hoping that he might start the breakfast, and then eased back into the pillow.

Suddenly, she was wide awake. The children should be up by now, and yet the house was deathly quiet. She bounded up, stepped into jeans and was pulling a tank top over her head as she walked out of her bedroom. Both doors at the far end of the hall were open, and there was no one in either of the bedrooms.

"Gordon!" There was an urgency in her voice that sobered him instantly.

"What is it?" He was already up and searching for his underwear.

"They're gone. She has the children."

"Gone where?" He was hopping into his loafers.

"I don't know. There's no one in the house," she called back from the head of the stairs, then she quickly ran down.

Gordon was right behind her, wearing only his trousers and shoes. "She probably took them down to the beach so that we could get some sleep."

Ellie looked into the kitchen and then stepped out onto the empty screen porch. "They're not on the beach," she called back.

Gordon was past her. "I'll check the garage." They met again in the driveway. "She took the Range Rover. Didn't she leave a note?" He raced up the steps to the house.

She tried to keep up. "I didn't see any note."

They had just reached the porch when they heard a car turn into their driveway. Both of them froze. The car bumped over the loose gravel and skidded to a stop somewhere behind the house. Doors

163

opened and instantly the air was filled with voices. They heard Molly announcing exactly who would get which doughnut, while Timmy kept repeating that he wanted the chocolate one. Next there were footsteps on the outside stairs.

"Where have you been?" Ellie demanded.

Molly pushed open the screen door and headed straight for the kitchen. "We went down to the village. We bought doughnuts."

"I want the chocolate one," said Tim, who was right at his sister's heels.

Theresa came behind them, taking the steps with much less energy. "They were up early. I thought I'd get them out of the house so you could get some sleep."

"You should have told us," Ellie answered. "We were worried."

"I left a note under the coffeepot. I thought that was the one place where you couldn't miss it. And you had to figure that they were with me."

"Still—" Ellie began, but Gordon cut her off with a tug on her elbow.

"Let's get that coffee going," he said.

They kept watching Theresa for signs of distress and anger. Did she know that her date had been under the boardwalk with another girl? Had she known that she was being two-timed all along? Was she planning some diabolic revenge? But there was nothing. She set the plates, poured the milk, and wiped the chocolate from Timmy's face every time he took a bite. In between chores she picked at a French cruller.

"Did you have a good time last night?" Ellie ventured.

"Great," she answered with honest enthusiasm. "The girls were all very nice, and the guys were lots of fun. A couple of them even danced with me. And I want to thank the both of you for letting me go. I mean, getting another sitter and buying me my dress and all . . ."

Gordon waved away the expression of appreciation. "We enjoyed having you with us," he mumbled through a mouthful of Danish.

"Was Don . . . attentive?" Ellie said, knowing that her question sounded ridiculous. But she couldn't ask if he had taken *her* under the boardwalk.

"Yeah, but it wasn't like that. Everyone was sort of with everyone. None of us were really paired off."

Boy, did you miss what was going on, Gordon thought. Don and

Trish were about as paired as two people could get. He watched quietly while Theresa cleaned up after the children and started them up to their rooms to get ready for the beach.

"She doesn't have a clue," Gordon said. "She probably thinks lifeguards always have sand on their suits."

"Or else she's great at covering up her feelings," Ellie added.

As soon as Theresa and the children left for the beach, Ellie got back to her dissertation. It had printed out to over one hundred and fifty pages, and she carried it out onto the porch with her second cup of coffee. Laboriously, she continued with her pencil corrections. She had planned to have Theresa enter the changes because the girl was much more facile with the computer. But now she was going to make the changes herself. She wanted to build a firewall between the girl and the paper.

Gordon got into jeans, a T-shirt, and an old pair of sneakers. He was going up into the attic to look through the stored luggage, and other piles and boxes where the tape could be hidden. If that didn't work out, he was planning a much more thorough search of the garage, and then a trip into the crawl spaces under the front porch. Sometime along the way he planned to suggest to Ellie that they should probably take another look through the young girl's room.

He tried to look casual even though his anxiety was growing into terror. She had told Don something about the videotape. Probably she wasn't planning on showing him the bedroom scenes because once their liaisons were made public she would lose the power she held over the Acton family. But she had told him enough so that he would mention the existence of the video. It was a way of reminding Gordon that his total destruction would take little more than a few seconds.

Where in hell could it be? he tortured himself as he started through the stored luggage. She'd never entrust it to Don or any of the young people. *"Keep this secret for me"* would practically guarantee that it would be the feature film at the next sleepover party. If she had taken it home, or if she mailed it to her foster family there would be every chance that they would play it just to see how she was spending her summer. She wouldn't want that. So, it had to be here, in the house. Or in the garage. And he had to find it and erase the damning scenes.

It was just a few minutes after noon when the telephone rang. "Can you get that?" Gordon called down from the top of the attic stairs. Ellie got up slowly, reading as she walked, the pencil clenched in her teeth. "Hello," she mumbled without dropping the pencil. She knew the call was threatening as soon as she heard the first sound of the voice.

"Tell your son-of-a-bitch husband that he's been cheating with the wrong girl."

The pencil fell as her jaw dropped. "What?"

"You know Gordie has been getting action on the side, don't you?"

Ellie nearly laughed. "Who is this?"

"Just tell your husband that his little secret is out, and that what he's been doing is beneath contempt."

There was a tone of outrage in her voice. Whoever she was, she wasn't making it up. Ellie felt her mouth go dry, and then the first hint of nausea in the pit of her stomach. "Who is this? If you don't tell me I'm going to hang up the phone."

"Ask Gordie who it is. He'll come up with a name."

Ellie slammed the phone down, and then felt her hands begin to shake. The girl was truly distraught over something Gordon was doing, something unspeakable. And she was shaking uncontrollably because she knew that it was true.

"Who was it?" Gordon called from the top of the stairs.

Ellie turned her head in his direction but she couldn't bring herself to even raise her eyes.

"Ellie! Who was on the phone?"

She looked back down at the telephone, and her hands recoiled as if it were too hot to touch. If she lifted it, the accusations would still be there.

She heard footsteps on the stairs. "Ellie, are you all right?"

Her jaw was set, and her eyes were squeezed shut to fight back the tears. He came across the living room to her. "Ellie?" She felt his hand on her shoulder and instinctively she pulled away.

"What's the matter?" Gordon stepped around to get in front of her. "For God's sake, who was on the phone?"

"Someone who says your secret is out. You've been screwing the wrong girl."

For the first time since she had met him, Ellie saw Gordon's face go white with terror. There was no need for him to say anything. His expression told her that he had been caught.

"Who?" he managed to get out.

"Why don't you tell me? Or are there a couple of girls you've been with?"

"Ellie . . ." There was no fight in his voice, not even a hint of denial. He was evaporating right in front of her. "Ellie, I swear to God I didn't mean it. She set me up . . . so she could blackmail me. Just like she's blackmailing you."

For a fraction of a second she was bewildered, but she didn't need to analyze who might be blackmailing her. In a flash of clarity she saw her husband with her young mother's helper.

"Oh no." It was a groan of agony. "Sweet Jesus, it was Theresa. Poor Theresa."

"Ellie, you can see how stupid it is. How . . . shameful. She's got me, and there's nothing I can do about it."

"Theresa? You had sex with Theresa? Where?"

"I was on the porch. It was the day . . ." He was going to tell her about the day when the whole club had turned against him, and how he had been drinking too much. But she cut him off with a scream.

"Here! In our house? You laid her in our house?" And then it was all coming up: last night's drinks, this morning's breakfast, even the ginger ale that she had been sipping while she was editing her dissertation. She pushed him away and ran past him into the bathroom. She fell on her knees and hung her face into the toilet.

Gordon followed instantly, but stopped at the door when he heard her retching. She vomited, then moaned, and then vomited again. He moved slowly into the room and dropped to his knees next to her. He put his arm around her to steady her as she continued being sick.

Ellie pushed his arm away. "Don't touch me. Leave me alone."

"Ellie, please . . ."

"Could you just leave me alone . . ."

"I can't leave you. I love you."

She turned and flailed with her fists against his chest. Gordon made no move to defend himself, which only made Ellie feel that much more powerless. She folded her arms across the spattered rim of the toilet, buried her face, and began crying uncontrollably. Gordon kept his arm around her, feeling the tremors as she sobbed.

Minutes passed before she was able to stop, and still more minutes before she felt strong enough to get to her feet. "Could you give me a few minutes alone?" she asked wearily. "I need to get cleaned up."

He nodded, backed out the door and closed it behind him.

Ellie wiped the rim of the bowl and flushed several times. Then she dabbed at a spot that she had gotten on the front of her tank top. She rinsed her mouth, gargled, and ran a comb through her hair. She took down the rarely used makeup so that she could disguise the whiteness in her cheeks and the dark smudges that had filled in under her eyes. She was barely presentable when she stepped out on the porch and let herself down into a chair across from her husband. For several seconds they both sat in silence.

Gordon knew he had to go first. "I've been sorry ever since it happened. Sorry, and sick with shame."

She kept staring through the screen out over the bay.

"But, in a way, I'm glad you know. Because I never could have told you, and keeping it a secret was killing me."

"I must have looked damn foolish," Ellie said, more to herself than to Gordon. "I'm playing mommy to the girl, and she's playing wifey to you. I know she must have been laughing at me. How about you? Did you think I was pretty much of an ass?"

"God, no. I wasn't laughing. I knew I had hurt you. And I was sitting at the table with the girl who helped me do it to you."

She jumped up and hovered over him. It seemed that if she had been holding an ax, she would have been chopping at his skull. "Then why did you want to keep her around? Why, every time I said we have to get rid of her, did you jump to her defense? Why did you keep telling me that we shouldn't be hasty? That we owed her another chance?"

He stood and grabbed her wrists. "Because she'd be talking to reporters ten seconds after she got home. Because we'd be looking at live footage of me screwing her on the evening news. I told you! She conned me into bed, and then took a video of us . . . together." His voice softened on *together*. It was the gentlest way he could describe the hot, panting sex that she had probably captured on tape. "And now she's blackmailing me."

Ellie laughed derisively. "Blackmailing you! Give me a break, Gordon."

"She is, damn it! Not in so many words. Not with notes demanding payment in unmarked bills. But she tells me how much money she's going to need, and if I don't have my wallet out fast enough, she casually mentions the great video footage she has of us. It's the same thing that she's doing to you. I'll need a new dress for the dance. I'll need accessories and shoes. And by the way, exactly what is it that you want me to say to your academic board?' This girl is too goddamned smart to ask outright, or to put it in writing. But she's got us both on a short leash, and she's just waiting for us to figure out the cost of being set free."

He dropped her hands and Ellie turned away to the screened windows that overlooked the bay. She was silent for an instant, and then she laughed softly. "I was a damn idiot. When we were searching her room, and when you wouldn't give up and kept searching all over the house, I thought you were concerned to save my doctorate. I felt real lucky to be married to someone who cared enough about me to help me get through my mistakes."

"I was," Gordon told her. "I was concerned about your doctorate."

She turned on him. "Bullshit! What you really were concerned about was saving your own ass. Your political career makes everything all right, doesn't it?"

"They're the same thing," Gordon shouted back, but then instantly regretted raising his voice. "Please, Ellie. Don't you see she has both of us? If either one of us goes down, we both go. If I turn up a child molester, what kind of a position are you going to get in education? And if you're a fraud, I won't be able to get elected as a bridge inspector. That's why I didn't want you to send her packing. We need time for her to answer any questions they raise at your hearing. We need time to find the damn tape."

Ellie was listening and understanding, but she was a long way from believing. She had no trouble agreeing that Theresa was untruthful, devious, and maybe even dangerous. But Gordon's charge that she had set both of them up, and that she was going to charge a price for her silence seemed to give the girl too much credit. She would have to be some sort of sick genius to have been maneuvering them all summer.

"Just give it a couple of days," Gordon begged. "A week at the most. She's running out of time if she's going to take that scholarship. Within a week, she'll find a way to tell us what it's going to cost us. I swear to you! It was a setup! She'll prove it for me."

She nodded, not in agreement, but simply to indicate that she had heard. "I'm going over to the club to see my children." She picked up the car keys from the table by the front door, and then thought to pick up her sunglasses to hide the redness of her eyes.

"I'll go with you," Gordon offered.

"No. I want some time alone. I'll take the long way." She was past him and starting down the steps.

"Ellie, please be careful. If you feel upset, pull over."

She stopped long enough to send him a withering glance. Then she was down the steps and out of his sight.

THIRTY-ONE

Ellie started toward the club, but she passed the access road and continued north to a winding, sandy path that led down to the water's edge. She got out of the car and walked out on a rocky outcropping where she could see the club in the distance. Farther south were the shapes of the large houses where her own house stood. She sat down and fought back the urge to cry; she needed to think.

The view helped. It was as if she were having an out-of-body experience, looking down at the landscape where the recent acts of her life had been played. Her children were at the club, and they would have to come first in any decision she made. Gordon was at home, agonizing over his future. She had truly loved her husband, and even when she began to understand that she would always take second place to his ambitions, she had never second-guessed her commitment to spend the rest of her life with him. When he needed space, she had found a bit of space for herself.

She had suspected that he had other women, but had chosen not to look for proof. If she scrutinized his laundry for traces of lipstick and searched his pockets for hotel receipts, there was always the chance that she would find what she was looking for. And that would lead to the private detective who would, sooner or later, confront her with the shockingly graphic pictures that simply couldn't be ignored. She had chosen not to learn anything that would force the end of their marriage. Why? Why didn't she want to know?

Ellie found herself skipping pebbles across the water from her perch at its edge. Why? Because she was a coward who couldn't stand the possibility of a confrontation? Maybe, but she had often confronted Gordon on other issues. Or was it because of the children? She and Gordon had always been careful that the children never see the difficult

170

moments in their marriage. Perhaps she was afraid of what angry confrontations would do to their sense of security. There was no doubt that she would do almost anything to keep them from losing their father.

But there was more. She enjoyed an overwhelming sense of security. As Gordon's wife she had easy access to everything she could want, and all the resources needed to pursue her cherished career. Her status would be drastically altered by a divorce. She didn't know whether she was strong enough to start from scratch even with a very generous income.

But now the confrontation seemed unavoidable. She might be able to ignore his demeaning selfishness — his total devotion to just his own prospects — for at least the weeks left until the election. She might even be able to get through a dalliance with another woman who was at his side in a moment of great need. But the seduction of a young girl barely half his age. Someone closer to his little daughter than she was to him. That seemed to change everything. How could she endure a man who could do such a thing? Or love someone who had done something so obscene? Hadn't he promised Theresa his protection when he took her into his home? And then grossly violated that trust?

She squeezed her eyes in a useless effort to shut down her imagination. She didn't want to see the two of them together with Gordon as the strong, overpowering letch, and Theresa a frightened child knowing she had to please her patron. How could she go on living with such a man?

She remembered his tireless search for the video. *She might have copied her notes, or photographed herself at the computer,* Gordon had warned her. His concern for her had been a bold-faced lie. He knew what she had copied, and knew exactly what it would say about him. The bastard! All he wanted to do was destroy the evidence of his sin.

Would he ever have told her? She doubted it. This wasn't an affair with a reasonable woman that he could hope his wife might understand and forgive. This was the abuse of a child, and that was unforgivable. This was a base act of pure lust, and there was no way he would ever be able to explain it.

She didn't want explanations. She wanted the girl out of her house *now,* not after a week. And she wanted her husband at the other end of the house where he wouldn't be able to reach out and touch her. Then, she could let events unfold. If Theresa produced a tape that destroyed Gordon, that would be no more than he deserved. And if she claimed coauthorship of the thesis, then the esteemed doctoral board would just have to sort out the pieces. Her strength had been that few universities would go out of their way to embarrass the wife of a congressman. But, by the same logic, no university would feel compelled to rescue the reputation of a child molester's wife. So probably they would decide that she had assigned too much of the work to an assistant. And if they did, Ellie would just have to live with it.

But could she walk away from the whole support structure of her life? Could she leave behind her colonial heritage to find a school in some cow town? Could she give up the house in Newport, her place at the Cape? Could she be happy with a man who wasn't to the manor born, and a rising star in public affairs? Ellie knew that her whole life was privileged. Could she survive with just the every-day ordinary?

She had to, damn it! Some things were unforgivable. And taking the au pair in the house he shared with his wife and children certainly reached that level. *She conned me! She set me up!* Lame excuses for a man who was used to making decisions. Pathetic excuses from someone who always knew how to take charge.

Theresa was no hopeless infant, she'd grant him that. The kid was smart, and not just school smart. She had the street smarts to maneuver people and set up events in order to get her way. And she had the equipment. There was no denying that she was attractive. Mata Hari would have given anything for a body like Theresa's.

Then there was the tape; it was a two-edged sword. It proved that Gordon had been in bed with the girl, but its very existence proved that the sordid event had to be Theresa's idea. If Gordon had dragged her clothes off, it didn't figure that either of them would have stopped to set up a camcorder. The tape was really Gordon's best defense. If there was a tape!

She had all the evidence she needed for murderous rage, but there were also a few circumstances that, if true, would clearly be mitigating. Ellie argued both sides of the case in her head as she climbed back into her car and headed south to the yacht club.

Theresa was just leading the children out of the water, back to the towers and hallways of the sand castle that they had been building. The kids ran straight to the castle. Theresa waved to Ellie and walked toward her. "Feeling better, Mrs. Acton?"

"I guess so," Ellie answered.

"I was going to keep them here for half an hour more. But, if you want, we can pack up right now."

"No," Ellie answered. "I'll just sit here and watch them." She sat down and began pushing sand over her toes.

Theresa looked concerned. "You sure everything is all right?"

"Yes, fine. Everything is all right."

Theresa backed away a few steps and then ran back to Molly and Timmy. Instantly, she was on her knees with them, scooping up wet sand for their construction project.

Why wouldn't Gordon be taken in by her? Ellie thought as she peered over the tops of her sunglasses. She's bright, energetic, and beautiful. All he would need would be a little encouragement, and Theresa would certainly know how to be encouraging.

But she was just nineteen, legally an adult but still closer to a child. Ellie was watching her giggling and pretending as she dug in the mud with Molly and Timmy. She seemed so much at home in their world, and so awkward around adults. No matter what was happening, Gordon should have been able to handle it.

At home, she was still wearing her sunglasses even though the sun had already set, and the lighting on the porch was soft. She was clearly locked within herself, sitting quietly next to the conversations, and offering only one-word answers. She would wait until the children were in bed. Then she would call Gordon and Theresa together in the living room and get everything out into the open. She would tell them she knew what had been going on. Then she would suggest that Theresa pack so that she could leave with Gordon when he went back into the city. When she was alone with her husband, she would ask him to stay at the apartment until she could sort out her next step. She liked the idea of sending them off together in the same car. It was defiant, like telling them to do whatever they wanted with one another because it was no longer any concern of hers.

Theresa took the children upstairs for their showers. Gordon was overly solicitous in helping her with the dishes. "You feeling any better?" he asked at one point.

"Just dandy," Ellie answered, cutting off any hope for a conversation.

Then she heard the flute, and she stopped dead to listen. Gordon came out of the kitchen to stand near the stairs. It was the same sad melody that Theresa had played a few nights earlier. But now it was less fluid. Its emotion seemed much more superficial.

"That's Molly!" Gordon announced.

"No, it's Theresa."

They listened together for several seconds and then Ellie suddenly agreed, "It *is* Molly." She came from around her desk and stood at the foot of the stairs next to Gordon. "That's unbelievable. Molly really knows how to play."

There was a bad note. The piece stopped and replayed the offending portion, this time getting it right.

"They've learned so much from her," Ellie said of the girl she intended to throw out of her house. In her mind, the arguments began churning again. What would she tell the children when she suddenly sent their teacher away? What would she tell them when they weren't seeing their father any more?

Theresa didn't come back downstairs. She simply fell asleep with the children, and Ellie welcomed her momentary reprieve from the dreadful confrontation.

"I'm going to bed," she announced with no preliminaries, and started up the stairs.

"I've got a lot of catching up to do," Gordon told her. "I'll be staying down here."

"Thank you," Ellie answered in a tone that didn't seem grateful at all.

In the morning, she was happy to find that her husband hadn't joined her, but also anxious that their rift not become immediately obvious. She didn't want to alert Theresa that her affair with Gordon had been discovered, nor did she want to create any anxiety with the children. So she dressed quickly, put on makeup and fixed her hair. But she was too late, down in the kitchen she found Gordon already serving breakfast to Molly and Timmy, and Theresa getting their things ready for another day's outing. Gordon, rumpled and unshaven, was an announcement of discovery that Theresa couldn't have missed, even if Gordon hadn't whispered in her ear. And the children were unusually quiet, probably sensing that something ominous was in the air.

Ellie barely nodded at the good mornings from her husband and her helper. She went straight to the coffeepot, filled a mug, and announced that she would have her coffee on the porch. The ring of the telephone stopped her in the middle of the living room.

"I'll get it," Gordon said, delighted to have something to say to her.

"No, I'll get it," Ellie snapped in a tone that told him not to dare and pick up the phone. She guessed that yesterday's caller might be returning with more information about her husband's philandering. She wanted the news straight.

"Mrs. Acton?"

"Yes."

"Ellie?"

"Yes. Who is this please?"

"Dr. Drury, from the university."

Her manner changed the instant she heard her mentor's name. "Oh, Dr. Drury. Forgive me for not recognizing you. I was . . . distracted."

"No problem. It's probably the hour. But I did want to get you before you were off on a busy day."

"Yes, of course." Here it comes, she thought. He's not calling at eight in the morning to discuss some point of analysis.

"I was hoping that we could get together during the next few days. I think we should go over the . . . eh . . . allegation that you used someone else's work."

A polite, academic way of saying *the charges that you're a cheat,* Ellie knew. "Yes, of course. Anytime. I'm free all week."

"Wonderful," he said. "I'm afraid there's been another phone call, so the credentials committee can't just ignore this. If we can talk it through, then I'll be able to report that there's nothing to it when the board meets at the end of the month."

"I'm anxious to get it all cleared up, and I'm looking forward to the meeting." Actually, she was dreading it, but she knew it was inevitable.

"And would it be possible for you to bring all your rough notes with you?" Doctor Drury added, almost as an afterthought. "Just to demonstrate their origin."

"Of course."

She sat on the porch with the coffee mug shaking in her hand, not from fear but from rage. She would have to bring Theresa with her. What could she do? Show up at the hearing and say that the assistant in question wouldn't be present because she had fired her? How was she supposed to explain? *"Why yes, Dr. Drury, I did decide to let her go after I received your call."* It would look like a cover-up. She might as well tell him that her notes had accidentally fallen into the paper shredder.

So, there could be no confrontation. Gordon would go back to the city without packing all his things. And Theresa would still be taking care of the children. She was outraged, but, in a way, she was relieved that the decision had been made for her. For at least a week, it was out of her hands.

Maybe she should spend some of the time doing a thorough search for the videotape. Perhaps she should take Theresa's room apart section by section in order to be certain that nothing had been overlooked. And perhaps, as Gordon had suggested, Theresa would find a way to tell her exactly how much her cooperation was going to cost.

THIRTY-TWO

On Wednesday, she learned the price. Ellie had spent the morning searching carefully through her children's closets. She had never made any attempt to straighten them, and neither of the children would sort through their junk even to find a favorite toy. They were perfect hiding places for someone who had unrestricted access to them.

Today's search, like yesterday's, had come up empty-handed. Yesterday her problem had been to leave Theresa's bookshelf in the same order in which she had found it. Today's problem was to leave the children's closets in utter chaos even though she yearned to sort and stack.

She had been interrupted only once, by a phone call from Gordon that she had disposed of with the minimum number of one-word answers. He had been terribly solicitous, determined to display his affection, but she would have none of it. As she hung up she had realized that things could never again be normal between them, and that thought had strengthened her resolve to send Theresa away as soon as her meeting with Dr. Drury was over, probably sometime the next weekend.

She was at her desk when the children rushed through the door closely followed by Theresa. When Ellie joined them in the kitchen they were already smearing peanut butter on bread while Theresa set plates and poured the milk. Then the children took their lunch out onto the porch, leaving the two women together in the kitchen.

"Theresa, you remember me telling you about the problem I was having with my dissertation?" With that beginning, Ellie recapped the preposterous idea that Theresa had actually written the document, and explained why she was planning to meet with her mentor. "It would be helpful if you were there to answer any questions that might come up," she said as casually as she could make it sound.

"Sure," Theresa answered, even more casually.

"And I thought we ought to do it soon, before you're getting ready to leave for college."

"Oh, I won't be leaving."

"Well, even if you're going to stay at a local school," Ellie advised, "you'll still have lots to do in a few weeks."

"I won't be going to any college," Theresa said. "Even with the scholarship, the money is way too much. I figure that when you don't need me anymore, I'll go get a full-time job. Maybe I can save something and then a year from now I can go back to going nights."

Ellie couldn't hide her surprise.

"Unless you know where I can find twenty thousand dollars lying around."

The surprise turned to suspicion. "Twenty thousand?" she asked skeptically. "It can't be that much."

Theresa sighed. "Well, it's close. Not just for school but for my whole family situation."

Ellie kept her attention focused. She knew that Theresa wouldn't need coaxing to explain where she had come up with the figure.

"I used to send money every week to the couple I lived with. It wasn't much, but over the year it added up to around twenty-five hundred. They didn't ask me to keep it up, but I know they counted on the money. Then, I have to allow for my own upkeep. Food and clothing. It doesn't come to much when I'm working, but if I go to school I'll be eating in a cafeteria. And I'll have to have a couple of changes to wear."

Ellie nodded. Her friends with college kids had all bemoaned the endless costs. So far Theresa seemed pretty realistic.

"Then there are the fees. They're probably not as high at a local school, but at Yale the fees add up to another two thousand. And I also have to pay for health insurance because I'm not covered by my family." Ellie knew how much that was.

"Then there are books. Some of the textbooks cost sixty dollars. And you can't get them used because they change them every year. That's another thousand. And I haven't even gotten to the tuition yet."

"What about your scholarship?"

Theresa laughed at the irony. "That's from the local Yale alumni club. It's only five thousand, and it's only good at Yale. It would just about cover the board. So no matter where I go, I'm going to need to pay for credits. I need twenty-four a year, and it's fifty to a hundred dollars a credit depending on where I go."

In her head, Ellie was already closing in on the twenty thousand figure. More if she took the Yale scholarship, less if she went full-time locally. But either way, Theresa had done her homework. It was going to cost her as much to go to college as it was going to cost the Mapletons to keep Trish in college. Except Theresa had no one to keep her.

"Unless something crazy happens, I won't be going anywhere," Theresa concluded. "So, I can go with you just about any time. All I need to know is what I should say and what I shouldn't say at your meeting."

Deep in her gut, Ellie now understood exactly what Gordon had told her. *One minute she's talking about how much money she needs, and the next minute she's reminding me that she has videos of everything*. It was unmistakable. For twenty thousand, Theresa would say whatever Ellie wanted. Gordon was right, she had suckered in the two of them. For twenty thousand dollars a year they could have their life back.

She wasn't nearly so abrupt when Gordon called back later in the day. "I think you better plan on coming out to the Cape tomorrow. There's something we have to talk about."

"Ellie, I wish you'd think this over carefully before you make any decisions. There has to be a way for me to make this up to you."

"It's not that." Her voice went to a whisper even though Theresa was nowhere in sight. "Remember you said we were both in the same fix, and that it wouldn't be long before I found out the price?"

"Yeah . . ." He was uncertain where she was leading.

"Well I found out today. And I don't think I want to pay it. It might affect you so I guess we should discuss it."

"Okay," Gordon snapped, actually sounding thrilled to have something to talk about with Ellie. "I'm at a dinner tonight, so I'll sleep here and head out first thing in the morning. I'll be there for a late breakfast."

He did better than that. Gordon rolled into the driveway a little after eight in the morning, in time to make pancakes for his children. He idled about until Theresa had left for the club with Molly and Timmy in tow, and then he carried coffee out to the porch where he sat close to his wife.

"Twenty thousand," Ellie said without any preliminaries.

"In cash?"

"In school expenses. She told me she couldn't afford college, and had a very detailed budget showing a twenty-thousand-dollar shortfall. 'Unless the money turns up by magic,' she said. And in her next breath she asked 'Now, what was it you wanted me to tell your professor?' "

"Sure makes it simple," Gordon commented. "She told me pretty much the same thing. 'I don't have the money to go to Yale. Do you know where I might get it? And by the way, I have videos of *everything* that happened this summer.' It's all pretty straightforward. We can sit up nights waiting for Theresa to drop a bomb on us, or we can pay her bills and ship her off to college."

Ellie's face sunk into her hands. "What a mess! What a godawful mess."

Gordon risked taking her hand and was ecstatic when she didn't pull it away. "It's not that bad. I can afford it," he told her.

"I know you can afford it, Gordon. But I don't think I want to be a part of it. It's out and out blackmail. And it will go on year after year which is something *I* probably can't afford."

He winced at her statement. She was saying that she would be paying her own bills next year. Well, he could deal with next year. But he couldn't let anything happen until after the election.

"You're right," he said, "it's extortion. She's the criminal, not us. And let's take it one step at a time. By her midyear break, you'll have your doctorate and my election will be decided. There won't be so much on the line. A year from now anything that happened this summer would be old hat. I really think that if we can get through the next six months we'll be in a much better position. I say we tell her that we're going to send her to school."

"She'll know exactly why we're doing it," Ellie protested.

"And we know exactly what she's doing. It doesn't matter. Theresa has suggested very openly that we buy her silence. And we'll be telling her, very openly, that we agreed to the price."

"The whole thing is despicable. You make it sound like there's no such thing as right and wrong. Like the only thing that counts is cash flow."

Gordon sipped his coffee. "It is despicable. It's straightforward blackmail. But we're the victims and all we're doing is trying to put an end to the crime. We have to get through the next few months, that's all. But I can promise you one thing. We're not going to be victims forever. We're . . . you and I," he corrected, not wanting to challenge the implication that they might not be together, "aren't going to keep paying forever."

"I don't think I can just tell her that we'll pay for her silence," Ellie said.

"You don't have to tell her anything. I'll handle it. Just be there so she knows I'm talking for both of us."

Ellie knew she should protest. Instead, she just nodded.

He waited until Theresa had the kids bathed and in their pajamas. "When you're finished," Gordon called up, "could you join us on the porch? There's something we want to tell you." They sat patiently through Molly's flute lesson and Timmy's endless demands for a glass of water.

Gordon had something else on his mind. He might buy off Theresa, but he was uncertain of his status with Ellie. Carefully, he tested the water. "I know this is no excuse," he offered his wife, "but I really was conned by her. She picked the perfect time and she knew exactly how to pull it off."

"That's for another time," Ellie said.

"Okay! But you can see how she was into you without you suspecting anything. I hope you can have a little understanding for how she got to me."

"You're not saying that what I did is anything like what you did!"

"All I'm saying is that she knew how to get to you, and she knew how to get to me. I hope you can believe that it wasn't something that I wanted to happen."

Theresa came out onto the porch carrying a soft drink. "Sound asleep," she announced cheerfully, referring to the two children. Ellie and Gordon exchanged glances. Ellie's nod told him that she was ready for him to make the offer.

"Theresa, I understand from Mrs. Acton that you've changed your mind about college. She tells me you're going to put it off."

180

Theresa nodded. "It's not what I'd like, but I think it's the only thing I can do."

"When we were out sailing," Gordon went on, "you said you couldn't cut it at Yale. But I thought you were planning to try a local college."

She shrugged. "I thought so, until I added up all the costs."

"We've been discussing this," he said with a glance toward Ellie, "and we both feel strongly that you're making a mistake. The scholarship to Yale is a real breakthrough for you. It's a once in a lifetime chance."

Theresa looked puzzled, first at Ellie and then at Gordon. "I know, but sometimes things just don't work out."

"We want you to go to Yale. Mrs. Acton and I will put up the difference. We'll pay the school bills, and set up a drawing account to cover your other needs."

Theresa fell back into her chair. "You can't . . . that's not right."

"We can," Gordon said. "We've been very fortunate and your success is very important to us. You go to school. We'll worry about the bills."

Theresa was looking from one to the other. Her eyes were wide in amazement.

"I can't let you do this. That's not why I told you. I mean, you're like family so I could tell you what was happening, and you'd be able to understand. My own family and friends wouldn't understand what I was talking about. Twenty thousand dollars is more than anyone in the family ever had. But I wasn't hinting . . . or asking? I couldn't take that much money."

Ellie was almost convinced that the offer had come as a complete surprise to the young girl. Gordon was getting angry at being put through a faked emotional scene. "We want to pay the costs. You said twenty thousand, and we'll put up twenty thousand. So do whatever you have to do to get ready for Yale."

The girl should have been smugly satisfied. She had just beaten her economic betters in their own home court. Or, if she were still playing her part, she might be teary-eyed with gratitude. Instead, she looked embarrassed, as if the offer of twenty thousand dollars was a cruel insult.

"Now, I thought we would go over to meet with my advisor on Friday. Mr. Acton can be here then to watch the children." Gordon didn't know what his Friday schedule was like, but he knew that he would be canceling it.

Theresa nodded. "Okay . . ."

"And I would like to see that video you were going to show Donald," Gordon added with his best political smile. "You must be very proud of it."

She nodded again.

"Then everything is decided," Ellie announced.

Gordon stood up to indicate that the meeting was adjourned.

Theresa rose slowly. "I think I'll take a walk down on the beach, if it's okay."

"Of course," Ellie told her.

"I may be a while. I have a lot to think about. So, if I'm not back, maybe you could just leave the front door open." She pushed against the screen door, but then turned back. "Nothing like this has ever happened to me. I don't know if I can take it. The money, I mean. But I'll never forget that you offered it."

They both stood smiling like doting parents until she had disappeared into the darkness. Then Gordon shook his head slowly. "She's good. I'll give her that."

"God, but I feel defiled," Ellie added. "She wasn't the only one acting. It hasn't even started and we're already living a lie."

"It's just a business deal," he said defensively. "She'll take the money, and then tell your mentor that she's illiterate. It's just payment for a service."

Her glance was icy, and he remembered what service it was that *he* was paying for. "You won't mind if I'm not around when she shows you the tape?" Ellie said, turning her back on him.

They both waited up until Theresa returned from pondering her future. Her eyes were bright, liquid blue against her pure white smile. "I'm so excited," she said. "I know I'll never be able to thank you enough. But I'll work my butt off to make you happy about your gift. I really will."

Ellie might have thrown her arms around the girl, except she suspected that the youthful excitement had been just as carefully rehearsed as the stunned gratitude. Gordon kept thinking that she was the most accomplished con artist he had ever come across.

"You have that video?" he asked, keeping his business deal on track.

"Oh sure. I'll get it. You'll both get a kick out of it."

She dashed up the stairs leaving Ellie and Gordon dumbfounded and was back in an instant, the camcorder in hand. "The eight millimeter is still in the camera, so you can hook it up to the TV," and she began to connect the wires.

"What about the copy you made?" Ellie wondered aloud.

"Oh, I sent that to my foster parents. They like to know what I'm up to. Do you know that they used to go to all of my concerts?"

She started the tape for Ellie and Gordon, then said goodnight, and disappeared up the stairs. Scenes of the children at play began to flash across the screen, followed by shots of the yacht club activities, the day camp, and the children at home. There were sequences panning the club, showing its facilities, and then long shots of the house taken from down on the beach. Interspersed was footage where the camera was simply left running, photographing a panorama of all the children at play. In one of these shots, Theresa came out of the water, walking toward the camera in her white bikini. Gordon's throat tightened. It was the way she had walked to him moments before she led him up to her bedroom.

The images stopped, and the television displayed the electronic noise of blank tape passing over the heads. They watched the fuzzy markings for a full minute even though both of them knew that her frolic with Gordon wouldn't be there. Why would she want to embarrass them now that they had agreed to pay the money? That evidence would be on the copy that she had sent home for safekeeping.

Gordon mentioned the busy day that was ahead of him, and wondered aloud whether he should spend the night or go back to the city. Ellie suggested that he go back to the city. She had seen the shot of Theresa in her bathing suit, and her sympathy for her husband's plight had flamed back to anger and resentment. He was a long way from being welcomed back into her arms.

THIRTY-THREE

Dr. Drury was clearly embarrassed to be interrogating a student with Ellie's background and credentials. He alluded vaguely to a telephone call, and sheepishly produced library records that his office had requested from Harvard and Brown. "We took this as simply a poison-pen attempt. With your husband running for Congress I suppose that smears of this kind are regrettably to be expected."

Ellie smiled broadly to show that she understood and was in no way offended by the inquiry.

"But when the caller suggested that we check library records to see who was actually doing the work, we really *had* to follow up. And then it turned out that someone else had done a good deal of the research." He pushed the library responses across his massive desk for Ellie's inspection. She saw copies of her card with Theresa's signature. "It would seem," Drury went on, "that work you cite was actually accessed by a Miss Santiago."

Ellie nodded briskly. "Yes, of course. Theresa Santiago is my assistant. She's outside in your lobby ready to answer any questions you might have."

"Your assistant?" He said the question as if the idea were somehow foreign.

"Yes. I've noticed that many of the professors here list numerous research assistants in their work."

Drury smiled. It had been years since he had dug through card files for any of his papers. He had a steady supply of eager-beaver graduate students who did that for him as part of their education. They even paid tuition for the privilege. "Yes, that's quite true, and I suppose there's nothing wrong with a doctoral candidate having an assistant. It's just very unusual."

"Actually, Theresa is my *mother's helper*. But she's much faster than I am on a computer, so she downloaded a lot of my references. And, she ran a few library errands for me to get material that we couldn't download."

"A mother's helper? A babysitter?" Drury was amused.

"She's in junior college, and hopes to put together the money for college. Considering her background, she really has achieved a great deal." Then Ellie told the professor about Theresa's deprived family life, and her astonishing achievements in computer science and music. She kept the stress on her Hispanic background and the poor quality of public schools in her area, conveying the impression of someone who, while reaching beyond her circumstances, would never be expected to handle graduate work. And she avoided any mention of a scholarship to Yale precisely because the honor would be a tip-off that this was no ordinary high school graduate.

"So, she was really just saving you the trouble of driving to Boston and Providence," Drury concluded.

"Yes," Ellie agreed. "That, and saving the libraries the havoc my two children would create if I brought them while I was digging in the stacks."

He glanced curtly at the notes and rough drafts that Ellie had brought. "And this is all in your handwriting," he said of the notes.

Ellie elaborated, apologizing in some cases for her scribble. She had carefully culled out most of the notes that were in Theresa's far more legible hand, leaving only those that conveyed no real analysis.

"Well, I'd like to meet this young woman," Drury said, making his request sound more social than professional.

When Theresa entered the room, Ellie realized for the first time how carefully she had dressed for the occasion. A sweatshirt, over rumpled jeans and sneakers, took her back from being a young woman to a child. And her entrance was almost laughable. She came in looking bewildered that Drury had such a large office, dazzled by the original oils that hung on his wall, and afraid to step on the Oriental carpet that surrounded his desk. When she took her chair, she flashed a rehearsed smile, and then concentrated on her fingers to avoid having to make eye contact with the austere academician.

Don't overdo it, Ellie thought to herself.

Drury complimented Theresa on being such a big help to Mrs. Acton and asked her if, in the process, she had learned anything about research.

"I guess so," Theresa answered stupidly, as if she wanted to leave it at that.

Drury pressed for details and Theresa decided that she had learned how much you could find on the Internet. Mrs. Acton had shown her how to phrase questions for the search engines. The library was pretty much like the one in her high school, only much bigger and much more confusing. Fortunately, Mrs. Acton had told her exactly what she needed, and the librarians had been very helpful. All in all, she made it sound as if she had done nothing that Molly couldn't have done if grade school girls had drivers' licenses. Ellie half expected the professor to reach into his desk and offer the girl a lollipop.

"Well, that's fine," Drury said standing to signal the end of the meeting. "I've done my duty to the sacred trust I bear," he announced sarcastically, "and I hope with the very minimum of inconvenience to you."

"Then I should go on with my final draft, and submit it on schedule?"

"Certainly," he answered, coming around the desk. "It's pretty obvious that this was an election-year slander, and that this young lady isn't a ghostwriter. I'll be able to tell the board that I pursued the charges and found them not only baseless, but ludicrous." Then he whispered to Ellie, "Telling them your *research assistant* is really your babysitter should put the entire affair in proper perspective."

Ellie could hardly look at Theresa as they walked to her car. They both knew that the meeting had been a parody of the important part that the girl had played in her dissertation. Even more, Ellie knew that the role of a very limited street urchin had been an embarrassing one for Theresa to play. But, she reasoned it was the same act that Theresa had used to get into her household. And at twenty thousand dollars she was certainly doing better than union scale for professional actors.

When they got home, Gordon had Molly and Timmy down on the private beach. Theresa changed clothes and went down to relieve him, and then he joined Ellie on the porch for an evening cocktail. Ellie ran through the Drury meeting. Her description of Theresa left Gordon shaking his head. "I guess when you have to live by your wits you get pretty good at it."

Ellie agreed. "She's good at it. Probably the best!"

"Well we're paying for the best," Gordon moaned. "I sent off the deposit check to Yale. Five thousand up front, and the rest in four easy payments. But there are fringe benefits."

Ellie showed her full attention.

"The whole thing can be deductible. The company attorney is setting it up as a charitable donation. Can you believe that Theresa is actually going to have a foundation named after her?"

"Is that legal?"

He laughed. "Probably not, but that's why we have a legal department. And the other benefit comes on Election Day. Henry says I'm close to carrying every neighborhood in the district. I'm damn near even in Theresa's ward, and Henry thinks that word of a scholarship should make me a neighborhood hero. Champion of the downtrodden, and so forth."

"Congratulations," Ellie said with more sarcasm than praise. She might be working with Gordon to save their mutual careers but she

186

was still a long way from forgiving him. He got the message, and downed his drink with a finality that indicated he was going.

"I've just got a couple of papers to go over with her. Curriculum stuff that she has to return. Her preferences on living accommodations. And a couple of legal documents connected with the trust. Then I'll be heading back to town."

"Why don't you meet her out on the porch. I'd like to be spared of seeing you two together."

He changed his clothes, gathered the papers, and met Theresa at the top of the steps. He did his best imitation of a civil clerk as he indicated what she had to read and sign, and pointed out the due dates of certain forms. Through the entire process he didn't once look her in the eye.

Suddenly he was aware of her hand touching his. He nearly jumped away.

"She knows, doesn't she," Theresa announced.

Gordon looked back blankly.

"Yesterday, at the professor's office, I could see hatred in her eyes. She hated me because she needed my help. And now you hate me because she's blaming you."

He held up the check stub. "Does this look like either one of us hates you?"

"That's why you're doing this, isn't it? You're sending me to college so that I won't be an embarrassment to you." She pointed at the check. "That's really a payoff, isn't it?"

"Don't be ridiculous. Why would . . ."

"Because I'd never cause problems for either one of you. You've both been very good to me. I'm grateful to her, and . . . I'm in love with you."

Gordon writhed in frustration. Part of him wanted to throttle her for taking over their lives; part of him wanted to embrace her. And part of him needed to explain to her why she certainly couldn't be in love with him. Out of all this, "Please, Theresa. Don't say such things," was all he could manage. He gathered up the signed papers and stuffed them into his pocket. Then he went inside and kissed his daughter.

Ellie was at her desk when he crossed back through the living room. "I'm going now," he said, and hesitated in mid-step to see if there would be any reaction.

"Have a safe trip," she mumbled without looking up from her work. It was something that she would say to a delivery boy.

He was back in his downtown apartment studying his schedule and realizing that he wasn't committed to a single political social event for the entire weekend. In fact, the preliminaries were over with. He wouldn't be involved full-time in his race for Congress until after Labor Day.

It should be a perfect time, he thought. Ellie was wrapping up her thesis, Theresa would be heading to school. They would have a whole month to devote to each other and their children.

Maybe that was the way he should present it to Ellie. He could spend a few days clearing his desk at the company. Then he would be able to devote his full time to her as an apology for his transgressions. "At least give it a try," he would say to her. "I don't want our marriage to die out of spite. And I don't want either of us to walk away from it. Let's spend the rest of the summer falling back into love."

In his gut, he felt that Ellie really wanted to forgive him. She had experienced Theresa for herself and, at a minimum, had to know that his momentary lapse wasn't entirely his fault. But she couldn't just say, "It's okay," because she couldn't trivialize what had happened in her own house. She needed a reason, an event that could help her turn a corner. Something had to make it possible for her to say, "I'm self-sacrificing enough to try to work it out." Then later she might say, "I forgive you, Gordon. I really do." And sometime after that she would be able to say, "I love you."

Maybe a trip, he thought. Three weeks at someplace she really loved. That would be much more special than his simply coming home to the house on the Cape. And he could specify accommodations with twin beds. That would at least get him back into the bedroom.

Or a gift. He could buy her another engagement ring to present with a note that said simply, "I'm sorry." That would make it easier for her to say, "We'll try again," and for him to promise that this time he would get it right.

Through his concentration he was gradually aware that his telephone was ringing. He lifted the receiver absently. "Hello," and then he sat bolt upright when he heard her voice.

"It's me," Theresa said.

"Theresa. What? Is something wrong?"

"No, I just needed to talk to you."

His hand went to his head. "Theresa, you can't call me . . . person-ally. Mrs. Acton would never understand."

"She won't know."

"She gets a telephone bill, and she damn well will remember that she wasn't speaking to me at the time."

"I'm not at your house. I told her I had to buy some stuff so I could call from the supermarket. It's okay. I know what I'm doing."

The call was dangerous at best. At worst it could be an attempt to entangle him even further. "I can't talk with you, Theresa. Not like this."

"Well how, then? Because I need to talk with you. Alone!"

Her words sounded ominous. "Why? What do we have to talk about?"

"I can't go to college. Not now!"

He listened open-mouthed.

"I think I'm pregnant," she said.

"Oh, Jesus . . ."

"And I need to know what to do."

THIRTY-FOUR

He knew it was true. And then, ten minutes later while he paced back and forth across the apartment, he was certain that she was lying. She was just upping the ante, giving him a reason to spend another ten or twenty thousand on her.

"I need to know what to do," she said, and that was a bold-faced lie. Theresa knew exactly what to do, and had probably done it once or twice already. He hadn't been her first lover. This might not be the first time she had gotten herself into trouble, or at least thought that she had. There were only two choices.

What she was really saying was "I don't know what you're going to do." And whatever he decided was going to cost him money. Lots of money.

Which was why he was pretty sure that it wasn't true. Just the sug-gestion would force him to hand over the money, and probably in cash. She knew he would never write a check to an abortion clinic. He wouldn't even want her name on a patient record. And he certainly couldn't finance her through full-term to delivery. That would involve arrangements that Ellie would recognize and leave a paper trail that his political opponents would trip all over. He knew how the conversation would go. "If you don't want your baby, I'll need fifteen thousand to take care of everything." She'd probably have an itemized bill of goods like the educational budget she had presented to Ellie.

He noticed a hint of light in the eastern sky, and realized that he had been pacing and churning through most of the night. And there was no end in sight.

How could he be sure that he was the father? She had spent time with Don McNeary and probably with some of the other young hulks in the gang. Even if she were pregnant, it wasn't impossible that it could be someone else. But Theresa wouldn't miss the fact that she was better off if the child were his. And what could he do? Demand blood tests? Run DNA analysis? That would obviously become public knowledge, and in the end he couldn't be sure what the results might show.

No, he had to trust her, and pay. And only God knew how much and for how long. If she wanted to keep the baby he could end up financing another family.

If there were a baby!

By dawn, he had dropped across his bed, the comforter still in place and his clothes still on. His eyes were shut and he was breathing deeply. But he was still awake enough to rerun all the dozens of scenarios that he had developed during the night. The only thing of which he was sure was that his nightmare would never come to an end. Theresa had him, and she could string him out for the rest of her life. Action Boats had a new stockholder who would eagerly be awaiting her dividends.

There was no way out. And no matter what he did it was only going to get worse. Tell her *no,* and she could take him to court. No matter what the verdict he would come out the loser. The tabloids would put out special editions. Ellie would have little choice but to leave him. Pay her the money and he might get by for a while. But it was certain that Theresa would come back for more, and likely that sooner or later Ellie would find out.

Twice he had put his hand on the telephone in order to call Henry Browning. The man who had paid someone to come on to his mistress in order to break up a politically damaging relationship could probably figure a way to stop Theresa. But Henry would know that the young girl and her baby were a ticking time bomb that could destroy Gordon Acton any time in the future. He would stick with Gordon through this election, but then he would probably find himself another candidate whose future was more secure.

What would Henry do? Maybe arrange a marriage for Theresa to someone her own age. He'd even give the bride away and pay for the reception. Or, he might shortcut the whole problem and hire a hitman to take Theresa completely out of the picture. But then, of course, they'd be blackmailed by the hitman.

It was during that part of his agonizing that he had thought about killing her. Not seriously, because murder wasn't anywhere in his profile, but practically. As a practical matter, getting rid of her was the only answer. But how could it be done without bringing in an outsider? His fevered brain had tossed about a number of scenarios.

He could give her a car to take to college, and saw halfway through the steering linkage. There were more than enough trucks on I-95 to assure the destruction of a runaway car. But he had no idea of how to cut a steering linkage, and if she were only injured his situation would be even worse. In fact, even if she were killed, there would probably be an autopsy that would discover her pregnancy. That would certainly warrant a police investigation.

That scenario framed others. Whatever he did, he had to make sure that her body couldn't be examined. Maybe a fire! An inferno that would destroy all evidence. Except that there was always evidence. Medical examiners could tell whether someone was dead or alive before a fire started. Investigators usually could tell when a fire had been purposely started. And besides, Gordon had his hands full just starting his charcoal grill.

A boating accident. That would be perfect. Take her for a ride and dump her over the side. Of course, he'd have to take her well out to sea to be sure that her body didn't wash ashore. And wouldn't people wonder what a married man was doing on an offshore cruise alone with his babysitter? The wags at the club already had them linked romantically just because she was living in his house, regardless of the fact that his wife and children were living there with them. To be safe, the whole family would have to be aboard, and there was no way he could bring his children to the scene of the crime.

By the time he was standing in the shower, he had rejected murdering the girl, but not because of his moral compass. Theresa's attack had been without any moral principle, and all he would be doing was fighting fire with fire. The truth was that he had dismissed the thought of murder simply because he saw no possibility of getting away with it.

He would have to pay.

Now a new question began torturing him. Should he tell Ellie? He might get away with one payment to Theresa. But Ellie knew how to read the company's financial statements and kept close track of household finances. She wouldn't miss a series of sizable cash transactions instituted by her husband.

Maybe just this once, he decided. Pay her off and get her out of their lives until after his election. There was always the chance that she wouldn't come back for more. And if she did—really *when* she did—then, he could talk to Ellie. He could argue that he made the payment just to spare her any further embarrassment and pain. But he could almost hear Ellie asking if he didn't think she had a right to know that he had fathered another child. She might forgive his one momentary transgression. She would never forgive a planned, lifelong lie. He had to tell her. She had to be part of any decision he made, either to stand up to the blackmailer, or face up to the costs.

He waited until late morning, when Theresa would be at the beach or at the club with his children. Then he phoned the house. Ellie picked up on the second ring, probably because she was working at the desk.

"Hello," she said pleasantly.

"It's me."

"Oh!" she answered, still polite but several degrees colder than her original greeting.

"We have to talk. Alone. We need to be clear of Theresa and the kids."

"Fine," she said, without emotion. "Today they should all be at the club between two and four."

"I don't want Theresa to know that I've come back out to the Cape. Can't you shake free to come into the city?"

"Of course not," Ellie snapped. "I wouldn't leave them alone all day."

He thought during a long pause. "How about at church, tomorrow morning?"

"Church?"

"Leave them at the house while you go to church. I'll meet you there and we can talk after the service. I only need an hour."

"Okay," she agreed. "And just so I come prepared, would you like to let me in on whatever it is that's so damn urgent?"

"It's Theresa," Gordon answered mournfully. "She seems to be upping the ante."

"Oh my God," Ellie blurted. They were both silent for a moment and then Gordon said, "I'll see you tomorrow morning."

Now it was Ellie who used the whole night to wrestle with all the possibilities. Her first instinct was to avoid the problem entirely. Just pack up her children and head down to the house in Newport. Let Gordon figure out a way to escape from the consequences of his own sin. If he paid her off and kept her quiet, fine. But if his affair burst into the public forum then she would simply file for divorce. She could probably get by as the offended wife, especially with the kind of divorce settlement that she would be entitled to. The problem with that approach was that she still hadn't come to grips with a life without Gordon. Strangely enough, her rage hadn't killed her affection. Quite to the contrary, her feelings for her husband inflamed her rage. Nor did she simply want to get by. It was Gordon's status that gave her status.

Her next choice was to support Gordon through his difficulties. He could come to a financial settlement with Theresa that would be fair and final. Then she and Gordon could stand together, he as a man who had done the honorable thing and she as the loyal and forgiving wife. But the fair settlement for a rich man taking advantage of a poor young girl would probably be astronomical. And the public might not see anything honorable in buying the damaged girl off.

Well what then? Maybe they should beat Theresa to the punch in going public. Gordon might call a press conference to announce that a young girl who had caught him off guard was blackmailing him. He could admit the indiscretion but publicly refuse to be compromised. There would be a very difficult period, but Theresa would have little public sympathy once her blackmail was made public. Gordon still might win the election. Worst case, he would be forced to withdraw from politics, which would still leave her family intact.

From time to time during the night, Ellie had wished simply that Theresa would die. That would be the simplest and most permanent solution. She remembered how she felt when Don McNeary's boat had been missing, and there was a chilling possibility that Don and Trish were lost. Though she had fought against it with all her strength, she hadn't been able to hold back the happy thought that all her problems were over. If they were the ones making malicious calls to the faculty then the calls would stop, and there would be no one to testify against her. She had the same sense of salvation as she thought of Theresa's death. If Theresa had been Don's crew and had gone overboard in the accident then she probably wouldn't even know about Gordon's infidelity. And even if she did, it couldn't possibly have the same frightening consequences.

But she recoiled from thoughts of Theresa's death. First, she wouldn't let herself wish for the young girl's demise. Second, wishing her dead led to thoughts of causing her death and she couldn't accept herself as a murderer.

Her final thought had been that it was really Gordon's problem. Let him deal with it any way he could. She would stay with him for as long as his disgrace wasn't harming the children or making her own life unbearable. That wasn't something she had to worry about right now.

But her worst imaginings hadn't prepared her for the news that Gordon delivered over breakfast. "Pregnant?" Her mouth fell open around the rim of her cup. "There's a child!"

He gestured to her to keep her voice down. They were in a corner table, but the popular Hyannis breakfast spot was jammed. The anonymous couples at the nearby tables were only a few feet away. And with all his campaign activities, Gordon was certainly not anonymous.

"Jesus, I don't believe this," Ellie said, her voice only slightly lower.

"I don't either," he whispered. "I think it's a damn lie."

"Do you know it's not true? Can you be sure?"

He dropped his eyes and shook his head. His hands came up in a gesture of hopelessness. "I hadn't made advanced plans to . . . it happened so quickly . . ."

"Well, don't you have to find out?"

"Oh, sure," he said sarcastically. "I'll get a court order demanding that she be tested. And then I'll file for DNA studies. Do you think the tabloids are going to wait for the results before they decide what to do with the story?"

"So then you have to accept it at face value . . ."

"I have to accept that there's a chance it could be true. And if I want to keep it quiet, I have to act as if it's true."

"So you'll pay for an *abortion*." She said the word with disgust.

"I suppose so, even though there won't be an abortion because there probably isn't any baby. I'll just hand over the cash, the same way I sent in the tuition deposit."

Ellie's eyes were down. "And if she decides to have this phantom baby . . ."

His hands went up in despair. "If there is a baby then there's no way I can avoid being discovered. I suppose I'll be paying child support forever."

A head at the next table turned slowly in their direction. Gordon hid his face behind his hand.

"I don't know what to tell you," Ellie said.

He sneered. "What are you going to tell yourself? You know she can wait until you're secretary of education, or something, and then show up on your doorstep with her complete notes on your dissertation."

Ellie set her cup down with a clatter, her eyes wide open.

"It's the same thing," Gordon explained. "She can ruin either one of us any time she wants."

The waitress pressed up to the table and set a fruit crêpe in front of Ellie and waffles in front of Gordon. "More coffee?" she asked. Neither one of them answered. She filled the cups without comment and made a hasty retreat.

Gordon restarted the conversation. "You know, last night . . . probably early this morning . . . I was actually thinking of ways to kill the little bitch."

Ellie's face colored slightly. "I wasn't doing that, but I was wishing that she were dead. I was thinking about Don's boat sinking, and the moments when we thought that Don and Trish might be lost. There was an instant when I hoped that they really were gone. Last night I was thinking that it might have been Don and Theresa."

He picked at the edge of his waffle, and then set down his knife and fork. "If she really is pregnant, the boat race wouldn't have been any help at all."

Ellie was puzzled.

"They'd find the body and in the autopsy learn that she was pregnant. Guess who'd be the prime suspect on the deck at the yacht club."

"Just rotten, slanderous gossip," she said.

"Papers print gossip!" He spent a few seconds staring down at his food. "No, it would have to happen far out at sea, where there wouldn't be any body."

Ellie set down her knife and fork.

Gordon sensed her interest. "And there would have to be witnesses. Unimpeachable witnesses who could swear to the accident, and swear that I did everything I could to save her."

Her eyes narrowed. "You really have been thinking about this."

"I guess so. Christ, I'm trying to save our lives, and I'm getting a little desperate."

"Who would be the witnesses?" Ellie asked suspiciously.

He looked straight into her eyes. "You. You and the kids."

Ellie fell back startled. "You can't mean it. Me . . ."

Gordon leaned in close, his face nearly to the center of the table. "Suppose I take her out cruising alone. Just the two of us. And when I get back I announce that, unfortunately, Theresa fell over the side. How many people would believe me? Wouldn't everyone be wondering what a married man was doing out cruising with another woman? Wouldn't they all have ideas about why he had to get rid of her?"

"I suppose so," Ellie admitted.

"But suppose we were all out cruising. You, the kids, our babysitter, and me out for a cruise up to Maine. And then I get on the radio and call the Coast Guard, frantic because we've lost someone over the side. It's tragic. It's heartbreaking. But it's perfectly innocent."

Ellie was staring at him, too shocked to respond. For a moment their eyes were locked together. Then Gordon suddenly looked down and picked up his fork. "Anyway, that's how it could be done."

"In front of your children?"

He ate a bite of his waffle, and glanced at the surrounding tables as he chewed. No one seemed to be paying any attention to them. Then he turned his attention back to his wife. "No, of course not. I'd wait until evening when the kids were asleep in their bunks. You'd go below. Maybe to check on them, or maybe to use the head. That would leave us alone in the cockpit, and I'd ask her to clear a line, or something. She'd be standing at the edge of the cockpit, and I'd just push her. She'd be over the side and into the water before you came back up. It would all be over in an instant."

He saw that her attention was riveted to him, and went on with the scenario. "We would just keep sailing for a few hours. Maybe past midnight. And then I'd get on the radio with an emergency. I'd give the position that we were at, not the one where she went over. And then we'd just wait for them to come out and search."

"Suppose they found her?" Ellie finally managed.

"Where? Her body would be fifty miles from where they were searching. It would have sunk hours earlier."

Again, they found that they were staring at one another. This time Ellie broke it off and dabbled with her crêpe.

The waitress came back to refill their cups. She left the check as a hint that they were tying up a table.

Ellie ended the silence. "You know that we're sitting here an hour after church, discussing the murder of a nineteen-year-old girl."

"We're only talking about how it could be done without anyone getting caught."

"Getting caught? That would be the least of our worries. Think about the children. They'd be traumatized; scarred for life!"

"We'd shield them from the awful truth, just like any parents would do. 'Theresa had to leave us. She'll be back after she's finished with school.' When they're older, we would explain the terrible boating accident."

"What about me?" Ellie demanded. "Do you think I could just stand by and watch?"

"You wouldn't have to watch anything. Just go below, wait ten minutes, and then come back up."

Her eyes were staring and her jaw was slack. "You're serious, aren't you? You want me to agree to this?"

"No I'm not," Gordon answered. He picked up the check and began fishing for his wallet. "I'm just fantasizing about ways to end all our problems. But I'm not up to killing anyone. I'd rather just pay for the rest of my life. And wait for the time when she goes public and destroys the two of us."

They were walking across the parking lot when Ellie suddenly asked, "What if she has left evidence with someone? Suppose your tape is in an envelope that gets mailed to the police if anything happens to her."

"Or her copies of all the notes for your thesis," Gordon added.

"Okay, that too. How do you know that everything isn't packaged and stamped and ready to drop in the mailbox? She could have done that to protect herself."

"How does it protect her if she hasn't told us about its existence? If Theresa thought she was in danger she would have to make sure we knew that getting rid of her wouldn't do us any good."

Ellie stopped, thought for a moment, and then nodded. It made sense. To do her any good Theresa would have to tell them what would happen in the event that she had an accident.

"Now who's serious?" Gordon reminded her.

She shivered. "No. Maybe it could be done, but not by me. I couldn't have any part in it. Killing an innocent young girl . . ."

"She's not innocent. She's a cold, calculating blackmailer who has already hit us for twenty thousand and is now hinting for ten thousand more. And besides, you wouldn't have any part in it."

"I don't want to talk about this," Ellie decided, and she walked briskly toward her car. Gordon was right on her heels.

"So, I'm just going to pay her. And then we'll wait and see what happens next. Is that what you want to do?"

"I don't want to do anything," she answered. She unlocked her door and climbed up into the Land Rover. "You're the one she has trapped, not me!" Her eyes were filled with tears of frustration and anger as she pulled the door shut and started the engine. Gordon watched her back out and then watched the car until she had disappeared over a hill.

THIRTY-FIVE

Theresa and the children were gathered around a board game on the floor of the front porch, but only Timmy jumped up to greet her.

"Can we go swimming?" he asked.

"Just as soon as we finish this game," Molly said, answering for her mother.

Theresa smiled and shrugged her shoulders. "We seem to have a difference of opinion."

"Have they had lunch?"

Theresa said they did and explained what she had fed them. Ellie decided to change into her beach wear and take Timmy down to the private beach. Theresa could bring Molly down whenever they finished their game.

She was in her bedroom, stepping into her bathing suit, when she fully appreciated what had just taken place. She had just had a friendly, productive conversation with a young woman whom, not half an hour earlier, she had discussed murdering. The memory of her breakfast conversation gave her a chill. They had talked about how Theresa could be done away with as if she were a pet that had to be put to sleep. And then she had found her, a young girl just entering womanhood, on her hands and knees playing a game with a child. What was happening to Gordon and her?

It was Gordon, she decided, coming apart under the strain of his relationship with Theresa. Gordon was a decent man, whose weakness was his own ambition. Theresa was threatening to bring him down, and now he was fighting for what he thought was his life. Was his future as a public servant important enough for him to actually push a young girl over the side? Did he really think that he could win back his wife by involving her in the murder of her rival?

But it was more than that. She had to admit to herself that she had listened eagerly, and used questions to test the soundness of his plan. If she had been outraged she would have screamed, thrown her coffee at him, and rushed outside for fresh air. But she hadn't been outraged. She had been interested. Intrigued by the subtle points her husband was making about how they would behave to protect their children. Even excited that the plan promised to bring all of their troubles to an end.

Both of them were coming apart, she had to admit. She was just as much threatened by what Theresa might do to her career ambitions as Gordon was by Theresa's threat of exposure. She was just as anxious to find a way to escape. She had been sorely tempted by the fact that Gordon would do the actual . . . work. All she had to do was go below for a few minutes, and then support whatever story her husband told.

Then she saw Theresa, still kneeling on the floor next to Molly, and she was filled with self-loathing. How could she allow herself to even think such things? There had to be an answer. Some sort of understanding they could come to that would be fair to the girl and reasonable for them. As she took Timmy's hand the thought of harming any child, even one as adult as Theresa, made her hate herself.

On the beach, she tried to give Timmy her full attention. But her mind kept wandering back to the morning. She *had* given Gordon's idea her full attention. She *had* been thrilled when he had an answer to every objection she could raise. And she knew why. Theresa was a threat not just to Gordon and herself, but to the children and to the whole life they were building for their family. Ellie knew that she was reacting like any other mother, going to any length to protect her home and her children. She was being attacked and she was fighting back. But there had to be another way. An agreement! A price! Something that would allow them to take up their lives without the threat of destruction hovering over their beds each morning.

Molly came down the steps with Theresa right at her heels and immediately waded out into the light surf. Theresa joined her and then Ellie took Timmy by the hand and helped him jump over the waves.

They were standing together in knee-deep water, watching the children. It seemed to Ellie that if they could work so well together they ought to be able to solve their problems.

"Theresa," she started, "I suppose I haven't really thanked you. You did yourself a terrible disservice in making so little of the help you've been to me."

"It seems like nothing compared to what you and Mr. Acton are doing for me," she answered.

"Well, we want to be certain that we set everything right between us."

"Oh, I know what work I did," the girl answered. "I have copies of all the web sites and all the library references. I loaded them into your computer so you'll have them when you do your bibliography."

Ellie was stunned. "You have all of it documented?"

"Chapter and verse," Theresa answered. "And now you have it too. When you get a chance to look at it, tell me what you think."

A wave nearly washed over Timmy. Ellie had forgotten to lift him over the crest.

That evening, she pretended to be absorbed in the domestic chores of getting dinner and then helping the children off to bed. But she could hardly keep her eyes off the computer. *I have copies of everything,*

Theresa had warned her. And she had loaded it all onto the computer so that Ellie could see just how damaging it was.

Ellie was at the machine the second that Theresa had taken the children upstairs, racing through her files. *Dissertation; Theresa's Notes.* She opened it and scanned it quickly reading the sequence of citations. The headings of all the computer documents were posted to an e-mail box in Theresa's name. Downloads were delivered to her at Ellie's computer address. From the Internet correspondence you couldn't tell that Ellie had done any of the research.

Library books were marked with date and time, which would lead any investigator to Theresa's name and signature on the sign-out slips. The dissertation's author had not accessed a single page.

Then there were the notes. With each item there was a memo of where it would best fit into the discussion, and Theresa's reminders to Ellie of other research that was suggested. Ellie's hands began to tremble as she scrolled from page to page. She closed the file and shut down the computer.

"I'm going for a walk," she called upstairs.

"Okay," Theresa's voice called back. "We're just starting our flute lesson."

Ellie had to hold the hand railing as she walked the steps down to the beach. Her mind was reeling with outrage, confusion, and fear. Theresa's notes penetrated every corner of her work. At the meeting with her mentor, Theresa had claimed no credit at all, presenting herself as incapable of an original thought. Now, her notes hoarded all the credit. There was virtually nothing that she hadn't researched, evaluated, and organized for Ellie. There were long passages that were even in her own words.

She sat on the bottom step, looking out at the moonlit bay. How could she do this? Ellie kept asking herself. Why? The only answer was the one that Gordon had suggested. *She's got us both. She can bring us down any time that she wants.*

"It's my work," Ellie told herself. Then she began a line-by-line review of all the information she could remember from the notes she had just read. She had explained the thesis to Theresa and outlined her strategy for proving her point. She had given the girl the starting points for each area of exploration, and the guidance that had kept her from working her way down dead-end streets. And she had selected the relevant points from the bulging files of data. That was what was missing from Theresa's notes; the expertise that Ellie had brought to the project.

But why should Theresa mention that? All she was doing was organizing the source material for Ellie's reference. And it was certainly true that Theresa had done most of the grunt work on the research. That's why her name appeared in nearly all of the headings. Filed in the computer for Ellie's future use, the documents would be of great help. But delivered to an outside investigator they would support the conclusion that Theresa was the author of the paper. Or, at a minimum, that she was an important contributor of information and analysis, which should have been the work of the author. That was the damnable part of the files. They were either incredibly helpful or terribly damaging depending on who was reading them and what the reader was trying to accomplish. The question kept circling back. What was Theresa trying to accomplish?

Ellie was aware of the strains of the flute coming from the house behind her. The music was soft and sentimental, almost a soundtrack for the beauty of the evening. Who could find such music within themselves? A conniving, blackmailing liar? It seemed impossible; too ridiculous to deserve another minute of her attention. And, yet, there was the obvious linkage to money. She had agreed to meet Dr. Drury in nearly the same breath that she had hinted at twenty thousand dollars. She had linked her video of Gordon to the cost of her college tuition. And then she had threatened Gordon with still more costs. And now this: a well-organized record of her work in writing Ellie's thesis.

What would come next? What new price would she suggest for keeping her copy of the records to herself?

She made her way wearily up the steps, pausing twice to listen as Molly played one of the tunes she had memorized. Certainly, it was a child struggling to imitate her teacher. But there was something of the teacher in the tone and the tempo. Something beautiful. How could it possibly be the same person who had seduced her husband and compromised her integrity? How could it be the same woman who was threatening to ruin them all?

Ellie went to the kitchen and poured a glass of wine from the jug in the refrigerator. She was crossing out to the porch when Theresa came down the stairs.

"I thought I'd take the kids shopping with me tomorrow," she announced.

Ellie focused slowly. "Shopping?"

The girl was bubbling with enthusiasm. "I've saved up some money and I thought I'd get started on my college wardrobe. Molly wants to help me pick it out, and I think we can keep Timmy entertained for an hour. Unless you wanted to come too? That would be super, and I'd really value your suggestions. Unless . . ." The excitement drained. "Unless there's something you have planned?"

"No, no! That sounds fine."

"Would you be able to come with us?"

"Yes, certainly. I'd like that."

"Great!" Theresa nearly shouted. "And is it okay if I walk down to the beach? Don said he might be coming by and . . ."

"Of course," Ellie said. "I'll be here if Timmy wakes up. Take your time."

Theresa dashed out the door and danced down the long flight of steps that Ellie had just climbed.

Her college wardrobe! Ellie had no problem visualizing the scam. Theresa would visit all the aisles and displays, fondling and ogling everything from sportswear to cocktail dresses, from spiked heels to sneakers. Molly would be urging her to buy everything, and Theresa would protest that it was all beyond her modest budget. Her face would be heavy with disappointment when she picked out sturdy shoes and all-purpose jeans. And the sales clerks would be staring at Ellie, waiting for her to reach into her purse and pull out her credit cards.

It wouldn't be much. Certainly nothing that she couldn't easily afford, and probably no more than what she willingly would have spent to send her mother's helper off to college. But it was just the beginning. Her opportunities to support Theresa would come one after the other, like cars on a train. And each occasion would bring a subtle reminder of the performance she had put on in Dr. Drury's office and the thesis notes that were ticking inside her computer.

Gordon was right. It was never going to end.

THIRTY-SIX

Gordon walked past the electronic navigation devices that were at the front of the store and went straight to the chart section in the rear. On the wall was an oversized chart of the New England coast, with all its component charts outlined and numbered. He wrote the numbers for the cruising charts of Cape Ann and the Gulf of Maine, and the harbor charts for Boothbay Harbor, found them in the files, and took them to the counter.

"Planning a vacation, Mr. Acton?" The manager had been running the store for years and had sold Gordon most of his equipment and fittings.

"A short one, Harry. I have to get some cruising in before the summer ends."

Harry glanced at the charts as he rolled them. "Maine, eh? When you going?"

"Over the weekend, weather permitting."

"Along the coast, or straight out?"

"Straight out, if there's a wind and the seas are calm. Along the coast if it looks marginal. I don't have to be anywhere, but I'm leaving Saturday, and I'd like to put into Boothbay on Sunday morning. Heading straight up will save me four or five hours."

He walked back to the apartment and spread the cruising charts out on the table. If he rounded the Cape and headed up the eastern shore, he would lose landfall twenty-five nautical miles after he set sail. Four to six hours depending on the wind. Then he would be looking at a hundred and twenty miles of open water until raised Monhegan. That would be fifteen to twenty more hours. A bit less if he had good winds. Not much more because he would use the engine if the wind died. He would reach the midpoint of the cruise in the early morning hours. At that point, he would be about fifty nautical miles from the closest land. He had made the journey several years before, and the charts confirmed the schedule he remembered. Leave the yacht club at first light and he would be farthest from land at the time of maximum darkness.

The vague plan that had been drifting in and out of his mind now had firm dimensions. Theresa would go over late at night, just about fifty miles dead east of the small New Hampshire coastline. He would sail on for another four hours until he was east of Kennebunkport. That would put the girl about twenty-five miles back in his wake. Then he would send an emergency message to the Coast Guard, and begin running a search pattern. It would be a few hours until daylight, enough time to satisfy everyone that the body was probably lost. The Coast Guard would run a perfunctory search, but they would be looking in the wrong area. Theresa would be gone with no chance of ever being found. The threats and the blackmail would be over.

A perfect plan, Gordon told himself. And then he began listing all the reasons why it would never work.

First, Ellie would never be a part of it. She would never set foot on a boat headed out to murder, much less ever bring her children aboard. That would leave him sailing with Theresa, which would immediately make him suspect, or at least the target of rumors. If Ellie wasn't a part of it, it could never happen.

Another problem was that Theresa might not go. She was a smart kid, and could well be suspicious of a sudden invitation to a dark cruise on an empty sea from the two people she was blackmailing. All she would have to do was protest that boating made her seasick.

And then there was the act itself. It was easy to fantasize the moment when he bludgeoned the blackmailer and threw her over the side. But it would be quite another thing to bring a marlinespike or a winch handle crashing down through the skull of a young woman. There was nothing in his makeup that could prepare him for that moment. Or, for the long, drawn-out hours when he would be sailing away from her sinking body.

Finally, there would be the inevitable inquiry. Could he maintain a consistent lie through several sessions of intense questioning? Could Ellie? Wouldn't they begin to trip themselves up?

What evidence would emerge? Would there be clues of his crime still aboard the boat? Gordon couldn't think of any. But there were clues that hadn't been thought of every time a murderer was convicted. What made him think that he was an exception?

Who would come forth to testify? Would the foster mother appear with the videotape showing the true nature of his relationship with the girl? Would Don McNeary swear that Theresa had told him she was pregnant with Gordon's child? Or maybe Trish Mapleton was the one making phone calls about Ellie's dissertation and his unfaithfulness. Wouldn't she love to give the coroner and the press an earful?

A perfect plan, he thought. Except that there were any number of reasons why it wouldn't work. He was much better off if he just wrote the check and took his chances. And yet, that probably wouldn't work either. She would demand more and more until he was forced to go public just to stop her.

He answered the ringing telephone and was amazed to hear Ellie's voice. "Can we meet someplace this evening?"

He was thrilled. "Sure! Anywhere! I could come home."

"I'm not sure that would work. It's about Theresa and she might be here."

"Tell her I'm coming home and that she can make plans for the evening. Or tell her she's watching the kids while we go out and have dinner."

Ellie hummed into the phone. "I suppose that would work," she decided.

"I'll leave right now!" Then he added as an afterthought, "Is everything all right?"

"No," Ellie answered. "Everything is terribly wrong."

Theresa seemed concerned when he showed up at the house. She eyed him suspiciously, as though she could guess that there was a sinister reason for his unscheduled visit. He made small talk until Ellie was out of earshot in the bathroom upstairs.

"I'm trying to work something out," he said confidentially. "That's why I came home, to see if we couldn't get some time together to talk."

Her eyes brightened. "When?"

"Maybe over the weekend. Ellie has friends in Maine that she likes to visit. If we sail up, you and I can have a day on the boat to work everything out."

She nodded. But then she said, "I could find a reason to go over to Providence. We could meet there for a little while."

"No, that's much too chancy. If I can get Ellie to make the trip, everything will be perfect."

Theresa shrugged, and in the next instant Ellie was coming down the stairs. She gave Theresa the phone number of a small, waterfront restaurant where they could be reached. Then she and Gordon walked down the steps to where his car was parked. He closed the passenger door behind her, and by the time he walked around to the driver's door, she was crying hysterically.

"Ellie, what's the matter? What's wrong?"

She was crying too hard to answer. She gestured to the road, indicating that he should drive away. Gordon had lapped past the restaurant twice before Ellie was composed enough the talk.

"I spent the whole day paying her off," she said. Then, while she reapplied her makeup in the vanity mirror she told him about the day's shopping spree. She went from store to store, remembering every item Theresa had handled and her soulful looks as she put each piece back. She told him about Molly's enthusiasm, insisting that Theresa get everything she liked. And she admitted that she had paid and paid.

"Six hundred dollars," Ellie concluded. "I'll bet the Mapletons won't spend that much on Trish. I knew exactly what she was doing, and I was helpless to stop her. That was the worst part of it. I was afraid to put my foot down and say, 'No.' I was actually afraid that if I disappointed her, she might destroy me."

He gave the car to the parking attendant at the restaurant, seated his wife by a window and ordered her the martini that she rarely drank. Tonight, she held it in two hands and sipped eagerly.

"Gordon, can't we get a lawyer, or go to the police, or do something? Do we have to be afraid of her forever?"

"Go to the police and there's a record," he answered. "Get a lawyer, and as soon as he steps into court, there's a record. Then we're on the front page, you with a phony thesis, and me with a phony baby."

They ate their food without enjoyment, picking and probing and finally putting down their forks in frustration. Gordon poured the last of the wine, and waited for Ellie to look up from her plate. "I got the charts. Provincetown straight up to Boothbay."

"Please," Ellie said, waving the information away.

Gordon persisted. "We're farthest out in the middle of the night. No one would see anything. Nothing would ever be found. Everything would be over."

"Gordon, we can't—"

"Then we keep paying her, because I don't see another choice. I keep writing big checks, and every time she nods, you jump and take out your credit card."

They were silent while the waiter tidied up their table and brought them their coffees. Ellie spent the time remembering how helpless and used she had felt during the day. "What would I have to do?" she finally asked. "Because there's no way I could . . . kill someone . . . no matter what they were doing to me."

"Nothing," Gordon answered. "Absolutely nothing. All you have to do is be there."

"But there would be questions. The Coast Guard . . . the police . . ."

"All you have to do is tell them exactly what you heard and what you saw. You were below. You heard me scream. You came up and I was coming about, yelling that Theresa had gone overboard. I called on the emergency frequency. You held the lamp. We searched back and forth until dawn when the Coast Guard cutter came and the helicopter was overhead."

"That's all?"

"That's all. Whatever was wrong with the rigging that she was trying to clear was all taken care of by the time you came topside. You don't know anything more."

"What was she doing in the cockpit in the middle of the night?" Ellie challenged.

"We were all in the cockpit, enjoying sailing under the stars. You went below to . . . use the head? Or maybe because you thought you heard one of the kids. Or maybe you were up as a lookout, and when you got tired you went below, sent her up as lookout, and went to bed."

Ellie gave her full attention to the coffee she was drinking. Gordon stared at her, trying to guess what was going on in her mind.

She was repulsed by the idea. Theresa was hardly more than a child—scheming, lying—but still only a child. There had to be *something* they could do to set her straight. She had remarkable talent that she simply needed to focus on the right objectives. She needed help, not killing.

And yet, it was too late. Her husband had already been seduced. Her academic integrity had already been compromised. They had already begun paying the blackmail, in college expenses, formal dresses, and now a college wardrobe. She already had them in her pocket. What could they possibly do? Tell her that what she was doing was wrong? Who were they to lecture after the way they had compromised her? Or maybe offer her a deal. Agree to pay for this child and this year at college, but after that she was on her own? Why would Theresa accept that? They would stop paying when Theresa decided that they should stop paying. She was in control; they had no bargaining power at all.

It really came down to choice of who was going to be destroyed. Her and her family because that was where the blackmail scenario would inevitably end. Or Theresa, who was the instigator of all their problems? Except, as she had to admit, they shared the responsibility for their situation. Gordon didn't have to take her bed, and she didn't have to let the girl do so much work on the dissertation.

"Gordon, it's really our own fault, isn't it?" Ellie finally said, almost as if announcing her decision.

"Ellie, did you really plan to have a junior college kid ghostwrite your thesis?"

She was shocked. "Of course not. But the biggest part of our problem, Gordon, is that you really did take her to bed."

His eyes dropped in apparent defeat. But after a moment he reached across the table and took Ellie's hand. "I didn't want to tell you this because I thought you might not believe me. But I have to tell you so you can appreciate what we're up against." He leaned confidentially into the center of the table so that their faces were only a few inches apart.

"When you sent her to Brown to look up some of the references . . ."

"I didn't send her," Ellie interrupted. "She insisted on going."

"Sure," he agreed, "because she had another agenda in mind. She came up to the apartment and let herself in with a key she had borrowed from your car-key ring."

Ellie's breath had the sound of shock.

"I came home from a political thing," Gordon went on, "and she was sitting on the couch, knocked back, shoes off, making herself right at home. I was flabbergasted. I told her she couldn't come to my apartment, that there was nothing between us, and that what we had done out at the Cape was terrible and could never happen again."

He paused. Ellie's interest was obvious, so he told her, "She got up and walked into our bedroom, shedding her clothes along the way. I was stunned. Absolutely stunned. This wasn't our little babysitter. This was a woman who was right at home in a man's apartment, luring the guy into her bed. She was a professional hustler. A damn call girl. And she thought she owned me. Just like you said about your shopping trip. She glanced and dropped her jeans, and I was supposed to fall over myself rushing to get on top of her."

Ellie stared at him for an eternity. There had to be more to the story. "And, then you . . ." she coaxed.

"I told her to get out!" he lied. "But there was no place for her to go. It was late at night, and it would be even worse if she went downstairs and slept in the lobby. So I left her in the bedroom, and I sat up in the living room. Sat up! I was afraid to go to sleep. But finally, early in the morning, I must have dozed. When I snapped myself awake, Theresa was gone."

Ellie was staring at him, not quite believing, but not ready to call him a liar. He hurried on before she could question him.

"I cleaned up and went right over to the Brown library. And there she was, working on your notes. She greeted me as if we hadn't seen each other in weeks. So I took her outside and we found a bench on the campus. I told her that there was nothing between us. I had made an awful mistake, but I wasn't about to make it again. And she told me I'd do whatever she wanted. You might as well enjoy yourself, she said, because you're already in jail. Once is all it takes."

Ellie was open-mouthed.

"It's the same as her letting you take her shopping. You might as well enjoy it because you're going to be doing a lot of it for a long time."

It *was* the same, the way Gordon explained it. That was exactly the feeling she had experienced while watching a store clerk run her credit card. She might as well enjoy it because there wasn't a damn thing she could do about it.

"She's destroying us, Ellie. We have to protect our marriage and our kids."

Ellie said nothing while he settled the bill and walked around to get the car. They were halfway home when she said, "All I have to do is go with you. Be there. That's all?"

"That's all," he answered.

"When?" she said.

"This weekend."

Her expression went to shock.

"Waiting is dangerous," Gordon told her. "Besides, I checked the weather forecast. There's a high moving through New England. The weekend is supposed to be warm and clear."

THIRTY-SEVEN

Theresa looked delightfully surprised when Gordon announced the overnight cruise to Boothbay. She had doubted that Ellie would want her along on the trip, particularly if she knew about her relationship with her husband. Certainly, she wouldn't want to leave them on the boat together for a long period of time.

But Ellie seemed to be completely on board, joining Gordon in a display of happy anticipation. "It will be so much fun," she promised Molly, whose immediate reaction had been a frown. She raised images of an adventurous cruise where Molly might get to steer, of swimming from the back of the boat when they reached port, and of the quaint shops they would visit. For Timmy, there was the promise of sleeping aboard the boat, which really wasn't anything like having to go to bed, and the assurance that he could live on sandwiches and soft drinks.

Ellie went through the preparations mechanically, shopping for food that would store well and be easy to fix. She involved Theresa in gathering the children's clothes—hats and long shirts for the sun, slickers in case it rained, sweaters in case it was cold—and sporty things that they could wear ashore. She made several trips to the boat to check the bed linens, the head supplies, and all the other household things that Gordon would certainly ignore. Intentionally, she kept herself busy around the clock with trip preparations in the day, and work on the thesis late into the night. The one thing she didn't do was let herself think about what *might* happen on the cruise.

Ellie had not completely joined in the conspiracy to commit murder. In her mind, she had not yet agreed to anything. She was committed to nothing more than having the boat and the family ready to sail, and had no plans for taking any action against Theresa. All she was doing, she convinced herself, was considering how she and Gordon might escape the net that had entrapped them. And she was moving toward one possible solution just to be ready in case that was what they decided to do. Maybe something else would come along and they would cancel the cruise entirely.

There were moments when, despite her best efforts, the truth forced its way in. She realized that she had no real agenda for their visit to Boothbay because she knew they would never get there. When she worked on the dissertation, she knew her work wouldn't be challenged because Theresa would no longer be in the picture. But she pushed such thoughts aside. She was going sailing, that's all. Part of the time she would be below, which was perfectly normal. Gordon probably wouldn't do anything, and if he did, it wouldn't be her fault. There was nothing she could do to shape events. She would simply deal with the eventualities, whatever they might be.

Gordon was busy with the boat and with all the details of the cruise. He brought the mechanic aboard to check out and tune the engine, and test the generator and electrical system. He recalibrated the electronic navigation equipment. In the dry midday heat, he laid out and refolded his extra sails, and even climbed the mast to check out the rigging.

"Where in hell are you going, to Australia?" Tom Cameron asked as he watched Gordon from the dock. "You don't need to be doing all this. Christ, you can make it to Boothbay in a rowboat."

"I'm taking the family," Gordon answered as he lubricated blocks along the deck. "I don't want any problems."

"Stay near shore," Tom advised.

"That's okay down here," Gordon said. "But up in Maine the shoreline is a lot more dangerous than open water. And if I get a bad weather forecast, I'll run for a safe harbor."

Jack O'Connell, whose boat seemed permanently fixed to the pier, was full of seafaring advice. He warned of everything short of icebergs. Phil Stucky offered to lend his oversized tender. It was too big for Gordon to carry aboard and he didn't want to tow it behind for fear of losing speed. Stucky argued that it had never slowed him down.

One by one, Gordon involved the club members in his plans for a cruise to Boothbay. He wanted lots of witnesses who could testify to the thoroughness of his planning and his obsession with safety. He also plotted out evidence to show that he really intended to spend a few days in Boothbay Harbor. He had the yacht club manager phone ahead to assure that a mooring would be open for his use when he arrived. He called to verify that launch service was available late into the night.

On Friday afternoon, he phoned his office and left radio communications instructions in case they needed to reach him while he was too far out for his cellular phone. Then he gave them an itinerary that had him in Boothbay through Tuesday morning. He promised to be back at his desk on Thursday. He also phoned Henry Browning who approved of the vacation as a preparation for the difficult campaign ahead. Henry was ecstatic when Gordon mentioned that Theresa would be coming along. "We'll make good use of photos that show her as part of your family," he promised.

Friday night, after an early dinner, the family went down to the dock and moved aboard *Lifeboat*. Gordon made quite a show of checking out all the life preservers as members watched from the decks of nearby yachts. Then they put the children to bed in the vee berths that were fitted into the curve of the bow, and made up the bunk above the dining bench in the main cabin for Theresa. Ellie and Gordon had a nightcap with their neighbors before turning in to the double bunk in the captain's cabin.

He was good to his word of getting an early start. Before any of the others were awake, Gordon threw off the lines, started the engine, and nosed out of his slip. He caught the sunrise behind the barrier beach as he hoisted the boat's mainsail, and ghosted out of the harbor on the light morning air. By the time Ellie came up with his coffee, he was turning the southern tip of the north beach and setting a northerly course along the vertical coast of the Cape. The winds stayed light, but they came out of the west putting him on a broad reach. The boat powered up to better than six knots.

Theresa poked her head topside to announce that the children were enjoying the novelty of their forward berth. "They want to play there for awhile, so I thought I might come up and take in the sights." She sat at the windward rail, her legs dangling over the side, and looked pensively toward the shoreline that was drifting past. "This is beautiful," she said at one point. And then minutes later, "I don't think I've ever been happier."

The children came to the foot of the ladder, and Theresa went below to get them dressed. Ellie went down to start the breakfasts and helped Molly and Timmy carry their cereal bowls topside. Then she brought up the sausage and toast she had fixed for the adults. The wind freshened, bringing an increase in speed and excitement. While they all watched, the shoreline began to recede back toward the west. Their course was carrying them gradually away from Cape Cod and out into the open water.

The breeze softened in the midday heat, but it still left *Lifeboat* on a broad reach. Speed was down, but only a bit, and the flat seas kept the sailing pleasant. Timmy was occupied with a drop line that streamed out from the stern. Gordon kept telling him that he would certainly catch a fish even though he doubted that the sausage he had used as bait would attract anything that swam in the ocean. Molly was sitting with Theresa on the windward deck, listening to a story about an opera-singing whale. Gordon held the wheel to keep the compass oscillating around his course. He took a satellite fix every half hour, enabling him to adjust for the drift of the tide.

Ellie was below in the galley, cutting fruit for the salad she had planned for their lunch. She was doing everything she could do to keep herself busy and to keep her mind off the girl who was reading to her daughter. It was a perfect cruise, with decent winds and flat seas, and with all the sun her light skin could stand. She had looked over Gordon's shoulder as he plotted a fix, and could see that they were right on course, and probably half an hour ahead of schedule. She would take the evening watch so that Gordon could grab a few hours of sleep in the cockpit. Then she would climb into her bed, and when she awoke in the morning she would be looking into Boothbay Harbor. That was the scenario she kept repeating in her head like the melody of a favorite song. She wouldn't let herself think of Gordon's sinister intentions, nor of any of the conversations that would make her a conspirator.

When she brought lunch up, Gordon was using the binoculars over the starboard bow. She could see another sailboat up ahead, on a converging course that would bring them closer together in the evening. "Where's she coming from?" she asked.

"Further out. Bermuda, maybe, or even from Europe," he answered, still frowning into the glasses. She was a big sloop with a towering mast, more than enough boat to have taken a dozen people across the ocean. But more than her size, he was interested in her course. He didn't want another boat close at hand when the moment came to get rid of Theresa.

Theresa took the children below for a nap induced by the hot sun and the steady drift of the sea. Once they were off, she came to the cockpit and told Ellie that she was going to catch some sleep herself. When the afternoon wind freshened, Ellie and Gordon were alone on deck.

Gordon plotted another fix that put them thirty-five miles north-

northeast of the Cape, roughly forty-five miles east of Cape Ann. He was running too far ahead of schedule, and would reach his farthest point from land before sunset. He had to lose an hour, maybe even more to allow for stronger winds in the evening. He eased out the mainsheet, letting the sail spill a bit of air. It was sloppy seamanship, but the boat straightened and lost speed.

"Let's keep going," Ellie said when she realized what he was doing. "Let's sail straight into Boothbay, just the way we planned."

He looked at her curiously, not wanting to consider that she might be losing her courage. "That's where we're headed," he answered.

"I mean . . . *all* of us," she told him.

"Ellie, I can't live my life this way. You know that."

"And I'm not sure I'll be able to live it after something happens."

"We're almost free," he said.

She answered immediately, "We'll never be free. Not if we do this."

"Then what's the answer?" Gordon persisted.

Her eyes went down and her head shook slowly. "I don't know the answer. But I don't think I can be any part of . . . this . . ."

He took her hand. "You won't be, Ellie. I promise. I'll never ask you to do something that you can't do."

But he left the sail out where it was fluttering at the top and spilling air. And he was steering farther out to sea, where he could cross well astern of the sailboat that was closing ahead of them.

In the distance, fishing boats were crossing his course on the way in and out of Gloucester. He'd have to keep well clear of those as well. They would answer his distress call in seconds, and with satellite navigation electronics, they could be at the scene within minutes. He had to make sure that he put her over the side after dark, when there would be no chance of their seeing him. And then he would have to allow time to sail thirty miles farther so that he would be well away from the body when the fishermen came to his assistance. He had assumed that he had some leeway with the timing because it would take the Coast Guard hours to get a boat to the scene, and until daylight to put a helicopter in the air. Now he was working with much tighter margins.

He swept his glasses across a distant commercial fishing boat, a big ocean-going vessel with miles of net coiled up on its fantail. He could see crew members scurrying about, probably icing over the catch. The bow wake told him that she was running at full speed. He glanced back toward the boat's stern and once again noticed the enormous coil of netting. At that moment he felt cold and let the binoculars fall loosely around his neck.

"Jesus," he said in a whisper.

"What is it?"

He hesitated for an instant. Then he explained, "Those things really move. I'll bet he's doing twenty knots."

Ellie studied the boat for an instant, and then stared idly back out to sea.

Fishing nets, Gordon thought in sudden panic. The fatal flaw in his perfect plan. Fishing fleets were dragging nets out this far. Any one of them might pull up her body, which the coroner would claim for forensic evidence.

He tried to calm himself. A long shot, he thought. Incredible odds. What were the chances of someone circling a net around that one spot within a day or so after she went into the water? Because after that, there wouldn't be any body. The fish would take care of that.

But it could happen. That could be the unexpected thing that he hadn't planned on, the kind of random happening that always seemed to blow holes in perfect plans. And if someone pulled up the body fifty miles from where he said she went over, that would certainly arouse suspicions.

What if nets had already been placed? Fishing boats trailed nets out for a day, and didn't pull the circle closed until the next day. If he waited until the dark of night he might be dropping Theresa right into the loop. Probably it would have to be done while there was still some light in the sky so that he could be certain he wasn't in the middle of a fishing fleet.

His hand went automatically to the winch and he began cranking in the mainsheet, pulling the huge sail tight across the wind. *Lifeboat* heeled slowly to starboard. Gordon could feel the speed pick up instantly.

Ellie noticed what he had done. She stood up off her bench and looked out over the bow to where the huge sloop was still converging on their course. "We'll pass close by her," she said. "We should get a good look at her."

Gordon nodded, but not because he shared her excitement. She had just summed up his problem nicely. He now wanted to reach his farthest offshore point before dark. But just about then, the sloop would be close aboard. It suddenly seemed as if every boat in New England was moving into the area and thousands of pairs of binoculars were trained on him. It wasn't going to work! His perfect plan was unraveling.

Spray came over the bow and rained into the cockpit. The wind, still out of the west, was blowing harder and turning up swells on what had been a flat sea. Gordon guessed that they were doing eight or nine knots, which was fast for the boat's commodious cruising hull and its single-sail layout. He looked at the sun, now clearly in the western sky. Three more hours to sunset. Events were beginning to rush toward him.

Ellie heard Timmy's voice and dropped down through the hatch into the main cabin. Theresa was a step ahead of her. She had already swung down from the pilot berth and was moving forward.

Timmy sprang eagerly into Theresa's arms, and she rocked him affectionately to calm his sobs. Molly announced that she wasn't feeling well. Ellie guessed that it was the heel of the boat that was disturbing them, and decided they would feel better up in the air. She helped Theresa get them into their life jackets, and suggested that the girl put on her own. Theresa took the children up while Ellie began searching the ice chest for a finger-food dinner.

It would never work, Gordon decided with resignation. The kids had napped, and they would be up in the cockpit until well past sunset. Theresa was wearing a life jacket, which would assure that, if she went over, she would be found quickly. And there would also be an audience aboard the ocean-going sloop that was close and drawing nearer. He couldn't do anything until long after dark, and then he would be taking his chances with fishing boats.

He saw that Theresa was looking directly at him, admiring his eye on the compass and his hand on the wheel. "You really look like you're in charge," she laughed. "Like you have everything under control. I ought to take a picture of you for your campaign."

Molly thought it was a wonderful idea and dashed below to get the camera. Gordon looked at Theresa. "In charge," he repeated in a mocking tone. "Everything under control."

Theresa posed him with his two children, one on either side. Then she had each of the children take a turn at the wheel with Gordon standing proudly behind. Ellie came up with a tray of sliced fruit and wedges of a quiche that would serve as supper in the cockpit, and

Theresa moved her into the photo session. Caught up in the fun of posing with her children, Ellie actually broke out into laughter, a sound that brought an expression of shock to Gordon's face.

"Smile, Mr. Acton," Theresa said from behind the camera, and Gordon forced a grin.

"Now you," Ellie insisted, changing places with Theresa. She posed Timmy on Gordon's knee, reaching out to the wheel. Theresa sat next to Gordon with an arm around Molly, drawing her near. Timmy laughed out loud, and for an instant Ellie felt the black tension that had hovered over the boat disappear.

"Did we bring the camcorder?" Theresa asked suddenly.

"Yes," Ellie said without enthusiasm.

Theresa got up and moved toward the hatch. "Should I get it?"

Ellie lowered her eyes.

"After we eat," Gordon volunteered. "I'd like to get a picture of that sloop."

They followed his gaze and saw that the huge boat was clearly visible, off the starboard bow, and still on a course to cross just ahead of them. They could see several figures moving about in her open center cockpit. Gordon knew that they would pass her close astern just before sunset.

The children were in a happy mood, playing a game of finding shapes in the clouds. Theresa had gone first, finding a cloud that looked like a rabbit. Molly found a horse, and then Timmy broke them up by pointing out a vanilla ice-cream cone. Ellie watched curiously. How could the girl be so child-like and innocent at one moment, and be a lying schemer a moment later. This was the girl who had wrapped a college professor around her little finger, sent Ellie a threatening letter in the form of a computer file, and then shaken her down for a new wardrobe without ever losing her smile. And now she was squeezed into a corner of the cockpit with the children, completely involved in a child's game.

She noticed the set of Gordon's jaw, and the hard, thin line of his lips. Just the mention of the camcorder had turned him into ice, reminding him that Theresa had everything on tape.

They came astern of the sloop, no more than three hundred yards away. Gordon's plot had them sixty miles east of Kittery, about the point where he had planned to get rid of Theresa. Instead, he was waving at a crew of beautiful people who were holding their glasses high in a toast. He figured that, judging by their course, they were headed into Portland, which meant that they would be in plain sight well into the night.

To the west, the sun was beginning to spill its blood-red color into the sea. A glistening line of crimson stretched across the surface all the way to their boat. The sky was turning to fire. Gordon looked to the north and saw the shape of another boat. Through the glasses, he identified another fishing boat moving slowly in a wide turn. Picking up her nets, he thought, or maybe spreading them out. He could only wonder how many more were behind her, working back and forth across his course.

The children watched until the sun disappeared, and then began finding new shapes in the glowing clouds. Only gradually did the sky go from red to pink and then to a final shade of lavender. Molly yawned and Timmy closed his eyes. Theresa took them down below.

"You should get some sleep," Ellie said to Gordon. "It's been a long day."

She was right, and normally he would have gone below and left Ellie on the evening watch. She was a good sailor and a cautious captain. But he was concerned about the fishing boats, and the possibility of getting fouled in their nets.

"I'll sleep up here," he decided, and began rolling a life jacket to serve as a pillow. "The wind will hold steady so you won't be tacking. Just hold course, and wake me if you see running lights or net markers." He made himself comfortable on the leeward bench and fell asleep in an instant.

Ellie settled behind the wheel, and began to feel terribly alone. Theresa had created a chasm between her and her husband that was much wider than simply his infidelity. She had stripped away his veneer of confidence and revealed the rot in the underlying wood. Before, he had been a business leader managing corporate affairs and growing the prosperity of his company. He had been a fledging government leader aspiring to do more for his community. Perhaps, some day, a presidential candidate. He had been a father determined to be an inspiration to his children. Now he was a frightened man, whining that he had been compromised and cheated, plotting murder to save his prospects and image.

And it wasn't just Gordon. Theresa had magnified her failings as well. Ellie had thought of herself as a fully liberated woman, managing

219

her home and her profession with equal skill. Now she felt paralyzed, adrift in her own fears, dependant on her husband to find a way out of their problems. She had been an innovator in education, hoping to lead the revitalization of public education. Theresa had turned her into a cheat. She had been courageous in promoting her ideas, risking censure, and fighting for her beliefs. Now she was a coward, unable to mount any counterattack of her own, afraid to take a firm stand against Gordon, and shocked at the thought of working with him.

They both were exposed as little more than polite animals, well trained in the niceties of the genteel, professional life, but still dangerous beasts. And where once they had been able to hide the truths from one another, now the truth was naked for all to see. How could they possibly love one another? How could they love themselves?

That was Theresa's most reprehensible crime. Not that she had entrapped her husband, nor compromised her own work. Not even that she was extorting a subtle blackmail as the price of leaving them with their reputations and their public images intact. Her most hateful deed was that she had made them see themselves for what they were. Now neither she nor Gordon could face themselves or each other. She had left them alone, frightened, and desperate.

Ellie could still see the cabin lights of the sailing sloop that was headed off to the west. It seemed alive in contrast to the deadly silence aboard *Lifeboat*. Up ahead, there was only darkness, and she was sailing into it with the wind at her back. She picked up the running lights of an approaching boat, probably a fishing vessel. It was inside her course and headed farther inland, so there was no need to wake Gordon.

Theresa came up from the cabin and was surprised to see Gordon sleeping and Ellie at the wheel. "I didn't know that you were a captain," she said in a whisper.

"Hardly that," Ellie answered softly. "All I'm doing is keeping us headed in one direction."

Theresa climbed into the cockpit, saw that Ellie wasn't wearing a life jacket, and took off the one she was wearing. "Is this okay?"

"Sure! It couldn't be better sailing weather. But keep it handy, because you never know."

She sat close to Ellie where she could see the chart and the compass, and began asking questions about their voyage. How did you choose a course? How do you know where you are? Does it matter which way the wind is blowing? Ellie responded with simple answers that conveyed the bare basics. She kept apologizing that she was no expert, and nodded toward the sleeping Gordon as proof that she couldn't take the helm by herself. They drifted into silence, sitting together and admiring the starlit night.

Ellie was struck by dilemma that Theresa presented. Here she was sitting close by like a best friend or even a daughter. Yet she had stolen Ellie's husband and left her life in ruins. Could she be so clueless as to be unaware of the damage she was causing? Could she be so cynical as to grab for her chance no matter whom she had to push aside? Why? Didn't she know that she had become part of their family? They probably would have given freely all that she had extorted. But she remembered early in their relationship when she had accused Theresa of lying and then said she understood what the girl was up against. "You don't have a clue," Theresa had told her, in a voice that seemed amazed that Ellie could be so dense. That was probably the answer. Even though they were leaning closely against one another, Ellie really didn't know what had brought Theresa to the point where she would ravage her benefactors in order to get ahead. She had lived the summer with the girl, and still, she really didn't have a clue.

"Theresa," she said, "I think you and I should pay another visit to Dean Drury." It was more than a suggestion. It was an order from someone who was taking charge. "I want to bring your complete computer file with us, and I want us to go over it with him, page by page, line by line."

Theresa blinked vacantly, caught completely off guard. "I thought . . . I mean he seemed to understand. He even said it was a closed issue . . ."

"You took too little credit for all the work you did. I want him to see how important you were to the project. Then he can make a fair judgment on whether it's my work or yours."

Gordon's eyes blinked open. But he lay perfectly still and kept up the rhythmic pattern of his breathing. He listened, beginning to fear what he was hearing.

"Won't you be . . . sort of . . . making trouble for yourself?" the girl asked.

"I've already made trouble for myself. I've compromised my integrity and put my whole future at risk. I want to get everything straight. Between the professor and me, but more important, between you and me."

Theresa nodded as if she understood. "Okay . . . whatever you want. I just thought I was helping you . . ."

"And now I'm helping you," Ellie said. "If we invent a lie together, neither one of us will ever be free."

"We didn't lie . . ."

"We didn't tell the truth, did we?"

Slowly, the girl shook her head. "I guess not."

"So that's what we're going to do. As soon as we get back."

Gordon stirred and sat up abruptly.

"Same heading, same speed, and no other boats near," Ellie reported. "Why don't you go back to sleep?"

"No, I'm rested." He switched on his satellite navigation unit, and entered a request for a position. The response, flashed on the display, put them sixty miles due east of Kennebunkport, Maine. The nearest land was about fifty miles dead ahead. He marked the chart.

"You're relieved from your watch," he told Ellie.

"Fine. But I think I'll stay up in the cockpit. It's such a beautiful night."

He understood her meaning. She was done compromising with the truth. She was no longer frightened of what Theresa might do to her, and she intended to stay topside all night to make sure that nothing was done to Theresa.

The girl stood, looked from one to the other, and then started down to her bunk. Gordon called after her. "Could you put on some coffee?"

"Okay," Theresa called up. "I'll bring it up when it's ready."

"You can turn in," Ellie told her. "One of us will get it. See you in the morning."

They heard the running water and the sound of the pot rattling against the stove rails. Then the cabin light went off, followed by a silence that made them both aware of the sound of the wind in the sail.

"It looks like you've come to a decision," Gordon said.

Ellie knew exactly what he meant. "I guess so, although it's really just a realization that I never made a decision to hurt her."

"But . . . you helped plan the cruise."

"While I was confused and afraid. I'm still afraid, but I'm not confused. I know what I have to do, and I think it's the same thing you have to do. Tell her you made a mistake but that you're not going to make another. Let her know that this year is on us, but next year she's on her own. Then you and I can sit down and work out our future."

"And if she calls up some reporter, or some television anchorman?"

Ellie thought for a moment and then said, "There's nothing the press can tell me that I don't already know. It will be embarrassing but I'll get through it."

He looked down into the cockpit, his head shaking slowly. "I'd never survive it . . ."

"Your political ambitions might not, but I think you're strong enough. And I'll help you every way I can."

He was silent, sitting motionless as he weighed all the uncertainties of his future. Then he jumped up and swung into the hatch. "Keep the helm for another minute. I have to hit the head, and then I'll bring up the coffee."

She sat alone, studying what she had said and trying to fathom his reaction. She guessed that he knew she was deadly serious. She hoped he understood what she was telling him. *Theresa goes free, and you and I take our chances. Together.* It was a good deal for him. Better than he deserved.

Gordon stood in the head, braced against the heel of the boat, and searched through the medicine cabinet. He found the sleeping pills—mild, over-the-counter tablets that were good for sleeping when the rest of the crew was partying. He shook two out into his palm, then decided on two more. As he was putting the bottle away, he reconsidered and doubled the dosage again. Then he put the empty bottle into his pocket.

He came through the hatch with two steaming mugs, and handed one to Ellie as he slipped behind the wheel. He sipped at his while she sat waiting for some reply to her suggestion.

"I won't tell her now," he finally announced. "But I will tell her right after the election. I guess I want to buy a little more time. I'm not really ready for a what a scandal like this will do to me."

Now it was Ellie who pondered their future before answering, "I guess that will be all right. But I want to go to Dean Drury now. I don't want to risk that it would all come out at my commencement exercises."

"You could wait until after your degree has been awarded," he suggested.

"No I can't!" She wasn't allowing herself any loopholes.

Ellie drank her coffee, never taking her eyes off the stars. "You know, I really feel good. Better than I've felt since all this started."

Gordon just stared at her.

It took ten minutes for the pills to show their effect. She began blinking as she tried to force her eyes open, and then snapping her head up when she caught her chin beginning to settle.

"It's been a difficult day," she told her husband by way of apology, and then a few seconds later she allowed that, "I guess I really need to get some sleep."

"I can handle it," Gordon said, referring to managing the boat. "Go down and get to bed."

She nodded. "Okay." And then repeated, "I really need to get some sleep."

Gordon listened as she made it down the ladder. He heard her bump into a bulkhead, and a second later slam her cabin door. The light from their cabin came on and reflected out over the water. And then, after only a minute, it went dark.

He waited for several minutes, giving her plenty of time to sink into her mattress. Then he scanned the horizon carefully to make certain that there was no other boat in sight. He slacked the mainsheet so that the giant sail could swing freely. Then he locked the wheel and slipped below.

Gordon looked forward to where Theresa was sleeping in the pilot berth. Then he checked the vee berths to be sure the children were asleep. He moved slowly aft, using the starlight that came in softly through the deck hatch and the portholes. When he leaned against his own cabin doorway, he could hear Ellie's steady, heavy breathing. He went back to the main cabin and nudged Theresa, then raised a finger to her lips to keep her silent.

"Come on up," he whispered. "We have the cockpit to ourselves."

She was wide-awake in an instant, already swinging her legs over the edge of her bunk. Now his finger went to his own lips, reminding her not to make a sound. He left her to dress in privacy and went topside into the cockpit.

THIRTY-EIGHT

Gordon breathed deeply, suddenly aware that his heart was pounding. He stood up from the bench, bracing against the heel of the boat. Carefully, he searched out to the west. There was no sign of the big sloop. He'd be astern of her and probably wouldn't see anything of her running lights. They might still be able to make out his port and mast-head lights, but nothing more than that. He guessed that they would have opened up several miles between them. Ahead, there was only darkness. The starlight gave him reflections from the wave tops, and he could just make out a change in color that indicated the horizon. There were no lights.

He lifted a storage cover beneath the starboard seat cushion and felt ground inside his toolbox. He fingered a hammer and several screw drivers before he found what he was looking for. Silently, he lifted out a large spanner wrench—a heavy, machined tool with a two-inch open-ing at one end, an inch and three quarters at the other. He closed the lid, replaced the seat cushion, and lay the wrench next to him. Then he brought the boat back to its heading, settled behind the wheel, and waited.

Fear seized him when Theresa came up into the cockpit and he was aware of a tremor in his hands. What little planning he had done for this moment suddenly abandoned him, leaving him stuttering as she handed him a mug of coffee.

"Black, right?" she said.

"What?"

"The coffee! You take it black."

"Yes, yes. This is perfect."

The coffee sloshed over the rim, burning his hand. He was afraid to try raising the cup to his mouth.

"Is it cold? You seem to be shivering."

"No, no, it's nothing. Just sit. Get comfortable."

Theresa smiled. "I'll just get my tea, okay?"

"Sure! Fine. I'll wait right here."

Get hold of yourself, Gordon chastised. Think! Don't tell her to get comfortable. Get it over with. You know what you have to do. Do it!

He tried to remember what he had seen himself doing over and over again during the past three days. Distract her. Get her to turn away. And then . . .

She came back up slowly, cradling a mug in her hands, and moved toward the high, windward bench.

"No, not there," Gordon said quickly as if she were endangering the boat. "Over here, this side." He pointed with his coffee to the leeward bench, closer to the water because of the heel of the boat.

Theresa looked confused for an instant, and then crossed ahead of him to the bench he had indicated. She sat carefully, and then looked up at clusters of stars that reached farther and farther into space. "What a beautiful night!"

"Isn't it," Gordon answered without looking up. His brain was searching for a way to get her standing up on the bench, leaning out over the side, where she would fall out and not back into the cockpit. He tried to sip his coffee but the tremor had gotten worse. He knew he would spill it down his chin.

He felt her eyes on him, almost as if they were casting beams of light. When he looked, she was smiling at him angelically. So young and so beautiful! How could he think of harming her? Gordon responded with a quick, flashed smile and then turned his attention back to the compass.

"Is it hard to steer it on course?" Theresa asked.

"No. Not really once you get used to it."

"Can I try it?"

"Yes, sure . . ."

She wedged her cup between two cushions and slipped between Gordon and the wheel. His arms came around her as they were both steering for a second. He realized that he was pressing against her and pulled back abruptly.

The compass rose began moving slowly, away from the heading indicator. Theresa made the novice mistake of trying to steer the compass back onto course, and began moving the wheel in the wrong direction. Gordon's hands came up and steadied it.

"No, no, move the marker toward the heading. Remember, the compass never moves. It's the boat that moves around the compass."

He started her turning the other way, and she giggled when she saw the movement stop and then the heading marker moved back to the course.

Gordon felt her up against him and remembered how exciting she was. As soon as she was back on heading he dropped his hands again, and watched over her shoulder.

"Try to anticipate," he advised. "The boat turns slowly but once you get the bow swinging it's hard to stop it. Bring the wheel back before you reach the course. That's it! Just like that! You see, it drifted a little bit past but then settled back."

She narrowed the swing of the bow from ten degrees to five, and then to one or two either side of her heading. Gordon followed the process, but he took no pleasure in her success. Get her leaning over the side, he kept ordering himself. Now! Do it now!

Below deck, Ellie turned over in her bunk. In her dream she was fleeing from Gordon—a gross diabolical caricature of Gordon—who was coming toward her with an ax raised over his head. He was shouting at her but his voice was silent. All she could hear were blasts of Theresa's laughter. She was running but her feet were frozen to the spot. There was no escape. And then they were standing over her, Gordon in his dinner jacket and Theresa in the pale dress she had worn to the clambake. They were holding their hands out over her face, dropping a trail of dust into her eyes. A flute was playing the mournful adagio that Theresa had taught Molly. So, it must be Molly who was playing, but Ellie couldn't see her anywhere.

"You're doing great," Gordon told his pupil. "You seem to have a real knack for it." His mind was disassociated from his words. All he could envision was the wrench crashing down on her head. His tremor was even worse, and his resolve had abandoned him. Do it, he kept ordering himself, even though he knew that the moment when he could have done it had passed him by.

Theresa leaned back away from the helm and kissed him on the cheek. Gordon jumped away and stood staring as if she had just infected him.

"What did you want to tell me?" she asked.

"You shouldn't do that," he said in a whisper.

"I wanted to," Theresa answered as if that were an adequate explanation. Then she added, "I love you. You know that, don't you?"

"Damn it, don't say that!" His tone was brutal and she recoiled as if she had been slapped.

Gordon pushed up to the wheel. "Drink your tea," he ordered.

Theresa backed away. "I'm sorry. Don't be angry with me!"

His jaw was set and his eyes suddenly blazing. Theresa took her cup in one hand and steadied herself by clutching the taut mainsheet. She leaned out so that she could see under the sail and look ahead. Gordon set his coffee carefully in the binnacle cup holder. His hand skimmed over his cushion until it found the wrench. He lifted it silently in a tight, white-knuckled grip.

"This is the most beautiful night of my life," Theresa said toward the dots of light that danced on the water. Gordon's hand came off the wheel. He sidestepped toward her without disturbing her. In an instant, he was right behind her, close enough to reach out and embrace her. Maybe she knew he was there. Maybe that was what she was expecting or hoping for. An affectionate gesture of apology for making her unhappy.

Gordon decided in an instant. He raised the wrench high in the air.

Theresa felt the stirring; her head turned and her eyes found him for an instant. She never had time to glance up and see the wrench starting down. She wasn't able to raise a defensive hand, or even tip her face away from the blow.

The wrench struck with cutting sound, like an ax crashing through the bark of a tree and sinking into the wet sap underneath. Theresa's eyes flashed like a light bulb at the instant it burns out. The flash died into dull lead.

As her body began to fall, Gordon pushed with his free hand. Her form cartwheeled over the lifeline and splashed into the rushing sea. A backsplash jumped up over the gunwale and sprayed over the cockpit. Gordon turned aft and glared out over the stern. All he could see was *Lifeboat*'s wake. There was no sign of Theresa. Not even a stain from her open skull.

Gordon turned back to the compass. It had all happened so quickly that the boat had turned down only a few degrees. He grasped the wheel and was startled to hear the clang of the wrench against the wheel's chrome finish. Looking down, he could see the weapon in the red glare of the binnacle light. The entire wrench looked crimson in the light from the compass. The blood at the end of the spanner appeared jet black. He flung his arm out, firing the ugly weapon out of his hand. It hit the lifeline and clattered back into the cockpit. Gordon ran around the wheel, picked it up from the deck, and flung it over the side. He saw a small water spout where it plunged in, and then, like Theresa, it was gone.

He steadied the heading, and then reached back into the tool locker and lifted out a cloth. Carefully, he blotted up the droplets of gore that were spattered along the gunwale. He folded the rag, and used a fresh surface to wipe the stain of the wrench off the cushion where it had landed, and the spots from the deck where it had clattered down. He reached for the cockpit light switch, but instantly pulled his fingers away. If he lit the cockpit, he might still be seen from the tall sloop. Any fishing boat on the horizon could see the bright floodlight. He would have to make due with the glow from the compass in order to make sure that everything was wiped up.

Gordon worked quickly, dashing from the helm to the edges of the cockpit, looking for evidence that he could obliterate. He looked over the side, and saw splash marks on the outside of the hull. Blood stains, he thought, and dipped the rag into the passing sea to wipe them away. But when he lifted the cloth, the stain was only tea, thrown out of Theresa's mug as she fell. He fumbled in the tool case for another heavy object, and found another spanner. He tied it into the cloth as a sinker, and threw the parcel over.

He heard a thumping, and looked around quickly to find what was beating against the hull. It took him a few seconds to identify the pounding of his own heart. His chest was about to explode. Heavy sweat was running down his face and falling in drops. He could feel that his shirt was soaked through. Gordon took several slow, deep breaths. His head began to clear, but in the deathly quiet his heartbeat sounded louder. He eased back onto the bench, and sat quietly, wondering whether he was going to live or die. It took him nearly half an hour to decide.

The time? When did she go over? Gordon realized that he hadn't been thinking of anything except his survival. He had planned to note the exact time, and then sail four more hours before radioing his emergency. He guessed it had been twenty minutes earlier which would put the moment at about eleven-thirty. So, at three-thirty he would put out the call. He could check his position every hour to make sure that he was making at least seven knots. That would put the body about thirty miles from the point where the Coast Guard would begin searching. It was okay. Everything had gone pretty much the way he had planned it. All he had to do was keep his head through what would certainly be a few difficult days. Then it would all be over. The blackmail would end, and he and Ellie could pick up the pieces of their life.

He felt exhilarated. The horror he had felt the moment when he struck was gone. The loathing that had risen up within him as he mopped up bloodstains was scarcely a memory. The tremor was gone from his hands.

Now, the story! How had she gone over the side? Why wasn't she in a life jacket? Why wasn't she able to keep herself afloat for even the few minutes it would take to drop the boat's only sail, start the engine, and get back to her? He had to be ready with answers, and he had decided that the best answer would be no answer at all.

She was looking out, thought she saw a light, and leaned out to look under the sail. Just leaning out, holding her tea in one hand, and keeping her balance by holding the mainsheet. It certainly wasn't seamanlike, and he had told her to be careful. But she was in no danger. The seas were calm, and the boat was steady. Sure, it was heeled, but only ten or fifteen degrees. Twenty at the most. And then it all happened in an instant. She seemed to lift her knees from the bench so that she could lean out farther. Gordon was more concerned with holding course. He warned her again not to lean out, but he would have to admit that his warning was only half-hearted. More reflexive than real, like telling your child not to run so fast. Just the kind of thing that you say automatically without really worrying that something might go wrong. He guessed that her foot slipped off the bench, or that the seat cushion she was standing on might have moved. But she was suddenly cartwheeling over the lifeline, tumbling around the hand that clutched the mainsheet. He remembered a thump against the hull. Her hand or her shoulder striking it, he had thought at the moment. But, in retrospect, it must have been her head. She must have knocked herself out cold because she never uttered a cry. Nor did she come back up. When he snapped his head around, he expected to see her clearly in the wake, probably no more than a few feet behind the boat, but he saw nothing. Not even ripples where she had plunged through the surface. Not a trace.

He did all the right things for a man-overboard emergency. He pulled the life ring from the rail and threw it into his wake. He came hard into the wind, luffed the sail, and freed the halyard, letting the sail drop into the wishbone cradle. The engine started instantly.

He screamed down to Ellie, and she was up on deck just about the time he crossed back over his wake. There was a handheld lamp in a fitting on the forward bulkhead. Ellie pulled it free as she came up. She had light on the water instantly. We were back running over our wake that was still perfectly visible within a total time of thirty seconds. Maybe a bit more, but certainly nothing like a minute. We expected to see her! We had to be within fifty feet of the spot where she had gone over. I pulled off my windbreaker and picked up my life jacket. I was positive that I would be leaping over to grab her and bring her back to the boat. But we couldn't see her.

Ellie started calling her name, and then I was calling her name. I kept going for maybe fifty yards until I was positive that I had gone back too far. I came about sharply and we ran back up the track. I was concerned, for sure. But not panicked at all. It wasn't possible that she could be gone so quickly. I still expected to see her or hear her voice.

Then I remembered the thump. Suppose she had hit her head? Oh, Jesus, she might be unconscious. Maybe her voice was too weak to hear. I killed the engine and we stopped dead. There were no waves or troughs to speak of. I took the lamp and aimed it all around the boat. We both kept calling her name, and I still expected her to answer. We drifted for maybe a minute, searching with the light. And now I was getting frantic. I ran from side to side, looking and calling. I thought of firing up a flare. But she couldn't be more than thirty yards from where we were. She would have to see the lamp and hear our voices.

I snapped on the cockpit light, which gave us a lot more ambient light out onto the water. I stared at individual spots, certain that I would see her floating just below the surface. And I thought, there's still time. If I see her, I can dive in and get to her instantly. I can hold her head up and get her breathing as I pull her back to the boat. The two of us will have no trouble getting her back onboard.

Maybe Ellie said that we needed help. Or maybe it suddenly dawned on me that we weren't going to find her. We were monitoring the Coast Guard emergency frequency. I picked up the microphone and broke in with an emergency man-overboard call. What time? Jesus, I never noted it in the radio log. But you must have a record of when I put in the call. How long? God, it's really a blur. I'll guess no more than five minutes after she went over. Probably a lot less than five minutes. When I think about what we did, it should only have taken us two or three minutes. But it seemed like it went on forever.

We kept searching back and forth over the same spot. I threw over a couple of dye markers so that we wouldn't lose the place. We were still searching when . . .

Gordon didn't know what would happen next. There might be a boat nearby that would answer the call, and he might fire a flare to help the boat find him. Or he might have to wait a few hours for a cutter to make it out from the shore. But whatever it was, they would find him running search patterns back and forth over the dye stain. Then they would all join in looking for her even though the Coast Guard professionals would know that she was dead. They would keep searching until Gordon showed some awareness that she couldn't still be alive.

He had been sailing over an hour, and still the only sound was the lap of the waves and an occasional rattling or whistling from the sail. He took a satellite fix and was able to figure that he was making good about seven knots. Everything was holding. By the time he called for help, Theresa would be thirty miles away.

His new fix put him thirty miles east of Biddeford, and twenty-five miles south of Boothbay Harbor. He was ahead of his planned schedule. He had run faster when he had decided to kill her before full darkness in order to be aware of fishing nets. Then it had been later than he planned when Theresa had come back up on deck. He wanted to sail three more hours away from the point where he had dumped her over, but he was only twenty miles from the nearest point of land to the north. He would have to compromise.

Gordon swung from his northerly heading to the northeast, out toward Monhegan Island. That put the wind astern, which meant he would lose some speed from the heading he had been holding. But it allowed him to maintain his distance from the shore while opening more space between the boat and Theresa's body. He would hold the heading for another hour, possibly an hour and a half depending on the speed he could make good. When he radioed his emergency, Theresa would be at least fifteen miles behind, perhaps as much as twenty. And he would still be twenty miles off the beach.

True, he would be a bit to the east of the logical track between the Cape and Boothbay Harbor. But he would explain that as a precaution to keep him from approaching the coastline before daylight.

The boat wallowed with the wind on its stern and the seas coming off its starboard quarter. Steering became more difficult, but Gordon found the added workload a blessing. It helped him keep his mind off the fact that he had just committed a cold-blooded murder.

He knew there was justification. He had been fighting to defend his family, and Theresa hadn't left him with any choice. Her demands would have increased as she saw how safe and easy extortion was. His only way to end it would have been to admit his sins, and that would have been even more disastrous than the payments. There was righteousness in striking back at a blackmailer.

But still, it was murder. He had destroyed her with the heaviest blow he had ever struck. It was more obscene than the sins it was designed to hide. He couldn't let himself dwell on the facts of his guilt. He had to learn to understand what he had done in terms of the protection of his wife and children. He had to relish his newfound freedom rather than suffer through the memory of his depravity.

He took another satellite fix. Even though the boat was hardly leaving a wake on its new heading, it was holding its speed. Another hour! That was all that it would take.

THIRTY-NINE

"Ellie! Ellie! Get up here! Now! Get up here!"

Gordon's voice broke through her stupor. She heard frantic footsteps on the deck over her head, and when she tried to climb out of her bed she realized that the boat was making a sharp turn across the sea.

"Ellie! I need you up here!"

She heard the engine crank over and explode into life. The vibration reached her through the mattress. She had been sleeping in her underwear as she always did when they were underway. She pulled on her jeans, pushed her bare feet into her docksiders and started out of the cabin. But her hand flashed out and grabbed the doorjamb. She was suddenly dizzy, the confined space below decks whirling around her. She steadied herself as she made her way to the foot of the ladder.

"Ellie! Ellie! Get up here! Theresa went over. She's in the water."

She was trying the steps on her hands and knees, shaking her head violently to break through the fog. Theresa couldn't be in the water.

She was standing beside Gordon dropping dirt into her grave. And Molly was playing the flute, although Ellie realized that she couldn't hear the music anymore. Everything seemed disjointed. She couldn't decide which part was a dream.

The night air hit her. She knew she was alive. Gordon was calling to her as he dashed from rail to rail and looked frantically down at the water. Then, the pieces began to make sense.

"Where is she?" Ellie screamed.

"Out there. Just off the bow. Get the lamp. Give me some light on the water." He held the wheel at arm's length so that he could peer out over the port side. "There, on the port bow," he screamed. "I can see the life ring!"

She fumbled with the lamp while Gordon shifted into neutral. The light beam found the orange ring immediately, floating only a boat length ahead.

"Theresa!" Gordon screamed.

Ellie circled the light around the life ring.

"What happened?" Ellie demanded.

"She fell over." Gordon began backing away from the life ring. "Get up on the bow!"

Ellie jumped out of the cockpit and found her footing failing her. She grabbed the handhold rail and carefully worked her way forward. Gordon turned on the cockpit light, casting a glow on the sea all around them. The ring drifted under the bow. He shifted to forward and threw the wheel hard over. The boat began to turn slowly across the spot. He ran quickly from one side of the cockpit to the other. Ellie looked to both sides, flashing the light about, even though she knew she would never see her. She remembered the plan that Gordon had outlined, and realized that Theresa was several hours behind them.

It was a pantomime staged to convince themselves that the terrible accident had just happened, as if going through the motions of anguish could dull the razor sharp knowledge of guilt. In their act, they were lying to themselves and lying to one another. Gordon was saying, "See, I didn't do it. It really was an accident." And Ellie was able to say, "I know you could never have done it. And certainly I never could have taken part." But even as she flashed her lamp back and forth across the water, Ellie knew it was a charade. He had thrown Theresa overboard. She must have heard the girl scream and simply blocked it out of her mind.

She flicked off the lamp and stumbled aft to the cockpit. Gordon saw her, and gave up his own pretense. He held out his arms.

"Ellie? Are you going to be all right?"

Her dead eyes looked back.

"It's over," he told her. "There was no other way."

She nodded slowly, signaling her acceptance of the fact. But she knew that there was another way. And she wondered whether it would have been as painful as the pain she felt now. She turned and moved slowly down into the cabin and then stepped quietly forward to be with her babies.

"Coast Guard, Coast Guard! This is *Lifeboat*. I have a man overboard! Man overboard! Do you read me?"

The response came in an instant. "*Lifeboat,* this is Portland station. Understand man overboard. Do you require assistance?"

"That's affirmative," Gordon said. "A passenger went into the water a minute ago. I'm searching, but she's gone. No sight of her. I need assistance in the search."

"*Lifeboat,* give me your position."

Gordon gave the latitude and longitude readings he had gotten from the satellites. Then he quickly gave his range and bearing from Cape Elizabeth, just south of Portland. The Coast Guard officer repeated both sets of figures and Gordon confirmed them.

"We have a chopper taking off right now," the officer assured. "We'll have boats heading toward you within a few minutes."

A new voice broke in. "Coast Guard, this is the yacht *Commander*. I'm located one zero five Portland, twenty miles. I'm turning to zero nine zero. On engine, I'm about three hours away from *Lifeboat*."

The Coast Guard officer acknowledged. Then he asked Gordon if he had a dye marker aboard, and told him to throw it over to mark the spot. "Do you have emergency flares aboard?" Gordon said he did. "Have them ready to fire at the chopper pilot's request. And at *Commander*'s request. Keep your GPS fix up to the minute. We're on our way."

Ellie came back through the cabin and saw the stale coffee on the galley stove. She touched the cold pot and examined the stain on the inside of the glass. Then she noticed the dried tea bag left on a saucer in the sink. Gordon would tell the Coast Guard that Theresa had just made him coffee and fixed herself a cup of tea. The remnants in front of her were obviously several hours old. She threw the tea bag in the trash and filled the coffeepot with water. Don't wash it, she told herself. No one would ever wash the pot before bringing the coffee topside. She sneered at her deviousness. The lying was starting all over.

She went back up to the cockpit, lit the electric lamp and began sweeping it idly over the side. She knew she had to be immersed in her role when the rescuers came on the scene. The light hit a dark red stain and she fell back in horror. "Blood?"

"Dye," Gordon told her. "To mark where she went over."

Ellie moved back to the rail. "What was it like?" she asked suddenly.

He pondered his answer. "Very quick," he said.

"Did . . . she scream?"

"No, nothing. She was leaning out, holding the sheet. Her feet came out from under her. She spun over the rail and hit the side of the boat. I saw the splash, but I never saw her in the water."

Ellie turned and stared at him. "The truth," she demanded.

"That is the truth," he answered instantly. "It's all the truth either of us has to know."

"But you told me. You planned for her . . ."

"We planned for nothing," Gordon snapped at her. "We took a mother's helper into our home. If we planned anything wrong it was only that we might use her for some publicity. We never planned what she would do to the two of us. God knows, we never planned to harm her."

Ellie's face contorted as she struggled to fight back the tears. Gordon reached for her and drew her into his arms. "We were victims, Ellie. Victims of extortion. Victims of malice that would have ruined us and destroyed our children. Now it's over. I'm not happy that Theresa is dead, but I'm glad that she's out of our lives. You should be, too."

They waited, huddled together, until the helicopter crewman's voice broke in on their radio and requested a flare. Gordon took the pistol, loaded a cartridge, and fired it over the mast. A burst of light exploded above them, setting the sea aglow with a pink flame. Before the flare had died in the water, they heard the whopping sound of distant helicopter rotors.

Ellie went down with the children who were frightened awake by the roar of the chopper as it hovered overhead.

"Where's Theresa?" Molly demanded.

"She has to leave us," Ellie said. "She's going away in the helicopter."

Molly tried to bolt up but Ellie held her back. "Not yet, honey. It's dangerous up there. You can come up and wave when the helicopter is leaving."

Molly screamed, "Why is she going?"

"Someone is sick at her home. They need her."

Timmy started to cry. "I want to see the helicopter."

The chopper circled around the dye marker, using a powerful search-light to keep the sea illuminated. Then it began a careful search back over Gordon's course line cutting back and forth in ever widening arcs in a fanlike pattern. It was no higher than the boat's mast, and its rotor wash was flattening the sea. The light was bright and crew members in wet suits were hanging out both sides ready to dive in at any sighting. They were still searching feverishly when the sky began to lighten in the east.

A masthead light appeared in the west, and then the running lights of a tall ship that was heading straight toward them. As it drew near, there was enough light in the sky for Gordon to recognize the ocean-going sloop that they had met at sunset. Through his glasses, he could make out the name *Commander* on the bow, and see the concerned faces lined up along the rail. There were four or five couples, along with a crewman standing on the bowsprit. Her sails were down, but she was making enough speed to kick up a sizable bow wake. She had power to spare in her engine room.

Commander began running a search pattern under the helicopter's search pattern, then she began moving away to the southwest following the drift of the prevailing current. She kept floodlights burning on her mast until the glow was erased by the rising sun. It was morning, and they were all searching furiously. They had seen absolutely nothing.

The Coast Guard vessel came on the scene. She was a small boat, more like a center-console fisherman than a military ship. But she was bristling with antennas and spinning surface-search radar. She came alongside, and a young officer, carrying a laptop computer, jumped the gap to land on *Lifeboat*'s deck.

"Lieutenant Myers," he said as he climbed down into the cockpit, offering his hand. Gordon recognized the voice from his earlier radio conversation. He sat on the bench next to Gordon after ordering his boat to cast off and join in the search.

The lieutenant got right down to business, entering the name and registration of the boat on a computer form. He asked for the insurance policy and copied pertinent data, inventoried the life jackets and the life raft, checked the first-aid kit. Gordon flashed his impatience, but the officer plodded ahead, taking information about Theresa. Next, he wanted personal information on everyone onboard. When he asked Timmy's age, Gordon snapped, "Why in hell is that relevant to anything?"

"It isn't," the officer admitted. "But it's on the form. I have to ask."

He noted the position fixes on the Gulf of Maine chart, entered information on the make and model of navigation systems and radio gear, described the layout of the cockpit, and only then got around to asking Gordon exactly what had happened.

Gordon told his sparse story. Theresa had been awakened by one of the kids. She came to hatchway and asked him if he wanted coffee. A few minutes later she came up into the cockpit with coffee and tea.

"She didn't put on a life jacket?" Lieutenant Myers interrupted.

"No. There was no reason . . ." Gordon responded. "There didn't seem to be any danger. The sea was calm and the wind steady." He looked up with despair in his deep-set eyes. "How could anyone fall over?"

He went on to describe how she had gone to the rail and steadied herself by holding onto the mainsheet. "She thought she saw a light, and she leaned out just a bit, and then bent over so that the sail wouldn't block her view. I said 'Be careful!' but the words were hardly out of my mouth when she tumbled over. I guess she was counterbalancing the weight she was leaning out over the water by jamming her leg against the lifeline. Then her foot slipped, and the weight took over. She went head over heels, as if she were diving and trying to do a flip."

Next Gordon described his instant response. He had pulled the life ring from its fitting and thrown it over the stern.

"How long did it take?"

"My God, five seconds at the most. I saw her go and I reached for the ring." The officer noted the time.

Gordon then demonstrated how quickly he had been able to come about. The boat was designed to be handled by one person. The mast was far forward and there was only one sail. "I know the boat so I was able to move damn quickly. I had the sail down and was running under power within another few seconds. I came about and was back on my wake in no more than thirty seconds. Even a nonswimmer should have still been afloat."

Next, Gordon offered the only possible explanation. He told of the thud against the side of the hull as Theresa tumbled. She must have hit her head hard enough to knock herself out. "But if she were still breathing, wouldn't she have stayed up? For a little while at least?"

Myers shrugged. "Hard to say. Without a life jacket . . ."

Ellie came up into the cockpit. The children had been confined below for several hours. She had to get them up on deck, but she didn't want them to realize what had happened to their friend. The officer sent Gordon below while he took her statement.

She had been awakened by her husband's cry, Ellie said. She came up instantly—probably within a few seconds, but certainly less than a minute. She was already half dressed. When she reached the deck, the sail was down and the boat had already come about. She took the lamp and went forward, fully expecting to find Theresa in the water. It had been such a short time. They had found the ring within a minute, so Theresa had to be right there within a few yards of the boat. But there was no trace of her.

"How long was it between the time you heard your husband and the time when he called on the radio?"

Ellie thought in silence and then shook her head. "I can't be sure. We went back and forth over the spot several times. We kept calling her name, and then listening. We even shut down the engine so we could hear her voice. We knew she had to be close by. We both expected to find her."

"Ten minutes," the officer suggested.

"I don't know. Probably longer. It seemed like an eternity. Maybe twenty minutes."

Lieutenant Myers suggested that Gordon head for shore and tie up at the Coast Guard station in Portland. He would stay with the search party until they had exhausted every hope. He would radio Gordon on his administrative frequency if they discovered anything.

"You think she's dead, don't you?" Gordon asked, trying to put some sort of closure to what was probably obvious to everyone.

Myers nodded. "It looks that way. But as long as there's any chance at all . . ."

FORTY

The story hit the wire services that night, thanks to a young reporter with a Portland newspaper who found irony in a passenger drowning from a boat named *Lifeboat*. He linked the yacht with Gordon Acton's company, and a telephone call gathered the information on Gordon's congressional candidacy.

His lead, stating that a young woman had been lost off Acton's boat, started a frenzy of rumors that quickly reached the networks. Only after they had aired partial reports filled with innuendos of impropriety did they identify the woman as the children's babysitter, and stress the fact that the candidate's wife was aboard. At that point, the story became routine, and disappeared from the electronic media. Newspaper coverage drifted to the back pages and then vanished. Except in Providence, where the story had political ramifications, and on the Cape where it was snapped up by the social set.

In his Rhode Island political district, friendly local papers played up the fact that Gordon had hired Theresa from a disadvantaged background, and had already committed to paying most of her college costs. Hostile papers noted that the Actons apparently had not provided the same level of supervision and safety to their hireling as they did to their own children. Henry Browning polled the constituency and found that the original negative reaction, based largely on the early, incomplete reports, had pretty much dissipated once the full story was out. A later poll picked up hints of sympathy for the candidate and his family. "It shouldn't change anything," Browning told Gordon in a phone conversation. "It's still going to be a landslide."

On the Cape, the story settled into the town papers, which no one read carefully or took seriously. There were photos of the boat, and remarks about the exclusive club from which it had sailed. Photos of the Acton family appeared with backgrounders on the family business and history. Society editors paid much more attention to Ellie's background as a descendant of the founder of Rhode Island. The coverage was sympathetic.

Shock and sympathy were the socially acceptable reaction of the yacht club members. Jack O'Connell referred to the loss of a *child,* even though he had publicly lusted to get into Theresa's pants. Pricilla Mapleton told everyone how close she had come to feel toward the dear girl. Trish cried at the loss of a true friend, and hugged other teenagers as they shared their grief. Theresa, the local weekly reported, had won a place in all their hearts. The tone was *inner-city waif taken in by the best people.*

At the bar and on the docks, where the true sailors gathered, the opinions on Gordon were judgmental but forgiving. He shouldn't have allowed an inexperienced sailor out on deck without a life jacket during a deep-water voyage. There should have been a blinking light attached to the life ring. Even more fundamentally, why plan to sail overnight? He could easily have followed the coastline and put into port at night. What was his hurry? But, they all agreed these were matters of the captain's discretion. Gordon certainly wasn't a reckless sailor, and there was no reason why he should feel personally responsible. The sea, after all, was a cruel mistress.

Gordon had rented a limo to take him and his family back to the Cape, and sent a hired crew to bring the boat back. He made his first appearance at the club to meet *Lifeboat,* and was joined on the dock by sympathetic well-wishers. He checked his lines, went aboard briefly to pick up some of the clothing items that had been left aboard and the still unopened bottles of rum and gin. He thanked the others for their expressions of friendship, and then drove back to the house. Ellie was down on the beach with the children, and the emptiness of the house was upsetting. He opened the gin.

He was sitting down on the porch with his second drink when he heard a car rumbling across the crushed stone in the driveway. He went to the window, and saw a man he vaguely recognized starting up the front steps. It was only when the man looked up that Gordon was able to see the piercing eyes and identify Sergeant Wasciewicz. He backed into the house, slipped his drink into the refrigerator, and waited in the living room until the man knocked.

"Mr. Acton," the sergeant stated.

"That's right," he answered through the screen door. "And you're the sergeant who's working on the semiconductor case." He pushed the screen door open as an invitation to enter.

"Right! Sergeant Wasciewicz." He looked around as he entered the living room and seemed to approve of the modest decor.

"How can I help you?" Gordon asked, gesturing for his guest to make himself comfortable. "Maybe a cold drink for starters?"

"Iced tea. Or a soft drink."

Wasciewicz was standing at the fireplace admiring the family photos on the mantle. "Nice kids." He took a Diet Coke and settled into the sofa. Gordon sat on the front edge of a soft chair.

"How's your investigation going?"

Wasciewicz shrugged. "We got our guy. And I guess we'll never know about your young lady." He shook his head slowly. "I want to express my sympathy. That must have been a godawful ordeal."

Gordon nodded solemnly.

"But I really need to ask you and your wife a couple of questions. You might be able to help me bury this punk."

"She's not in," Gordon said. "And we've both given full statements to the Coast Guard. There's not much we can add."

"I'll try not to take you through the same things again," Wasciewicz promised as he flipped the pages of a notepad. "But it's a different jurisdiction. Different interests."

Gordon sat across from him, looking pained but resigned.

"Did you know Theresa Santiago was pregnant?"

Gordon's face fell. If he had been expecting the question and rehearsed his reaction, his expression could not have been more stunned. The man had just trifled with his darkest secret.

"I guess you didn't know," the sergeant said dryly.

Gordon stared at him and then answered, "I don't believe it."

"Yeah, kids these days. Hard to believe, aren't they? But she was. She went to a doctor over in Providence. A clinic really."

"Oh my God . . ."

"Any idea on who could be . . . responsible?"

Gordon shook his head. He tried to speak but his tongue was pasted to the roof of his mouth.

"Was she seeing someone that you know of?"

For an instant he thought of mentioning Don McNeary, but he decided that would be adding another crime, maybe even worse than the one he had already committed. He shook his head again and pursed his lips. "No one in particular. She knew a lot of young people. The kids here seem to hang around in a crowd."

"It wouldn't be this crowd," Wasciewicz interrupted. "She was three months pregnant. It would be back in Providence when she was first working for you."

Air rushed from Gordon's chest as if he had been punched. "Three months . . ." His mind whirled. Three months ago he hadn't even met the girl. "Then she was . . . expecting . . . most of the time she's been working for us."

"You never knew? Never even suspected?"

"No, of course not! Why should I?"

"What about Mrs. Acton?"

Ellie's voice sounded clear and controlled. "What about Mrs. Acton?" she said.

Wasciewicz climbed to his feet, dropping his notebook in the process. Gordon continued sitting, letting his face sag into his hand. The sergeant looked from one to the other, waiting for some kind of introduction. Then he took a step toward Ellie. "I'm Sergeant Wasciewicz. I'm finishing up my notes for the coroner's inquest . . . concerning Theresa Santiago. I was just asking your husband a few questions. Routine background stuff."

Ellie didn't budge from the doorway. "What about Mrs. Acton?" she repeated.

He looked toward Gordon for help.

"You better sit down," Gordon suggested. Ellie glanced warily from one man to the other and then took the chair nearest to the door.

"The sergeant was just informing me that Theresa was pregnant. Three months pregnant. She had already been to a clinic."

Ellie's hand flew up to her mouth, a soft groan escaping from her lips.

"I guess you didn't know, either?" Wasciewicz concluded. Ellie made no response. He sat down again, picked up his notebook and turned a page.

"Did Miss Santiago ever mention, a guy named Karl Sinder . . . or Cat Sinder?"

Ellie and Gordon looked at one another, and Gordon answered for both of them. "Never heard the name."

Wasciewicz went on, "Did she have any meetings that you know of, outside the house? Did she ever meet someone in another town?"

Gordon got to his feet. "Sergeant, you said routine questions about Theresa's accident. Why are you asking us about her private life? Or her life before we even knew who she was?"

243

"Because it might not have been an accident."

Ellie flinched. Gordon's face drained of color. Then he recovered and turned to a snarl of anger. "Now what the hell is that supposed to mean? If it wasn't an accident, what was it?"

The sergeant answered a question with a question. "Could it have been a suicide?"

Now Ellie flashed anger. "That's outrageous. A lovely, young woman out enjoying a vacation. Why would she want to . . ." She left the question unfinished.

Wasciewicz closed his pad. "I'm sorry, but there's background here that creates some problems. Theresa . . . Miss Santiago . . . was suspected of being involved in thefts from the place where she worked. Computer codes and passwords were fabricated so that expensive components and assemblies could be taken out of inventory without anyone knowing. It was going on for nearly a year, before she quit and went to work for you."

"Theresa?" Ellie was shocked. Gordon nodded in her direction, confirming what the sergeant had said.

"Karl Sinder is probably the guy who was running the operation. He got very close to Theresa. Took the girl around to the best places and gave her a taste of the good life. He may be the father. Theresa had access to the security software. She could have been the one who set up the codes, although so could a lot of others. But Sinder tried hard to keep Miss Santiago from quitting. And when the investigation began focusing on him, he had every reason to try to bring her under control."

"Theresa?" Ellie repeated in total disbelief.

"So, if she knew she was going to have his baby, she was faced with maybe having to go back to her old life. Or maybe she thought she was going to be implicated in the robberies and would be taking her baby off to jail."

"But, she slipped," Gordon said, now sounding much less sure of himself.

Wasciewicz reopened his notebook and flipped through to an entry. "That's what raises the question. Because you told the Coast Guard that she just flipped over the side. One second she was there, the next she was gone. You said that she *must have* slipped. So my question is, are you sure she didn't jump?"

"Ridiculous," Gordon snapped.

Ellie's eyes began to fill. She stood up abruptly. "Excuse me, Sergeant. But I wasn't there. I have no way of knowing whether she slipped or jumped. And I have to check on my children." She hurried out, trying to control her growing hysteria.

"She didn't jump. She was still holding her teacup. And she grasped at the mainsheet to try to catch herself. That's what spun her back into the side of the boat."

"But she didn't answer when you called. She didn't swim back to the surface."

Gordon bristled. "She hit her head on the hull."

"Yeah," Wasciewicz went along, "but apparently not very hard. The Coast Guard says there were no marks anywhere on the hull. And hitting the cold water like that usually revives people."

"Well, it didn't revive her," Gordon said.

"Or, maybe she didn't want to be saved. You see my point? You and your family are giving her everything. But she knows she can't have it, and that she's going to end up living with a cheap hood, or maybe even living in prison. The police are asking a lot of questions. Maybe she thinks we're right on her heels. That she's going to be arrested as soon as she reaches shore. So, she doesn't want to get there. She wants it all to end right now, while she's with her new family."

Gordon settled back into his chair. "I can't buy that. There would have been some sign, wouldn't there? She was playing with our kids. Taking pictures with us. The last thing she did was make sure I had a cup of coffee. There was no hint that she had a problem, no look of sadness, no nervousness."

"So you're positive that she slipped, hit her head, and was helpless in the water?"

Gordon thought. "No, I guess I'm not positive. Her position was a little careless, but not terribly dangerous. I guess I concluded that she slipped because I didn't know how else she could have fallen. But I certainly didn't think that she had jumped. And the way she was right up to the last second, I can't believe she had any thought of suicide."

Wasciewicz seemed to be satisfied with the answer.

"Although," Gordon said, to stop him from putting away the pad, "I can't, in all honesty, rule out the possibility."

The policeman mumbled a thank you and a few words of sympathy as he left. Then Gordon walked down the steps to the beach where Ellie had gone to rejoin the children. She was sitting on the bottom step, watching Molly and Timmy as they played in the distance. He sat down quietly beside her.

"It wasn't your baby," Ellie said, summarizing what she had been thinking.

"I never thought that it was," he answered.

"Then why was she such a danger? She couldn't have hurt you."

"Yes she could. She knew I couldn't take a chance on even having the question raised. If it came down to it, I couldn't swear that I had never had sex with her. And that would have been the end of everything."

Ellie lowered her face and began drawing in the sand with her finger. "What's everything? Your political career? My degree? What was more important than her life?"

"Ellie, she was going to saddle us with another man's child. And then use it to bleed us to death. We didn't have much of a choice."

"You think we were right?"

Gordon weighed his answer. "As right as we could be under the circumstances."

Ellie glanced out into the bay. "Then why do I feel that I died with her?"

Gordon put his arm around her to draw her close but she kept her distance. "You had nothing to do with it. You weren't even there."

"If I had just stayed up the way I planned. I knew if I stayed on deck that nothing would happen to her. That you wouldn't . . ."

"You were tired. You can't blame yourself for that. You'd been up since sunrise without a break."

"I think I knew what would happen. And yet I went below. I went down to the cabin and pulled a pillow over my head. Doesn't that make me guilty? Doesn't it mean that I really wanted to be rid of her?"

He stood up. "Stop this Ellie. Nothing makes us guilty. She was the one who was guilty."

September

FORTY-ONE

The service was in an old Catholic church, built by immigrants and then passed on to a new generation of immigrants. The Portuguese had built it, pledging donations from catches that hadn't yet been born in the sea. Their names were on the stained glass windows, and most of the pews toward the front. Next came the Italians, who stayed just long enough to learn English and put their children through the parish school. And now it was Hispanic, bringing together Puerto Ricans, Dominicans, Salvadorans, and Nicaraguans.

The service was in Spanish, with a priest presiding who looked to be no more than twenty. Ellie and Gordon couldn't understand a word. But they gathered from the reactions of the mourners that he was depicting Theresa in the embrace of the Virgin. The women in the half-filled church were dabbing at their eyes, and the men were sitting straight, their arms folded, and their faces as fixed as stone. Theresa had obviously made an impression on the community, and her loss was shared by many.

They had learned about the service only the night before, when Henry Browning had called Gordon to suggest that he might attend.

Gordon understood; it was an exercise in damage control. There was little to be gained by attending, but a great deal to be risked if he didn't.

Ellie felt hypocritical at the thought of joining the mourners. She hadn't put it in so many words, even to herself, but they had wanted the girl dead and she felt tainted at the idea of pretending to be grief stricken. They had driven through a devastated neighborhood looking for a place to park, and then had seen every eye turn toward them as they entered the church. They went halfway up the aisle, stopping well behind the chief mourners who were bunched together in the front pews. They were trying to show that even though they were not really family, they loved the girl like a daughter. Twice during the priest's homily, they noticed eyes turning toward them. The expressions held no hostility. Apparently, their interest in Theresa was being acknowledged and praised.

And then the formal service was over. People in the congregation were lining up to take a carnation from a basket and place it on the altar. Ellie and Gordon fell into place, walked slowly up the steps, and paused for an instant with feigned memories of the girl. In truth, they felt awkward, out of place, and were simply pantomiming what others had done before them.

They waited until the priest processed down the aisle, and until the front row mourners had followed him. Then they moved into the center aisle, and took their turn in thanking the celebrant. They were on the outside steps, trying to remember the direction to their car, when an elderly couple came up the steps toward them.

"Mr. Acton," the woman said. "I'm Mrs. Hernandez." She gestured to include her husband but never introduced him. "We were parents to Theresa. She lived at our house."

Ellie cut in front of Gordon and embraced the woman sincerely. "She talked about you every day," she said. "You were her family."

The woman smiled. Her husband shifted awkwardly from one foot to another. Gordon held out his hand to the man. "I'm happy to meet you at last," he said, assembling a combination of sadness and joy. "Theresa spoke about you constantly."

"*Sí*," the man said, smiling pleasantly. He didn't speak English, and had no idea what Ellie and Gordon were saying.

"She was such a lovely girl," Ellie told the foster mother.

The woman shrugged. "She was young. You could either hit her or hug her. Sometimes she was happy."

"She loved you," Ellie said.

The foster mother wasn't terribly impressed. "Theresa didn't want to be like us. She had big ideas. I think she wanted to be like you."

Ellie struggled for a comment. She settled for another friendly embrace.

The woman backed away, opened her handbag, and took out a videotape, still in its paper container. "She sent me this. She said it showed where she was living and that I would love the children she was minding."

Gordon's eyes locked on the cassette. There *was* another copy. She had sent it home, and now someone else knew his secret.

"We thought you might want it," the woman said.

Gordon responded immediately. "We certainly would want to have it. Can we pay you for it?"

She pressed the tape into Ellie's hands. "No pay! We don't have a player. Just a television. But she said you were good people and that she loved the children. So I think it has to be about you." She looked at Gordon. "You have a player. You can see what Theresa liked."

Gordon clutched the tape tightly as they walked to the car.

"No VCR," Ellie said in disbelief. "The evidence that was going to destroy us has been sitting next to people who couldn't even look at it."

"So why did she send them the tape?" he asked, in a tone that said he already knew the answer. "She didn't want them to see it. She wanted them to mind it."

He drove back to their apartment, and paced nervously as he waited for the elevator. "Do you want to see this?" he said as they came through the door. He was headed directly toward his entertainment center.

"No, I don't think so. I don't want to see Theresa with the children, and I certainly don't want to see you with Theresa." She closed the bedroom door behind her.

Gordon started the video, and stood directly in front of the screen. There were lines and electronic noise patterns, followed by a second of black silence. Then Theresa appeared on the screen, a talking head looking directly into the camera.

"Hello Rita! Hello Juan! I hope you're both well and that everything is okay." Her eyes glanced down, probably at some notes she had written. "I wanted you to see the place where I live and the people I'm living with. It's right out at the end of Cape Cod, where I showed you on the map."

Ellie heard Theresa's voice and couldn't resist. She opened the bedroom door and stood leaning against it. Theresa went on describing the beach, and the club, and then the children. Molly, she said, was so talented. Timmy was precious. As Gordon looked at her he could see her bed in the background. The camera was sitting on the bookshelf, just where he had found it. He had been right that by leaving it running she could photograph every move of their lovemaking.

Her voice stopped and her picture disappeared. And then there were the home movies she had made of the children, the family, and the various settings that they lived in. It was the same tape she had given them and Gordon recognized the sequences. He came to the part where the camera had been left on the clubhouse porch and had caught her coming out of the water.

"She's gorgeous," Ellie said, startling her husband. She had crept up next to him while he was absorbed in the image. He grunted in agreement, his eyes never leaving the screen. Together, they watched the events of the summer; the sand castles, cookouts, beach games, swimming events. There were frequent cuts to Timmy, sound asleep while family activities or children's games were happening all around him. And then it ended, just as the copy that they had already seen ended.

"Nothing," Ellie said. "She never had any pictures for us to worry about."

"There's another half hour of tape," Gordon answered.

Theresa reappeared, once again standing in front of the camera in her bedroom. She repeated the nice things she had said about the Acton children, and then promised Rita and Juan that she would see them soon. And then the screen went dark, playing nothing more than the markings of blank tape.

Ellie turned and went back to her bedroom. Gordon sank into the sofa, staring at the crackling screen, waiting for the damning footage to appear.

But it wouldn't appear, Ellie realized. Theresa hadn't been that devious and cold-blooded. Maybe she had seduced her husband, or simply submitted willingly to his advances. She wasn't inexperienced, as they had learned from the police sergeant. And maybe she did think that she could get something in return. She wanted a better life, and the Actons were probably her best chance. But she hadn't staged her husband's crime and then coolly photographed his performance just to entrap him. And it was probably Gordon's guilt more than her intent that made her hopes sound like threats. She may have been a young woman on the make, but she probably wasn't a blackmailer.

Could the same thing be true for herself? Perhaps all Theresa had done was try to score points by reminding Ellie how much work she had done on the dissertation. Maybe the blackmail was a product of Ellie's own sense of guilt.

FORTY-TWO

The coroner, a geriatric judge from Plymouth who had been given a bench on the Cape as a reward for party loyalty, wore his robes in the conference room and sat at the head of the table. Ellie and Gordon were side by side a few places down one side. Ellie was wearing a simple black dress in keeping with the solemnity of the inquest and as a token of mourning. Lieutenant Myers from the Coast Guard rescue boat sat to the judge's left. Sergeant Wasciewicz was directly across from Gordon, and there was a middle-aged woman behind a stenographic machine seated near the table's open end.

There were three people in chairs along the near wall, introduced as reporters for papers in Providence, and from the local weekly. Judge Gamble had closed the proceedings to the electronic media, but it was an idle gesture. There wasn't enough interest to send camera crews to the scene.

Presentation of the facts was completed in just a few minutes. Gordon repeated his version of what had happened aboard *Lifeboat* three weeks before. He stressed the word *slipped* in referring to Theresa's fall into the sea, and argued that his first and lasting impression was that her foot had slipped out from under her. Still, under questioning by Judge Gamble, he repeated his comment that he couldn't be absolutely certain that she hadn't jumped.

Ellie recounted the delightful day spent aboard with her family which, she said, certainly included Theresa. "To the children, she was a big sister, and to me an older daughter." She told of taking the helm while her husband got a few hours of sleep in the cockpit. Then, when he was rested, she went below to her bed. She was up instantly when Gordon shouted, and joined him on deck in just a few seconds, probably less than a minute. The boat had already dropped its sail and come about. They found the life ring in the water almost immediately and were sure that Theresa was close by. Only gradually did she begin to realize that the girl was lost.

Her eyes were filled, and she occasionally dabbed with a tissue. Her grief was obvious and genuine, leading the judge to extend a few soft words of thanks for her ordeal in testifying. But he resumed his gruff demeanor when he turned to the Coast Guard officer.

The lieutenant read from the report of the accident, going into an excruciatingly detailed description of the boat, its paperwork, and its equipment. His summary conclusions:

No body had been found at the scene or recovered later.

The victim's effects were still onboard.

The yacht was perfectly seaworthy and well-equipped.

The actions that Mr. Acton said he had taken immediately after the incident were the correct man-overboard procedures. He was a skilled and experienced captain who had performed properly in the emergency. The only discrepancy was in the time it had taken to radio the Coast Guard. Mr. Acton's original message had said the girl had gone over only a minute earlier. Mrs. Acton recalled that they had searched for several minutes before they radioed for help.

The victim should have been wearing a life jacket and both Gordon and Ellie's testimony indicated that she had been wearing one earlier. Undoubtedly, both she and the captain thought it was unnecessary because she was not going to remain up on deck, and because the seas were calm and the boat was sailing on an even keel.

"Is it against the law to be out in the open on a boat without a life jacket?" the judge growled.

"No sir, not at all! The law requires life jackets to be available. It's up to the captain whether passengers and crew should put them on."

"But the jacket would have saved her?"

The officer went to his water glass, and then answered, "In all likelihood, yes."

Judge Gamble glared at Gordon. "So, why didn't you make her put on a life jacket?"

Gordon nodded toward the Coast Guard officer. "For the reasons the lieutenant suggested. The weather was nonthreatening. Theresa wasn't going to remain up in the cockpit."

"Why didn't you keep her away from the side?"

"She thought she saw a light, and leaned out for a better view. I told her it was dangerous and told her to get back inside. She was gone almost before I finished the sentence. The whole incident took about five seconds."

The judge looked displeased but satisfied with the answer. Gordon assumed that the inquest was over until Gamble looked up and said to Sergeant Wasciewicz, "Okay, what have you got?"

Wasciewicz introduced a deposition from a doctor in Providence. Theresa had been late in her first trimester of pregnancy. She had refused a referral to a women's clinic because "there was someone she had to talk with first." There was nothing unusual about that. Theresa's visit became unusual when a detective entered the clinic moments after she had left, and told the doctor that the girl was under police surveillance. Gordon was instantly alert. *Surveillance.* Had she been followed the night when she stayed in his apartment?

Next, he presented the report of an ongoing investigation of theft from Theresa's workplace. Karl Sinder had been arrested and was awaiting trial. He had admitted a relationship with Theresa Santiago, and had used that relationship to get her to alter security procedures at the company. Sinder didn't know that Theresa was pregnant, and thought that her baby could be "a lotta guys'."

Both Ellie and Gordon were stunned when Don McNeary was brought in as a witness. Wasciewicz had interviewed all the young people at the club who knew Theresa, and found McNeary's testimony particularly relevant.

"She told me she was pregnant," he said, focusing all his attention on the hands folded in his lap. "And she was real scared. She didn't want to tell the guy because she didn't want to have anything to do with him ever again. And her foster parents couldn't help her because they didn't have any money. She figured she wouldn't be able to go to college, or anything."

Did Don consider helping her? "Heck, no. I didn't need to get involved with someone else's baby."

Did he offer Theresa any advice? "Yeah, I told her to go to Mrs. Acton. But Theresa said she didn't want Mrs. Acton to know anything about her past. So I told her she could trust Mr. Acton. He seemed like a decent guy at the club, and he had lots of connections. She didn't say anything for sure, but I got the impression she might ask Mr. Acton to help her."

No, Don couldn't say for sure whether she had ever told anyone besides himself. But he had to agree that she was really scared. "It was like all of a sudden she had more than she ever dreamed of. And now, she was afraid that she was going to lose it all."

The judge looked straight at Gordon. "Did she ever ask your help?"

Gordon thought long and hard before answering. "She did ask if we would have a chance to talk during the vacation. But she didn't say what she wanted to talk about. I guessed she wanted to ask me something about her college arrangements. And both Ellie and I were anxious to help her."

"So, she might have been trying to work out her problems," Judge Gamble suggested.

"I think she would have," Gordon said. He reached over and took Ellie's hand. "Mrs. Acton and I certainly would have helped her. Theresa was a remarkable young woman."

The judge glanced at the detective. "I don't think there's nearly enough for a presumption of suicide."

Wasciewicz bowed in defeat. He had hoped to link Theresa's death to Cat Sinder's crimes. If the district attorney could suggest that Sinder had corrupted a decent young woman and then driven her to suicide, the jury would be more apt to demand the maximum sentence.

But Ellie bristled at even the suggestion of suicide. She spilled her purse contents on the table and picked up a packet of photo prints. Without a word to anyone, she sorted through the pictures and set three or four of them into a separate group. She pushed these in the general direction of the judge.

"These were taken a few hours before Theresa died. I don't understand how anyone could think that she wanted to end her life."

Gordon came halfway out of his chair to deliver the photos to Gamble, and the judge sorted through them several times.

"She doesn't look suicidal to me," he said, pushing the photos back toward Ellie. "So, the coroner's inquiry finds that the cause of death was accidental drowning at sea." He picked up his papers and stood abruptly, as if he were late for a tee time. "I want to thank all of you. And offer my sympathy to the Actons. It seems as if they've lost a daughter."

He was out the door in a flash. Wasciewicz gathered his own notes, nodded curtly toward Ellie and Gordon, and left. Don McNeary came up to apologize if he had caused the Actons a problem. "I got a subpoena that said I had to be here." Gordon patted him on the shoulder.

It was over. The verdict had been delivered. Gordon was relieved. But Ellie was sinking further into despair. Theresa had had no one to turn to with her impossible problem. And when she turned to her and Gordon, they had crushed her skull and tossed her overboard. There was no court on earth that could exonerate her.

FORTY-THREE

They sat in the Land Rover outside the courthouse, watching the lieutenant, the sergeant, and the judge drive away. The stenographer locked the front door when she left and didn't even glance in their direction when she pulled out of the parking lot.

"It's over!" Gordon announced.

Ellie kept looking at the photographs she had given to the judge. Gordon put his hand on her knee. "You going to be all right?" he asked.

"She didn't want to blackmail you," she answered. "She just didn't know where else to turn for help."

"Ellie, don't torture yourself. What she was doing is obvious: she was carrying a child, and there were two men she could name as the father. One was a small-time gangster on his way to jail. The other was a millionaire with maybe enough political clout to keep her out of jail. Theresa knew exactly where to turn for help."

"But why would she need to threaten you?" Ellie wondered in a voice that was fighting hard to keep from breaking.

"Why would she make a phone call and tell you that we had . . . been together?" Gordon said. "She didn't want our help. She wanted you to kick me out so I'd be free to take care of her."

"I don't believe it!" Ellie insisted.

"Why else would she tell you about me? And if all she wanted was our help, why would she have threatened to take credit for your dissertation?"

Her tears began to come. She stuffed the photos back into her handbag.

"Don't sanctify her, Ellie. The girl was a street-smart schemer. She worked a scam on the company that paid her, and left the poor thug she was sleeping with to take the blame. Then she worked us over for social status, college tuition, and even a complete new wardrobe. And she was just getting started. Face the facts! She was going to stick me with the hoodlum's baby, and let me pay all the kid's expenses for the rest of my life. The girl was bad news. The only thing she didn't count on was that we might fight back. And that's what we did. That's *all* that we did."

He started the car, and moved slowly out to the highway that would lead them back to the house. Gordon grilled a light dinner, which Molly and Timmy ignored. They were still angry that Theresa had left them to take care of someone else. Ellie took the children through their night-time rituals, and sat with Timmy until he fell asleep.

Then she went out and sat morosely on the steps to the beach, sipping vodka on the rocks and looking out at the starlight reflections on the bay. She was pondering what they had been through and trying to define her role in Theresa's death. Gordon was probably right. Theresa had held them hostage, and ransom would continue to rise as she grew bolder. But still, she was hardly more than a child. A child who had learned to scheme and steal for everything that she needed. She didn't deserve to die. She was entitled to whatever help was needed to overcome her incomprehensible background.

"You don't have a clue," Theresa had told her. And she was absolutely correct. She might threaten her and Gordon, but they had all the resources needed to turn the girl around. There was no reason to fear her. They should have been able to help her. God knows they had everything and Theresa had nothing.

Gordon sat beside her and pulled her close. His hand brushed her hair away from her shoulders and he leaned close to kiss her neck. Ellie tried to accept his advance, but the thought of burying themselves in one another turned her cold. They had a horrible crime between them. They couldn't act as if their lives had never changed.

"It's late, and I have to be back in town in the morning," Gordon whispered. "Let's go up to bed."

She tried to say yes, but she couldn't. "Not yet, Gordon. There's a lot I have to work out before I can pick up where I was. I feel . . . dirty . . . defiled."

"You shouldn't," he said. "You know that I love you."

"I think I know that Gordon. But I'm not sure I love myself."

He kissed her good night at the foot of the stairs, and tried to find a comfortable position on the living room sofa. Early in the morning, before the sun rose, he dressed, wiped the dew from his car, and drove back to Providence.

FORTY-FOUR

She was up early, and had breakfast waiting for the children when they came down. She outlined the day she had planned. First, they would spend the morning on their own beach. Sand castles, swimming, and ice cream and juice from their camper chest. Then lunch back at the house, and then a trip off the Cape to Plymouth, where they would shop for new school clothes.

The uprising began instantly. Molly wanted to go to the club and join in the day camp. Timmy didn't want to go to any stores. Ellie cajoled; the children sulked. She knew that she should do everything possible to get them back into their routine. But she didn't think she was ready to face the sympathy and concern of the ladies at the club. To break the impasse, she did the worst possible thing. She screamed at her children and told them that she didn't care what they wanted. She endured an hour of their anger until she admitted to herself that she didn't want to go shopping for back-to-school clothes either. "Okay," she finally said to Molly. "Let's start all over again. What do you guys want to do?"

She left them playing on the beach and started up onto the deck. But she stopped on the stairs as soon as she was high enough to see the clusters of members at the outdoor tables. God, but she didn't want to face them. She eased quietly down the steps and decided to take a long walk along the water's edge. She had only gone a short way past the club when she heard someone coming up behind her.

"Mrs. Acton . . ."

She turned and found Don McNeary trotting toward her.

"Mrs. Acton. Hi. I just wanted to talk to you for a minute. If that's okay?"

"Sure Don," she said, but she turned and kept walking, letting him scurry to catch up.

"I just want to say how sorry I am. For what happened, and for showing up at the coroner's inquest. I didn't want to go. But my dad's lawyer told me they could make me. And he said that if I didn't answer their questions I could end up in jail."

"I didn't want to be there either, Don. I heard things about Theresa that I never wanted to hear."

"Well, I knew *some* of it, because she talked to me a lot. What someone tells you in private, as a friend, ought to be a secret. But the lawyer said that at a coroner's hearing, there couldn't be any secrets. I felt like a rat talking about what she told me."

"You shouldn't blame yourself. You had no choice."

"Yeah, I know. But there's something else you might be hearing, and I want to set it straight."

Ellie stopped walking and gave McNeary her full attention.

"Theresa never said that she was doing your work for you. That was something that the girls thought up."

"The girls?"

"Yeah, the ones in the crowd. Theresa was talking about all the great stuff she was learning. Maybe she was bragging a little about a doctoral thesis, and this important professor who thought that your stuff was great. But see, these girls have all been to terrific schools, and most of them are in name colleges. And they just couldn't take this . . . foreign . . . girl being so much smarter. They figured she was blowing smoke, and someone came up with the idea of getting her in trouble."

"Who?" Ellie asked softly. "Trish?"

"I don't remember," Don lied obviously. "All of them together really. They were going to send you a letter telling you that Theresa had been bragging that she was writing your doctoral thesis. Then someone said 'Not Mrs. Acton. She'll never do anything to Theresa.' So they sent the letter to the professor instead. They wanted to take her down a peg or two. When I heard, I told them it was dumb. You were the one they'd be hurting. But they had already sent it. They were even working on another one and planning to make phone calls."

Ellie was open-mouthed, wide-eyed, and turning pale.

"It was a rotten trick, and I know I shouldn't be telling you about it. But I didn't want you to think that Theresa had done it. I know how much you meant to her, and she never would have done anything to hurt you."

She buckled and dropped down into the sand, first to her knees and then to her haunches. Don didn't realize what was happening until she was down, and then he didn't know whether he should be helping her back up. He went down on one knee beside her.

"Mrs. Acton, are you okay?"

Her jaw was locked and she was shuddering as she held back grief that was filling up inside her.

"Mrs. Acton, can I help you?"

"Please, just leave me."

"Where? Here on the beach?"

"Just go. Please."

"I can't just leave you here. Are you all right?"

"I'll be fine. I just need to be alone."

He got up slowly and then backed away a few steps before he turned and started back to the club. But he kept slowing, turning, and glancing back over his shoulder. His expression was worried, even frightened.

Ellie sat back on her heels. Her fists were locked against her sides and her shoulders were rigid. Her neck swelled as she fought to hold back a scream. Suddenly, she was crying uncontrollably. She rolled onto her side and buried her face in her arms.

Don turned and ran back to her. "Jesus, Mrs. Acton, I didn't mean to upset you. Please, let me help you back to the club."

Ellie kept her face hidden and just shook her head.

"I can't leave you this way," Don insisted.

"Just leave me, please. I'll be all right."

He stood slowly, and walked away reluctantly. She was still curled up in the sand, crying hysterically.

Minutes later she lifted up slowly, running her forearm across her eyes. She stood, brushing the sand from the front of her shirt and shorts. She walked back along the beach until she reached the place where her children were playing. Then she sat in the sand next to them, watching the small waves wash in and out.

FORTY-FIVE

Gordon slept late in the morning, showered, and called Henry Browning while he was still wrapped in a towel. "What do you hear?" he asked.

"Well, our telephone poll is encouraging. Most people think you're a good and caring man who has just suffered a terrible loss. There are a few who think you should have taken better care of her, but even they express sympathy. But that's only the telephone calls, and it's not really all that certain."

"When will we get the hard stuff?" Gordon asked.

"Tonight. We should have some tabulations done by morning. Why don't we have dinner? There are some events coming up that I need to cover with you."

They ate at Henry's club, a very modest men's escape with indifferent food and little interest from the younger set. Gordon called it a tomb, but Henry defended it as the one place he could eat without having politicians and lawyers join him for just a moment, and stay on talking until they could join him for coffee.

He made small talk until his fish was served and then asked Gordon for his opinion of the inquest. Gordon dismissed it as pretty much routine, except for the salacious details of Theresa's criminal past.

"Some of that was news to me," Henry said in one of his rare admissions of fallibility. "I knew, of course, about the police investigation into the theft of semiconductors, and I had heard that she was under some suspicion. But I had no idea that they had closed the noose so tightly. And as for her being with child . . ." He shook his head in disbelief.

"A shock," Gordon agreed. "But nothing about her past can change my opinion of her. She was a bright, caring young woman. If she had been charged with a crime, I would have spent a fortune on her defense."

Henry paused with his fork in midair. "Now, wouldn't that have been something? Gordon Acton defending a guilty-as-sin Hispanic kid from criminal charges." He shook his head, moved his fork and chewed vigorously.

"You would have played it up big?"

"Most certainly. I would have worked to have the trial moved up to before the election. You'd be on the evening news every night, sitting at the table with her. And Ellie would be right behind you."

"I suppose you would have bought the jury, too?" Gordon asked cynically.

"Of course. I'd have paid anything for a guilty verdict. And then the election would occur while you were battling for an appeal. Tell me how many of Theresa's neighbors would have voted for your liberal opponent then?"

Gordon laughed. "You're much too much, Henry. But wouldn't you worry that some of our conservative districts would turn against me? They think everyone who isn't like them should be in jail."

They both enjoyed the irony of a candidate from the establishment taking up an immigrant cause. But Henry got back to the topic at hand and predicted that—barring some unforeseen catastrophe—Gordon's landslide would make him an instant subject of speculation for the governor's mansion, or maybe even a Senate seat. "We have ignition," Browning said. "Now the only question is how high will the orbit be?"

" 'Governor'," Gordon repeated, liking the sound of the word. "Do you really think it's possible?"

"One job at a time," Henry cautioned. "Although I don't see why not. You're rich. You bathe daily. And you have no passionate causes that are a threat to anyone. That just about covers all the prerequisites."

They felt so good that they ordered dessert.

It was over coffee that Henry got to the troubling news. "You remember the arrangement that I made to end your . . . friendship . . . with Miss Lambert, your PR counsel?"

"Of course," Gordon said, the fine spirits fading from his expression. "I've got to figure out some way to make that up to her. Although I don't look forward to telling her. She'll go crazy when she finds out that we hired somebody to put a move on her."

"She found out," Henry announced without fanfare.

Gordon dropped his fork onto the tablecloth. "Christ, she didn't! How in hell could she find out?"

"Her suitor actually became infatuated with her. He wanted a real romance, so he felt obliged to confess the nature of his earlier feelings. She struck him with a bookend, and dislodged several teeth."

"Jesus!" Gordon's face sank into one of his hands.

"There shouldn't be any problem with him. I gladly paid all medical bills to assure that his jaw was wired shut. But I think you ought to arrange a business meeting with the lady. In the privacy of her office where she won't want to make a fool of herself. I passed the word that you knew nothing about my little deception. But I think it would be a good idea if you assured her as well. As I said before, hell hath no fury . . ."

Pam obviously didn't want to meet in her office. She fumbled for excuses, and came up with her summer interns who used her office for their conferences. "They're always in and out. Why don't I come over to your place?"

Gordon didn't want her announcing their affair in the lobby of Action Boats, and he couldn't ask her to stop by his apartment. He suggested a small Italian restaurant that they both agreed had the lightest pasta in the city. Pam grumbled that the tables were too close together, but finally gave in. She was already at a corner table when Gordon came through the door and squinted into the darkness.

They danced around anything of substance, making small talk about the menu, deciding on an expensive Brunello, and then asking about family and friends. Their dishes had been served and the waiter dismissed before Gordon hinted at a weightier topic. "Pam, there *is* something we have to talk about. And I'm terrified about getting into it because I know it's going to make you mad as hell."

"Don't worry about it," she answered softly. "I knew it was coming."

He set down his fork. "You knew *what* was coming?"

Pam looked confused, and then blushed to a deep red. Gordon hunched his shoulders to signal that he had no idea what was going on.

"That you were going to drop us, take your account away. And I don't blame you. My only excuse was that I was with a friend, and we were both smashed. Maybe a little stoned on top of it. But by the next day . . ."

"Pam, what in the name of God are you talking about? I came here to apologize to you."

"You did?"

"I had dinner with Henry last night and he told me that he had arranged for . . . your *suitor*." The word sounded ridiculous. "The guy you dumped me for."

She nodded. "Yeah?" Her tone said "What's the rest of the story?"

"Well, Henry thought it was a political necessity, and I guess that keeping us apart was a good idea. But when I heard that he had recruited the guy and put him on to you, I was incensed. We were at his club, and I made a terrible scene."

"So did I when I found out. I thought it was the worst, most deceitful thing that anyone had ever done to me. I hit him with a bookend. Luckily, it hit his mouth. If it had been higher up on his head I probably would have killed him. Then I called a girlfriend for some sympathy. We got blotto, and then smoked some stuff. I haven't done that in about fifteen years. But we were really gone when I made the telephone call."

"I don't blame you at all . . ." Gordon started, but then he heard what Pam had said. "What telephone call?"

She laughed ironically. "Boy, are we on different frequencies." She paused for a moment to gather herself. Then she said, "Gordon, I'm so sorry that I called Ellie. I mean, I was blistering mad, and I probably would have killed you if you had been handy. But I never would have dragged your wife into it, if I weren't . . . wasted. I hope to God you know me well enough to believe that."

"You called Ellie?" His expression was wide open in disbelief. "You told her . . . we . . ."

"Oh my God, she never told you," Pam concluded.

Gordon was stuttering. "It was *you*? You told her about *us*?"

Pam looked back at him in stunned silence.

"It was *you*," he said more to himself than to Pam. Something unbelievable was coming together in his head. "*You* . . . not *her* . . ."

"She *did* tell you," Pam realized. "And you thought it was someone else?" Her eyes narrowed with a hint of brewing anger. "I've been agonizing over my stupid call and you didn't even know that it was me."

He snapped back to his senses. "No, that wasn't it. Ellie told me about the call, and we figured it was political. Someone on the other side was trying to stir up trouble. We didn't take it seriously," he lied. "Ellie didn't cut my allowance."

She reached across the table and grasped his hand. "Gordon, I can't tell you what a relief this is. I was sick over all the agony that I was causing your family. I'm so glad that she didn't believe me." She laughed in her sense of escape, and smiled at him, waiting for him to explode in laughter at the pain she had caused herself.

But there was no humor in his expression. His eyes filled and his jaw was showing a tremor. He looked vacantly in her direction, oblivious to her words. He seemed to be having some sort of spell.

"Are you all right?" Pam asked with concern.

"Yeah, sure. But I just remembered something." He looked at the uneaten lunch and the still-filled wine glasses. "Pam, could you just put this on my bill? I've got to do something."

Gordon rose slowly, and picked up speed as he neared the door. He never looked back at Pam, nor did he return the greeting of the bewildered owner. Pam called the waiter and asked for the check.

He drove like a robot, unaware of the turns he was making or the traffic he was negotiating. His mind was numb, churning the same images and phrases, but unable to bring them into order where they might build to a conclusion. Nothing had happened the way he had seen it. None of the things that he knew had ever been true.

She hadn't taped him in her bedroom. The video images had existed only in his mind. And it wasn't his baby. Theresa had never said that it was. Nor had she tried to break up his marriage. He was the one who assumed that the telephone call had to have come from her.

And yet, she threatened him. She kept telling him how much money she needed. She maneuvered him into writing the checks for her college expenses. She threatened Ellie, and coerced her into her school wardrobe. But she hadn't really said "Pay up or else." Maybe she just hoped that they would help her. Maybe they were the ones who had coerced themselves.

What were the words? Exactly what had she said? Gordon couldn't remember with any certainty. All he remembered were words that fit with his reactions. Did she really link the money with the videotape? Or had the linkage been in his own imagination?

What had she said to Ellie? Hadn't she talked about money the day before she and Ellie went to the university? And hadn't she shown Ellie the records of all the work she had done on the dissertation just minutes before she mentioned the cost of her school clothing? No, wait! What did Ellie say? Theresa said she was going shopping and asked Ellie to come along. Wasn't that the same thing? Didn't she know that Ellie would go overboard? But that wasn't the same as threatening! Or demanding payment! Except that Ellie thought that was precisely what Theresa was up to. Did Ellie remember the words?

A car horn blared next to him. He was turning onto a ramp, cutting a car off in the process. And for an instant he wasn't sure what ramp it was. Then he noticed he was heading back to Cape Cod, which wasn't where he had intended to go. He had meetings with supporters that Henry had lined up. His desk back at the office was scattered with items that had been neglected too long. He needed to be in the city.

But he had to talk to Ellie. What exactly had Theresa said? He wanted to go over the computer file that she had left. Was there a chance that it was there simply as a ready reference to help Ellie with her paper?

He suddenly realized that he didn't want to talk with his wife. He couldn't let Ellie know that the phone call had been from still another woman. Maybe she could manage to forgive his mistake with Theresa. After all, she herself had been taken in by the girl. But could she forgive a habit of philandering? If there were two other women, there were probably even more.

There was still another reason why Ellie could never find out that Theresa hadn't been the one who arranged for the damning telephone call. Ellie was stretched to the breaking point. The only thing that was keeping her from wiping the blood from her hands as she walked the halls was the notion that she had no choice. She could make it through, maybe even build on the notion of self-defense. Knowing that Theresa was willing to destroy her and her family made it possible for her to live with her feeling that she had conspired in guilt. But if she ever found out that Theresa wasn't threatening anything! If she even guessed that the girl had cared for her! Gordon knew Ellie would never make it through the truth. Her guilt would rise up and devour her.

Carefully, now aware of what he was doing, Gordon eased to the right and pulled into a side street. Then he turned back to the apartment. He needed to rest. Perhaps call Pam with some lame apology. Then he needed to get back to his company, and back to his campaign. If he could just pick up his life where it had been before Theresa. He was a candidate for Congress. His wife was about to earn her doctorate. They were a charmed couple with great things before them. That's where they should be. But could they ever get back there? Or, were they launched aimlessly into space?

October

FORTY-SIX

The yacht club stayed open well into October, hosting members and guests who cruised the New England shoreline for the reds and oranges of the fall foliage. But during the weekdays, the building was a deserted hulk. Most of the members returned to the mainland cities for the start of the school year. The dock boys, tender skippers, and lifeguards were off to colleges that stretched from Indiana to North Carolina. The professional help headed for tennis and golf resorts in Florida.

Ellie came out to the Cape on weekends, loading the Range Rover on Friday afternoons, and driving up from Newport during the night, when the children could sleep and the roads would be empty. Gordon came out from Providence on Saturday. Then, the first weekend in October, a Canadian cold front brought the season to a close. Gordon and Herman, the caretaker, put up the shutters and drained the pipes. An ex-chief from Newport's navy years came up with a wharf-rat friend and together they took the boat back around Woods Hole to its winter home in Newport. Gordon got Ellie and the children settled, and then he headed north to Providence, and the most demanding month of his campaign schedule.

"She *will* be joining us?" Henry Browning assumed when Gordon apologized for Ellie's absence from a fund-raising dinner.

"I hope so," Gordon answered, not sounding at all confident.

"More than half the campaign workers are women," Henry reminded.

Gordon snapped, "I know that, and Ellie knows it too. But she still hasn't gotten over the accident. She clings to Molly and Tim as if she's afraid that they're going to be next."

"Mourning isn't the answer. She needs to get back into the swing of things."

"I'm sure she will," Gordon promised.

But he wasn't sure at all. Ellie was now certain that all the dangers Theresa had posed had been in their imaginations. They had killed her for no reason.

"You didn't kill her," he told her over and over again, hoping to see some light in her empty eyes. "*I* did what *I* thought I had to do. I still think she planned to lay her baby at our doorstep and take us for everything she could get."

"She wasn't the one who called the university. Why did I believe that it had to be her?" And then Ellie would go back through all the evidence they had assembled, and insist that Theresa hadn't been responsible for any of it.

He phoned her every afternoon and every night, always hoping that she would be out doing something, or that she would gush over with details of an exciting afternoon. But she was always there, picking up on the first ring, which told him that she was in her bedroom. Their conversations were stilted and her voice almost a monotone.

His political light began to grow dim. He was barely going through the motions of campaigning, distracted when he should have been involved. Henry made excuses for him and even tried to rouse some sympathy. But he could feel the enthusiasm of Gordon's supporters dying around him.

He suggested a psychiatrist. "A very close friend who still believes in privacy," Henry said. "No one will ever know that she's seeing him, and he may be able to help her unburden herself."

Gordon dodged a decision. How could he tell Henry that the last thing he wanted was for Ellie to begin unburdening herself? She wanted desperately to confess to someone; to tell in detail exactly what had happened, and hope to be convinced that she wasn't guilty. It might save her mind, but it would most certainly destroy his future.

He just had to be patient. It was only another few weeks until the election, and even if his majority was slipping a bit there was still no doubt that he would win. Then he would move her to Washington, which would be an exciting new beginning with new challenges for her and the children. It would take time, but surely a new life would help her pull herself out of the wreckage of her old life. They didn't need a psychiatrist, all they needed was time.

"They found Theresa's body," Browning said over the phone early one morning. Gordon, who had reached for the phone without opening his eyes, was suddenly upright in bed.

"When?"

"Yesterday afternoon. It will be in tonight's paper, buried toward the back. They have to report it, but I've been assured that it won't get extensive play."

"Where?" Gordon asked.

Henry sighed. "Where she went over, I suppose. A fisherman pulled her up with a net full of fish."

"They're sure it's Theresa?"

"Not yet. There isn't much left to identify, so they'll need to look for dental records. But Sergeant Wasciewicz seems to think that what *can* be identified fits her description."

"Sergeant Wasciewicz? The guy with the stolen semiconductors? Why is he still involved?"

Henry assured Gordon that it was the same policeman. "He's still trying to connect her death with that hoodlum. If he can show that the gentleman drove her to suicide, he thinks he may be able to get a stiffer sentence out of the court. At least he hopes it will keep them from letting the thug off with probation."

"How does he hope to prove it was a suicide? Was there something unusual about the body?"

"I'm sure it will be in the paper," Henry said. "I called because I thought you might want to be with Ellie when she hears about it. You should be able to get down there and still make it back for tonight's dinner."

He raced down to Newport where he found Ellie sitting on the porch outside their bedroom as if she were a recovering invalid. The children were with a nanny who had taken them to buy school supplies. He sat beside her for awhile, admiring the remnants of the fall colors that were still visible across the Narragansett. Then he told her that Theresa's body had been found.

Ellie acted as if she already knew. Theresa, she had decided, would never be out of their lives. The fact that her corpse was back only confirmed her feelings.

"What will they find?" she asked.

"Exactly what they'd expect to find. The badly decomposed corpse of a drowned girl. They already know that it's her, from her jewelry, her height, and weight. They're going to check dental records just to be certain."

Ellie simply nodded. Everything he had said made perfect sense. Theresa had no choice. She had to come back.

"None of this is your fault," Gordon told her again. "But we can expect more inquires from the press. They'll want our comments and our thoughts. That's about all we can give them."

"We're glad they found the body so that she can finally rest in peace," Ellie said.

Gordon was surprised, "That's fine. Exactly the kind of thing we should say."

"And then I'll add that this will help her family and her many friends to reach a point of closure."

"Fine . . . fine. That's great."

"And then, I should add that we had to kill her because we thought she was blackmailing us. Only, she wasn't blackmailing us at all. It was all in our imaginations, but we knew she was scheming to be just like us. You see, Theresa thought that we were pretty wonderful. She never knew . . ."

Gordon pulled her to him and pressed his lips against her mouth. There was no response. It could have been a final kiss to a dead person.

"That's the truth, isn't it," she said as soon as he had pulled away. "All she wanted was to be like us. Good breeding, good school, and a trust account."

"Ellie . . ."

"Why, Gordon? Why would anyone want to be just like us?"

He rocked her in his arms as he tried to calm her. He was still holding her when the front door burst open and the children rushed into the downstairs hallway shouting for him. Ellie was immediately alert and was down the stairs well ahead of Gordon. She was on her knees, hugging Molly in one arm and Timmy in the other by the time he reached the bottom step.

He asked the nanny to stay over for the night. "There may be some calls for Mrs. Acton, and I think it's best if you just tell them she's not at home." He laid out the sleeping pills on her night table before he returned to Providence.

Sergeant Wasciewicz didn't use the telephone. He drove up to the front door early the next morning, moments after the nanny had taken the children to school.

"Mrs. Acton. I hate to bother you so early, but there are a few loose ends . . ."

"You're the police sergeant, aren't you?"

"Yes, Sergeant Wasciewicz," he answered, holding up the leather case with his badge. "I met you out on the Cape."

"And at the coroner's hearing," Ellie said. "And now you're here to tell me that Theresa's body has been found."

"You know already?"

"My husband told me. And the news put me right back into a funk. I was beginning to survive, and now I'm back to step one." She pulled the front door wide open and stepped aside. "I was just going to make some coffee. Would you like a cup?"

Wasciewicz followed her into the kitchen and then went to the sliding doors so that he could look out over the patio and see the bay. "Boy, this is beautiful," he told her without taking his eyes from the panorama of water and shoreline.

"Do you live in Newport?" Ellie asked.

Wasciewicz wandered back to the table and sat. "No. I'm from Fall River. It's nice, but nothing like this."

She leaned against the counter, the coffeepot gurgling behind her, and looked down at the sergeant. "You didn't come all the way down here just to tell me about Theresa's body."

"Well, yes. But then there are a few inconsistencies I've been hoping to clear up."

"How can I help?" Ellie asked. Wasciewicz asker her to run through, once more, everything she could remember about the night when Theresa went over the side.

She went back to the day before and detailed minute by minute all the events leading up to sunset. She told how they had sat in the cockpit until the sun set behind the sloop that she later learned was the *Commander*. Then she described Gordon sleeping on the bench while she held course, and mentioned how easy it was because of the light air and the flat seas. Then, after eleven, Gordon awoke and took over. She went below and fell fast asleep.

She was graphic in describing the emergency that had awakened her. She took the sergeant through the search, the life ring, and their confidence that they would find her any second. And then, the slow realization that she was gone. Even when they knew she was dead, and had called the Coast Guard, they continued to search just on the chance that she might still be out there, struggling in the sea.

She interrupted her narration while she poured the coffee and brought cream from the refrigerator. She was sitting across from him when she said, "We left the boat and climbed into the limo Gordon had rented. I haven't been back aboard the boat since."

Wasciewicz had pulled out his notebook while she was still standing by the coffee and began writing notes. He was writing and flipping from page to page for a full minute after she finished.

"That's pretty much what you said in your deposition, and at the inquiry," he finally said, still referring to his notebook.

"What were you expecting?" Ellie asked.

Wasciewicz looked up directly at her. "I thought maybe you might want to tell me the truth."

She didn't seem shocked. She just stared at him, wondering what it was that he didn't believe.

"A couple of things we found out just don't jive with what you just told me," he went on. "Like, for example, there's no way you could have missed finding the body, because it didn't sink for several hours. She would have been floating right next to the life ring."

"Why?" Ellie asked, more curious than frightened.

"Because she didn't drown. She was dead when she went into the water. So her lungs still held a lot of air."

Ellie looked puzzled.

"She might have gone under from the momentum of her fall, but she would have bobbed right back up to the surface. She wasn't breathing so her lungs didn't fill up."

"You mean she was right there where we were searching and nobody saw her?"

Wasciewicz sipped at his coffee. "That's the problem. She wasn't right there where you were searching."

"She wasn't?"

"No. She was twenty-five miles back, judging by where the fishing boat netted her body."

Ellie took a moment to register what the policeman had just told her. Then she said, "I don't think that's possible. I was still up in the cockpit twenty-five miles earlier."

Wasciewicz shrugged his shoulders. "That's where they found the body."

"Well then it must have floated over there."

"Against the current?" he asked.

"Maybe she was dragged by another fisherman's net."

"Then why didn't he pull her up?"

Ellie sat staring across the table for a moment, and then jumped to her feet. "I can't help you with your problem, Sergeant. I know she was still aboard when I turned in, and that couldn't have been more than a couple of hours before my husband sounded the alarm. I can't explain your problem with a floating body, or which way the current was running."

Wasciewicz made no move to get up. Instead, he flipped back through his notebook. "You said Theresa had already gone to bed before you went down for the night."

Ellie nodded. "Yes, that's what I remember."

"And the next thing you knew, your husband was calling you."

Another nod.

"So then," he reasoned, "sometime before, Theresa got up from her bunk in the main cabin, got dressed, made coffee and tea, brought it topside, and you never heard a thing?"

Ellie didn't nod. This time she stared curiously and slipped slowly back into her chair.

"And yet," Wasciewicz continued, "when your husband called, you heard him right away and were on deck immediately. How do you figure that?"

"I don't know," Ellie mumbled. "I hadn't thought about it . . . like that . . ."

"You see the problem. According to your husband's timetable she fell over right after she came up on deck. So that means there couldn't have been more than a few seconds between the time she fixed the coffee and the time she fell over. She was right outside your door when she was banging around in the galley and you heard nothing. But your husband calls from up on deck, and you're wide awake."

"She must have been very quiet."

"Do you always sleep so soundly?"

"I don't know, maybe it was the sea air," Ellie guessed.

"Did you have a lot to drink?"

"I hadn't had anything to drink."

"Did you take something to help you sleep?"

"I don't take sleeping pills . . . at least, I didn't then."

He paused, weighing the danger in his question. Then he asked, "Could your husband have given you sleeping pills?"

Ellie's face registered recognition, and for an instant Wasciewicz thought she might be about to tell him something. But then she went back to her blank, bored expression. "Sergeant, I've really told you all that I know. I have nothing more to say." She stood at the table, signaling him to get up and leave, but he wasn't taking the hint. He was still involved in turning through the pages of his pad.

"I have a very tight schedule," Ellie said, "and I'd really like to get started. There's nothing more for you here."

"Just a few more thoughts," he said, settling on one of his notebook entries.

"No," she insisted. "If there are going to be any more questions I'll want my lawyer to help me answer them. Would you like his name so you can set up an appointment?"

His eyes came up slowly, filled with sympathy rather than anger. "Why don't you just tell me what happened out there, Mrs. Acton? I think you want to talk about it. Sooner or later you're going to have to tell someone."

She began to tremble, and then her guilt broke through her act like a chick coming out of a shell. She collapsed back into the chair, buried her head in her arms, and began crying hysterically. Her body heaved with each sobbing gasp.

"Mrs. Acton," Wasciewicz said several times. Then he extended a hand and rested it on her shoulder.

Ellie took several minutes to get control of herself, and then sat still with her face still buried in her arms. When she finally raised her eyes, he was holding out a tissue. "Can I get you a glass of water? Or maybe another cup of coffee?"

She shook her head. "I'd appreciate it if you'd just leave."

He folded his notebook and slipped his pen into his jacket pocket. "It's not going to get any easier for you, Mrs. Acton. It just gets worse. You're going to have to talk to someone . . ."

"Please," she begged.

Wasciewicz dropped his card on the table. "Thank you for your time. And feel free to call me whenever you're ready."

Ellie waited until his car had disappeared. She stepped outside, lingered for several minutes at the top of the steps that led down to her dock. Then, when there was no sign of his returning, she raced down to the boat.

She stepped aboard *Lifeboat* carefully, almost as if she thought someone might be aboard. She glanced across at the lifeline that Theresa had fallen over, and back to the helm where Gordon had said he was sitting. Then she opened the hatch and climbed down into the cabin.

She went directly to her stateroom head, and opened the medicine chest. She pushed through the Band-Aids, the antiseptics, and the creams that eased anything from sunburn to bug bites. The sleeping pills weren't there. Ellie closed the cabinet and moved forward to the crew's head that was in the saloon. Again, she tossed through the medicines looking for the sleeping pills that she knew they kept aboard. No sign of them. She stood in the center of the cockpit thinking, trying to remember exactly what had happened that night. Gordon had gone down, and then he had come back with coffee. But it had taken a while. He said he was going down to the head, and yet she couldn't remember the noisy flush. If he had gone for the sleeping pills to lace her coffee, what had he done with the bottle?

She remembered the medicine chest that was kept just above the sink. She dumped it out on the saloon table and went carefully through all the bandages, salves, burn ointments, adhesive tape, iodine, and other typical contents. There were no sleeping pills.

Then she remembered the threadbare jeans that Gordon liked to wear when he was sailing. He had them on for the entire voyage. She went into their cabin and looked through the lockers. Nothing! Then she went forward to the foul weather locker behind the ladder. The jeans were rolled into a careless ball on the deck. Ellie lifted them, hung them on the open door, and started through the pockets. In the side pocket, her fingers hit a plastic bottle. She took out the container for the sleeping pills, twisted the top off, and turned the bottle over. All the pills were gone.

The drowsiness . . . the irresistible sleep . . . the vivid, frightening dreams. The bastard had drugged her. He needed her to be aboard the boat, but he couldn't let her interfere with his murderous plans. So he had put her out of the way.

And then he hadn't told her. He had let her go on feeling like an accomplice. Watched her whither and fail and let her believe that she had chosen to go below so that she wouldn't have to witness the crime.

FORTY-SEVEN

"What is it?" Gordon asked Ellie.

"I was hoping that you might tell me."

"I know what it is, Ellie. It's your sleeping-pill bottle. But I don't get the point you're making."

"This isn't one of the ones the doctor recommended. This is the one that was in our medicine chest aboard *Lifeboat*."

She saw a quick flash of recognition in his eyes, but then he went back to his bewildered look. "So?"

"It wasn't in the medicine chest. It was in the pocket of your jeans. The ones you were wearing when Theresa . . . was killed. And it was empty."

He threw his hands up in a gesture of bewilderment.

"You drugged me. When I said I wouldn't let you get rid of her, you drugged me."

He shook his head slowly. "Ellie, I don't know when I took those pills. Maybe a year ago. Maybe when I tried to catch a catnap up on deck. But drug you? Where did you get such an idea?"

"From the policeman. The detective. Sergeant Was . . . whatever."

"Wasciewicz? He was here?"

Gordon's expression had gone from bewildered to condescending. Now there was more than a hint of fear.

"He was here this morning, wondering how I could have slept through Theresa getting up and making coffee. I was confused about that myself. And then I remembered the sleeping pills that we kept aboard. Only they weren't aboard any longer, were they Gordon?"

"Ellie, Sergeant Wasciewicz is on some sort of personal crusade. He's grasping at straws."

She shook her head violently. "He knows!"

"Knows what?"

"Everything! That she was killed before she went into the water. That she actually went over twenty-five miles earlier. That we had the Coast Guard searching in the wrong place."

"Ellie, if he had any sort of evidence he wouldn't be taking advantage of your grief. He ought to have his badge pulled."

"But he knows!"

"He thinks he knows something, but he's not even sure what it is. He's chasing rainbows."

She shook her head. "He'll come back. He's not going to let go."

"If he comes back just tell him what you've already told him. In the meantime, I'll get his superiors to tell him to back off. You've given your statements. And you're not well enough to put up with endless police badgering."

The next day, Gordon returned to the campaign trail, but he became more and more alarmed in his daily telephone conversations with his wife. The signs of depression were clear, and becoming more obvious with each passing day. She still hadn't left the house, much less come up to join him in Providence. She was smothering the children, holding onto them as if she were protecting them from a tornado or a hurricane. The final draft of her thesis had progressed no farther. And then the damn policeman had conjured up images of Theresa floating in the sea, pointing an accusing finger at Ellie and the children. One afternoon, Ellie had thought she saw Theresa's body in the water, just off their bedroom porch.

He had been driving home to Newport nearly every day, in the mornings if he had a late night meeting, or after a dinner if the next morning were free. Over and over again, he had told Ellie that she hadn't done anything. He was the one who had made them susceptible to blackmail, and that he had simply done what was necessary to protect her and the children. "You have to put all this behind you and move ahead," he kept advising. "Theresa is gone, and we're all better off for it."

It was during one of his quick visits home that he realized he couldn't leave her alone. She was becoming the ticking bomb that threatened their future just as Theresa had. Theresa would have destroyed them out of malice. Ellie was going to destroy them out of guilt. Waiting here in the big, empty house gave her nothing to do other than recall the last day of their cruise. And that was what she talked about every time she was with him. She was on the verge of purging her guilt to the housekeeper, or maybe even to Molly. If the damn detective made another visit there was no telling how much she might tell him.

They were sitting at the breakfast table when he finally said, "I need you up in Providence with me."

Her answer was a look of complete bewilderment.

"We're down to the last two weeks, and I think the momentum is beginning to swing away from me."

"Gordon, I can't . . ."

"You can! Mrs. Laughton will stay nights. She can even bring the kids up to the apartment so they can be with us on the weekend."

"That's not what I mean. *I* can't. It's not the children. *I'm* not up to facing all those people."

"You handled it beautifully in the spring."

"In the spring I didn't feel like a murderer."

"You didn't murder anyone!"

"Well then I didn't feel as if I were living with a murderer."

He skipped a breath. "Is that what you think? That I'm a murderer? For God's sake, Ellie, I had to protect you and the kids. I was fighting for my family."

"You were protecting your precious career."

He sprung to his feet, his hand knotting into a fist. But he caught himself in time to let his hand fall slack and let the sudden rage in his eyes mellow into a look of sadness.

"You don't know what you're saying, Ellie. You're all mixed up. I can't go on thinking that you might do something to yourself. I can't leave you alone. Please, for both of us, get a few things together and come back to Providence with me."

She knew he was right. If she stayed by herself there was no hope for her. She nodded in agreement. "It will only take me a few minutes."

He brushed a kiss on her forehead as she moved by him and then sighed in relief. In Providence, he would be able to keep his eye on her. She had to be monitored until after the election. And then she had to be defused.

FORTY-EIGHT

Two days later, Ellie joined him at a Rotary luncheon, rising to acknowledge the applause when she was introduced. She chatted aimlessly with the committeewomen while her husband espoused pro-business policies to the men. In the limousine, Gordon was pleased at the way the meeting had gone. "You've got their votes," she asssured him. And after kissing her on the cheek he told her, "You've got their wives' votes."

The afternoon was a tour of a fish-processing plant where she allowed herself to be photographed with her finger in the mouth of a dead shark. Then there was a dinner for a children's hospital, and she said a few words about children being the only future that any of us have.

The rest of the week followed the same pattern. Gordon had a breakfast in a smoke-filled room. She joined him for luncheon with veterans' groups, chambers of commerce, church auxiliaries, and the Knights of Columbus. Then they visited a factory, a hospital, a senior citizens' shelter. The evening was a fund-raising dinner, or perhaps a private supper with a few CEOs from any one of a dozen industries.

They were awarded scrolls that praised Gordon's contributions to something or other, bronzed gavels from legal associations, honorary memberships in alumni chapters, and keys to cities too small to appear on maps. She tried on tribal hats from fraternal organizations, wore the kilts of an Irish brotherhood, and tasted squid prepared by the descendants of a Mediterranean port city.

But it was all an act, as Gordon found out each night when they returned to the apartment. Ellie immediately sank into her morose silence. And when she did speak to Gordon, all she could tell him was that Theresa had never threatened them, and that they had killed her without any reason.

Sometimes it was *we* who had killed the girl. Ellie felt like a conspirator simply because she had agreed to go on the cruise. "I knew what you were going to do," she reminded her husband, "and I understood why you needed me to go along. I could have just said 'no,' and that would have been the end of it. But I went along with you. I helped kill her."

There were other moments when she saw the details in a colder light. "I decided against it. I told you I wanted no part in it. So you drugged me to get me out of the way, and then *you* killed her."

Gordon kept insisting that he had never given her the sleeping pills. Yes, he had gotten rid of Theresa, but he had done it for her and the children. He saved them all from Theresa's intimidation and blackmail. She would understand what he had done if she would just get involved in their future and stop living in the darkness that Theresa had brought to the family. "Trust me, Ellie. Just try to trust me and believe me."

283

But whether she came to trust him or not, Gordon knew *he* couldn't trust *her*. Her guilt was boiling up inside her and would soon overflow. She would have to tell someone . . . anyone. He couldn't risk being away from her for even a moment. As they campaigned, he kept her on an ever-shortening leash. At first, she was never out of his sight. But by the end of the first week, she was never out of his grasp. He kept her beside him everywhere they went on the campaign trail. He even walked her to the door of the ladies' room and waited outside until she reappeared. He found himself intercepting her phone calls and opening her mail. He pushed his face into every conversation that she joined.

That was how he learned about the call from Sergeant Wasciewicz. It had been left on her machine, acknowledging her call to his office, and asking for a time and place where they could have the meeting that she had suggested.

Gordon felt himself falling into panic. There was only one thing that Ellie would want to talk to the police about. That was either to admit what *they* had done or to describe what *he* had done. He had erased the message, but he knew that either Ellie or Wasciewicz would call again.

He told Henry Browning that Ellie was ill. "It's that fucking police-man who has been trying to prove that Theresa was a suicide. He's been calling her and threatening her. You've got to do something, Henry. Can't you talk to his commander? There has to be someone in the department who can give the son of a bitch a job in the property room."

Henry considered for a moment. "We could clip his wings, but I wonder if that might not start others asking questions. The election is only a few days away."

"Henry, if he's on the loose I'm sending Ellie back to Newport and I'm hiring an armed caretaker. He's already driven her back into the worst depths of her depression."

"No, we don't want Ellie disappearing. That would just raise more doubts about her health and about the health of your marriage. Maybe I can arrange a meeting between you and Wasciewicz. If you satisfy his curiosity, he'd have no reason to keep after Ellie."

Gordon growled. "If I see that bastard, I'm apt to throttle him!"

"We're only days away, Gordon. This is not a time for you to be assaulting police officers. Let me get the both of you over to my club. I'll make sure that he behaves civilly. You can put his problems to rest."

"Okay," Gordon agreed. "But it has to be today. Or tomorrow morning at the latest. I've got to put a stop to this harassment. I have a wife who's hiding under the bed."

They met the next morning for breakfast at Henry's club, the only guests in a room of a dozen completely prepared tables. The waiters poured juice from glass pitchers with silver tops, and carried out over-sized plates with eggs Benedict in the center. During the service the three men sat in silence with Gordon and the sergeant looking away from one another anytime their eyes made accidental contact. Henry broke the silence as soon as the waiters departed.

"Sergeant, I'm sure you realize the distress that Mrs. Acton is under. I think we can all agree that she's been through a terrible ordeal."

Neither of his guests showed any sign of agreeing to anything.

"Mr. Acton feels that it was your visit to Newport that reversed her recovery. So he is understandably determined to keep you away from her. He has no intention of letting you speak with her."

"I think Mrs. Acton has a conscience problem," Wasciewicz answered. "Otherwise, why would I be upsetting to her?"

"Because you've accused her of lying about the circumstances of Theresa Santiago's death."

"She did lie. And so did you," Wasciewicz said in a matter-of-fact tone.

Gordon started out of his chair but was stopped by the simple touch of Henry's hand on his sleeve. He sat down slowly. The policeman never changed his posture or his expression. Henry waited until Gordon's temper was back under control.

"Sergeant, we can certainly appreciate your zeal to put away that . . . gangster . . ."

"He's not my prime concern anymore," Wasciewicz said.

"Oh?" Henry acknowledged gratefully. "Then why your insistence that this was a suicide?"

"I thought it was a suicide. Now I know that it was something else."

Henry looked over at Gordon who was staring icy daggers into the detective. Then he turned back to Wasciewicz. "I hope you're going to tell us about the *something else*."

"I can't," Wasciewicz answered. "It might have been a couple of things. Maybe Mr. Acton would like to tell us."

Gordon's jaw was set. He managed, "I've already told the coroner's inquest everything I know."

"But what you told the coroner wasn't what really happened."

Henry joined in. "But surely, Sergeant, aimless speculation—"

"Not speculation," Wasciewicz interrupted. "Facts. I can't be sure exactly what did happen, but I do know that it wasn't anything like the Actons' testimony at the inquest.

"Here's the first fact. Theresa Santiago was killed by a brutal blow struck to the back of her head. The medical examiner couldn't tell all the details of her death because the body was in pretty bad shape. But something cracked her skull open like a walnut."

"Perhaps the boom swung across," Henry speculated in Gordon's direction.

Wasciewicz shook his head. "There is no boom in Mr. Acton's boat. There's a wishbone rig and a free sail. Even if she were standing straight up on the bench, the wishbone would have gone a couple of feet over her head. Besides, an experienced sailor like Mr. Acton would certainly know if the mainsail jibed, wouldn't you, Mr. Acton?"

"There was no boom to hit her," Gordon agreed, still fighting back his anger. "I told you, the sail was out on a broad reach, and the sheets were taut over the side. She was holding onto the sheet when she fell. Nothing could have hit her. But I did tell you that she had struck the side of the boat. Probably that's what fractured her skull."

"Not likely," Wasciewicz answered immediately. "The side is a smooth, gently curved surface. A dull, narrow instrument inflicted the wound. Something like a crowbar or a tire iron."

"There are fittings on the deck," Gordon pointed out. "Cleats, chain plates, blocks . . . any one of them could cause the wound you describe."

"But she didn't fall on deck. According to your testimony, she flipped out over the lifeline. So then how does her head come back inside the lifeline and strike one of the fittings? And if it does, how does she once again get to the outside?"

"Damn it," Gordon snapped. "I told you it all happened in an instant. I have no idea how she might have hit her head."

"Could it have been the propeller?" Henry Browning tried.

"Engine wasn't running," Wasciewicz said, "and the *Lifeboat* has a low drag prop, doesn't she Mr. Acton?"

Gordon nodded and then explained for Henry's benefit, "The blades fold up against the shaft when they're not turning. They open out from the centrifugal force."

"Well there must have been something that her head hit," Browning concluded.

Wasciewicz looked at Gordon. "What do you think, Mr. Acton? Any ideas?"

Gordon puzzled for a few moments. "It sounded to me like the side of the hull. That's all I really know. I have no idea what shape or what fitting she might have hit."

"And she was in the water for a number of days," Henry said. "Anything could have crushed her skull. A passing boat. A sunken wreck. I don't suppose we'll ever know."

"She was dead when she went into the water," the sergeant responded. "The blow that killed her was struck aboard Mr. Acton's boat."

Henry was out of suggestions. Gordon had no additional comment. They sat around their cold breakfasts, all looking perplexed. Finally Henry tried to move on to the next step. "Have you brought this information to the district attorney?"

Wasciewicz answered, "Not yet. There are still too many loose ends."

"Those aren't *loose ends*," Gordon said. "They're wild speculations that lead nowhere. And they're damn poor reasons for stalking my wife and calling me a liar. The plain truth is that you don't have any idea what happened on the boat, and I do. So I'm telling you one last time. No matter what the size and shape of her head wound, it didn't happen aboard *Lifeboat*."

"Well, it certainly didn't happen when and where you told the inquest."

Gordon pounded his fist and set the silverware vibrating. "Once again, you're calling my wife and me liars!" He looked at Henry. "I don't have to put up with this. This is out and out police harassment."

Henry patted his arm. "I agree with you completely." But still he asked the detective, "What makes you think it happened in another time and place?"

Wasciewicz started to pour himself more coffee but a waiter appeared immediately. They were quiet while the cups were refilled.

"Because of where her body was found," the sergeant said as soon as they had their privacy. "It couldn't have gotten there from where Mr. Acton reported her lost. I've talked with the Coast Guard meteorologists and with the experts down at Woods Hole. Anything that goes into the water more than a few miles out in the Gulf of Maine moves onshore pushed in by the Labrador Current. The body was found almost thirty miles to the southwest of where she was reported overboard. The Woods Hole gang figure she had to have gone over at least twenty miles to the southwest. Right on the course you plotted on your charts, only about three hours earlier."

"Are you a sailor, Sergeant Wasciewicz?" Gordon demanded.

"No, sir. I just do a bit of fishing out of a rowboat."

"Well, then, let me tell you a few facts that every sailor knows. First, no matter what the spooks at Woods Hole tell you, there's no way in hell you can predict how something will move in the sea. The tides, currents, winds never come together in exactly the same way. Drop three objects in on three different days and they'll all come up in different places."

"Except they didn't," Wasciewicz said, not at all impressed with Gordon's superior knowledge of the sea. "I had our marine division rig up three parcels with the same buoyancy and decay rate as a body. We threw them over on three successive days, right where you said Theresa went overboard. They all washed ashore exactly where the Woods Hole guys said they should. On Pemaquid Point. That's nearly forty miles from where the fishing boat netted Theresa's body."

Gordon was no longer lecturing. Sergeant Wasciewicz had taken over the conversation.

"Couldn't a fisherman have netted her near the scene of the accident and dragged her south?" Henry tried.

"Of course," Gordon answered. "There are so many damn possibilities that where the sergeant's packages managed to wash ashore has nothing to do with anything. Theresa fell over where I marked on my chart, and she was found wherever in hell she was found. There are a hundred reasons how she could have gotten from one place to another."

"Well, it wasn't by being dragged in a fishing net. We've checked with all the commercial guys from Portland to Gloucester. Nobody dragged across both points. In fact, nearly all of them draw their nets in a circle. So they wouldn't have taken anything for a forty-mile ride. They would have pulled it back into the center."

Henry nodded at the inescapable logic. Then he turned to Gordon. "It sounds to me as if the sergeant has a very convincing case." He looked back at Wasciewicz with his eyes suddenly blazing. "So why don't you turn this mountain of information over to the district attorney? Let his office decide whether there are loopholes or fanciful flights from reality."

"Because I don't have a motive," Wasciewicz answered pleasantly. "And I don't have the murder weapon."

"Then you don't have a case," Henry suggested.

"Not unless someone confesses."

"Which is not very likely, considering that neither Mr. or Mrs. Acton have the damnedest idea of what you're talking about."

"Mrs. Acton does," Wasciewicz answered. "And she wants to talk about it. She almost told me at her kitchen table. A couple of nights ago, she phoned my office."

Gordon's face grew red. "Is that what you're doing? Trying to coerce a despondent woman into confessing to something that never happened?"

Wasciewicz settled back in his chair. "Some cases can't be solved any other way. Chances are the murder weapon—a crank handle, or a wrench, or a marlinespike—is at the bottom of the gulf. And only two or three people know the motive, with one of them now dead. A young woman has been killed. It happened aboard a boat where only two other people were present. So we won't be able to close the case unless one of them tells us what happened."

"I already told you," Gordon snapped.

"Yeah, but your version is full of holes. I think you're protecting your wife."

"Ellie?" Henry gasped.

"It happened during the time when Mr. Acton was sleeping." He looked straight at Gordon. "Maybe the fight woke you. Or maybe you slept through it and then woke up with a body on your hands. But I think you had to protect your wife, so you put the body and the weapon over and cleaned up the cockpit. And then you sailed well into the morning so that the Coast Guard would be looking in the wrong place."

Henry whistled softly. "Well, I must say that *is* quite a flight of fancy. You won't believe, Sergeant, how absolutely ridiculous all this sounds to someone who has known Ellie for many, many years. Since she was a child, really."

Wasciewicz nodded, accepting Henry Browning's testimony on behalf of Ellie Acton. He raised his eyes to Gordon. "Well if that isn't what happened, why don't you tell us what did happen? There were only two people on the boat who could have done it."

Gordon had listened to the logic of the case against Ellie. He had slowed the boat down in order to delay its arrival at the farthest point from land. The change hadn't been marked on his chart or recorded in his log. So it was logical for Wasciewicz to conclude that whatever happened had occurred on Ellie's watch. He was juggling the implications and beginning to recognize the outline of a last-ditch alibi. But right now, he needed to end this meeting before Wasciewicz convinced Henry that he was the killer. He stood slowly, purposefully, until he towered above the sergeant. "What I'm going to tell you, I'll only tell you once. Your harassment of my wife and myself is going to stop right here, right now. And just to make sure it does, I'm going to your commissioner with a very simple message. *If you ever come near Ellie or me again, or if I ever hear this slander repeated, my first act as a congressman will be to launch a federal investigation into corruption in your department.* That should get his attention, and get you assigned to guarding the bodies in the morgue." He turned to Browning. "Now if you'll excuse me Henry." He fired his napkin down into his untouched eggs and stormed out of the dining room.

Browning and Wasciewicz sat in silence until long after they heard the elevator ring. Then Henry unwrapped his first cigar of the day and made a great show of lighting it. He exhaled a silvery cloud and then smiled through it. "I think you should take Mr. Acton very seriously," he said. "He has enough connections right now to have you on never-ending jury duty. And when he's a congressman? Well, I suppose you can imagine the favors he'll be able to call in then."

"They killed her," Wasciewicz said. "There's no other answer."

"Maybe not," Henry decided. "But I wonder if that's reason enough to throw away your career for a case that you're never going to win. And the reason you're never going to win it is precisely because they were the only two on the boat. You're challenging the word of a direct descendant of Roger Williams, and a man whose family saved thousands of sailors off sinking ships. A United States congressman and a champion of education for the poor. Frankly, I don't like your chances."

Henry signaled for the bill and signed his name. Then he stood and walked from the table, leaving Wasciewicz to trail him to the elevator.

Henry went directly to Gordon's office to tell him the finale of their meeting. "I think you made yourself very clear," he told Gordon. "But just in case Sergeant Wasciewicz was still not convinced, I gave him even more reasons why he should drop his stupid investigation. I don't think we'll hear from him again."

"I hope not," Gordon said. "Ellie can't take much more."

Henry smiled shrewdly. "I share your hope, because I wouldn't want the sergeant's views to get a public hearing. He makes a very convincing argument." He paused waiting for Gordon's response, but when none was forthcoming Henry asked, "I assume the girl *was* dead before she went over the side?"

Gordon studied his mentor. Then he nodded slowly.

"The sergeant had it just about right?" Browning assumed.

Gordon sighed. "She was blackmailing Ellie. The kid had done a lot of grunt work on Ellie's dissertation but she made it look as if the whole thing was hers. She came up into the cockpit and told Ellie how much her silence was going to cost. Ellie told her she wasn't going to pay anything, and that she was going to turn Theresa over to the police. The girl attacked her and Ellie struck back. She swung a winch handle. She had no idea how much damage one of those things can cause."

He was speaking softly, his eyes downcast.

"Good God," Henry allowed. "And you helped her cover it up."

Gordon nodded. "What else could I do? I love her."

"It would have destroyed both of you. If you hadn't deep-sixed the girl, your political future would have gone to the bottom."

"At the time, that never crossed my mind. I knew Ellie would never survive the scandal. Now I'm afraid she won't survive the secret. Henry, I'm terrified that Ellie is going to kill herself. That's why I won't let her out of my sight. I think she's determined to end it all."

Gordon accepted Henry's sympathy and listened to his advice about seeking psychiatric treatment. He had his arm around the older man as he walked him toward the door. "You're a true friend, Henry. I never wanted you to know this. I owed it to you to build a firewall so you wouldn't be in a position of abetting a crime. And I swear, I'll never tell anyone that you know."

He had laid the groundwork for Ellie's suicide in case it became the only way of silencing her troubled conscience.

291

November

FORTY-NINE

The dinner was in the heart of enemy territory, in the working towns along the Massachusetts border. This part of the district, continually nourished by new waves of immigrants, had voted Democratic since the first Roosevelt administration. Nobody from Ocean Drive could hope for more than a few dozen votes.

But according to Henry's unending polls, Gordon would win over a third of the ballots; a percentage that had been rising ever since Theresa Santiago had become the Acton's mother's helper. This was her hometown where her achievements had been common conversation and her picture universally recognized. This was the community that had gathered to cry at her memorial service.

Originally, the dinner had been a luncheon scheduled by the Rotary club at a small Italian restaurant. There weren't many Rotarians, and even though they took over the room, they never filled more than half the tables. But now, because of Theresa's notoriety, tickets to the luncheon were in such demand that the agenda had been switched to dinner at the union hall. It was the last place in the area where a Republican could expect a place at the head table, but in this crowd, Gordon Acton wasn't thought of as a Republican. He was the man who had treated Theresa as a daughter, and had planned to put her through Yale.

"You're going to end up winning this ward," Henry told Gordon as they sat side-by-side on the dais spooning down their fruit cups.

Gordon looked at the crowd, five tables deep across the entire room. "It's hard to believe this many people knew Theresa."

"Legends grow," Henry said. "They all remember that they loved her like their own child."

"Even though she was stealing from her employer?"

Henry snickered. "That was a frame-up by racist police determined to keep the immigrants in their places."

Gordon turned to his other side where Ellie was smiling over her salad. "I think you may have to say a few words," he warned.

Her smile vanished. "I don't think that's a good idea. I don't know if I can handle it."

Gordon kept his smile toward the audience while the anger leaked from the corner of his mouth. "Of course you can handle it. What are you going to do, snub all her friends?"

"Gordon, I don't know what I can say . . ."

"Two sentences, for God's sake. 'It's a pleasure to be here honoring Theresa and so on. I'll miss her as much as you will.' What's so hard about that?"

"It's hard because I helped kill her . . ."

His fake smile vanished. "Jesus . . ."

"But I'll try, Gordon. I'll think of something."

He turned back to his fruit cup and found that it had lost its flavor.

It wasn't going to work, Gordon knew. Ellie wasn't going to get any better, not now before the election, and not right after the election. Her guilt over Theresa's death was burned too deeply into her conscience. He had to do something. He couldn't spend his every waking hour watching over her to make sure she didn't talk to anyone. Nor could he risk that one of her innocent conversations would suddenly turn into a confession.

He thought of a sanitarium. One of those private places in the country that watched over the drunks, drug addicts, and arsonists from the best families. Publicly, he could make it look as if she needed time to recover from the shock of losing the girl she loved like a daughter. "A short rest," he might announce a few days after the election. "No, nothing serious. It's just that this has been a difficult year for Ellie. More difficult than I could have ever imagined when I accepted the nomination. And then, with the loss of Theresa . . ."

Gordon liked the idea because it would reflect well on both of them. He would be the concerned husband and her only problem would be that she loved too much. There would be no long-term stigma that might rise up in his next political campaign. Ellie would gradually put everything in perspective and would return home cured.

But there would be no way to stop her from talking inside the sanitarium. That's what psychiatrists and psychotherapists were supposed to do, encourage their patients to talk. At first her descriptions of the events leading to Theresa's death might be seen as part of her illness. But within a short time, her graphic and detailed descriptions would be recognized for what they were. Ellie's doctors and nurses would quickly understand that she wasn't suffering from delusions of guilt, but was burdened by actual deeds. And then what? The doctors at these places made their livings by being discrete. But someone would certainly take Ellie's tale to the authorities.

There had to be another way. He needed to be assured of her silence. He had thought he was buying her cooperation when he made her part of the crime. After all, she couldn't destroy him without destroying herself. He never imagined that she would ever see destroying herself as salvation from her guilt.

"I'm ready," Ellie suddenly whispered to him. "I'll tell them how Theresa taught Molly to play the flute."

He nodded. "Great idea. Just perfect." He repeated her remark to Henry who broke into one of his infrequent smiles. It was a harmless story that had nothing to do with Theresa's death, yet was perfectly illustrative of the affection that had bonded the girl into his family.

As the waiters were clearing away the chicken, the chairman of the event began clearing his throat behind the microphone. He introduced Gordon as a man with the strength to get things done and the humanity to know what should be done. The applause was polite, but cautious.

Gordon did well with his prepared remarks, talking about the end of old divisions and the new era of community. "None of us are going to succeed if we don't all succeed," he announced in a raised voice. "We are one family, just as Theresa Santiago was part of my family."

The diners rose in a spontaneous ovation. They had come to hear about Theresa, not to discuss government policies or political nuances. Gordon wasn't even back in his chair when the chant began for Ellie. No one, the crowd figured, had been closer to Theresa during the last tragic months of her life.

Ellie stood bravely, and made her way to the podium. She listened to applause that was more generous than the greeting Gordon had received. She stood smiling at the microphone until the crowd grew quiet and settled back into their chairs.

She recited the usual opening words of gratitude to everyone involved in the affair that she had learned from all of the previous campaign stops. Then she repeated Gordon's one-family theme, which led seamlessly into a few words about her intimate knowledge of the district's people. "I had a daughter who lived here," she said, "whom I loved as much as you did."

There was a tomblike silence. Not a plate clattered nor ice cube rattled.

"I can recall so many things. But one incident in particular comes to mind."

She glanced across the audience, and then spotted a newcomer who had joined a table up front to her left. Sergeant Wasciewicz was pulled in close to the table, leaning forward so as to catch her every word. In a sea of faces, his were the only eyes.

Her knees wobbled, and she clutched the side of the podium with white-knuckled fingers. She looked away, toward the far back of the room, but Wasciewicz's face shone like a flare at the edge of her vision. Her glance wandered back to him. He was smiling up at her, daring her to tell the truth.

"Theresa was very close to my children. Particularly my daughter Molly, who thought of her as a big sister." She looked to the other side of the room, but still saw the sergeant. "It's hard to trust your children to someone . . . someone you don't really know. Theresa once told me that I didn't have a clue. I knew nothing about her life. And she was right. It was easy to be suspicious of her."

Her faltering voice was the only sound in the deathly still room.

"Theresa was a musician. She wrote this . . . theme. A sad theme that was . . . well maybe the sound track for her life. God help me, but I still hear it. Sometimes at night I have to hold my hands over my ears. Theresa taught Molly to play that theme. So maybe it's Molly that I hear at night. Molly has . . . in a way . . . become Theresa. I think that's why I'm so afraid for her. It sounds silly, but I think mothers will understand. You always wonder what you should have done differently . . . and then you begin to be afraid. I'm afraid that if Molly ever became a threat to us . . . to our position . . . that we'd have to get rid of her too."

In the audience, people began stealing glances at one another. What was the woman talking about? Who was a threat to them? Theresa?

Gordon's head came up. He realized that Ellie was lost and was wandering into deadly territory. He shook his head when Henry said, "Where in hell is this going?"

Ellie searched for a friendly face, but the only face she recognized was Sergeant Wasciewicz's. She could tell that he knew, that he understood. She looked right at him.

"It's not as simple as you think. We thought she was threatening us. She wasn't, but we didn't really trust her because we didn't know her. As she told me, we didn't have a clue."

"For God's sake, shut her up," Henry snapped into Gordon's ear. Gordon slipped out of his chair and began making his way behind the dais guests toward the podium.

Ellie closed her eyes, grasping for the right words to explain what had really happened. Her breathing could be heard through the speakers. "I think part of it was that we thought we were better than she. Our lives were more valuable than her life. We didn't think of what she might become but only of what she might prevent us from becoming . . ."

The faces in the audience still did not comprehend. What in hell was the woman talking about?

"And, we were frightened. Do you know what it's like when you're threatened? When someone is going to take away everything you need. Even if you love the person, you still have to do something . . ."

Gordon pushed in next to her. He twisted the microphone away, sending a shrill shriek through the amplifiers, but Ellie seemed not to notice. She kept talking, loud enough to be heard on the dais. Loud enough to be heard at the front tables.

"We were just going to take her out to sea and leave her behind. But I couldn't. The closer we came to the time, the more I knew I could never hurt her. You have to believe that. I loved her, but I was afraid of her. I wanted to be rid of her, but I couldn't hurt her . . ."

Gordon wrapped his arms around her and physically lifted her from the podium. Henry rushed over to help him and the toastmaster stood and took Ellie from Gordon's arms. Several of the head table guests surrounded her and led her out behind the dais. Gordon stepped back to the podium and rearranged the microphone.

He heard the rumble of voices as people at every table turned to one another. When he looked up he saw stern faces that wanted answers. If they could believe what they had heard, the candidate's wife had just confessed to a crime. She had been telling them that she and her husband had planned to get rid of Theresa. Didn't she say that they had no intention of bringing her back from the cruise? And the dinner guests knew what they had seen. Her husband had shut her up. Gordon

Acton had ripped the microphone away from her and dragged her from the podium.

"My friends," Gordon tried, but the buzz of conversations continued. "Please, if I can have your attention for just a second . . ."

Faces looked up and locked on. Voices from the audience demanded quiet and silenced the hiss of whispers.

"My wife," Gordon said, "is not well. As you can see, she feels terribly guilty over the loss of Theresa Santiago." His words were followed by a deathlike stillness. He looked around and saw some expressions of sympathy. A few of the women had their hands up to their open mouths.

"She believes that if we hadn't planned the vacation, and taken Theresa sailing, she would still be alive. I suppose that's true. It will take her a while to remember all the wonderful things she did for Theresa and the plans she had for her."

The hostility in the audience was fading.

"I've been terribly worried about her. I begged her to rest, but she insisted on being here. She wanted to be with Theresa's friends. I know she'll be sorry that she caused you anxiety. When she's better, I'm sure she'll want to come back here and tell you all how much she loved Theresa Santiago."

The murmur began again, now accompanied by shuffling as the audience turned toward the exits. A few of the guests lingered and came up to shake Gordon's hand.

FIFTY

"It's all very positive," Henry Browning reported in the morning. "She was seen as distraught over the memories of the girl. Your comments were inspired."

Gordon was pacing in circles around his desk. "For Christ's sake Henry, she came unglued. She made a public confession of murder."

"That's not the way the audience saw it. They saw her break down in grief. The response we're getting is 'see how she loved her.' We're playing up the distraught and exhausted angle."

"It was all that fucking policeman! How did he ever get on the guest list?"

"The Police Benevolence Association had taken a table. There was no list of names, and he didn't show up until you were getting your standing ovation."

"And now he's trying to get her arrested. Can't anybody control that son of a bitch?"

"He won't be able to get a warrant, and he'll never be able to pick her up," Henry Browning explained calmly. "There isn't a judge or a police chief who wants to incur the wrath of the district's next congressman."

"That's not what the newspapers are saying." He gestured at the scattering of dailies that were on the floor next to his desk. "Troubling questions! Disturbing evasions!" Gordon recited from the headlines. "They're saying that the coroner's inquest was hurried to avoid embarrassing me and hurting my candidacy. One of the papers says the inquest was nothing more than a cover-up."

Henry nodded. "The press will have its day. But the election is still three days off, and we're already putting out our spin. There are two psychiatrists going on the afternoon and evening news who will say she's a classic case of despondency with all the guilt and self-loathing that is entailed."

"What about the papers?" Gordon demanded.

"We've carefully leaked that you're bringing her home to rest and requested the papers to leave her in peace. That just about assures that they'll all have photographers waiting at the front door."

"But . . ."

Henry raised a calming hand. "And then you'll say a few words about her recovery being the only issue."

"And I just stay there, at the house . . ."

"Exactly," Henry said, reaffirming the plan. "That will keep the press from asking you any questions, and it will show that you're a family man first and a politician last. Believe me there won't be any downside. By the time the polls open you'll be a hero. You'll carry ninety percent of the women's vote."

"Shouldn't I put out some sort of statement about the Theresa thing?"

"Not now!" Henry answered "Right now we're concerned about

damage control. We don't want to remind anyone of what she said at the dinner. Once you're elected, we'll have plenty of time to get Ellie back on her feet and to sweep her Theresa comments under the rug."

"I feel like a real bastard," Gordon said.

Henry shook his head. "I don't care how you feel. Just make sure you keep acting like a concerned husband. Every time the press reports that you've abandoned your campaign to be with your wife, you'll pick up another two points."

Gordon brought Ellie home to the house in Newport, looked concerned as he led her past the expected photographers, and said the few words that Henry had recommended. Then he brought in hired guards from Action Boats' security company. Ostensibly, it was to make certain that Ellie's needed rest wasn't disturbed. "You don't know what the supermarket tabloids might try," he had explained. "And you never know what some political crackpot might do in the last days of a campaign." But, in truth, he wasn't really afraid of pushy reporters or disappointed opponents. The security force was simply to assure that Sergeant Wasciewicz never got to turn into the driveway. A security woman inside the house screened incoming calls to make sure that he never got through on the telephone.

Publicly, Gordon was upbeat. "She'll be fine," he assured friends. "As soon as the election is over, I'm going to take her house hunting in the Washington area. The change in scenery and the new responsibilities will be great for her." His tone made light of her problem. He was intimating that the change would put an end to her mourning. But he knew it wasn't just mourning. Ellie needed to confess their crimes.

"She keeps blaming herself for the girl's death," the inside security woman told him. "She says she should have put a stop to it the first time you raised the idea." Then she asked, "What idea is she talking about?"

Gordon fumbled for a few seconds and explained that his wife felt she shouldn't have brought the girl on the cruise. Then he had the woman removed from duty inside the house. Wasciewicz hadn't tried to call, so maybe he was no longer an issue. Certainly not as immediately dangerous as the possibility of Ellie providing more explicit information to the people who were minding her.

Wasciewicz had given up on the chance that Ellie would break her silence and had taken his evidence and the excerpts from her speech to Judge Gamble. Now, the day before the election Henry Browning had learned that "new evidence has been brought to the attention of the coroner, which may result in reopening the inquest." Browning immediately drove to the Cape for a personal consultation with the judge.

"The information is certainly persuasive," the judge said as soon as they got past the niceties and down to the issues. Then he led Henry through the problem of the girl's skull fracture, the fact that she had been dead before she went over the side, the location of the body that had drifted against the tide. Henry listened gravely as if he were hearing the damning evidence for the first time.

"We didn't have any of this information at the time of the inquest," Gamble pointed out, "so we certainly should reopen the case long enough to get some answers."

Henry countered the legal issues with a strong dose of political reality. Gordon Acton was the party's link to the benefits bestowed by the federal government. Opening an inquiry hours before Election Day wasn't a very smart thing to do. And, God help us, any hint of impropriety or negligence could hurt Republicans all over New England "Republicans created this branch court for you, Judge. But the Democrats would probably want to move the bench back to Boston."

Judge Gamble vehemently resented the idea that crass politics could leach into the judiciary, but Henry insisted that he was just advising prudence. "None of this can come to anything definitive because of the uncertainties of the sea," he preached. He told Gamble that the head injury could have come from striking a deck fitting. The body could have been caught up in a fishing net and dragged to where it was finally recovered. "You lay this whole thing out and you won't know for certain whether the Actons did something wrong, or whether the tides and currents have just played tricks on us. But you can be damn certain that the papers will come up with some very unsavory innuendos. And our opponents will mine them for all they're worth."

Judge Gamble could see that Henry's worst fears might be realized. Just as important, he couldn't see himself giving up the pastoral pleasures of Cape Cod for the hellish uproar of Boston. "I see your point, Henry," he concluded. "Let's just leave it alone and stick with the original verdict."

That night Ellie told Gordon she was going to see Judge Gamble.

She had to be sure he understood that she had decided not to silence Theresa, that she planned to take the girl with her on a return trip to her academic review board. Gordon promised her that he would go with her "as soon as this damn election is behind us." He had agreed that they would both be better off if the truth came out. Then he had told the security guards that Mrs. Acton was not to leave the grounds under any circumstances.

Election Day morning he was on the phone, chatting with Henry about the arrangements for the victory celebration. Henry figured that the contest would be over before noon, with the rest of the day simply adding to his obvious victory. They decided that Gordon should return to Providence early to be on hand for his opponent's concession. Gordon agreed cheerfully. He seemed to be home free!

As he hung up the phone he saw that one of the extension lamps was lit. He gasped when he realized that Ellie was on the phone, sprung out of his chair and raced up the stairs to her room.

"Who were you talking to?" he demanded angrily.

"I wasn't talking with anyone. Nobody called."

"I know nobody called. But you called someone. Who was it?"

"I had to talk, Gordon. I can't stand this any longer."

"Ellie, for God's sake, who was on the phone?"

She turned to her window. "I don't want to talk about it."

"Damn you!" He picked up the telephone and pressed the redial button. He heard a number dialing while he watched Ellie walk out onto the balcony.

"Detective Sergeant Wasciewicz," a familiar voice answered. Gordon clamped his hand over the mouthpiece. Slowly, he lowered the phone.

"Hello, this is Sergeant Wasciewicz. Who's calling?"

Ellie's hair was blowing in the onshore breeze. Her chin was raised slightly as she looked out into the sparkle of Rhode Island Sound.

"Hello, are you trying to reach the police? This is the police department. Sergeant Wasciewicz speaking."

Gordon hung up the telephone.

She was more dangerous than Theresa had been. Theresa knew that he was an adulterer. Ellie knew that he was a murderer. He had to put an end to her morose brooding. He had to make certain that she never confessed to anyone. There was no other way.

He pulled the telephone cord from the socket, rolled it around the handset and took it with him as he left the room. He locked the door, left the phone on the carpet outside the door, and then walked slowly through the house.

They were alone. The children were away at one of their activities with their nanny. The security guards were all outside the house, gathered at the gate at the far end of the driveway. Gordon went from window to window making certain that no one was on the grounds outside.

He knew he had to do it now, before he left for his campaign headquarters. Alone in the house, she would certainly find a way to reach Wasciewicz, or Judge Gamble, or perhaps some friend of Theresa's. He knew he had to get it over with quickly, before either of them could realize exactly what he was doing. He wouldn't be able to look at her. Given enough time to imagine her terror, he would never be able to go through with it. And there could be no turning back. Once she understood what he intended to do she would have no hesitancy in naming him.

It would be just like a suicide. She was buried in her grief. She had shown an entire hall full of people that she was irrational. He had spelled out clearly to Henry his fears that she might take her own life. He had even hired security guards to mind her.

It wouldn't matter what she had said to Sergeant Wasciewicz. It would be apparent that she was out of her mind. Why else would she jump from her balcony onto the rocks below? Wasciewicz might stir up some problems before his superiors could silence him. But anything he said would be countered by Gordon's testimony, by the thoughtful verdict of the coroner, and by Ellie's obvious instability.

He walked slowly back up the stairs, looked up and down the corridor even though he knew no one was there. He turned the key, opened the door and then moved the key to the inside of the lock. Carefully, he reconnected the telephone and checked to make sure that there was a dial tone. He looked out to the balcony where Ellie, wearing a sweater over her jeans, was sitting in a deck chair. He breathed deeply and then started out to join her.

Wasciewicz knew he was driving dangerously. His speedometer was running up into the eighties on the short straightaways, and his tires were screeching when he braked into the curves. Each time he raced into a turn he was praying that there wasn't another car coming the other way.

He had listened carefully to Ellie Acton's telephone confession, understood that she had toyed with the possibility of silencing Theresa Santiago, and believed her when she said that she couldn't go through with it. He had understood clearly the significance of her finding the empty sleeping-pill container in Gordon's jeans. And then, he had advised her that her best hope was to come into the station and make a formal statement. He had heard the real fear in her voice when she said that Gordon wouldn't allow her to talk with anyone, and the sergeant had offered to send a car to pick her up. But despite her guilt and her fears, Ellie had balked at the idea of a formal statement.

"Wouldn't that be the same thing as betraying my husband?" Ellie had said. And Wasciewicz had counseled that there could be nothing wrong if she simply told the truth. Ellie had promised to think about it, and had hung up.

It was only a few seconds later when his phone had rung again. There was someone on the line, but whoever it was had kept silent. The sergeant had been puzzled for only a second. But then his caller ID had flashed the same number that Ellie Acton had called from, and he understood what was happening. Someone in the house had used redial to find out whom Ellie had called. When he identified himself, he had signed Ellie's death sentence.

He tore around still another turn and then saw the house directly ahead. The sound of his engine alerted the people at the gate, and all of a sudden there was a private army blocking his entrance into the Acton property. He gave a moment's thought to driving right through them, but at the last minute decided that he needed their help. The car left a trail of smoking rubber as it braked with its bumper just inches from the gate.

"It's beautiful up here," Gordon said. "The whole bay looks like silver."

"Gordon, I want to explain about that phone call . . ."

"Don't worry," he interrupted. "I think I knew all along that we would end up visiting with the sergeant. I think it's the right thing for us to do."

"Then you're not angry?"

"I wish you had told me about it. It was sort of a nasty surprise. But you're right. We have to tell someone how she was threatening us, and why we did what we had to do. I know I don't feel at all guilty about protecting you and the kids."

Her glance dropped down to her hands. "But there had to be a better way. I feel completely guilty about . . . taking her out on that cruise. I could have saved her . . . I could have saved us . . ."

He reached a hand down to her. "Come up here where I can put my arm around you. The waves hitting the rocks are really spectacular."

She stood confidently and moved to the rail next to where he was standing.

"Someone's going to get killed in there!" Wasciewicz shouted at the security guards. He had his badge out and was hanging it through his open window. "We just had an emergency call. There's no time to lose."

The guards looked back and forth at one another.

"Open the fucking gate!" Wasciewicz screamed. "Now!"

A guard answered that they should call Mr. Acton for permission.

"Mr. Acton may already be dead," Wasciewicz lied. "Open that gate or I'll shoot out the lock." It was bravado. His small caliber revolver probably wouldn't chip the paint off the gate. And Acton's security guards were brandishing automatic weapons.

"I'll have to go with you," the guards spokesman insisted.

"Fine! Get your ass in here now and open that gate!"

Ellie was leaning against the balcony railing, pressed close to Gordon and welcoming the security of his arm around her. She felt completely relieved. There would be no more lies, no more cover-ups. Gordon and she would put everything into the hands of Judge Gamble, and trust he would see the intimidation they were under and the pressure they felt. Maybe Gordon wouldn't make it to Congress. And certainly she would never find a prestigious position in education. But at least they could take up their lives without worrying about what might come to light tomorrow.

His arm tightened around her shoulders. He was pulling her close as if to lock her in his embrace and kiss her. She turned to him, leaving her back against the high iron rail. Suddenly the rail was pressing into her back. She was being bent over backward. She felt her canvas shoes dragging across the deck.

The guard fumbled with a ring of keys and finally turned the lock on the front door. Wasciewicz pushed past and rushed into the foyer. Then he heard Ellie's scream from the bedroom at the head of the stairs. He charged ahead, taking the steps two at a time.

Ellie was tottering on the top of the rail, clutching Gordon's shirt in one hand, and flailing at him with the other. Gordon was forcing her slowly over the top while he tried to untangle her fingers from his shirt. His eyes were squeezed tightly shut to save himself from seeing what he was doing. He didn't even feel the feeble blows that Ellie was landing on his head and back.

"Gordon, please! Jesus!"

He didn't answer. He hated what he was doing. But, as with Theresa, he had no choice. Ellie could ruin him and there was no sure way to stop her. He had to force her suicide.

His shirt began to rip. The blows stopped as she grabbed frantically for the railing. Gordon could feel her slipping away.

A man flashed by him, lunging at Ellie and catching her arm. Just as she lost her grip, the reaching hands stopped her fall. Gordon looked over at Sergeant Wasciewicz, and then down at his wife who was dangling by one hand and reaching out with the other. She caught the railing, and then Wasciewicz leaned far out and with his other hand grabbed her arm.

Gordon reached down and began unwrapping Ellie's fingers from the railing. He could see that Wasciewicz wasn't going to be able to lift her over. If he held on, Ellie's weight would probably pull the sergeant over the edge.

He felt a hand at the back of his neck. He was dragged back and then fired like a rag doll into the corner of the porch. As he slumped to the floor he saw one of his uniformed guards catch Ellie's other hand. Together, the two men were able to lift her face above the top rail, and then shift their grip to her waist. A second later, she was sprawled along the top of the rail, and then she rolled off into their arms.

Gordon began to think. "She was going to jump. I held her but I couldn't pull her back."

"Bullshit! I saw what you were doing," Wasciewicz snapped. He was steadying Ellie as he walked her into her bedroom.

"She was jumping," Gordon appealed to the security guard.

"Fuck you!" the guard screamed back. He followed Ellie and Wasciewicz off the balcony leaving Gordon cowering on the deck in the far corner.

Ellie seemed bewildered. "He was going to kill me . . ."

"He tried everything else," Wasciewicz said. "He lied to you, drugged you, blamed you, and planned your suicide." He kept an arm around her as he led her down the stairs and out the front door of the house.

Gordon saw that the guard was talking on the telephone. The man was sitting on Ellie's bed with his pistol drawn, blocking off the only path of escape, and undoubtedly talking to the police. Gordon heard words "Tried to kill her . . . Another second and she would have been gone . . . Yeah, he's with the lady, but he'll need a car to bring the bastard in . . . No, we won't touch anything . . ."

He looked over the rail and saw the sea crashing against the rocks far below. He had to act now. If he thought about it, he probably wouldn't be able to go through with it. And there was no alternative. He knew he could never survive the disgrace.

FIFTY-ONE

"Gordie! Gordie! Gordie!"

The crowd in the hotel ballroom was hysterical with joy. The results of the election had been obvious two hours after the polls opened. It was Gordon Acton by a landslide.

He was carrying the well-off, conservative Republican vote by a ten to one ratio. The liberals at the university and the college were supporting him by three to one. And most startling, he was carrying the working class neighborhoods by almost two to one. The updated tally on the stage said he had 82 percent of the vote counted, and projected his final winning margin to be 79 percent.

Henry Browning was walking the dance floor, accepting congratulations from all sides. "Jesus, Henry, this is wonderful," said a probate judge. "He pulled in the whole ticket. Sheriffs, court clerks, commissioners. Everyone won."

"Henry! Henry! What a job you've done," said a justice of the peace. "The only office we didn't win was truant officer."

"I'm not conceding that," Henry laughed. "It's still too close to call."

The governor dropped by the hotel early in the afternoon as part of his tour of voting districts. "Henry, you're to be congratulated. Six months ago, I thought we might lose this one."

Browning smiled modestly. "I wouldn't let you down, Governor. Now you own the whole state."

"Where *is* the new congressman?"

Henry glanced at his watch. "He's late! We talked this morning and agreed that he'd be here by noon. I'll call up to his room and let him know that you're here."

The governor accepted a glass of fruit punch from one of the committeewomen, and raised it in toast to the campaign workers.

"Governor!" someone shouted, and then a new locomotive cheer began screaming his name. He raised his arms and embraced the applause.

In the midst of the euphoria, a police captain pushed his way through the crowd and took the governor by the arm. "I just got it on the radio. Gordon Acton went off his balcony and into the water."

"What?"

"About an hour ago. Police were called to his house but he was dead when they got there."

The governor's mouth was hanging open, his eyes perfectly round. "It can't be. Are you sure?"

"I called down to confirm it. Couldn't believe it myself."

"Jesus, why? Why would he do such a thing?"

"Something about his wife. They were both out on their balcony . . ."

Henry Browning reappeared at the edge of the crowd and pushed his way through. His expression was stunned and his color drained. The governor didn't have to ask him if he had heard the news.

"He jumped," Henry said as if he were trying to make himself believe it.

The governor nodded. "It's on the radio. But how? Why?"

"I don't know," Browning said, confirming the astonishment that was written across his face. "He was down there because he was afraid that his wife might have been going to do something foolish."

"Could he have fallen?" the governor wondered.

"I was told he was trying to avoid arrest. The police had been called to arrest him."

"Oh my God! How are we going to handle this Henry? The man has just been elected to Congress."

"I'll say something. In the meanwhile you better give some thought to whom you're going to appoint. We'll need a replacement until we can put together a special election."

"I better get out of here. I don't want to know about this until I've figured out what to say."

Suddenly there was a scream from across the room. Someone else had just learned about Gordon's death. And then the news spread like fire, changing the expressions on face after face. The celebration ended within a matter of seconds, leaving the campaign workers staring blankly at the rows of Gordon Acton posters. Each showed him in action with an attributed quotation from his platform in bold type.

Henry worked his way slowly to the stage. His path was blocked by people wanting information. Was it true? Was he dead? How? When? He waved them away with shrug and a blank stare that said he was as mystified as any of them.

When he reached the microphone the hall fell silent.

"As you've heard, we have just been informed that Congressman-elect Gordon Acton died in a household accident sometime this morning. My understanding is that he fell from the balcony of his house."

There was a single cry of despair, and then individual voices vented their grief.

"I have no further details," Henry said. "The governor was here when the news was received, and he is rushing down to the Acton home to offer his condolences to Gordon's wife Ellie, and to . . ."

He stopped in mid-sentence. Ellie, he thought. The grieving mother of an adopted daughter. The strong wife, carrying her children through the tragic death of their father.

He saw that his audience was still waiting on his word. ". . . to assist in making the appropriate arrangements. I know we will hear from the governor as soon as he arrives on the scene. But that may be several hours, so there is nothing more that I can add this afternoon."

He drew a handkerchief from his pocket and wiped his eyes. "This is a terrible tragedy," he said, turning away from the microphone.

His thoughts went back to Ellie. She wouldn't really have to do anything. All she would have to do was lend her name.

Henry arrived at the Newport police barracks an hour later. The police captain who had accompanied the governor had already thrown his rank around the station house, and taken over one of the private offices. "It's a goddam mess," he moaned to Henry. "I'm not sure I can keep it under wraps. There's a detective here who says he was in the process of arresting Gordon for murder and attempted murder."

"Ridiculous," Henry insisted.

"Yeah? Well there's a private security guard who says that Gordon was about to throw his wife off the balcony."

"Where is he?"

"Picking out the job he wants in the state administration. If he remembers that Gordon fell while he was trying to save his wife, he's going to be a seventy-grand-a-year bridge inspector."

"Is that how you're playing it? That Ellie was going to jump?"

"That was the idea. But the local detective down here won't go along."

"Local? You mean Sergeant Wasciewicz?"

"Yeah. They've got him in the squad room but they can't keep him there forever. And there are reporters all over the place. I guess you noticed the satellite trucks outside."

Henry found his way to the squad room and slid into a chair across the table from where Sergeant Wasciewicz was writing up his report. The sergeant recognized him immediately, and put down his ballpoint pen.

"Are you here to suggest what I might have seen?" he asked.

Henry smiled. "No. Just what you might want to write in that report."

"You want me to save Congressman Gordon Acton's reputation."

"No," Henry said. "Gordon Acton is dead. He's no longer a concern of mine. But I thought you might want to do a favor for Mrs. Acton. Unless you still believe that she's the one who killed Theresa Santiago."

Wasciewicz laughed. "I never thought she had hurt anyone. I figured the bastard drugged her and kept her around as his alibi. I just hoped that if I accused his wife I might force his hand. But he'd have thrown her into the gas chamber if he had to. Christ, when I got to the house he was trying to throw her off the balcony."

Henry nodded. "I never thought she could have hurt anyone. And even though I needed Gordon as a candidate, I really didn't think much of him as a person."

"Then we agree. So tell me, Mr. Browning, why are you here?"

"I thought you might want to do something for Mrs. Acton.

Resurrect her career and, if you enjoy a little cynicism, help her to have the last laugh."

Wasciewicz did want to do something for Mrs. Acton. He leaned forward, his attention obvious. "I'm all ears," he told Henry.

An hour later, Henry Browning was able to assure the governor that all their political problems were over. "Sergeant Wasciewicz has decided that Gordon's fall was probably an accident."

The governor was amazed. "Christ, Henry, what did you have to promise him? We're already overstaffed with bridge inspectors."

"Sergeant Wasciewicz is that rare honest man who wants nothing for himself. But he would like us to do something for Ellie."

"Of course. What does he want?"

"He wants you to nominate her to fulfill her husband's term, permanently, or at least until we can arrange a special election."

"What? But she's mentally ill . . ."

"Who do you know in politics who is completely sane?"

"Why would she want to do it?"

Henry smiled. "She has some very strong beliefs about the education of disadvantaged children. I think she'd welcome the opportunity to put them into operation."

"That's the most ridiculous . . ."

Henry's hand was up to hold off the governor's onslaught. "Gordon had about eighty percent of the vote," he reminded. "Can you think of anyone who would be a more popular choice than his widow?"

There was a long silence as the governor weighed the idea. A smile gradually formed on his ass-tight lips. "I suppose we'd have no trouble controlling her."

"I don't know," Henry answered. "If Gordon could have controlled her he wouldn't have gone off the balcony."